MY TWO CENTS

A Collection of Shorts Stories

Arthur Dean

FIRST EDITION

Little Red Tree Publishing, LLC,

First Edition, 2015, manufactured in USA
1 2 3 4 5 6 7 8 9 10   LSI   20 19 18 17 16 15

Book Layout and Cover Design:
Michael J Linnard, MCSD

All photos included in this book, and the cover, were taken by Barbara Dean and are used by kind permission.

In this collection the majority of the stories were first published in the Southeastern CT *Jewish Leader* newspaper in the author's column called "My Two Cents." Sports related essays were originally printed in the *Waterford Times*. Three of the stories: "My Father's Shoes," "The Kiddush Cup," and "A Family Found," were published in the *Masorti/ Conservative Judaism magazine*, an international publication distributed to members of the Conservative Movement throughout the United States and Canada.

Library of Congress Cataloging-in-Publication Data:

Dean, Arthur, 1953-
  My Two Cents: A Collection of Short Stories / by Arthur Dean. -- 1st ed.
      p. cm.
  Includes glossary.
  ISBN 978-1-935656-40-1 (pbk. : alk. paper)
  I. Title.
  PS3614.O9A79 2015
  811'.6--dc22

Little Red Tree Publishing, LLC
website: www.littleredtree.com

DEDICATION

This book is dedicated to my wife, Barbara. We met on line 40 years ago while students at the University of Pennsylvania before that meant a computer aided encounter. We have rarely been separated since. She's edited my stories, and encouraged me, fueling me with her enthusiasm, listening to my ideas at all hours of the day or night. At times I think I write just to see if I can make her smile.

CONTENTS

INTRODUCTION

I have always envied writers who lived through difficult times—war, famine, international intrigue. If they followed the old adage, "Write what you know," they had plenty of material. When I first began to write, in my mid-forties, often at 4 or 5 in the morning, I feared that my "ordinary life," as a first generation Jewish-American, was far from interesting. Yet, despite my misgivings, I plunged ahead, letting my everyday concerns surface in my writing.

Frequently I felt my stories wrote themselves, with characters and plots that seemed to jump from my subconscious. Conflicts with children, parents, and teachers pervaded my early morning ramblings. Doubts about the proper way to live my life and raise my children resurfaced, steeped in my memories of a childhood spent trying to assimilate.

To my delight, readers seemed to find a connection with my characters' struggles, ordinary as they might be. So I continued writing, working out my protagonists' conflicts when mine were much harder to resolve.

My sensibilities reflect the Jewish-American experience of a generation born in the fifties to immigrant parents. I was born in New York in 1953, to Jewish parents from Austria whose lives were shattered by the holocaust. Miraculously, as teenagers, they each escaped Vienna on the Kindertransport, lived out the war years in London during the Blitz, and eventually settled in America. They met in Philadelphia on an arranged date. Within a short time they married and settled in New York City to pursue the American dream, in the Washington Heights neighborhood, a stone's throw from the George Washington Bridge. That's when I came into the picture, blithely unaware of my parents' travails, or the tragedy that had befallen our family at the hands of the Nazis in the shtetls of Eastern Poland.

So, there I was, growing up in one of the most culturally diverse neighborhoods in America, with children of all races and nationalities. We mixed in the schools, on the baseball diamonds, and in the schoolyard, where the art of stickball and punchball seemed far more intriguing than the traditions my parents hoped to instill. They longed to preserve their heritage, despite all that had been snatched away. I attended Hebrew School and synagogue, as instructed, but, I admit my mind was not always fully engaged.

Wanting desperately to fit in to my American homeland, I felt strangled by the traditions of my parents. I wanted to be an American first and foremost, not a reflection of my parents' values. While they clung to their European roots and emphasized religious observance, I pulled away, pursuing baseball and basketball and all things American.

The 60's and 70's were turbulent times. The Vietnam War and loosening cultural taboos polarized an already confrontational New York City, often pitting the baby boom generation against their parents. Perhaps generational conflict is common to the immigrant experience in America, or perhaps I was a bit of a rebel. Either way, early conflicts were hard to overcome.

Life experience changes us. I married. I raised a family. I got older. I began to see value in maintaining my heritage and traditions. I raised four children with my wife, Barbara. I had hoped my own conflicts might help lead my children through the mine fields of youth. Instead, as the children grew, they developed opinions and values of their own, often sponsoring vigorous debate as they navigated through their teenage years. Sometimes, I would find myself taking positions that sounded much like my own father's, an irony that continues to surprise.

I began writing essays for the Jewish Leader newspaper nearly twenty years ago when I was asked to write an article about our yearly synagogue baseball game, an event I had helped organize. Later I gravitated towards fiction. My stories often reflected things that were going on in my own family, a catharsis that might have helped me cope with the challenges of parenthood.

I started a biweekly column for the Southeastern CT *Jewish Leader* newspaper and called it "My Two Cents"—thus the title of this short story collection. I've been writing for the *Leader* regularly for 15 years, publishing more than 300 essays and stories. I consider the pieces in this collection my best. Most are from my work for the *Jewish Leader*. Many of the sports related stories appeared in the *Waterford Times* newspaper. The trio of, "My Father's Shoes," "The Kiddush Cup," and "A Family Found" were picked up and republished in the *Masorti/Conservative Judaism* magazine, a national publication that reaches Conservative Jews throughout the United States and Canada.

Most of my characters happen to be Jewish, but I believe their challenges are universal. Some grapple with questions of faith. They have conflicts with their fathers, or mothers, or perhaps their own children. Some have turned their back on their religion, or their family, and want to make amends. Some are estranged from their children and yearn for a second chance. In the story, "My Father's Shoes," the little boy who stayed out of services too long on the day of Yom Kippur is perhaps a metaphor of my own life experience. The boy plays tag outside the synagogue, loses track of time and then falls and rips his pants. He returns to the Synagogue, bathed in sweat, ashamed to face his father. Years later the boy, now a man in his fifties, remembers the event, and thinks, "I did come back. It just took longer than I thought."

If you're a sports enthusiast there's plenty in this collection for you. Check out the, "Let the games begin," chapter. Love baseball? Try, "Yankee Fantasy Camp," or, "The Anniversary Gift."

I've reserved some of my longer stories for, "The Big Picture," chapter. In "You Can't Go Home Again," a young man is forced to deal with the rifts in his family when he is mistakenly accused of child abuse. In "The Big Picture," a man nearing retirement reconnects with his estranged daughter and infant granddaughter putting his savings and, ultimately, his life in danger.

The "Holiday Blues," chapter contains stories with the Jewish Holidays as a backdrop. If you like a good dog story you might enjoy "Celebrating Chanukah," the story of a lost dog whose love of latkes ultimately reunites him with his family. For fans of Charles Dickens, you'll recognize his influence in "'Twas the Night before Passover Story," a parody that shows even the most hardened heart can repent, and find a meaningful life. I suppose that is all we can hope for.

The stories in "Reflections on Raising Children," were written over a ten-year period while my four children were still at home. It was a tumultuous time. One of my New London readers once lamented to my youngest son, "I only like when your father writes stories about himself." To which my son laughed and said, "Every story is about my father." Our children only think they know everything, but on this occasion he may have been right.

For those trying to raise teenage children, you know how humbling it can be. Our kids are married now, some with children of their own. I look forward to seeing my children raise their own children. I doubt it they'll ask for my advice, but if they do, I'll try to hide my smile.

CHAPTER 1

MY FATHER'S SHOES

MY FATHER'S SHOES

Last year, when my mother sold her house, she cleaned out boxes upon boxes stored in her garage. With my father gone there was no longer any reason to keep the house. I was given a share of the loot. To the casual observer this treasure trove would bring little interest at a Christie's auction. I found cassette tapes (remember those?) of famous operettas. I smiled to remember how their shrill notes would chase me from the living room as a teenager. A jumbled spider's web of old ties filled one box. Notebooks that my father used for a course on Jewish History filled another. One item tugged at my memory—a pair of worn canvas sneakers.

My father was not an athlete. He wore sneakers for a few hours each year, on the day of Yom Kippur. I ran my hands along a rubber sole that knew only the linoleum floor of his orthodox shul in Washington Heights. When the Jews of the neighborhood fled New York for the suburbs back in the seventies, the shul went under, and was eventually demolished. A multicultural public school stands where once we chanted Kol Nidre.

As I ran my hand along the yellowed canvas that once housed my father's feet, snippets of memory flashed before me. I remembered sitting between my father and grandfather on the men's side of the mechitzah, my toes barely touching the ground. Suddenly everyone stands, and my father's hand on my shoulder guides me from my seat. All around me men are pounding their chest and shaking. I do the same. We sit again. My father points to a line in his book and then shows me the place in mine. Two minutes later my mind begins to wander.

"Daddy, can I go out for a few minutes?"

"You just went out," he answers. "Why can't you sit still?"

I shrug my shoulders. "Please. Five minutes, I promise I'll come back." He rolls his eyes, but lets me go anyway. Outside my friends are waiting.

"Tag, you're it," one boy yells as he taps me on the shoulder. The group scatters. I run after them. I forget all about my promise. I fall, rip my pants and skin my knees. Finally I return to the shul a half an hour later with grimy hands. My forehead glistens. My father frowns. He hands me a handkerchief, but says nothing.

Kid stuff, you might say. But I can still feel his disappointment. That interlude set the tone of many of our skirmishes, whether it was my taste in literature, music, or politics. I know he wanted me to take religion more seriously in those early years. I just couldn't. Maybe I wasn't ready. Maybe my head was too filled with baseball and basketball and just wanting to fit in with my friends and have fun.

3

Several years later my father told me of his own past. "I never got a good Hebrew education in Vienna," he said. "Then the Nazis came when I was 14. I always wished I could read Hebrew and daven better. That's why I want you to learn more than I did."

That's an awful lot of pressure for an adolescent to bear. Still, my father was surely not the only parent who wanted his child to make good on his regrets.

Fifty years have passed. I've raised four children of my own and tried hard to learn when to take a stand and when to back off. Passing on my Jewish heritage seems very important. As for Jewish learning I'm no Talmud scholar, but I've made an attempt to go beyond my early difficulties. I rarely leave services before the Aleinu, and I try to look the other way when my children do. Sometimes I lead the morning minyan. This past Yom Kippur Rabbi Astor asked me to chant the Yom Kippur Haftorah at Beth El—quite an honor, one that made me swell with pride at the same time it made my heart quicken. What if I mess up in front of all my friends, I thought. I studied. I practiced, but mostly I worried. Like a Bar Mitzvah boy with a guilty conscience I thought of my early years under my father's watchful gaze. *What would he say if he saw me on the bima? If only he could.*

Finally Yom Kippur arrives. This year it fell on Shabbat—sure to bring out an even bigger crowd. I wake at five. I practice the parsha for hours until the letters begin to blur together. My wife comes downstairs. "Good morning, you sound really good," she says. "Better get dressed."

My insides twist. I pick out my best blue suit, my favorite red tie and a pair of black loafers. I check my appearance in the mirror. I take a deep breath and head down the stairs. An idea flashes in my mind. I retrace my steps. I rummage in my closet and find my father's canvas sneakers. In 30 years in my conservative synagogue I have never worn sneakers on Yom Kippur. But on this particular Yom Kippur, it just feels right. I remove my black loafers and slip on my father's sneakers. They fit like I've been wearing them all my life.

I arrive at the synagogue early. Somehow I keep my anxiety in check, and then it's time. I glance down at the sneakers and I smile. I make my way to the bima. I look into the faces of friends and family. I clear my throat. I begin. The words flow. I even manage to maintain some semblance of the proper trope. Certainly I am no chazzan, but somehow I manage to pull it off without embarrassing myself. The Rabbi congratulates me. The president of the shul shakes my hand. Before I leave the bima I glance down at my father's sneakers. I hope he would have smiled to see me wear them, almost as if he were in some small way taking part in the Yom Kippur service. I return to my seat and my wife kisses my cheek. I take a deep breath and exhale.

Some weeks later I wake in the middle of the night aroused by a most unusual dream. I am sitting in the front row of the synagogue. A tall man with bushy hair walks to my side. He places his hand on my shoulder. I can't see his face, but I am certain it is my father. In the next few days I tell everyone who will listen about the sneakers and the dream. I refrain from trite metaphors about filling my father's shoes, but truthfully the thought is there.

Many thoughts cross my mind when I think of my father. I think of how we both felt insecure about leading services. I realize that our disagreements from so long ago have lost their sting. I think he'd be proud to see how his grandchildren are turning out.

I think of the promise I gave my father so many years ago in shul. "I promise I'll come back, Daddy." Well, in the end I did come back. It just took a lot longer than either of us ever imagined.

THE KAMINSKY PAPERS

The sound of the Wall Street Journal hitting the plasma screen TV would have shocked anyone sitting beside Josh Kaminsky in his darkened room. Through good times and bad you could find Josh glued to the financial news each morning. He would switch between CNBC, Fox, and Bloomberg, clicking the remote like a Gameboy on speed, the market figures flashing the bottom of the screen in a never-ending stream of worry. Often as he watched he would fondle the key to his safe deposit box that he kept on a string around his neck, as if constantly calculating the value of his holdings.

That week the news was especially worrisome: a budget deal that pleased no one, a plunging stock market, and renewed fear of a global recession. "Damn politicians gonna ruin the country," Kaminsky mumbled as the Russian housekeeper entered with his breakfast. "First thing cut off all the welfare we dole out," he said to the newscaster, as if his opinion was to be broadcast on "Meet the Press." The woman averted her eyes. Then turning back she presented the silver tray. "For God's sake, Mister Kaminsky. You're going to give yourself another stroke. Now eat up you eggs. You know what the doctor said about losing more weight."

Kaminsky poked his eggs with a fork a few times, grimaced and then pushed the plate to the side. "You want me to call your son?" the housekeeper said, when Kaminsky put a hand to his chest.
"No, not on your life," he said with far more vehemence than the question required. "Just gas, Olga. It'll pass. But turn off the TV and fetch me some Bourbon from the living room. These idiots don't know what they're talking about." Then he pushed the tray off the side of the bed, the cacophony of crashing plates an exclamation to his discontent.

Olga shrugged. She struggled to remain silent. After all he was her boss, and even a cranky and temperamental employer was not someone to be disrespected—not in this economy. She cleared the mess from the floor, exited, and returned with the snifter of liquor he seemed to be asking for earlier and earlier each day.

Sometimes she thought of her three sisters back in Minsk. How she dreamed of the day when she'd have enough money for them to be together. Some days she dreamed of having a husband and a house of her own. But most days she daydreamed of living on a deserted island with peace and solitude—no dishes to wash, no sheets to launder, and, above all, no old Mr. Kaminsky.

Kaminsky finished his brandy and fell into a deep sleep. He dreamed he

6

was a young man once again, running with his girlfriend along the shore in Harkness Park. In his dream he hadn't yet made his fortune, hadn't even finished business school. He relished the intoxicating cocktail of youth and unlimited possibilities. As he slept the television droned on: Dow drops 500 points. Jobless report disappointing. European debt threatens Italy and Spain. Beneath the sheets Kaminsky's withered legs twitched as if they alone could sense the fear of another economic Armageddon.

Kaminsky never had visitors. Except, of course, if you count his lawyer and accountant who came to his bedside to have him sign papers. All Kaminsky ever talked about was business, and how the country was going to the dogs. To all this Olga merely nodded, going through the paces of her day with a thin-lipped smile and a wish to be somewhere else.

As the shadows grew long in the room Olga knocked briefly and opened the door. "Its time for your walk Mr. Kaminsky." His eyes fluttered open. He struggled to rise as if he'd forgotten his own disability.

"What I wouldn't give to be young again," he said. "If only I'd stayed with Rose."

Olga's eyes glanced at Kaminsky's key resting on his chest. How often she wondered why he kept it so close to his heart. What lock did it open? Why had he never removed it in the five years she'd been his caretaker? If only he'd cared as much for his wife and son as he did for that key, perhaps he'd have someone in the world who cared if he lived or died.

In quiet moments Olga often fantasized about a life of luxury, a life of big business deals, stocks and bonds. So it was with rising fascination that Olga helped Kaminsky get dressed, for, on this afternoon, upon waking from his nap, Kaminsky announced, "Olga, today I want you to take me to the bank."

KAMINSKY'S TREASURE

"Today you're taking me to the bank," Kaminsky said to Olga with the certainty of a man used to getting what he wanted,

"Yes, sir," Olga replied, her eyes darting to the key suspended from the lanyard around his neck.

Never in the five years that Olga cared for old man Kaminsky had she ever seen him without the key. She never dared ask its purpose. Kaminsky rarely left his apartment anymore. With his sallow eyes and the way he clutched his chest when he coughed, Olga assumed that the secrets the key held would follow him to his grave.

As she helped her employer get dressed a devilish thought ruminated in her mind. She imagined Kaminsky dead, and the reading of the old man's will. *I leave all my earthly possessions to Olga, my faithful housekeeper.* She suppressed a chuckle imagining her two sisters' glee when they flew in from Minsk to share in their younger sister's good fortune.

"Well, woman, I don't pay you to daydream," Kaminsky barked, jolting Olga from her revelry.

"Call for the limo, and bring me my walker. And be snappy about it!"

"Yes, Sir," Olga said, hiding clenched fists behind her back.

Kaminsky shuffled forward, clutching the arms of his walker while Olga stood by the door.

"Don't keep me standing here waiting."

"Of course, Sir," Olga said. Then she opened the door and waited for Kaminsky to shuffle to the elevator before she followed. She pictured the elevator door opening and Kaminsky tumbling forward into an empty shaft, his walker clattering all the way down to the basement.

Kaminsky eyed Olga as she rode beside him in the elevator. *I'd fire her in a minute if I could find someone less incompetent. Why bother with so little time left?*

On the limo ride to the bank Kaminsky closed his eyes and tried to sleep, but his thoughts surfaced as they always did. He thought of the day his son was born, a perfect moment still unspoiled by the pain of a loveless marriage. He felt a great sense of loss, and the pain of missed opportunities. *Why didn't I find a way to stay close to my son?* He thought of the last time they met almost a year earlier, their last argument so bitter, so final. *Convert to Buddhism? Unthinkable,*

Impossible! Of all his failings as a parent perhaps this was the worst. He thought of his own father's words in the hospital that last day as he pressed his most treasured possessions into Kaminsky's hands. *Some things can't be bought. One day you'll realize that.*

Kaminsky clutched the key in his hand and took a raspy breath.

Meanwhile, as Kaminsky's eyes fluttered in the back seat of the limo, Olga sat quietly watching. *Look how he clutches the key. Must be millions stashed away.* She pictured herself ensconced in Kaminsky's penthouse apartment, with a maid of her own preparing meals fit for an heiress.

The limo crawled to a stop. Olga helped Kaminsky as he struggled to the bank door. She put an arm on his shoulder, noting the way his chest was heaving, the beads of sweat covering his forehead.

"Stay with the car," Kaminsky wheezed, when Olga followed him into the bank. Olga nodded and retreated. She pictured Kaminsky alone in a bank vault surrounded with his most treasured possessions: diamonds, rubies, heavy bars of gold lined up like so many Lego blocks.

A half hour passed. Olga began to wonder if Kaminsky would ever return. Finally he appeared huffing and puffing outside the door of the bank carrying a shopping bag bound closed with twine. He motioned to Olga with frightened eyes. She ran to his side, catching him just as he seemed to be collapsing. She saw immediately that the key around his neck was gone.

"Mr. K. what's wrong?" Olga said, feigning concern.

"See that my son gets the contents of this bag," Kaminsky said in a whisper. Then his eyes rolled back in his head, and he slumped forward, his forehead hitting the pavement as Olga stood in stunned silence. Her eyes flew wide, as her employer lay at her feet, her pulse racing, her throat opening in a shrill scream.

In a matter of seconds, the sidewalk was filled with frantic strangers: a bank president wringing his hands over one of his best clients, a security guard shouting into his walkie talkie, a family of Asian tourists being ushered away by a protective tour guide. Olga's mind whirled as an ambulance pulled up to the curb. As they loaded old man Kaminsky's motionless body into the back Olga wondered where she would find a new place to live. The doors closed with a clang of finality. Olga raised her hand and took a few steps forward towards the speeding ambulance, but her call was more like a whisper, than a shout. Ensconced around her wrist was the handle of Kaminsky's shopping bag.

"All right, break it up. The show's over," a cop barked. Olga's eyes darted away from his gaze.

Her heart felt as if she was running a marathon, and her breath came in little gasps. "Yes officer," she muttered. She walked to the subway station on the corner. She took the subway directly to JFK airport where she booked a ticket on the next plane to Minsk with the last bit of her savings. She ran to the ladies' bathroom, and into the handicapped stall. She locked the door after peering right and left, seeing that the rest room was almost deserted. *The Kaminsky family treasures, and no one will be the wiser.*

She untied the bag and emptied the contents onto the floor, the clatter of silver breaking the silence. Olga put a hand to her mouth to muffle a stream of Russian curses. On the tile floor before her she found no diamonds or rubies, no stocks or bonds. Instead she found only a misshapen Kiddush cup, a tiny prayer book and a yellowed tallis that had belonged to old man Kaminsky's father so many years before. A note in Kaminsky's handwriting read: To my only son—I leave to you the only things my father left me. He would have wanted you to have them.

KAMINSKY'S LEGACY

While old man Kaminsky lay in intensive care at Lenox Hill hospital, his housekeeper, Olga, stole stealthily into the rest room at JFK. She dumped the contents of Kaminsky's safe deposit box—all that remained of his father's legacy onto a floor that smelled of urine and ammonia. Rather than the portfolio of riches she expected she found instead relics from a world gone by: a yellowed tallis, a tiny prayer book and a Kiddush cup.

She scooped them back into the shopping bag and ran to the ticket counter.

"There's been a terrible mistake. I need a refund on my ticket," she said, fighting back tears as she held up her boarding pass.

The man at the desk looked up from his computer screen and took a deep breath. "Minsk? We don't give refunds."

Olga's eyes flashed. "But I just bought the ticket! This is outrageous!"

The man shrugged, his face blank, with the demeanor of one who long ago learned to placate fliers with frantic demands. "All I can do is reissue the ticket for a later date."

Olga crumpled the boarding pass in a fist of blanched fingers. *I can't go back to Russia peniless.* An image of old Kaminsky's face rose before her as she relived the way his limp arm fell to the pavement when she removed the shopping bag from his wrist. She had pivoted and scurried towards the taxi stand, Kaminsky's shopping bag held tight under her arm. She pictured being trapped behind bars as the yellow cab drew to the curb. *Might still be time.* She handed the taxi driver her last $20. "Take me to 256 Central Park West."

Meanwhile an unconscious Kaminsky remained in the intensive care unit, the steadily spiking EKG paying tribute to his tenacity.

Once back in the apartment Olga's options fluttered through her mind like the flapping of a vulture's wings. She went through the contents of the shopping bag again and again looking for some secret inscription, perhaps the combination to a vault that would snatch victory from Olga's humiliating defeat. The Kiddush cup was simple, unadorned. She leafed through the prayer book, looking for some marking that might reward her efforts. Aside from a penciled inscription in Hebrew on the back page she found nothing. She wrapped the items in the yellowed tallis and stuffed them back in the bag.

Only one way out. She picked up the phone and dialed 911. "I'm looking for Mr. Joshua Kaminsky. We got separated this morning after he went to the

Citibank on Broadway." She waited for what seemed like hours. Then a voice barked on the other end of the line. A small smile curled at her lips. She left the apartment and strode towards the Lenox Hill Hospital.

"I'm Olga Vischencka," she said, when the guard barred her way. "I have something that Mr. Kaminsky dropped," she said. A doctor passing in the hall paused, noting the fringes of a tallis protruding from Olga's shopping bag.

"Let her in for five minutes," the doctor said, while Olga dabbed at her eyes with a Kleenex.

In a room filled with blinking machines Olga stepped around IV poles and approached Kamisky's bedside. She put a hand to his cheek, making sure that the nurse observed her gesture. To her shock Kaminsky's eyes flew open and he began to mutter, "Give to Aaron, please. Important." Then he was silent.

As Olga walked towards the subway she mulled over her cards like a Texas Holdem gambler in Vegas. *If Kaminsky recovers I'll still have a job. If he dies I could be in the will. Either way if this junk winds up with the son, no one will be the wiser.*

When Olga found Aaron's third floor walkup in Flatbush she cringed. The lobby was filthy, the halls marred with graffiti.

Kaminsky's son ushered her in reluctantly. With his Buddhist robe and shaved head Olga would never have recognized him from the framed Bar Mitzvah picture hanging in old man Kaminsky's bedroom.

"Your father's at Lenox Hill." she began. Then, before leaving, she outlined all the wonderful things she had done for old man Kaminsky over the years.

"He always told me he'd take care of me," she said with glistening eyes. Kaminsky's son nodded. "Of course you can stay on in the house until my father recovers," he said.

"He wanted you to have the contents of this bag," she said before leaving.

Aaron went straight to the hospital. Kaminsky remained in a coma, yet his son came every day and read from the little prayer book, hoping that despite their big rift over religion he might make amends. Olga remained in Kaminsky's Central Park apartment. She drew her salary and watched television.

As the days passed Aaron began to think about the words in the prayer book. And, after a month, he began to use the words Shema Yisroel as his mantra during meditation. After two months he began reciting the Shema each morning and night. After three months he substituted the reading of the Amidah for his meditation. After four months he let his hair grow in and stopped wearing his robe. After six months when his father weighed 96 pounds Aaron stopped going to the Ashram in Bensonhurst, and began to pray with increasing fervor at his father's bedside.

Olga called Aaron once a month to inquire about her employer's condition. "Don't worry, Olga," Aaron would always say. "As long as my father breathes you'll have a job."

On the day an earthquake rumbled through New York, old man Kaminsky opened his eyes. He smiled to see Aaron by his bedside. Then he closed his eyes and was gone.

Aaron resolved to say Kaddish each day in a little shul in Flatbush, not far from where his father grew up. At the reading of the will the following week the lawyer informed Aaron that his father's wealth had dwindled. Apparently the stream of income from Kaminsky's investments with Bernie Madoff had long ceased. The Central Park apartment was sold at auction to repay Madoff's cheated investors. When all was tallied Aaron received a check for $270. Aaron took all in stride with a shrug and a smile. After all, his needs were few. Olga returned to Minsk bitter and penniless.

After a year of saying Kaddish Aaron approached the elderly Rabbi at the end of services. He extended his hand. "I've found comfort here," Aaron said. "But my year is over, and I'll be moving out of the neighborhood."

The Rabbi smiled. "I knew your grandfather. He would have been proud to know you wear his tallis." While Aaron removed his tefillin, the Rabbi picked up the little prayer book and thumbed through its pages. With a crooked yellowed finger he tapped the scrawled inscription on the last page.

"I never could understand my grandfather's message," Aaron said. "My Hebrew's not that good."

"The Rabbi laughed. "But it's not Hebrew."

Aaron shrugged.

"Yiddish is also written with Hebrew letters."

Aaron's eyes grew wide, and his heart began to pound, as if about to receive guidance from the grave.

The Rabbi translated in a halting voice. "First Immigrant Savings corner of Delancy and Rivington. Safe deposit box 2491. And then there's a combination."

That day Aaron took the subway to the lower east side and found the Immigrant Savings Bank. They did indeed have a listing for Aaron's grandfather, and a record of his safe deposit box, last opened in 1957. Once Aaron presented the combination the bank president led him to a basement storage area and opened a rusted strong box. "This is where we keep the inactive accounts."

Aaron spent a half hour sifting through faded photographs. There was a picture of his own father on the day of his Bar Mitzvah, snapshots of long-dead relatives, and a diary written by his grandfather when he first immigrated to New York from Poland. Most of the things he found were fascinating details of the Kaminsky family in Europe. It was not until Aaron got everything home that he found the tattered certificate at the bottom of the pile. He had never seen anything like it before, nor had anyone else of his generation. For back in 1957 companies still had to issue certificates when they sold stock. Aaron squinted to read the gilded lettering. "Berkeshire Hathaway Company, twenty shares."

He found a receipt from a brokerage house for 175 dollars. It was not until the following day that Aaron learned of the miraculous wealth that Warren Buffet had created for his shareholders. His grandfather's modest investment was now worth three million. Back at the shul Aaron asked the Rabbi why his father had never discovered the inscription in the prayer book.

"He would have had to open it," the Rabbi said.

Some men would have let money like that go to their head, but Aaron was not like other men. He made a hefty donation to the little shul in Flatbush and funded a community park in his neighborhood. He did move to a nicer building down the street from the little shul. While his new job didn't allow him to attend minyan each day, he often showed up on Shabbat with the yellowed tallis around his neck and his grandfather's prayer book in his pocket. While his needs were simple, things did get a little more complicated when he married Rachel, a dark eyed beauty with a heart of gold, much like Aaron's. Although they lived frugally, the money did come in handy after she and Aaron had the first of their five children.

As for Olga, she toiled for years at a job she hated in a factory outside Minsk. She often thought of the Kaminsky family. "The son got just what he deserved—a bunch of old junk," she muttered to anyone who would listen to her story of the Kaminsky legacy.

THE STORY OF JOHN DAVIDOVITCH

Cleaning out his father's house the week before Christmas was not a task John Dovkovitch relished. Buried beneath old magazines and clippings dating back to the fifties, John wondered whether he could, in good conscience, throw out everything he found without going through it. With his father entering the nursing home, everyone in the family thought it best to give up the family home in New Jersey. *Why did Dad keep every bit of junk he ever found? At this rate I won't finish till Christmas Day. Not that Dad ever cared about religion.* In fact he raised his son, John, to view religion as the opiate of the masses, an antiquated crutch for the poor.

After four tedious hours, sorting items on the garage floor, John began to throw things into a large garbage can. There were yellowed copies of Hardy Boy mysteries, Mad magazines dating from the sixties, a pack of bazooka bubble gum purchased before the Dodgers left Brooklyn. As he delved deeper into closets he found family relics aged earlier and earlier: a ticket stub from the 1953 World Series, a flyer from Roseland Dance Hall advertising dancing lessons. *Funny to find out these things only after Dad's health fell apart. I didn't even know he could dance.*

It was in an old shoebox buried beneath papers in his father's desk that John found the first item that would change his life forever—a picture of Russian troops posing in front of a prison camp somewhere in Europe. John had known since childhood the Dovkovitch family saga—father born of peasant Ukranian stock. After studying engineering in Moscow he was conscripted into the Russian army to fight the Nazis at Leningrad, serving as an intelligence officer, and then rising in the ranks of the Communist party—only to defect in 1948. As a child John knew better than to ask his father too many questions about his past. Whenever pressed for answers the elder Dovkovitch clammed up, a hardened look transforming his face. His father never talked about his childhood, let alone any of his experiences in the Russian army. "Orphans have no history," he liked to say, whenever John insisted. He studied the picture, staring from face to face, hoping to recognize his father's strong jaw and prominent nose—no luck. John ran a hand through his hair. *Why would Dad keep this photo hidden?*

In another draw John found a parcel of faded black and white photographs held together with bits of shoestring. He flipped through pictures of men and women he did not recognize. Men in long black coats, women with kerchiefs covering their heads stared back with sallow eyes.

The next day in a closet he found a silver cup in a red velvet bag. Engraved on the cup he could make out a date, 1923, and engraved letters that looked like chicken scratches. Within the cup was a yellowed passport with the name Uri Davidovitch. The picture was torn away. He flipped through pages stiffened with age. Instead of the Russian he expected he found lettering that looked more like the markings on the silver cup. *Could this be the passport my father used to come to this country?*

The hours flew by. John sorted through the remaining items. He placed anything of interest in a manila envelope, and took it along with the silver cup to his home. For some reason he hid the items in a drawer of his desk and never mentioned them to his wife. Although he visited the nursing home each day his father seemed to not be aware of his presence. One day he brought in the cup and the pictures. "Where did these come from," he said. His father turned his face to the wall.

Christmas Eve came. As usual John and his wife exchanged gifts, then went out for Chinese food. That night John tossed and turned. Dreams haunted his sleep. He rose at the first gray of dawn with a premonition of disaster. As he groped around the kitchen preparing coffee the phone rang.

"I'm sorry to call you on Christmas Day," the nurse said. "But your father's very agitated this morning. He keeps shouting, 'I'm a fraud,' …the doctor's afraid for his heart."

John went to the desk and drew out the manila envelope and the red velvet bag. He broke every speed law, but got to the nursing home in minutes.

When John arrived his father was silent, but his eyes darted from side to side.

"Pops, what's wrong?" John whispered in his father's ear. His father's eyes flew wide, and he dragged a bony hand across his forehead as if to sweep away the past. He stared up at the ceiling. "I lied, all these years. Just wanted to start over." His breath came in gasps.

John swallowed hard. He drew the pictures out of the envelope, and held up the tarnished silver cup. "Who are these people?" John said. His father raised a trembling hand and then clutched his chest. An alarm sounded at the nurses' station. Two doctors raced in. They placed a mask over his face and carried him to a waiting ambulance. John's father survived the crisis, but that was the last time he uttered a word.

A week later John brought the items from his father's desk to a meeting with Mr. Ira Schwartz, the curator of the Museum of Immigration based on Ellis Island. "My father was a Russian soldier," John said, "but I want details of his admission to the United States." When he showed Mr. Schwartz the yellowed passport he punched up the number on his computer. Mr. Schwartz exhaled sharply as details appeared on the screen:

"Uri Dovkovitch. Decorated Russian soldier. Captured Jan 5th, 1943, by the Germans at the battle of Leningrad. Imprisoned at Treblinka. Liberated by Russian soldiers. Stowed away on a British cargo ship on its way to Palestine. Decorated by the Irgun, the Hagana, and the Israeli Defense Forces in Israel's War of Independence."

"But why would he do all that?" John muttered. "He hated religion. And why would he hide his past?"

Mr. Schwartz shrugged. He took the silver cup from John's hand and read its inscription. "Avraham Davidovitch, May 4th, 1923, Tarnapole. Mazel Tov."

"But why would my father keep a wine goblet?"

Mr. Schwartz shrugged. He put a hand on John's shoulder, a kind smile creasing his lips. "There's more," he said pointing to the computer screen. "Mr. Uri Dovkovitch, born as Avraham Davidovitch, given political asylum in the United States in 1948...that's a distinction usually reserved for intelligence officers who passed Russian technological secrets to the United States after the war. I'm surprised the KGB never found him."

John felt as if his world of safe assumptions was falling apart. *What else didn't Pops tell me?*

"And just for your information, Mr. Dovkovitch, your father didn't keep a wine goblet hidden all these years. I'd say with some certainty that this was the Kiddush cup from his Bar Mitzvah. And these pictures were likely his family."

Thoughts swirled through John's mind. He stood meekly, numb to the information overload. Unsure of his future and much of his family's past, John kept the revelations from his wife. But when his father passed away in his sleep the following month, John had a Rabbi perform the funeral service. Although it was difficult and required the Rabbi's tutoring, John recited the Kaddish each day for a year. It took another year for his wife to come around, but they plan to visit Jerusalem this summer, by way of the Ukraine, to look for lost relatives. And, as you might expect, John is thinking of changing his name back to Davidovitch.

THE KIDDUSH CUP

On one of my last visits to my father's house he asked to speak to me in private. We sat on his couch and a melancholy smile crossed his lips. I gazed at my father and waited for him to speak. He looked all of his eighty-one years, tired of doctor's visits and blood tests, arthritic knees, and pills. Only the sparkle in his eyes gave hint to the young soldier he had once been in the years that England fought Germany.

He placed a simple silver cup in my hand. I stared with immediate recognition at the lone adornment, a worn inscription 'JD' engraved on the cup's face.

"This was your grandfather's Kiddush cup," my father said, with uncharacteristic gravity.

I refrained from protest. "Don't you still want to use it?" I asked, innocently, feigning ignorance of his latest oncologist's report.

"Did I tell you how I had this made for Poppa?" he said.

I nodded slowly. "You did, a long time ago, but tell me again."

He leaned back in his chair and his eyes became unfocused, spinning the tale I had last heard when I was a boy.

A Jew born in Vienna in the twenties had limited possibilities. My father was one of the lucky ones. At the start of the War he escaped to England on the Kindertransport. He spent his teen years in London, and enlisted in the English army in 1943, at twenty-one. After the war he was stationed in Stuttgart, Germany, as part of the occupying forces. As an English soldier, who spoke perfect German, my father spent his time as an interpreter.

Paper money in postwar Germany was nearly worthless. So when he wanted a special gift for his own father, bartering was the preferred approach. He traded English coffee and cigarettes for German silver coins.

"Make me a cup from these," he told the German silversmith, placing a fistful of coins on the counter. "And engrave JD for Poppa's name. (Joseph Diener)."

How uplifting to know that the cup my grandfather used to make Kiddush was made from melted down German coins. As a boy I liked to imagine that the transformation of those coins into my Grandfather's cup would in some small way strike a blow to the terrible Nazis who had exterminated so many of my relatives.

My father brought the cup back to London, where his parents lived through the horrible years of the Blitz—the frightful German bombing runs on civilian areas designed to break the British spirit. From there the cup made it to America when Dad and his parents immigrated to the States in '51. My earliest memories of that cup include its use on Passover for Elijah's Cup. In our house the Seder was a serious affair, which my Grandfather led in Hebrew. The only time I was supposed to utter a sound was to recite the Four Questions. By the time we reached Elijah's Cup at the end of the Seder I could hardly keep my eyes open. Grandpa would tell me to open the door. When I returned he'd point to the cup and ask me if I thought the level of wine was lower. It always was. That Elijah was a tricky Prophet.

One Passover night when my grandfather was 70, everything changed. We came to his home, as was our custom every year. All was prepared as before—the horseradish, the matzoh, and the wine. But on this particular night, although he filled the cup for the blessing, he was unable to chant a word. That night my father took over the leadership of the Passover Seder. My grandfather listened, but said nothing, his only response a shrug when we asked him if he was ok. When weakness of his left side appeared the next day the doctors told us it was a stroke. He never spoke again. When he passed away a number of years later the cup reverted to my father, who used it at every chance he could to honor his own father—until he passed it on to me.

I treasured that cup, for, in what remains of our family, the cup is a priceless heirloom. I made sure to use it every Friday night for Kiddush. On Passover it never left my side. And, after my father finally succumbed to his illness, it felt especially important to honor his memory.

One week we hosted my wife's parents on a Friday night. All went well. We did Kiddush and Motzi and had a fine Shabbat feast. After the meal I heard a high-pitched metallic shriek from the kitchen. I approached the sink calmly, while my wife and mother-in-law struggled over a jammed garbage disposal. We'd had many such incidents—trapped spoons, knives and forks swallowed whole by a mechanism that knows no restraint. Most we freed by inserting the round end of a broomstick in a twisting and rocking motion. It was the least I could do to relieve our disposal of its dinner of cutlery. I went to get the broom, but when I returned, the panicked look on my wife's face gave rise to my own unease.

"We can't find your father's cup," she said with a sideways glance at her mother.

"What do you mean? We used it tonight. I left it on the table after the Kiddush, myself. How could it have disappeared?"

The two women shrugged. Then my mother-in-law's eyes wandered ever so slowly toward the clogged sink.

My eyes nearly bulged from their sockets. There, lodged in the drain, as if it had been designed as a silver cork, was my father's cup.

I reached in. Tenderly I grasped the edge and rotated. I used my broomstick trick.

Nothing, nada, zip. No movement. A flashlight directed into the mechanism revealed the awful truth. The beautiful soft silver, which had served my family so well, was no match for the disposal's jaws. My treasured cup was skewered from all sides.

It took a vice grip and a pair of pliers to finally free my heirloom. What was left of fine German workmanship looked more like a warped strainer than a Kiddush Cup.

My made-in-America KitchenAid disposal had made quick work of my sacred trust. I suppose it could have been worse. I know Bosch makes a very good unit. I don't know if I could take the idea of a German machine crushing my grandfather's cup. I took a deep breath. *How will I ever tell my sister and my mother?*

"We'll fix it," my wife said, renewing my adoration for a woman who thinks nothing is impossible. I pictured an alchemist melting the remains down with a blowtorch and casting it anew. Instead we took the ill-treated cup to a jewelry store known for doing repairs. "Can't do anything with this," the saleslady said. "This is your only hope." She handed me the card of a silversmith in the area known to take on hopeless causes. The man had a name that suggested his ancestors came off the Mayflower. Would he do his best for a man whose ancestors came from Poland? My wife insisted we go find his shop immediately.

The Leonardo da Vinci of silver repair turned my treasure over in his hands.

"It's a Kiddush Cup," I said.

"I know. I've seen something like this before."

I wanted to tell him the story of the cup's birth, but the words dried up in my throat.

"I'll need time to get in the mood for this one," he said with a low whistle. "Could cost 3 or 4 hundred. We'll see." He put the cup in a desk drawer. "I'll call you when it's ready."

For five months we heard nothing. In the meantime, my son, Jason, whose initials are also JD, like my grandfather, asked if he could one day have the cup for his own Shabbat table. I loved his enthusiasm. His timing could have been better. "We'll see," I said, averting my eyes. "Maybe someday."

I could wait no longer. Passover was coming up soon. My son and his wife agreed to come to our Seder. If the Kiddush Cup were missing, there would be questions. I called the silversmith.

"No, I haven't gotten around to it yet. Check again in two weeks."

Two weeks came and went—still no word. "He hasn't even started," my wife said.

Everything happens for a reason. At least that's what my grandparents used to say. A week later my wife and I took a vacation in New York City. We planned to explore neighborhoods we'd never seen—The Lower East Side, Little Italy, Brooklyn.

While in Brooklyn, my wife wanted to take a detour to Borough Park, the mostly Hassidic neighborhood.

Strolling down 14th St., the main shopping drag, we passed bakeries and Judaica stores galore. We stopped at one shop that displayed Shabbat candlesticks in their windows. My wife was interested in a new pair. We've given silver ones to our children, but the silver plate ones we use are dented and tarnished.

"By any chance can you repair a Kiddush Cup?" she asked.

They gave her a number. "Call Yisroel. If any one can do it, he can."

She called. Yisroel listened to the storied history of my little cup with fascination, as if his own family heirloom had been so mutilated.

"Melted German coins to make a Kiddush Cup. Of course, I understand," he said, as if this was his specialty. "Send it to me by mail when you get back to Connecticut. I'll fix it in two weeks."

When we got back home, my wife retrieved my multi-punctured cup from its tardy silversmith.

She sent it to Yisroel in Borough Park by Kiddush Cup Express. How do you insure something that has no value, but is priceless?

Good to Yisroel's word we received the cup back in record time. Between smelting, soldering, bending, and polishing, the repairs were nearly flawless.

My wife and I use our Kiddush Cup every Friday night with renewed pleasure. I think both my grandfather and father would be happy if they knew of the care we took with their legacy.

My son, Jason confirmed that he and his wife would attend our Seder this year. I plan to use our rehabilitated treasure for Elijah's cup. I hope Jason doesn't examine the cup too closely. If he notices the slight crease near my grandfather's initials, I'll have a long story to tell.

A FAMILY REUNION

I have been writing stories and essays for the Jewish Leader for many years. On occasion someone stops me to say they read my column. Sometimes I receive a phone call, or an acknowledgement from a fellow minyan attendant, that something I wrote made them smile. I like to hear from my readers, to know that a story I put down on paper struck their fancy.

To those who read this column you may remember a piece I did entitled "The Kiddush Cup," a story about a family heirloom that got the losing end of an altercation with a garbage disposal. This was no ordinary cup, purchased at a synagogue gift shop or perhaps on a trip to Israel. My unfortunate cup was made of melted-down German coins at my father's request, while he was a British soldier occupying Germany at the conclusion of the War. I detailed the trials and tribulations of trying to restore this damaged cup that my father gave to my grandfather in 1945. The magazine published photos of my father in uniform, and my grandfather as he appeared when he lived in London during the time of the Blitz. Also included—an explanation of how my father changed his name to Dean at the urging of the British army, while my grandfather retained the name of his Polish heritage, Joseph Diener.

While my ravings are usually confined to the local area, this piece was published by the Masorti/Voices of Conservative Judaism Magazine, an international publication that reaches hundreds of thousands of readers across the country. Well-wishers called my mother. Long lost friends called to say they'd seen my piece. A female Rabbi in Israel sent an email to tell me she was using the story in a course she was teaching about traditions. I have her Hebrew translation of my story to prove it. I was flattered by the attention and the chance to have my work read by so many people. But nothing could have prepared me for the call I got last week from Canada.

"Hello, you don't know me, but I read your story in the Masorti magazine," the caller began. I glanced at the caller ID. My eyes widened—we don't get many calls from telemarketers in Ottowa, Canada. "A couple of friends told me to read your story," he continued. "I really liked it."

"Thanks, I appreciate that," I said, flattered.

"From your story I see that your father changed his name from Diener to Dean during the War."

I listened, always happy to discuss anything about my writing.

Then he dropped his bombshell. "My name is John Diener. What town was your grandfather born in? Mine was from a little town in Poland named Grzymalow."

I called to my wife, who, organized whiz that she is, brought me a sheath of papers detailing our family tree, a document I had prepared after interviews with my family years ago. The breath caught in my throat, and I became aware of my heartbeat.

"My grandfather was also from Grzymalow," I said in a whisper. In all my years I had never met another Diener, and was convinced that they all perished in the Holocaust. My mind whirled. After the War my father had been stationed in Stuttgard, Germany, and he tried, to no avail, to find any remnants of his family.

"They were all slaughtered by the Nazis," he had told me when I was a boy.

I continued reading to John from my notes. "My grandfather, Joseph, had three sisters, Frima, Dina, and Freida, and his father's name was Ephraim. There was a long pause on the other end of the phone call. Had I bored my newfound friend from Canada? I wondered. "Hello, are you there?" I said.

"Ephraim was my grandfather's brother's name," John said. I stopped breathing.

"Artie, I think we're cousins."

I looked up at my wife, my vision suddenly clouded.

"What is it?" she said.

"I think I just found part of my family," I said.

What followed over the past week is a flurry of emails and phone calls that have electrified my usually calm household. It turns out that John is 58, exactly my age. His father, Nathan, survived a concentration camp. After the War he was sponsored by relatives Sam and Goldie in Canada and immigrated to Ottawa. When I had time to think I remembered meeting these two relatives when I was a young boy when they came to visit my grandfather in the Catskill Mountains.

John is a geneology buff, which explains why he took the time to find me. He writes a column on genealogy for the Ottawa Jewish Leader. A few days ago he sent me copies of documents that chronicle my father's history—the 1947 ship's manifest of the Queen Mary, listing my father and his parents as passengers on the trip that brought them to the United States—a letter that my father wrote to authorities in Germany hoping to find news of any surviving members of the family, a social security application my grandfather prepared, listing Grzymalow as his town of birth. The news is a bit overwhelming. I feel happy to know I am less alone in the world than I thought, but saddened to think that I might have found my family if I had only looked.

The latest wrinkle in the story: John contacted relatives in London and Paris, also distant cousins who remember meeting my father and grandparents at a Bar-Mitzvah in London before they left for America. I wish my father were still alive so I could share the news with him.

I'm not sure what will come of all this. Will I one day meet John Diener from Ottawa? I certainly hope so, and I suppose a trip to London and Paris to search out these other Dieners would be a reasonable quest. I am stunned that knowledge of newfound branches of my family tree grew out of a story for the Jewish Leader. Many of my friends are first generation Americans who lost their families in the Holocaust. Some travel to Europe to research their past. Some stay at home and use the Internet for their search. One thing is clear. We may not be as alone as we think.

IN REMEMBRANCE

I often think of my earliest years as a boy in New York City. My grandmother lived upstairs in our Washington Heights apartment building. She was an old fashioned Bubba born in Galitzia, Poland, the province of Eastern Europe that changed hands frequently at the whim of politicians' negotiations. During the twentieth century her tiny village of Skalat, near Tarnapole, was first part of the Austrian Hungarian Empire, then Russian, then Polish again in a progression of transfers since the First World War. It's Russian now, once again part of the Ukraine. But regardless of nationality the Jews of that region had a language and culture that stretched unbroken back in history. They spoke Yiddish.

With her love of family, her big boned features and warm smile she was the epitome of an old-fashioned Jewish grandmother. In an unguarded moment when I was two, I overheard my grandfather call her "Nunu," (meaning beloved in Polish.) I began to call her by that name. It stuck, and from then on our family called her Nunu, although her real name was Rose.

Our family's suffering during the years of World War Two was rarely talked about, but was never far removed from the surface. Every Jewish immigrant in our neighborhood who escaped Europe had a miraculous story of survival. One day, (I must have been about five) I took the stairs to her apartment on the fifth floor. I lived on the sixth. I stood in admiration and watched while she prepared her famous strudel.

"Nunu what is a Shwitz?" I had overheard my parents discussing the death camps earlier that morning.

She stopped kneading the dough and glanced up, her eyes searching my face for a glimpse of understanding.

"A Schwitz is a type of steam bath, Tattela. The Concord Hotel has a big one. It's good for you...cleans the skin."

"But how can it kill you?" I asked.

Her forehead wrinkled into a washboard of bewilderment.

"Wait a moment," she said and then placed the mound of dough in the center of a wooden board, sprinkled it with flour and covered it with a large glass bowl.

I pictured emaciated children sitting around a swimming pool, waiting their turn to invigorate themselves with a nice steam bath. Even at five I had seen pictures of starving children in the concentration camps. How would they get to the Concord?

"Daddy said the Nazis killed millions."

Her eyes flew wide. "Ach... Auschwitz," she muttered. She wiped her hands on her apron and led me to the couch in the living room.

"Sit, Tattela," she said, without the smile that usually etched her face. "I will tell you a story." I nestled beside her.

"Once upon a time the Jews of Europe were like a great forest filled with beautiful pine trees. The trees had grown for so many years that no one remembered a time when they had not been there. As each year passed, the older trees grew taller until their branches reached to the sky. Tiny saplings grew into young pines from the pinecones of their ancestors. When the older trees died, there were always younger pines to take their place. Do you understand?"

I nodded and held onto her apron, happy to hear a good story, for my Nunu was a wonderful storyteller.

"Then one day there was a terrible fire in the neighboring village. Flames leaped all around the forest. Now, trees being trees, they had big strong roots and they had to stay. The fire consumed them and the pine forest burned to the ground."

My eyes felt moist. I pictured a forest of burned trees like in the Smokey the Bear commercials on TV.

"Why didn't anyone put out the fire?" I asked.

A sad smile came over Nunu's face.

"They tried, Tattela. But for a long while no one believed that such a beautiful forest could burn to the ground. By the time people came to help it was too late." A single tear ran down Nunu's cheek. She seemed to be looking past me, her eyes unfocused and glistening.

"But what happened to all the little trees?" I asked, alarmed to see her so unhappy.

She didn't answer. I tugged on her apron. "The trees, Nunu, what happened? Tell me already."

She took a tissue from her apron, wiped her eyes and blew her nose. "The little trees vanished with the forest. Now let me go. I've got so much work to do."

"Finish the story," I begged.

Nunu's face brightened. "All right, so listen. When the fire was over, a great wind arose. The seeds from that pine tree forest were blown all over the world. Some landed in Israel, and some made it all the way here. You understand?"

This confused me. I had heard about forests in Israel, but from what I had seen of my New York City neighborhood, there weren't many trees at all—especially not pines. I nodded anyway because I wanted to hear the end of the story.

"And so the pine trees took root amongst the oaks and the chestnuts, the birches and the willows. And, in time, even though the pine forest never again grew so big and so tall, now there are pine forests all over the world." She smiled and folded her big hands in her lap.

"But will the big pine forest ever return?" I asked.

"Maybe not in my lifetime Tattela, but maybe in yours. Just make sure you take care of the seeds." She stroked my head. "Now come to the table and have a sugar cookie. I made them just for you."

She led me back to the kitchen, poured me a glass of milk, and placed a plate of warm cookies before me.

"I love you, Nunu," I said.

"I love you too, Tattela. Now eat up and no more questions for today."

A MIRACLE IN NEW LONDON

A short story in memory of the liberation of Auschwitz

I worked a double shift that day. Maybe that explains what happened—maybe not. Funny things happen when you're tired. I just can't keep this to myself anymore.

The restaurant was quiet—usually is on the fourth of July. I was tending bar. We'd been deserted most of the night, and the last few customers were leaving. I normally close at two, but I was hoping to leave early since business was slow.

The door opened and a figure draped in a wet blue poncho slid into the room and sat at the end of the bar. He'd be tall if it weren't for the hunch. I glanced over quickly not wanting to be too nosy. After midnight you know to mind your business. He wore a black beret slanted to one side. In the dark I couldn't see his face, but I had the impression from the way he moved that he was an old man.

As if he knew I wanted to leave he looked me right in the eye.

"Double whiskey, straight up," he said.

I poured the drink and brought it over. He paid with five silver dollars— don't see too many of those. Then he extended a bony hand.

"Name's Jacques—Jacques Rothenberg," he said with a vaguely familiar accent.

I took his hand hesitantly. His grip was a vice, his skin like sandpaper. He picked up the shot glass, tipped it towards me, and then drained the whiskey in one gulp. He sucked in a deep breath, letting it out slowly. I went back to the other end of the bar to start cleaning up, but I couldn't take my eyes off the old guy. He took off his poncho, checked his watch, and stared out over the harbor. A flash of lightning lit the sky, setting the water ablaze, silhouetting the fleet of bobbing sailboats moored in the river. After five years tending bar in this place you take the view for granted, but there's something magical about a storm on the water.

"I come here once a year on the fourth, at midnight, and she's never shown up," he muttered, stroking his beard.

The old guy seemed to be talking to himself. I looked away, started rinsing a few glasses. When I glanced back the old man put his head in his hands and wept.

Usually I don't mix in, but I couldn't help myself. I dried the last glass and approached him, a bottle of whiskey in hand.

I cleared my throat. "Who are you waiting for?"

He looked up, his eyes glistening. "My wife Anna," he croaked. She left for New York from Marseille with our two-year-old daughter, Rachel. They never arrived.

I poured him another drink, on the house.

26

"Flights don't come into Groton Airport from overseas—just domestic. You must have made a mistake. When did they leave?"

He leaned back and wiped his eyes, revealing a faded green number tattooed on his right forearm. The sight of it sent a chill through me, even though the bar was stuffy.

"1942," he said hoarsely. "But they didn't fly...lucky to get on a freighter, the Rotterdam."

I dropped my towel. "But that was more than sixty years ago."

He shrugged, and then drained the shot of whiskey. He put a bony hand on my arm, his coal-black eyes ablaze.

"She was a refugee ship. Cost me everything I had to get them passage... thought I did the right thing to get them out of Europe."

His voiced cracked. "I stowed away on another ship the next day...damn Nazis"

"Nazis?"

He stared at the empty glass. I filled it.

"The ship made it to Providence, but the harbormaster turned them away—no papers."

He sighed, pointing toward the mouth of the river, but his eyes had a glassy far away look. "They waited 'til nightfall, then sailed down the coast toward New London—must have thought they'd have better luck here."

I nodded, but said nothing; by this time I had forgotten all about leaving early.

The old man continued. "German U-boat picked them up around Montauk—followed them. Freighter must have figured the U-boat wouldn't follow him close to shore, so he slipped into Long Island Sound, around Ledge light, up the Thames, headed for New London Harbor."

The old man scratched his beard with a trembling hand. "Freighter made it to the state pier, when a torpedo split her in two. Four hundred people lost, and no one found any remains. It's as if they just disappeared off the face of the earth."

I shook my head. "Why do you keep coming back?"

The old man let go of my arm and wiped his eyes.

"Got to. Came to me in a dream the year after it happened...saw that ship sail right into New London Harbor. Saw my wife and child step off that boat and walk down the gangplank...walked right into my arms.

I felt sorry for the old guy. From the look in his eyes, I knew he believed that dream, no matter how crazy he might be.

"Why July 4th?"

"Saw fireworks go off across the harbor. Had to be the fourth. Been coming here every year." His eyes narrowed as he stared into the distance.

I scanned the harbor, trying to see what he was searching for. Tiny lights dotted the Long Island shore. The rain had let up, but lightning still flashed in the distance. A tug slipped by, but aside from the lone call of a seagull, the docks were silent.

"Ships don't come here much anymore, and they don't do fireworks on the fourth," I said.

The old man didn't respond. He just stared out at the harbor. Then he motioned with his index finger.

"Gimme another."

I checked my watch. "All right, but that's the last call." I poured him another whiskey.

"Nazis took everything I had in the world. I should have been on that ship."

The old man downed his last drink. "I dream of my Anna and little Rachel every night."

I glanced at my watch. It was 1:30. I wanted to leave, but I didn't have the heart to kick the old guy out. I walked to the door, locked it, then returned to the bar and took a drink for myself.

"Listen Mister. Do you have a place to stay? Don't be ashamed. There are city shelters. I'll find you a place to sleep." I reached for the phone.

"No!" he shouted. "Please...I know she will come. I will see Rachel again. They must come this year."

His wrinkled hands clasped together in the manner of a prayer. Small beads of sweat covered his pale brow. He swayed, and almost fell from his stool.

I shook him gently. "You all right? You don't look so good."

"I'm sick, but it will pass. Doctor says I have cancer. They give me six months."

I was about to call 911 when suddenly he rose, his face twitching, eyes wide with excitement.

"Good luck," I muttered, as he bolted to the door and ran towards the pier. I was surprised an old man could move like that, especially him being sick and all.

I washed his shot glass, toweled off the counter, locked the cash register, and closed up for the night. As I walked towards my car I stopped and looked out at the pier. The old man was pacing up and down at the end of the dock.

"Crazy old guy," I muttered, and turned away. A foghorn bellowed. I twirled around. A beacon of light knifed through the darkness, bathing the pier in an eerie glow. The old man waved his arms and did a little pirouette. I was afraid he was thinking of throwing himself off the dock. The horn sounded again.

He cupped his hands around his mouth and shouted something; I strained to hear.

"Anna! My little Rachel, at last!"

I shook my head sadly. *Poor fool—probably just a fishing boat coming in. He's chasing after ghosts.*

I got in my car and swung onto the access road to I-95. Before I got onto the highway, I looked one last time for the old man.

An old freighter pulled up to the dock, black smoke billowing in the wind, its lower deck bathed in light. I saw hundreds of people—old men, women and children, as they crushed forward along the railing.

I pulled onto the shoulder and rubbed my eyes. The image of the freighter shimmered, the lights of the opposite shore twinkling through the body of the ship. People ran down the gangplank, arms outstretched, laughing and screaming.

When I looked back at the pier, I couldn't see the old man—just a man about twenty wearing a blue poncho. A woman with a little child in her arms ran down the gangplank. The young man, hoisted the child to the sky, kissed her gently, and then embraced the young woman, their sweet laughter rising above the clamor of the crowd.

Just then an explosion startled me. I looked skywards towards the flash. Bright streaks of red, white, and blue burst over the pier, and then floated slowly towards the water. *What the hell? Crazy kids. Who the hell would light fireworks off at two a.m.?*

When I looked back at the pier the freighter had vanished. The pier was deserted. All I saw was a blue poncho, floating on a gust of wind, dancing in the air amongst wisps of white smoke. Suddenly it twisted, fell, and then slipped into the water. I ran to the pier, tried to find the spot where the poncho had disappeared, but it was too late.

I drove home slowly through a thick fog, but I couldn't stop thinking about the old man—couldn't stop thinking about what I saw that night. The next day I called my buddy who works at the New London Day. He did a little checking. The name the old guy gave me, Jacques Rothenberg, must have been an alias. Just the previous night an old man by that name was found dead, alone in a homeless shelter. The police report confirmed it. All they found in his wallet was an immigration card dated 1946, and a faded picture of a young man and a woman, holding a baby between them. I checked with the Coast Guard. No ships had docked at New London Pier the night of the fourth. Still, I know what I saw. Guess some things just can't be explained.

It Happened One Night in New London

As I stood shivering on the boardwalk at Ocean Beach, I stared out towards Montauk Point. I had blown off the invitation to attend Friday night services, looking instead for the solace of the ocean. My teeth chattered. Suddenly I became aware of a stranger sitting on a bench nearby.

"You break a da Shabbos," I thought I heard him mutter.

"Can I help you?" I asked, unable to hide the belligerence in my voice. He was dressed in a black coat, belted at his waist, and a white shirt, the collar stretched taught by his thick neck. Long tzitzits flowed from beneath his shirt and nearly scraped the floor. "Chabad must be having a convention," I muttered beneath my breath. I was about to tell him to mind his own business.

Then he stood. "Are you talking to me?" he said.

"Uh, no, sorry, never mind," I said in a breathless voice, my heart hammering in my chest, for not in my 27 years on this earth had I ever seen a man so large. He stood 7 feet tall, with shoes that looked the size of swimming flippers.

He stared down into my face with steel blue eyes so intense I had to turn away.

"It's not right to break the Shabbos," he said with a glance over his shoulder at my car parked in the parking lot.

"I know, I know." I said, feeling like a twelve year old being chastised by my Rabbi all those years ago. I wondered how the Chassid got to the beach if he didn't drive, but I didn't dare ask.

"Are you a Rabbi?" I asked.

He shook his head. "No, I'm not."

"So why do you care if I drive on the Sabbath?"

His eyes flashed as if I'd stabbed him with a red-hot poker.

"Where I come from we care about things like that."

From his accent I thought he might be from New Jersey. *Maybe he's one of those black hatters from Lakewood, out on a mission for the Rebbe.*

He held up the biggest hand I had ever seen and glanced at his watch. "It's time for services," he said. "We need you."

I grimaced, and opened my mouth to speak, then hesitated. I had intended to say "No, thank you," but instead I merely nodded obediently, amazed at the power this stranger had on me. "Where are we going? Beth El? Ahavath Chesed?"

He shook his head and turned the large gold ring he wore on his finger. I thought I saw Dallas Cowboys 1993 inscribed on its face surrounded by diamonds.

"Where'd you get the Superbowl ring?"

"I won it."

I laughed. "At cards?"

"I never gamble," he said. "I played offensive tackle for the Dallas Cowboys."

"Sure, and I'm the King of England."

A cloud passed over the moon, the darkness making his scowl even more ominous. "Even a football player can find God. Now come, services are starting any minute. Besides, this might change your life forever."

"What about my car?"

"You won't need that where we're going," he answered.

"Exactly where are we going?" I said. He opened his coat revealing a black and white folded tallis. He wrapped me in what seemed like ancient cloth, ignoring my protests. "Yerushalayim," I thought I heard him whisper in my ear.

Suddenly a gust of wind set my hair in a wild dance and seemed to be lifting me, as if a hurricane had swept in from the Sound. Just when I thought I might faint the wind ceased and the tallis slipped from my shoulders. I was standing in a narrow alley, the street lined with stone houses that might have been built in the Middle Ages.

I looked for my giant Chassid, but he was nowhere to be seen, only the sound of muffled laughter in the distance a clue to his disappearance.

"Praise Hashem, we've got our minyan," an elderly man shouted in Yiddish from an open doorway. "You're just in time. Come in."

I followed like a man in a trance. He led me into a small room with men lost in prayer.

"Is this the New London Chabad?" I asked. The man's eyes twinkled, but he said nothing.

"Can you daven?" he asked.

I shook my head. "Not so good. But where's all the snow?"

Again no answer. "Didn't the angel tell you where he was taking you?"

I cringed, my knees weak. *Angel? I must be dreaming.* While my mind said run, my legs seemed incapable of leaving the tiny room packed with nine shriveled men whose average age might have topped a century. All I could think of was that no one back in New London would ever believe my story. I found myself praying, uttering bits of Hebrew verses I thought I had forgotten soon after my Bar Mitzvah. I'm not sure what I was saying but when we finished, every one of those men shook my hand and kissed me on the cheek.

"It's a special honor to make the minyan," the last man said. "May it bring you masel." Then he thrust a silver goblet with schnapps into my hand. "L'chaim," he said. One gulp later my head was spinning. I staggered back to a chair and fell into a deep sleep.

When I awoke my teeth were chattering. The old men were gone. I was back in my car in the parking lot of Ocean Beach. Before I could come to my senses a cop drove by and eyed me suspiciously.

"We don't allow any funny business in New London," he said. "If you're a troublemaker, you came to the wrong town. I'll give you two seconds to clear out."

I drove away slowly, the effects of the schnapps wearing off rapidly. I would have thought it was all a hallucination except I found the black and white tallis folded neatly in the back seat.

A week later on Friday night I found myself drawn to the synagogue. I sat in the back, wrapped in the black and white tallis. I returned the next week, and the three after that. By the second month the rabbi knew me by name. He gave me an aliyah on that fateful Shabbat morning.

At the end of the service I noticed a huge man in the back row with a tallis wrapped around his head.

"Good Shabbos," he said as I approached. "My, my, never thought I'd find you here."

His hand was a vice, the golden Superbowl ring nearly severing my fingers.

"I'd like you to meet my daughter," he said as soon as the color returned to my face.

I followed him to the lobby, then glanced at the front door, prepared to make a run for it if the daughter looked anything like the father.

"This is Rachel," he said. "We're new in town." I glanced about nervously, then I noticed her dark eyes and shy smile. My eyes flew wide. The girl before me was the most beautiful girl I had ever seen. When I smiled, she averted her eyes.

"Come for Shabbat lunch," the man mountain by my side said, more of a command than a request. I hesitated. A religious family doesn't normally extend an invitation like this casually. I glanced at Rachel's father, his smile warm and welcoming, as if I were the only man in the world worth introducing to his daughter. *Why the change of heart?*

"So, you'll come?"

Again, I hesitated. The knuckles of my right hand still throbbed from our handshake. I pictured sitting at a beautiful table piled with delicacies. What harm could come from a home cooked meal? I imagined walking home with Rachel, perhaps a second meeting, or a third, and then who knows? I glanced again at my newly found benefactor, and wondered once again about that eerie night the previous month on the boardwalk of Ocean Beach. *Had my mystical trip to Jerusalem been a hallucination brought on by scotch and the start of the flu, as my physician had insisted? Can a hallucination be trusted to provide lunch and not ask for something in return?* I rubbed my hand absentmindedly. *What would it feel like to have those giant meat hooks wrapped around my scrawny neck?* I glanced at Rachel, who turned her face towards mine, her eyes flashing.

"Yes, do come," she said.

My knees felt weak. "Of course," I said, my trepidation suppressed. "What can I bring?"

"Only an open mind is required," he said. "See you around one?"

When I approached his home the aroma of simmering onions wafted from the window. My taste buds watered in a manner reminiscent of visits to my bubby's house all those years ago when I was a child. I approached the door and the sound of muffled laughter filled my ears. When I knocked the sounds ceased abruptly. The reverberation of heavy footsteps signaled that my host was at home. I waited. I raised my hand to knock again, but the door flew open. My eyes bulged at the site of the middle-aged man towering above me, his velvet yarmulke nearly flush with the top of the doorframe, an apron strapped around his middle. His sleeves were rolled up, revealing massive forearms. "Come in," he bellowed in a thunderous voice, his eyes twinkling, his face lit with a smile. I glanced around the room—no sign of Rachel.

"Oh, don't worry, she'll be along in a bit," he said. "She's visiting with the Rebbitzen. Meanwhile, sit with me in the kitchen."

I followed, my senses intrigued by the sights and aromas of an elaborate feast. Set on the table were delicacies fit for a wedding or Bar Mitzvah reception. There were plates of stuffed derma, kishka, and kasha varnishkes fit for a king. A pot of cholent bubbled gently. A heaping tray of roast beef sat beside noodle kuggle (all pareve of course). While my host turned his back to arrange a tray of garlic pickles I reached out to scoop up some chopped liver with a cracker.

"Here we wait until Kiddush and Motzi, my friend," he said, without turning around. I dropped the morsel as if it were poisoned, and folded my hands together.

"Of course," I said, shifting my weight from foot to foot.

"Let's go over this week's parsha," while we wait for Rachel," he said casually. He led me to a study, and motioned me to a leather chair. Then he pulled a Chumash from a bookcase and placed it in my hands. When I stared at him helplessly he opened the book with a flick of his finger. "Ah, that's it," he said, seemingly pleased with his accuracy. To my amazement the portion of the week was my own Bar Mitzvah portion. I read from the English, he from the Hebrew. He asked me questions, to which I mostly shrugged, and then listened while he explained at great length. I glanced at my watch, wondered what was keeping Rachel. As we continued to study, the memory of my long forgotten parsha resurfaced. Haltingly, I chanted the Haftorah, to my new teacher's delight. When I discussed its relevance to the Torah portion my host smiled.

After an hour Rachel bounced in through the door, her girlish laughter fading to silence as soon as our eyes met.

"We'll be done in a few minutes," Rachel's father said. "He's a natural."

"I didn't know you were a scholar," Rachel said, her eyebrows raised.

"I'm trying," I said, fully aware that my knowing the week's portion must have been a miracle.

"I admire scholars." Rachel said. "I like to study with Poppa on Saturday afternoons when he has time."

"I've got plenty of time," I said, my heart pounding to a wild klezmer beat.

"We'll see," she said, and scurried to the kitchen, the hint of a smile creasing her lips as she turned away.

After the meal I sat with Rachel and we discussed the portion, while her father hovered in the kitchen and did the dishes. I found it hard to concentrate, but I managed to keep my attention on the book, afraid of her father's reaction if he caught my eyes lingering on his daughter.

"So, you'll come again next week?" Rachel asked, when father and daughter walked me to the door. "We can study next week's portion."

I glanced up at the giant Chassid. He nodded his approval, but his eyes looked as if he were suppressing a laugh.

I spent the week in anxious preparation. I studied the portion on Aish.com. I got an English copy of the Torah Anthology from the synagogue library and reviewed the Sage's analyses. *How I wished I had paid more attention in Hebrew School.*

When I met Rachel again the following week she seemed surprised by my knowledge.

"Are you sure you didn't study in a Yeshiva?" she said when it was time to leave.

Her man-mountain of a father merely waved good-bye from the kitchen, his eyes full of mirth. I began to believe that my initial meeting with Rachel's father at Ocean Beach on that winter's eve was merely a hallucination, brought on by the freezing cold, and a glass full of scotch. I was afraid to bring it up, sure that the mention of my fantasy flight to Jerusalem for a minyan would convince Rachel that I was a lunatic. Instead I kept my doubts to myself, and since Rachel's father never mentioned it, neither did I.

A year of weekly Shabbat lunches and meetings with Rachel passed, under her father's watchful eye. I gained 15 pounds. I learned everything I could of our Jewish traditions. When with trembling hands I asked Rachel to be my wife, she glanced immediately towards her father, who with arms crossed over his massive chest, smiled and said merely, "Why not?"

That was almost a year ago. Rachel and I are expecting the first of what I hope will be many children. My father-in-law continues to be a guiding presence in our lives, but he's much more relaxed. Mixed in with his Torah discussions he fills me with stories of his previous life as an offensive lineman in the NFL. While he swears he wouldn't hurt a fly, I never want to see him angry. With everything going so well with Rachel his demand to meet me on Ocean Beach this Friday night caught me off guard.

I walked the three miles from my apartment despite the mind numbing cold. Once on the boardwalk I asked him to explain. He pointed to a forlorn looking young man who was leaning over the railing, staring out at the churning sea. Then my father-in-law handed me a black and white tallis.

"You know what to do," he whispered in my ear as he gave me a friendly nudge.

My mouth fell open, my protests swallowed by the whipping wind. My father-in-law's eyes narrowed and his massive hands balled into fists. "I'm counting on you," he said.

I approached the young man hesitantly, for I was not in the habit of talking to complete strangers. I could see he was shivering, his eyes wet with tears. I handed him the tallis, and much to my surprise he let me wrap it around his shoulders, and huddled in its warmth.

Turns out the unfortunate boy was homesick and alone, a freshman at Mitchell College. The other students in his dorm were gone for Presidents week vacation, while he had missed the last train home.

"You're coming with me," I said, prying his near frozen hands from the railing. "On Shabbat we always serve chicken and scotch."

This seemed to soothe his agitation. Whether it was the promise of "chicken a la Rachel," or a bottle of single malt, I'll never know. But I do know my father-in-law approved. And when the young man came to services the following morning, wrapped in the black and white tallis, and sat with our growing family, my father-in-law's face was lit with pleasure.

"Not bad, for a beginner," he whispered in my ear. "But there are still a few tricks I need to teach you before I leave."

"Leave?" I nearly shouted. "What are you talking about?"

He placed a hand on my shoulder in a gentle manner and stared into my eyes. "Even an old football player needs a replacement once in a while."

"But where will you go?" I asked, my voice shrill.

He turned his palms to the sky. "Boca, maybe Miami. Somewhere warm where they need a little extra yiddishkeit. But don't worry. I'll be back to check up on you in June."

I raised a hand to my forehead. "So, that night on the boardwalk, my trip to Jerusalem for a minyan, that was you? It really was a miracle?"

He hesitated. Then he shrugged. "You study our traditions and attend Shabbat services. You've got a wife who adores you and a child on the way. Why ask about miracles?"

Epilogue: As far fetched, as this story may seem it was inspired by the true tale of Mr. Alan Shlomo Veingrad. He played in the NFL for seven seasons as an offensive lineman for the Packers and Cowboys, winning a Superbowl ring with the Dallas Cowboys in 1993, blocking for the legendary Emmet Smith. He turned to religion after he retired and raised his children in the Chassidic tradition. He travels the country speaking of his experiences for the Chabad movement. I did indeed meet him one Shabbat afternoon on the campus of the University of Pennsylvania. He is a very powerful man, and I'm not referring only to his physical stature. He maintains a web site at www.alanveingrad.com.

Not Just Another Old Lang Syne

Harvey Rosenblatt approached Times Square with a mix of excitement and trepidation. He glanced at the package yet again, confirmed the address 2074 47th Street for the fifth time. *Why would an Orthodox Rabbi send me to the Diamond district on New Year's Eve?* He had thought of knocking off early that day, time and a half or not, but hey, in the last analysis, he needed the money.

He palmed the softball-sized package in one hand, then shook it gently, as if the rattle might give some clue to the riches inside. Not that he was usually the nosy type. No, Harvey had made a career of looking the other way and minding his own business, a quality that had kept him regularly employed in New York's Diamond District these past 5 years. Besides, he pondered as he fought his way up the packed steps of the Times Square subway station, *if I lose this job who else would hire a man with a record?*

Finding the streets impassable with would be revelers waiting for the ball to drop, Harvey decided to walk cross-town on 43rd and head up 5th Avenue. As he walked he passed a Salvation Army station. The sign read, "Feed the Hungry."

A smile creased his lips. He imagined dropping his package in the kettle and heading back to Brooklyn early. And he would have too, if not for that little voice in his head that said *what about Sarah?*

What about Sarah? That little phrase was the first thing he thought of when he rose, and the last thing he thought of each night before he dozed off. It was also the first thing his estranged wife had said to the judge, before they split. If only he had read the last paragraph of the divorce decree more carefully before he signed.

"Trust me," the ex said. "I want what's best for the child."

How could he have known the full impact of that lovely lawyerly phrase, *Child support in perpetuity?* The final mistake, of course, was risking everything for that crazy get rich scheme.

"What about Sarah?" was the phrase he muttered when the Feds came to his Merrill Lynch office and took him away in hand cuffs. And now that ten years had passed and his precious Sarah was at the NYU campus he worked sixty-five hours a week to help pay her tuition—not that she would ever know. He slept in a rat infested 4th floor walkup in Bensonhurst. *And now my little angel's a college girl.* He supposed silent support was better, after all the poison his ex had spewed to turn his only child against him. It had been ten long years since he'd last held his darling child in his arms.

"Let her keep thinking you moved to Australia," his ex kept saying.

He took a deep breath and turned up his collar to block the chilling wind that was blowing up the Avenue. *What I wouldn't do to put things right.*

As he turned up 5th Avenue a flood of possibilities rose in his mind. Again he held the package and rattled the contents, imagining the tiny thuds to be diamonds the size of grapes, sapphires like peach pits. *Think what I could do with that kind of money...pay for college and med school in one fell swoop.* But then the pang of those five years behind bars stabbed at his heart. *No, I made that mistake once. Can't let that happen again....would rather die.*

He continued up the avenue taking stock of his life, and making resolutions to make amends—after all, what else is New Year's Eve for? A momentary memory of his one remaining asset, his life insurance policy, rose in his consciousness, but he banished the evil thought that had been increasingly coming to mind.

"No, that's my last resort," he muttered as he reached 47th Street and turned west, his eyes searching for a sign to match the name on the box: David's Diamond Emporium. As his pace slowed he became aware of a scruffy figure dressed in a tattered pea coat who had turned up 47th when he did. *Didn't I notice that same man when he exited the subway back on 42nd, or am I losing my mind? Or maybe I saw him when I got on the train in Bensonhurst?* He shrugged off his creeping paranoia. He'd heard lots of stories of fellow deliverymen being robbed at gunpoint over the years, but for five years he'd avoided trouble.

As he continued he went over the litany of his failings. He thought of how his Hebrew School teacher had cursed him the day of his Bar Mitzvah.

"May you suffer for the torture you've put me through," he had whispered.

He thought of his father's favorite refrain, the one time he came to visit at the prison. "Once a bum, always a bum." And he thought of the hard curl of his mother's lips when he told her about the upcoming divorce.

It was then that he felt the hard prod in the small of his back. "Don't look back, and keep moving," a raspy voice commanded. Harvey froze. He thought he heard the click of a trigger being cocked, and then a voice whispered in his ear, "I said keep going."

A mist of sweat and whiskey washed across his face. Harvey fought the urge to retch.

"Look back and you're dead meat."

Clutching the package more tightly, his heart pounding, Harvey plodded west down 47th St. towards the neon sign of David's Diamond Emporium, now visible halfway up the block. He thought of the legions of cops milling about the station at 42nd. *Where are they when you really need them?* How he'd love to see one mounted on horseback ride to his rescue, just about now. But with most of the diamond district closed early for New Years, the street was relatively deserted. The shops usually brimming with life were eerily quiet...until they reached David's. A lone light lit the back of the shop, where a middle aged man wearing a kippah sat reading a thick leather bound book, clearly waiting for someone or something. The man behind Harvey moved into a doorway to avoid being seen. When Harvey glanced over all he saw was the muzzle of a gun pointed at his side.

Harvey hesitated. He thought of running. Perhaps a bullet in the back and a nice life insurance check for Sarah would be the best for everyone. Harvey reached out and tapped on the door. The man inside looked up and smiled. Harvey held up his package and pointed to the currier's cap on his head. The man inside kissed his book, closed it, and then hurried towards the door, a broad smile on his face.

"I was beginning to give up hope that you'd come," the man said after unbolting the door and opening it a crack.

Before Harvey could say a word the man with the gun scampered from his hiding place, pushed Harvey through the door, and then entered, holding the gun to Harvey's head.

"Give me everything you've got," the robber said. Then he shoved Harvey towards the jewelry store owner.

"Wish I could, believe me, I do," the owner said in a measured tone. "Everything's put away in the safe. Locked down for the night. Can't be opened until business starts tomorrow morning. That's how all the stores work in the Diamond Exchange. Why don't you come back at 9 a.m.?"

The robber glanced around the shop, noting the empty trays that an hour earlier had held millions of dollars worth of jewelry. He shifted his weight from foot to foot, glancing nervously through the store window.

The robber growled. "Why, I oughta put a bullet in your head."

Harvey edged towards the door. "Hey, you, gimme that," the robber said, gesturing towards the package and pointing the gun at Harvey's head. Harvey froze. The robber wrenched the package from Harvey's grasp.

"No, anything but that," the store owner said as he leaped forward, knocking the package to the floor and then jumping on it, shielding it from the gunman with his body.

"Must be a pretty big shipment of diamonds," the gunman said. Then he raised his pistol and pointed it at the store owner's cowed head.

"Hand it over, you filthy Jews."

Harvey looked on in terror, his hands to the sides of his head. *But I'm just the messenger.* He wanted to flee out the door and never look back—run back to his hole of an apartment in Brooklyn, safe to live yet another meaningless day. Yet something inside him made him stay. Harvey Rosenblatt was Jewish of course, even if he hadn't been inside a synagogue since his Bar Mitzvah.

"Hitler should have done a better job," the robber said.

Maybe it was the anti-Semitic taunts that Harvey endured as a child, or perhaps his knowledge that all his ancestors died in the gas chambers of Europe that made something click in his head. Or maybe, on that particular late afternoon, it was his mounting anguish over his daughter that catapulted Harvey Rosenblatt into action.

As the gunman placed the gun to the prostrate shop owner's temple Harvey Rosenblatt rushed forward and pounced on the robber's back. The fight took seconds, unfortunately for Harvey. When the gun went off and Harvey crumpled to the floor the robber ran for the door.

"Oh, Mister, Mister, what have you done?" the shop owner wailed, cradling

Harvey's head while the drone of a siren sounded in the distance.

"At least you got your diamonds," Harvey said, coughing, a trickle of blood oozing from one nostril.

"What diamonds?" the shop owner yelled, opening the package and dumping out a set of tefillin on the shop floor. "These were my father's. I had Rabbi Israel in Borough Park check the scrolls before I use them tonight. This is Papa's yartzheit."

Harvey turned to look into the man's eyes. *What kind of a man would risk his life for something like that?* Harvey coughed once more, the trickle of blood now a stream. He felt little pain, only the aching sorrow that now he might never get to see his Sarah. Later as they loaded him into the ambulance a weak smile came to his lips. *At least Sarah gets the insurance money.*

The shop owner stood muttering in shock.

"Mister, don't die, please, you saved my life. You can't die."

Conclusion

Harvey spent the next seven days in intensive care, slipping from oblivion to consciousness in a never-ending menagerie of tubes and IVs. Meanwhile Mr. Shmuel Katz, the jewelry store owner who was saved by Harvey's action, visited every day. Mr. Katz asked the nurses for updates. He brought fresh flowers. He davened in the chapel, praying for Harvey's recovery. He paid for the hospital's top pulmonary surgeon to fly back from a vacation in Mali to attend to Harvey's wounds. Katz was possibly the first person in the past five years who cared whether Harvey lived or died—pity Harvey himself had been so ambivalent.

"Everything happens for a reason," Katz muttered to Harvey's motionless body. "You can't die."

On the day after Harvey's selfless act landed him in the hospital an unnamed source at the police department leaked a grainy copy of the jewelry store security tape on YouTube—anonymous submission, anonymous location, with nothing to identify those on the tape.

Meanwhile, a week later, at the NYU cafeteria, Sarah Rosenblatt was clearing tables. She was a quiet girl, liked by all, even if she seemed a little withdrawn at times. The school psychiatrist called it mild depression brought on by an abandonment complex. She just called it the blues, brought on by overwork. Often she wondered why her doctor always wanted to bring the conversation around to her absent father—something she resisted. *Why talk about a man I haven't seen since I was eight? Besides, he ran off to Australia.* When she wasn't studying Organic Chemistry, stressed out over her workload, or bussing tables at the cafeteria, she volunteered at the local health clinic.

"Hey Sarah, check this out," a fellow classmate said, turning his laptop towards her, as she picked up an empty tray. "Here's something you don't see every day," he said. "A delivery man fighting off a gunman to save a complete stranger."

Sarah stared at the screen, the images a blur. She was still thinking of her

Chemistry exam and was about to turn away when for a brief second the delivery man's face came into full focus.

She could swear she'd seen his face before. But before she could watch the end of the video, her classmate had to dash off for class.

That night Sarah couldn't sleep. Her thoughts alternated between her next day's Organic exam and the grainy features on the video. So many times she saw someone she thought she recognized. She'd dwell on it for hours until all of a sudden the name would pop into her head. This time however, with the pressure of the exam looming, no name materialized, almost as if the man's features had been ripped from her memory.

Finally the alarm rang, and as she staggered to the shower she fought to banish this new obsession from her mind—at least until she could take her exam later that morning.

❖   ❖   ❖   ❖   ❖

Meanwhile, at the hospital, after the surgery to remove the bullet from his chest, Harvey Rosenblatt developed a staph infection that threatened to wipe out what little lung capacity he had left. In brief respites from his delirium his mind dwelled on one thing only. *At least Sarah will get the life insurance.* Day after day the doctors waited for Harvey's fever to break. They cultured, they sampled, they tested every fluid they could to find the right mix of antibiotics that could bring Harvey a cure. There was some concern his kidneys might be shutting down.

"The drugs should have worked by now," his surgeon lamented to the jeweler, Mr. Katz, three days later. "It's almost as if he's not trying to recover."

Mr. Katz redoubled his prayers, and then, just to cover all his bases, he contacted the head of Infectious Diseases.

"We can only do so much, Mr. Katz. After all, we're not miracle workers."

Although Harvey's employment records listed neither wife nor kin, Mr. Katz had a nagging feeling that someone somewhere must have at one time cared about Harvey Rosenblatt. Certainly, he felt, *I should notify someone.* Whether it was his guilt for having survived while Harvey lay in a coma, or Katz's gratitude, who can say? Either way Harvey Rosenblatt's physical and mental health became Mr. Katz's overriding concern. He resolved to hire a detective to search Harvey's bank records.

Sarah finished her exam and then rushed back to her dorm. She whipped open her laptop and searched "delivery man hero," on YouTube. She found the video and watched it four times. She studied the one faded photo she had of her father—the only one that her mother hadn't burned. Finally she was certain. With tears streaming down her face she called her mother. "How could you lie to me all these years?" the conversation began.

After one week Shmuel Katz had the answer to the enigma of Harvey Rosenblatt's life. Outside of Wall Street, financial records don't lie. Shmuel Katz had everything: the address where Harvey mailed a monthly tuition check, the old alimony payments, even the restitution he made to his former employer at the investment firm. Katz smiled as he pulled into the hospital parking lot. *So the man has a daughter.*

❖   ❖   ❖   ❖   ❖

Sarah Rosenblatt entered the hospital room followed by Mr. Katz. She was shocked at what she saw. Instead of the vigorous lion of a father she remembered from her childhood, Harvey Rosenblatt looked more like a corpse under a shroud.

"Dad," she whispered. "Can you hear me?" Sarah waited for an answer, but then, hearing nothing, she placed her lips close to Harvey's ear.

"I love you Dad," she whispered. Harvey's lips twitched ever so slightly.

"Just a reflex," the nurse explained, when she stopped in on her rounds. Sarah sat in silence, but for the rhythmic beep of the EKG and the sound of nurses murmuring down the hall. Avoiding his IV, Sarah placed her hand in her father's palm. She squeezed his hand rhythmically to the beat of the Beatle's "I Want to Hold Your Hand," a little shtick Harvey would do when he took Sarah for walks back before everything in his life went to pieces. Even at the age of eight Sarah knew it was corny, but now, with her chance to reconnect so tenuous, she wanted desperately to feel a response. After an hour sitting by her father's side Sarah leaned forward and in a trembling voice began to sing.

"Oh yeah, I'll tell you something,
I think you'll understand,
When I say that something
I want to hold your hand,
I want to hold your hand,
I want to hold your hand…."

Her voice trailed off. She bit her lip with her eyes gleaming. "I'll stay, you go," she whispered to Katz, the kindly jeweler.

Antibiotics are a godsend. But every physician will admit to their limitations. Some infections are too virulent; some patients are too weak to respond. Even the germs themselves have become resistant, particularly those introduced deep into the chest by a foreign object, such as a bullet. But the balance between death and recovery tipped in Harvey Rosenblatt's favor somewhere around 3 a.m. that morning. A fine sheen of sweat rose on his forehead. The color returned to his cheeks. Somewhere around 5 a.m. unbeknown to his overworked nurses Harvey Rosenblatt's eyes fluttered and then opened. And, in a quivering voice undetectable to anyone but his daughter, Harvey Rosenblatt croaked the lyrics:

"Oh please, say to me,
You'll let me be your man,
And, please, say to me
I want to hold your hand…
I want to hold your hand."

41

Epilogue

Sarah visited her father every day, as did Katz, the jeweler, until Harvey was discharged from the hospital a week later. Father and daughter found they had a lot in common despite the ten years they'd lost. They shared lunch once a week, and Harvey learned how to laugh again. He stopped dwelling on his life insurance policy. Sarah's bouts of depression never returned.

Katz the jeweler never forgot that terrible day when he almost lost his life. He urged Harvey to return to his roots—even got Harvey to attend minyan now and again. And when Shmuel Katz, a widower without any children passed away quietly in his sleep a year later he left a sizeable portion of his estate to Harvey—enough to pay off all of Sarah's college loans and leave enough for medical school.

Harvey finally moved out of his dive in Bensonhurst. I'd like to tell you that Harvey and his ex reconciled, but who would believe a story like that?

BAR MITZVAH BLUES

Little Simon Moskovitz squirmed under the watchful eye of the Rabbi.

"No, that's a final mem, not a suff," the Rabbi said. How many times do I have to correct the same mistake? It's almost like you're not paying attention."

The boy fidgeted in his seat. Four months of intense preparation for his Bar mitzvah and he seemed farther from the demanded perfection than ever.

"You know, I've never had to cancel a Bar Mitzvah before," the Rabbi said in a somber tone. "Should I call your father?"

Simon's eyes nearly bulged from their sockets. An image of his father's face, swollen with rage, rose before him. *Please, God, no, anything but that.* He thought of all the times his parents had fought about money in the past year, bickering about the cost of the caterer when they thought he was asleep in his bed. Granted he dreamed of pitching for the New York Yankees when he should have been working on his speech, but cancel a Bar Mitzvah for daydreaming? *Can a Rabbi really do that?*

The Rabbi picked up the phone. He dialed a number.

"Pleeeese. Don't," the boy whimpered with the look of a deer caught in headlights."

"Hello, Mr. Moskovitz," the Rabbi said. "There's something I have to tell you."

"I'll work harder, really." Tears hovered on Simon's lower eyelids. He drew in a big breath. *That would be the last straw.*

The Rabbi covered the phone. "Alright, one more chance," he said with a glance at Simon. "But don't disappoint me."

"Mr. Moskovitz, Simon is finished for the day. You can pick him up now. He's still got some work to do before this Shabbos."

Simon exhaled. "Thank you," he whispered.

Simon sat silently in the back seat of his father's Porsche with his hands in his lap and his eyes on his shoes. Oblivious to all but his own woes he ignored the newspaper on the back seat folded open to the help wanted section.

"So, I hope this lesson was better than the last," his father said before his cell phone rang.

"Down another ten points? You've got to be kidding me!" his father shouted into his cell phone before he flung it across the front seat. "Jesus Christ, they're killing me!" he muttered, his son's trope prowess all but forgotten. Then he turned up the Bloomberg stock market report on the radio, and ran a hand through his thinning hair.

As Simon sat in the back seat he went over the worries that had been plaguing him all month. He thought of the way his father never seemed to have time for him anymore, working long hours at the bank. He thought of how his mother's eyes so often looked red in the morning. He thought of how the pressure of his Bar Mitzvah seemed to be driving his parents apart. *If they get divorced it's my fault.*

"Go do your homework," his father said when the car turned into the driveway. "And no funny business."

Simon kissed his mother on the cheek. She gave him a hug, but he pulled away when he sensed her staring at his father as he trudged through the door. "Good evening, honey," she said in a cautious tone. "Any luck?"

He dropped his attaché case on the floor, and shook his head. "Nothing yet. And you?"

She took a deep breath. "I didn't get it." The color drained from Mr. Moskovitz's face. He shrugged his shoulders and managed a weak smile. "At least we can be proud of the boy. The Rabbi says he'll be great."

Simon's stomach did a backflip, but he said nothing. He made a silent pledge to spend every night of the week practicing his parsha. He spent all afternoon on his homework. After dinner he made a beeline for his room, pulled out his Haftorah, and then shut the door. He got halfway through the blessings when he got a text message on his blackberry. "Watching the World Series tonight? Come over—Ruben." Simon pushed delete and went on practicing. Ten minutes later the phone rang. "Did you see that homer?" he heard Ruben say. Instead of dropping everything and heading for his best friend's house he made an excuse and went back to his singing. "So what do you really want for your birthday?" Ruben texted. Simon put his hands over his eyes and whispered a silent prayer. Somewhere around ten thirty he pushed the pages away and started down the stairs. He stopped when he heard the sound of his parents, their muffled voices tinged with anger.

"Maybe if you sold that damn car," he heard his mother say.

"Things will turn around," said his father. "Can I help it if the caterer went up twenty percent? What do you want me to do, cancel the boy's Bar Mitzvah?"

Simon snuck back to his room and redoubled his efforts. When finally he dozed off around midnight he dreamed of a time when he was six. He was in the backyard of the family's first little house, and his parents were taking turns pushing him on the swing. They were laughing, and when they stopped pushing the swing, they swept Simon from the seat and kissed him, alternating smooches on either cheek. Simon's shrill screams of "Never stop," sent his parents into hysterics.

Every night of the week Simon resumed his dedication. At Wednesday's lesson the Rabbi actually smiled. "Better," he said, without a hint of sarcasm. That afternoon his father picked him up in an old Chevy, a car that Simon had never seen before. "Hey, Dad, where's the Porsche?" was met only with silence as his father's hands tightened on the steering wheel.

"We've made some changes," his father said at last.

On Thursday the Rabbi patted Simon on the shoulder as Simon chanted the last notes of the Haftorah. "Just polish up the speech and I think you're golden," the Rabbi said. That afternoon Simon's father showed up wearing a pair of jeans and a flannel shirt, instead of his grey three-piece suit. He seemed more relaxed than usual, and as they drove home, his father put an arm around his shoulder. That night he heard his mother whistling as she made dinner—fried chicken, Simon's favorite. On Friday, the day before his Bar Mitzvah, both his mother and father showed up for his final lesson, a full run through. His parents sat beside one another on the leather couch in the Rabbi's office. As Simon went through the blessings, he saw his father take his mother's hand. As Simon chanted the Haftorah, his mother's face looked kind of funny, and she dabbed at her eyes with a tissue. As Simon began his speech his father's eyes were shining, his face beaming in a way Simon had never seen.

On the way home Simon sat between his parents. His father placed his arm around Simon's shoulder while his mother ran her fingers through Simon's hair. When they got to the fork where they usually turned right, they went left, to Simon's quizzical look.

"We're giving up the big house," his father said matter-of-factly as they reached the driveway of the little bungalow they had bought in their first year of marriage. Simon raced to the back yard. Although the seat was rather snug Simon squirmed onto the swing and pumped his legs for all he was worth as his parents watched with their arms around each other's waists.

The next morning as they walked up the steps to the synagogue Simon's father stopped. He kissed Simon's forehead. His mother did the same. "We are very, very proud of you," Simon's parents said in unison. They walked into the synagogue.

"So, I never asked you what you want for your Bar Mitzvah," his father said as he placed the tallis around Simon's shoulders, and they prepared to enter the sanctuary.

"I already got it, Dad," he said. Then he linked arms with his parents as they strode towards the bima.

Part 2

As Simon Moskovitz strode towards the bima his pace slowed. While his parents went to greet the Rabbi, Simon stood immobilized at the front of the sanctuary. He turned to look at the congregation and his breath caught in his throat. *There's hundreds of people here.* Some he knew well, a few he recognized as distant relatives, but most he had never seen before in his life. His tie felt suddenly more like a noose, his new blue suit like a straight jacket. He glanced down at the wing tip shoes his father purchased only last week—how he longed for the comfort of his stained Nike sneakers. A crushing realization slapped his face. *I've got to read Torah and chant my Haftorah in front of all those people*—not that he wasn't prepared. Over the past week he had redoubled his efforts and knew his parsha cold. It's just that he'd never practiced for more than two people at a time. Usually he practiced alone in his bedroom. His concern over his parent's arguments had driven thoughts of this day from his mind. Just then Joey Stern, his fellow Hebrew school buddy, slapped him on the back.

"What's the matter, nervous?" Joey said with a chuckle. "Thank God my Bar Mitzvah was in Israel. We barely had a minyan. You're going to have three hundred at least. Better not mess up."

Simon steadied himself against an upholstered bench, beads of sweat rising on his forehead.

"Remember, whatever you do, don't stop if the Gabbi tries to correct any mistakes," Joey continued. "Aaron did that last month and lost his place—got so flustered the Rabbi had to finish the Haftorah."

An image of the Rabbi frowning rose before Simon. He pictured the entire congregation laughing as he stumbled over the hebrew words. He glanced at the door. He thought of running back to the parking lot, but then he saw his parents advancing towards him with grins on their faces. "This is going to be great," his father whispered in his ear. "Rabbi says he's never seen a student make such a turnaround."

Simon's stomach felt as if he were at the top of a rollercoaster, poised to hurtle towards earth. He opened his mouth to reply but all that escaped was a squeak.

His father placed a hand on Simon's shoulder as the service was about to begin. "Are you alright son? You look a little green around the gills."

"I need some air," Simon said with eyes wide. Then he bolted towards the door. He brushed by his great aunt Sarah, just then arriving, and ran for the bathroom.

"But I came all the way from Miami," he heard her say in the distance as he threw open the door.

He locked the door, turned on the water in the sink, and looked in the mirror. "You can do this," he mumbled and took a deep breath. He stared at his reflection, hoping to screw up his courage, but all that stared back were the eyes of a frightened mouse. He cupped his hands and brought ice-cold water to parched lips. He thought of the caterer setting up the luncheon, the party decorations adorning the social hall, the hundreds of people there to see him deliver. He pictured chanting his Haftorah at Yankee Stadium on opening day.

"Oh dear God, I'll never get through this," he said to his reflection. Then he threw up in the sink.

After a few minutes the color came back to his cheeks. He heard the door rattle. Then came a knock at the door.

"Simon, they're waiting for you. Unlock the door, this instant!" his father said. As Simon did, the door flew open. His father took one look at his son's face and his anger melted away.

"Simon, Simon, Simon," his father said in a gentle tone. He shook his head, with the hint of a smile on his lips. He took out a handkerchief and wiped Simon's face. He straightened Simon's tie.

"I can't do it," Simon whispered and buried his face in his father's chest.

His father said nothing. He passed a hand through Simon's hair. He kissed the top of Simon's head. "I understand, and I can't force you, but I'll be right behind you on the bima in case you change your mind. Tell me what you're afraid of. Sometimes it helps to talk."

"Just give me a minute alone," Simon said. When his father left, Simon closed his eyes. His lips moved soundlessly. Certainly he had repeated prayers before, reciting the words written by others, never really sure what he was saying. But now as he tried to summon his courage the words flowed effortlessly and his eyes glistened.

Meanwhile, in the sanctuary, Simon's mother's eyes darted around the congregation. As each minute ticked by she became more and more frantic. The Rabbi pointed to his watch and looked at her with inquiring eyes. "Where's Simon?" he mouthed silently. She shrugged and turned her hands up in resignation. Time passed. The creases on the Rabbi's forehead deepened and his eyes narrowed. Finally he could wait no more. As the ark opened the congregation rose. The president of the synagogue marched the Torah around the sanctuary. The Torah scroll was brought to the table and spread wide. The blessings were recited.

"Shimon ben Avraham," the Rabbi announced from the bima, calling young Simon to read the scroll. No one stirred.

The Rabbi called louder, **"Shimon Ben Avraham."**

Still no response. A murmur spread through the congregation as all eyes cast about for Simon. Simon's mother leaned forward and placed her hands over her face.

At that moment the doors of the rear entrance opened. Simon and his father appeared in the doorway, their arms linked. Silence blanketed the congregation.

"Thank God," Simon's mother muttered.

"Shimon Ben Avraham," the Rabbi called, with renewed hope.

Simon took his place in front of the Torah scroll for an Aliyah. The Rabbi handed Simon a slender silver yad and pointed to a word. Simon wrapped a tallis strand around his finger, touched the scroll, and then brought his cocooned digit to his lips. He glanced at the Rabbi, who nodded. He looked over at his father who smiled. Simon coughed like a man in a tuberculin ward. Once, twice, three times. He wiped his forehead. Then in a small voice he said a blessing, the congregants straining to hear.

Words written down in antiquity flowed from Simon's lips.

"Very good," the Rabbi whispered under his breath, just loud enough for Simon to hear. Simon's voice gained strength as he read. At one point he glanced up to see his mother's beaming face. When he chanted the Haftorah his voice filled the sanctuary. Even the stragglers chatting in the hall stopped and listened at the door.

The Rabbi stared at Simon's small figure, wondering at the boy's newfound vitality.

When Simon reached the last line the congregation joined in. Then total silence descended. If applause were allowed in a synagogue, Simon would have received a standing ovation. He shook hands with the Rabbi, the president, and the Gabbi, who was smiling in a way no one in the congregation could ever remember. When Simon rushed to his parents in the front row they wrapped him in their arms. Later after the service Simon and his parents came back to the bima. "Thank you," Simon's father said to the Rabbi. "Thank you," Simon's mother repeated. "Thank you," Simon said as well. But as his parents and the Rabbi discussed Simon's extraordinary performance, Simon's eyes were not on them. Instead his eyes were fixed on the ark and the flickering eternal flame above it that he had never quite noticed before.

A SHABBAT TO REMEMBER

As men approach fifty, the age of wisdom, some do silly things. Blame it on a mid-life crisis, but let's face it, there are a lot of us driving sports cars that are more appropriate for our children. A generation whose parents' idea of a wild getaway was a weekend at the Concord, was, until recently, more likely to take the plane by that name than stay at the hotel.

The half-century mark seems to be a potent milestone, one that conjures up images of fear and dread for some, and a wake up call for others. Time is infinite, but only in physics textbooks, not for the individual. Ah, there's the rub. As I reveled in the congratulations of friends and family for achieving an age where some think of slowing down, I could only think of speeding up. One thought tugged at my subconscious—"What should I do to commemorate the big five O?"

The adage "I'd rather burn out than rust out," comes to mind." My sports life is an active one, some would use frenetic as a more accurate term. I am no couch potato. *Should I train to run a marathon? Ignore my aching knees? How about a triathlon—swim, bike, and run in smaller proportions?* A thirty-year-old acquaintance insists I can do it. *Ski the Alps? No, too expensive, besides one wrong turn and you're toast.*

So, one Shabbat, lost in thought as I sat in the back row at Beth El, and the Torah service began, the answer to these questions came to me in a flash. *Don't do anything physical. You've got nothing to prove. Chant a Haftorah*—easy for some, (my Schechter educated children just shrugged, when I told them), but for me the mental equivalent of climbing Mount Everest. The idea grew in my mind. *I'll repeat my Bar Mitzvah portion.* (I had relearned it when I turned forty). *That shouldn't be so hard.* Since Rabbi Astor was away on sabbatical I broached the idea to Diane Maran, who, in his absence, kept track of Shabbat Haftorah and Torah portions.

She smiled warmly when I told her. "So you want to chant Va'eira? I think that's great. Let me check on the date. I'll get back to you."

That night I announced my intentions to my family. My wife loved the idea. I saw my son and daughter exchange a quick glance—then a smile.

"Wasn't your Haftorah a really long time ago?" my daughter asked.

"Very funny," I said.

A few days later I got a call. It was Diane. "Va'eira is on January 24th."

"Terrific," I said. "I'll sponsor the Kiddush."

"There's a little problem…"

"What's wrong?"

"It's Rosh Chodesh Shabbat. There's a special Haftorah."

My blood ran cold. "You mean I can't do the portion I know?"

There was silence on the phone. "Afraid not. Look it over. It's pretty long, but I know you can do it."

I immediately went to the bookcase, pulled out the Chumash, and nervously looked for the new portion. I noted the slightest tremor in my hand as I found the page. Twenty-four verses, four full pages, and lots of trope marks I'd never seen before—more than I was prepared to learn in a month. I decided to forget the whole thing.

Yet the idea refused to be ignored. When Rabbi Astor returned from his sabbatical we got together for a game of tennis. I told him of my disappointment.

He shook his head, and his eyes twinkled. "You've still got two weeks. I'll make you a tape of the Haftorah to practice from."

My heart fluttered. The sweat on the back of my neck felt strangely cold. Somehow I found myself saying, "Yes, I'll do it," but my mind screamed, "No, no you fool!"

The next day as I stuttered over the Hebrew words in the Tikun, my sixteen-year-old son looked over my shoulder, then sat down next to me.

"Here, let me show you how to do it," he said, as I relinquished the book with relief. He chanted ten lines flawlessly, pointed out my mistakes, and described the fine points of Haftorah trope. I sank lower into my chair. *So that's what they learn at Solomon Schechter.*

Later that night my daughter coached me as well. "You'd better get to work on this, Dad. You've got less than two weeks." I took the book up to my room and closed the door, trying to convince myself I wasn't totally crazy.

In the next ten days I chanted the new portion at least twice a day, and as the days passed a budding confidence replaced my anxiety. *Maybe I can do this after all.* I began to focus on the greater picture. This was a way to connect with the history of our people, to chant a Haftorah said for thousands of years in synagogues all over the world. And I would be chanting it on this special Rosh Chodesh Shabbat along with thousands of others in synagogues all over the world.

Finally the day arrived, a frigid morning in single digits. I got to Beth El early—there were only six congregants. *Good—no one will witness my humiliation.* I sat in the first row, joined by my wife, my twenty two year old son and his girlfriend, who had driven in from Boston as a surprise, my thirteen-year-old daughter and my sixteen-year-old son. (They had agreed to read Torah portions.) By the time the Torah service began I counted seventy people. My hands were cold and sweaty as they called me to the Bima. Visions of the horror of my own Bar Mitzvah filled my mind. At thirteen I had nearly passed out from fright. Perhaps that's why I wanted to do this—to overcome that early trauma.

In any event my children did their Torah portions with the ease of ducks swimming in water.

"Avraham ben Zalman," Jerry Fischer intoned. The moment of truth had arrived. I approached the lectern, recited the blessings and launched into the Haftorah portion. It must have been good because afterwards Rabbi Astor told me he had never heard the Haftorah chanted quite like that. Although I knew he was kidding, my blood pressure dropped back to 125 from what felt like 250.

When I got home my son put his arm around my shoulder.

"I'm really proud of you Dad."

My daughter hugged me. "Good job, really."

I broke into an ear-splitting grin. I know that as we age we reverse roles with our children. I just didn't know it would happen so soon.

A MINYAN TO REMEMBER

I have always been moved by the conclusion of the movie, 'Field of Dreams.' Kevin Costner laments to his wife that as a young man he had refused to have a catch with his father. Why? Teenage rebellion or perhaps a touch of disguised anger, who knows? But in the fantasy of Hollywood, his father's spirit as a young man returns in the flesh, wearing a baseball glove, and the two men have a go at it finally, saying little but tossing the ball back and forth with a look of purposeful fulfillment. As if the mistakes of a lifetime could be erased by that one simple restitution.

So it was with mixed feelings that I rose at 4:30 a.m. on a winter Sunday two years ago. I showered in the downstairs bathroom so as to not wake my children (under penalty of death, or at least a prolonged shunning.) By five I was on the road, fighting a freak snow squall that threatened to make my surprise early visit to my parents in Queens a big mistake. They were to leave for Florida, that Jewish sanctuary from the cold, in three days time for a prolonged hiatus from the absurd snowstorms of this cruel winter.

"Don't come too early," my father had said. "I have to attend minyan at eight. It's Mama's Yahrzeit." I always called my grandmother Nunu. She was an old-fashioned Bubba from Eastern Europe—a woman who made her own gefilte fish, strudel, and pierogies that melted in your mouth. She was always there to listen and to encourage, never judging harshly in an adult world that seemed severe and unforgiving.

"Maybe I'll come with you," I had said to my father.

"To the minyan? Don't be silly. You'd have to leave New London in the middle of the night."

"Ok, but maybe I'll surprise you," I said and hung up. Why was he so hesitant? So I'm conservative, and he's orthodox. How different could the minyan be? Was he afraid I'd embarrass him?

An image of myself as a ten-year-old sitting next to him in our little New York shul flashed in my mind. In those days I couldn't sit still for more than ten minutes in services.

"Dad, can I take a break?" I would say, tugging on the strings of his tallis.

He'd glance at his watch and roll his eyes. "But you just came back."

"Please, just for ten minutes. I need a drink of water."

He'd look around helplessly, the Yeshiva boys all around us shuckling and buckling, davening for all they were worth.

"Shh, the Amida is starting," he'd say, but I'd persist, until finally in exasperation he'd give in. "All right already, so go, but ten minutes only, and no running."

I'd navigate out of the service, evading the Gabbi like a running back heading for the goal line on Super Bowl Sunday, my father's admonitions already lost in the sheer excitement of my newfound freedom. There were my friends across the street, refugees from services, just now starting the morning's game of freeze tag. Forty minutes later I returned, sweaty, my shoes scuffed, holes in the knees of my new Shabbas pants. I gave my father a smile, trying to hide the scrapes on the palms of my hands.

My father glanced down at me. "Nu, you missed the whole service. What am I going to do with you?"

I'd shrug, grab a Siddur, avoiding his gaze, until he'd turn back to the service and forget about me.

That was forty years ago. I'm raising four children of my own now. Each has attended the Solomon Schechter Academy and can daven a lot better than I can. I try not to show my disappointment if they don't want to accompany me to Shabbat services when I go, but deep inside I get a glimpse of how my father must have felt all those years ago. I suppose I was a bit of a rebel as a teenager, but I've long since come to love our traditions, taking on my father's values as I've aged. He's learned so much since I was fourteen.

I tried to focus on the highway, as the snow intensified, coating the highway with a slick inch of slush. Just when I thought of abandoning my little pilgrimage the snow ceased and I noticed the first gray of dawn unfurling in the eastern sky. I pushed on, increasing my speed gradually, still hoping to get to the city for the minyan.

Funny the things you think of at six a.m. when there's nothing before you but the open road and a lone trucker or two. Was I crazy to drive in so early? I feel very spiritual, but I'm not a religious man. So why was this so important? One minyan in New York would not make up for all those Shabbats I spent in the schoolyard playing stickball, nor would it make up for the ultimate betrayal. I had moved away from New York City to the hinterlands of modern Jewry in New London twenty-five years ago, to join a conservative congregation to boot. How could one minyan make amends for that?

I watched the clock tick towards eight as I bent the speed laws coming over the Throgs Neck Bridge. God would understand, I thought, even if the judge wouldn't. Seven forty five, and I knock on the door of my parents' home in Queens. My father answers immediately, peers into my face in amazement, already wearing his overcoat and his trademark cap.

"Can't talk now," he says, "I'm late for minyan. Why don't you keep Mom company? I'll be back in an hour."

I wave to my mother who is sitting on a couch in the living room. I think of all the traffic infractions I committed on the way into the city.

"There's no way I'm letting you go by yourself," I say to my father, as my mother nods her approval.

"But you don't have teffillin," he says. I produce a little bundle from my coat pocket.

He shrugs. "So where's your tallis?"

"I'll borrow one," I say with assurance, fighting back the inclination to forget the whole thing and have breakfast with my mother.

"Nu, so lets go," my father says, and hands me an extra kippah. It is clear that he takes being on time to minyan very seriously.

At eight sharp we are sitting side by side at the minyan. I glance around the room, feeling a little out of place, even though I try to make minyan at Beth El Synagogue a few times a month. A few men have long scholarly beards that make them look like they lived during the writing of the Babylonian Talmud. Yet, when they begin to chant the prayers I realize they speak Hebrew with New York accents. I pick up a Siddur, all in Hebrew without an English translation. I put on my teffillin, just as Rabbi Greengrass taught me when I turned forty. Still, I eye the other men closely, adjusting my straps as if I might be graded. If I've made any mistakes no one seems to notice.

I feel like a fish out of water, trying to keep up with the service, but no one announces the pages. And although the leader sings in a clear strong voice everyone seems to be davening at their own pace, each with a different Siddur. I sit beside my father, chant the prayers I recognize, the Shema, the Amida, bits and pieces of the service springing to my lips through the cobwebs of memory.

When the Mourner's Kaddish begins I can't help but notice how difficult it is for my father to rise from his chair. His arthritic knees are getting worse. I hold out a hand to help him up. He shakes his head no, but I put a guiding hand on his elbow anyway. I stand in respect during the Mourner's Kaddish and say the prayer quietly under my breath. I know its only said for a parent, but my grandmother was like a second mother to me. If she knew I was there I think she'd approve.

When the Aleinu is finished a few of my father's friends come over and introduce themselves.

"So this is your son from Connecticut," they say, smiling broadly as I take off my tefillin.

"Yes he came all the way from Waterford for today's minyan," my father says, beaming.

"Oh, you're very lucky," one elderly man says. We all chat for a few minutes, and then the men slip away to get on with their day.

"Thanks for coming. It meant a lot to me," my father says as we leave the shul.

I take his arm as we cross the icy street.

"Your welcome," I say, without a hint of sarcasm.

We reach his car; he unlocks the door and turns toward me and for a moment I recognize in his face the features of my grandmother.

I clear my throat, smile, and say without hesitation. "You know Dad, it meant a lot to me too."

A Passover Redemption

Jonas Frobisher stood at the door to his father's home. *Ten years—can't believe it's been that long since Mama died.* Jonas had lived abroad for most of his career; Singapore, Bangkok and lastly the posting to London with the World Bank. Success had not come easily to Jonas. Truth be told, he had won respect by substituting perspiration for inspiration. He had outworked and outhustled every other junior executive from the day he graduated with his MBA from Wharton. Too busy for a vacation, working weekends throughout the year, Jonas had risen through the ranks of the business world by the strength of his will. As he prepared to knock on the door, a flood of childhood memories rose like a tidal wave of regret. Suddenly the idea of surprising his father seemed ill conceived. He stood with his fist hovering at the door. *How can it be I haven't been home all these years?*

He turned to leave, a sense of panic tightening around his throat like an iron band of shame. He had hoped to return a big success, bigger than his brother Jonathan, the neurosurgeon, bigger even than his brother Saul, the founder of the Internet dating site Wahoo. Then he noticed the cars lined up along the opposite curb. He counted sixteen. *What would bring this many cars unless...*He pictured the empty plot beside his mother's grave. *Can't be that. Saul would have called even if he hasn't talked to me since that scene with his wife.*

He approached the door again. He could hear the sounds of muffled song from behind the door, the undeniable guttural refrains of an unintelligible prayer. *Can't make out the words but that sure sounds like Hebrew.* The idea of bursting in unannounced and uninvited on his father's funeral seemed too much to bear. He chose instead to climb the fire escape up to the roof of the garden apartment, hoping to get a glimpse of the scene inside from the skylight. He used his sleeve to wipe away the grime and peered in through the glass. What he saw in the living room below made his jaw drop. There, aligned on both sides of a long table, were all the members of his family, kippahs on their heads, prayer books open, singing together with smiles on their faces. A look of bewilderment crossed Jonas' features. Then he glanced at his watch and checked the date, finally making sense of the gathering below. *It's not a funeral....it's a Seder!*

It was at that moment that the elder Frobisher looked up from his Haggadah and caught a glimpse of his son's befuddled face hovering above the skylight like an apparition. He clutched at his chest, fighting for air.

"Oh my God, it's Jonas!" he mumbled. Then his mouth went slack and his upper denture dislodged, splashing in the large bowel of matzoh ball soup on his plate. His face turned magenta. As son Jonathan began to perform CPR, a violent cough sent a projectile of half eaten matzoh shooting across the table, splattering the bowl of dark red horseradish his father had made from scratch the night before. The assembled guests gasped a collective sigh of surprise and pointed up to the skylight, simultaneously alarmed and elated, their mouths working in threats and entreaties.

"Come down," they seemed to be saying, or rather "You clown." It was hard for Jonas to discern through the skylight. But as was his way, in most altercations, he preferred to avoid confrontation and clambered down the fire escape. He reached the ground and ran towards his car, parked around the corner.

"Wait," he heard his brothers yell, as he reached for the handle of his BMW. "Pops wants you to come back."

Inside the house the elder Frobisher, Sam, sat gasping—not from his near brush with matzoh asphyxiation, rather from the shock of seeing his youngest son Jonas' disembodied face in the skylight.

It had been ten long years since their rift sent Jonas packing all over the globe. What little information Sam gleaned about Jonas he got off business websites. Jonas Frobisher meets with OPEC, Frobisher meets with the Bundesbank, Frobisher to help refinance Italian debt. What he wouldn't give to have another heart to heart father-son talk, the kind that stopped when Jonas turned 16. *What good does it do to know your son is a big success if you can't be part of his life? Didn't Jonas know that a simple call could have set things right. He's the one who should have called.*

The years had passed and Sam tried to make the best of things, turning his attention to his other two sons and their families. Still, in Sam's heart of hearts, on nights when sleep proved elusive, there was no denying that Jonas' alienation was never far from Sam's mind.

Jonas Frobisher froze with his hand on the door handle of his BMW.

"Come back," his brothers were yelling. Jonas glanced into the passenger seat, barely making out the shape of his well-intentioned surprise through the darkened glass. *Maybe they're just not ready.*

Jonas' first inclination was to hop into the roadster, burn rubber, and leave his narrow-minded family behind. *How could they possibly understand? What was I thinking when I conceived this harebrained scheme?* He had planned to see his father unannounced thinking that, after a decade's absence, time might have healed their differences. After all, the country had changed, why not have hope for Sam Frobisher? But this Passover scene packed with his brothers, their wives and their children... perhaps that was too much.

As his brothers approached, Jonas knocked on the window of his car. The window opened half way.

"Let's get out of here, Jules," Jonas said, in a breathless command. "They're having a Seder."

"Hey, sport. You haven't brought me and the baby halfway around the world to tuck your tail between your legs and run, have you?"

Jonas swallowed hard and nodded. He withdrew his hand from the door handle and straightened up. He had stood up to prime ministers and presidents, at least when it came to high finance. *Why can't I face up to my father?* He'd been planning a confrontation for a year. Only in his daydreams he hadn't pictured an audience of twenty.

"All right then!" Jonas said, a tremor in his voice. He turned to face his brothers, just now reaching the car.

"Michael, Saul, I've got someone I want you to meet." Then he sauntered around to the passenger side of the car and opened the door.

Sam Frobisher stood by the window watching Jonas run towards the car. His mind sidestepped the obvious What's Jonas doing here? *Certainly, he's come to apologize.* Parting the venetian blinds with his fingers, and squinting to see his favorite son, he nearly gasped at the sight of the large man getting out of the passenger seat. *Why would Jonas need a chauffeur to visit me?* Then he saw the man place an infant in Jonas' arms. While Sam watched from the window Michael and Saul stood before Jonas. For a moment Sam wasn't sure whether they were going to throw punches or embrace, but after a while the entire entourage turned away from the car and walked towards the house.

"I'm still not sure he'll understand," Jonas was saying to his brothers as he walked beside Jules.

"Hey, it's worth a try," Jules said.

The brothers said nothing. There had been so much talk over the years, now was not the time for reopening old wounds. Besides, that was always their father's specialty. Then the door of the house swung open.

"Jonas?" Sam Frobisher said. "Come in, come in. And who's this little guy?" Sam said, placing a wrinkled hand on the boy's head.

Jonas and Jules exchanged a glance. "This is my son, Pop."

Sam's eyes flew wide. "A son!! Oh, my God! I didn't even know you got married."

Jonas' eyes narrowed, and he fought the urge to glance at Jules who was staring at the ground.

"We drove up from Washington. I wanted to surprise you," Jonas said at last.

"Well don't just stand there. I want to hear everything. And bring your driver in too. I'm sure there's room at our Seder table tonight. You must be famished."

The extended Frobisher family filed into the foyer, unwilling to miss a word of this most unlikely of all reunions.

Jonas leaned over towards Michael and whispered in his ear. Then Michael and Saul herded the family back into the living room.

"Give them a few moments," Saul said, and nodded his head, winking at his wife.

"Pops, there's something I want to tell you, before we join the Seder," Jonas said.

Sam stared, and then began blinking incessantly, an involuntary response to the turmoil in his mind. He wanted to dismiss Jonas' driver, to be alone with his son, but the way Jules was staring into Sam's eyes gave him pause. A Rolodex list of possible misfortunes flipped in Sam's mind: *Divorce...why else would Jonas show up with his kid, alone? Maybe he's sick...just like Jonas to keep it from me.*

After an awkward silence Sam raised his index finger. "If its money you need..."

"What? No, Dad, It's not like that. I'm set."

"Marriage on the rocks? You can tell me."

Jonas glanced at Jules who nodded. "No, Dad, will you stop? Just listen." Sam took a deep breath, "Ok, ok, I'm listening. So talk."

"I came home because I want your blessing," Jonas said after a long pause.

Sam's blinking began anew. "You got married and had a kid and now you need my blessing? It's a little late for that, isn't it? I've never even met the girl."

Jules coughed and tapped his foot, but said nothing, averting his eyes as Jonas raised a hand, as if to silence his father before he made a fatal misstep.

"Really, Dad, don't you get it?" Jonas said in exasperation." There'll never be a girl. What do you think I was trying to tell you the last time we fought?"

Jules nudged a chair into position and Sam collapsed, his jaw going slack as if suddenly his tongue were too big for his mouth.

"But a son? I don't understand...never could understand."

"We're adopting."

"We?"

"Jules and I. We're adopting a child together."

A broad smile spread across Jules' face, but he seemed content to let Jonas do all the talking.

"We want your blessing. Actually it was Jules' idea. He's kind of a traditionalist."

Sam nodded with a blank stare, the blinking fast and furious. When Saul and Michael came in to urge everyone in for the Seder, Sam remained silent. In fact he said little the entire evening, staring from Jonas to Jules and back again, as if to fathom a riddle with no solution.

Epilogue

I'd like to tell you that Jonas and Sam got back to the heart to heart talks they had in Jonas's teen years, but that would read like a fantasy. The Frobisher household continued, however, their yearly Seder traditions, and a few years later little Jonathan, for that's what Jonas named his new son, said the four questions— beautifully I might add. Two years later Jonas and Jules adopted a second newborn son. They thought to call him David at first, but since having sons named Jonathan and David might be too obvious an irony, they settled on Samuel instead. And when they asked Jonas' father to be the Sondig at the bris he agreed without hesitation, choosing instead, once and for all, to keep his questions to himself.

THE MINYAN

Sam tucked the red velvet bag under one arm and made his way to the cinderblock building he had last seen the day of his Bar Mitzvah. A gaunt middle-aged man in a black suit grunted a welcome as Sam passed. "It's down the stairs," he said, as if there could be only one destination people considered once they entered the building.

Sam glanced about cautiously, walking on legs made weak by memory.

I wonder if they still have a Hebrew School here? How many times did I get kicked out of class?

He removed a handkerchief, blew his nose, and wiped his eyes. *Damn allergies.* Murmurs of Yiddish wafted from a room down the hall, peppered by the laughter of elderly men. Sam entered the room and all eyes turned. One man elbowed his neighbor and gestured towards Sam with a toss of his head, as if visitors were a rarity.

Sam glanced from man to man, each in various stages of wrapping their arms with black straps. He opened his velvet bag. Hesitating, he pushed the pouch with the tefillin to the side, glancing up at the chazzan who was just now beginning. He removed the tallis, placed it over his shoulders. *How long has it been? 4 years, maybe 5.*

As a boy he had always felt uncomfortable around religious worship. Whether it was the way they prayed, shuckling back and forth, or his own lack of fervor, it was hard to say. Perhaps it was the years of Hebrew School he had endured when all he wanted to do in the afternoons was play in the schoolyard. Too many times he felt he was just going through the motions to please his parents. *Isn't worship supposed to be more than obligation?*

Again he stared at the bag of tefillin. "I can't," he muttered. *Lack of respect.* Certainly that's what Papa would have said. *I can't even cry.*

An elderly man, his back bent with age, pointed a yellowed finger at Sam's arm. "Nu, aren't you laying tefillin?"

Sam shrugged, his eyes darting away.

"But you must. Please."

Sam glanced back as the old man placed a hand on Sam's bicep. "You put it up right here, near to your heart, and the other one here between the eyes," the man said, pointing to the black box affixed to his own forehead. Sam couldn't help but notice the faded number tattooed on the man's forearm. "No matter what, we Jews believe. You understand?" Then he smiled, revealing a nest of golden caps protruding from his lower lip.

Conflicting emotions ran through Sam's mind. He thought of telling this man who looked like he walked out of a shtettle to mind his own business. *If I can't do it, I can't do it, what's the big deal?*

"I almost didn't come today," Sam muttered, looking off in the distance.

"This is right where your father used to sit."

"You knew him?" Sam said, his voice cracking, despite his best efforts to stay in control.

"Of course. Everyone knew him. Sat beside me every Shabbat…a quiet man, a good man. Now put it up."

He grabbed the bag of tefillin and held it out to Sam.

Sam opened the bag slowly. The red velvet was faded and worn. He pictured the way his father would close his eyes during the service, mumbling the prayers by heart. *How many times did my father ask me to join him and I refused—so often that finally he stopped asking.* The scene from Field of Dreams where the father and son finally play catch together flashed in his mind. *If only Papa had asked that…*

Why was I so turned off by worship as a teenager? He pictured his father's disapproving scowl. *If only Papa didn't push so much.*

Sam removed the tefillin from his bag. He pulled at the straps, and the loose knot fell away. The black straps unraveled like coiled snakes ready for action.

"That's right, put it up, the old man said, nodding approval as Sam placed one tefillin on his forehead and the other around his bicep.

"Yes, yes," the old man mumbled, the hint of a smile on his lips while he watched with a supervisory glance,

"I'll help you," the man said. Sam held out his arm, but he began to wonder if he could escape out the side door, sooner rather than later.

The leather chaffed the skin on his bicep as the man cinched it in. "Vun, two, three times like dis, make a shin. Then make the yud on your fingers. Let me show you."

The puckered flesh on Sam's forearm seemed to be turning purple, while his fingers turned white, but he said nothing. "I'd rather do it myself," he said, gently, removing the tefillin, then replacing it himself, a long abandoned muscle memory guiding his hands.

The old man grinned, "Good, like you never stopped." Then he handed Sam a prayer book. Sam mumbled a few of the prayers he remembered, but felt lost most of the time. After a while the old man handed his book to Sam and pointed to the middle of the page. "Go ahead, say it."

Sam's eyes flew wide and his heart began to race. He had come to the minyan expecting to sit in the back, an invisible visitor from the past, unprepared to accept the yoke of generations of tradition.

As the old man stared at Sam a hush came over the worshippers. A pounding pain rose in Sam's temples. His mouth formed the first words, but then he hesitated, the letters on the page blurred and unpronounceable.

"Say it," the old man said again, insistently. "You must."

Sam nodded, then wiped his eyes on his sleeve. He turned back to the book.

"Yisgadol veh yiskadosh, shemai rabah," Sam began, continuing to the end, the Chazzan prompting him in a slow cadence.

"Your father would have been proud of you today," the old man said as the Alenu began.

Sam didn't answer. He pictured again the sights at the gravesite and the way the dirt bounced on his father's casket. He had stopped up his grief then, unable to cry, standing stone faced in the cold as the other mourners covered the casket with soil.

Men don't cry, he had told himself, and tried to think of the new project at work, blotting out the memories and the pain.

But, now, as the service concluded, a vision of his father as a young man teaching him to put on tefillin the week before his Bar Mitzvah rose before him. He crumpled into his seat and stared at the book, the words blurring once again. He fumbled with the tefillin, trying to return them to the bag.

"You know after the doctor bills were paid, this was the only thing my father could leave me," he mumbled.

A wrinkled hand adorned in brown spots rested on Sam's shoulder. "I'm sorry for your loss. See you again tomorrow? Same time?" the old man said, shuffling away. Then he hesitated, turning back towards Sam.

"You know your father would have been proud of you. All he ever wanted was to have you by his side."

Sam nodded and he covered his eyes with his hand. Then his body began to shake, the tears he had so long restrained flowing uncontrolled down his cheeks.

THE WEDDING

Moishe turned the invitation over slowly. He didn't recognize the foreign stamps across the envelope but he recognized Riva's perfect calligraphy, even if most of the words were in Italian.

"The honor of your presence is requested at 2 p.m. on August 11, 2005, for a wedding reception in the outdoor square of San Guisseppe, Florence," was engraved across the top of the rich velveteen paper. A small photo fell from the envelope. It was a portrait of his dark-eyed brooding daughter with her arms draped over the shoulders of a blond, blue-eyed Adonis worthy of the cover of G.Q. Funny, he thought, but in that pose Riva looks so much like my Sophie, may she rest in peace.

"Please come. Its time we were a family again—Riva," was inscribed under the picture.

"Oy a broch," Moishe gasped and let the photo slip from his cold fingers. *Forty thousand a year at an Ivy League school, and for what? So she can run off to paint for a year in Tuscany? Then marry the first non-Jew she meets.*

"At least my parents aren't alive to see her marry a shagitz," he muttered and sank into a worn kitchen chair.

He reached for the half empty bottle of Slivovitz that he had brought back from the Kiddush the previous Shabbat. An hour later Moishe slumped forward, his head nestling against his folded arms, the empty bottle crashing to the floor—sleep the only respite from the demons that plagued him.

But with sleep came the dream again, his wife's gravesite, the coffin opening slowly, a cold finger prodding him in the small of his back, his writhing body propelled into the grave, followed by the joyous laughter of his wild daughter. Riva stood, oil paints in hand, her unfinished canvas propped on an easel before her, painting the scene, an impassionate observer of his worse fears.

In the morning he didn't feel up to attending minyan. Just as well. The other men would probably see the worry in his eyes. No need rehashing the same old thing again.

And my brother's advice stinks as usual "It's a new world, Moishe. Maybe you need to be more flexible." *Of what use was such an attitude? Where would the Jewish People be if we all thought like that?"*

Later that day the cleaning lady stopped by to straighten up. She found Moishe Rappinsky still in pajamas, sitting in a darkened room staring at a snowy TV screen.

She walked to the window and lifted the shade, opening the window to let in a cool spring breeze.

"How can you live like this, Mr. Rappinsky?"

When Moishe didn't answer she waved a hand in his face.

"Jesus, Mary and Joseph, what's wrong?" she said in her lilting Irish brogue when she saw that his eyes were red.

"Oh, Mrs. Murphy, it's you," he said. "…you wouldn't understand. I can't talk about it."

"Nonsense! A body needs to share what's troubling him. Why don't you tell me what's on your mind?"

Moishe told her about the invitation. She listened without interrupting.

When he leaned back in his chair she put a hand on his shoulder. "You're going aren't you?"

His jaw dropped open. "To the wedding? How can I? She's turning her back on her religion."

"But you're the only family she's got."

Moishe said nothing, his hands clenched in his lap.

"Listen, Mr. Rappinsky, I've known you for twenty years and I've never given you a word of advice, but I'm sticking in my two cents now. Don't think so much. Just go!"

"We said so many horrible things to each other. I can't."

"Don't be an old fool. Your daughter's reaching out to you. Don't push her away."

Her eyes seemed to glisten with a distant sadness. "You could never understand," he said.

"I know what I'm talking about," she said, her eyes boring into his. "I wasn't always a cleaning lady. Back in Dublin all the men in the parish were fighting for my hand, but I married for love…may God rest his soul."

He studied the lines on her face. Funny, but in all the years he'd known her, he never realized that she must have been quite beautiful once.

"I married the most gentle, perfect man God ever put on this earth. But he was a Protestant and I was a Catholic."

Moishe said nothing.

"My family drove us away. We settled in America. You understand?"

Moishe nodded. "And your parents?"

"Never saw them or heard from them again. Is that what you want for your daughter?" she said choking back tears.

He tried to say something, but for once he was speechless.

A week later Moishe took a taxi to JFK airport, and caught the red-eye flight to Florence. While everyone slept on the plane he sat bolt upright in his seat, his mind seething.

The plane was delayed, but landed at last. He showed the invitation to a taxi driver, who let him off two blocks from the address.

"That street is closed to traffic. —some type of festival," the driver said in broken English and pointed towards a huge domed church.

Moishe paid the fare and walked down the street as a man walks to his execution, still unsure if he could go through with it. As he neared the church, bells began to chime. The doors flew open and a beautiful bride with a pasty, red headed groom emerged. Well-wishers threw rice over the heads of the young couple, who ran past Moishe without a glance and jumped into a waiting limo.

He nearly dropped the invitation.

"That's not my daughter!" He said, bewildered. After the car drove off, he showed the invitation to a man on the street.

"Next block," the man said and pointed a bony finger towards a small brick building. As he approached he saw a Star of David on the façade of the building and his walk turned into a run. He touched the Mezzuzah and kissed his fingers.

"Oh, please, God, I hope I'm not too late," he muttered and wiped his eyes with his sleeve. He burst into the sanctuary. His daughter was standing on the bima with the groom-to-be.

Riva glanced over her shoulder at the sound of the closing door. She left her young man to wait while she ran to Moishe sitting in the back row.

"Walk me down the aisle, Poppa," she whispered.

He rose and accompanied her with the step of a much younger man towards the waiting chuppa. The service was mostly in Italian, but when the Rabbi began the Sheva Bruchas, Moishe's voice rang out in a rich baritone.

After the ceremony Riva introduced Moishe to her blonde husband.

"Paulo, this is my father."

Moishe looked up into the young man's blue eyes, and for a moment words would not come.

"Shalom, Abba." The young man said, with a broad smile.

"He's learning Hebrew, Riva said. "Isn't that wonderful?"

"Yes that is," Moishe said. "That most certainly is."

And although his first impulse was to ask if it had been an orthodox conversion, for the first time in his life Moishe Rappinsky failed to tell his daughter what he really thought. There'll be plenty of time for that when I get them to move back to New York, he thought. As if she could read her father's mind Riva slipped her hand into his.

"I'm glad we're together today," she said.

Moishe stared into his only daughter's dark eyes, and a smile crossed his lips.

"I am too," Moishe said. That night he had a restful night, and awoke with the feeling that his dreams of the grave were gone for good.

CHAPTER 2

LET THE GAMES BEGIN

LET THE GAMES BEGIN

This Sunday, my oldest son, David and I took a long anticipated trip to a temple not often discussed in the Jewish Leader. "Beware of false idols," I thought I heard him mutter under his breath as we gazed up at the concrete and marble façade, the golden lettering proudly proclaiming to all who might enter: YANKEE STADIUM.

Unless you have been living abroad you know that the New York Yankees have a new home across the street from their usual digs in "da Bronx."

With a one and a half billion dollar price tag, I expected the new stadium would be filled with modern amenities. I caught glimpses of it last year while under construction, but this year I wanted to attend a game during the Yankees' first home stand.

With memories of my childhood baseball heroes dancing in my head, and a credit card handy, I bought 2 tickets on the Yankee website last week. When asked for seating preference I clicked best available. The computer's reply: **"Field Level Seating," 2 tickets directly behind home plate are being held for you for the next 2 minutes.** My heart pounded. *My son will love this.* Then I glanced at the price tag—$2400 each—throw in an extra 50 for service charges and the price of parking and you'd have an even 2500 bucks! *Who do they think I am—the CEO of General Motors.*

NO THANK YOU. *I'll sit in the nosebleed seats with the other victims of the recession. And I'll love it.*

As my son and I drove down I-95 towards New York, filled with anticipation, the conversation turned to playoff games we'd seen together over the years. I know the Bombers got bombed on opening day 10-2 by the upstart Cleveland Indians. And I will choose to forget Saturday's historic loss 22-4. Cleveland scored 14 runs in the second inning alone, more than any other team in a single inning against the Yanks. I refute the notion that the Yankees rest on Shabbat, although that is precisely what the lopsided score indicates. Although the weather forecast called for rain my thoughts were more positive: *This is Yankee baseball, I'm with my son, it's spring, and all things are possible.*

We arrived two hours early and parked a half-mile from the stadium to approach with the proper sense of awe. As we walked we joined other Yankee fans, all sporting their Yankee caps, many in uniforms, all with the wide-eyed look of children, despite their graying hair. There, before me, sat the old stadium, shuttered forever, deserted, a ghost of Octobers past. How many times had I waited outside those gates with my three sons, straining with anticipation, eager to catch an important game? I wonder if they knew that, more than the thrill of baseball, I longed to treasure their companionship and revel in their laughter.

We crossed the street, leaving the old stadium behind us, and there it was, the new Yankee Stadium. Looking very much like a modern version of the original built in 1923. The architects of the Roman Coliseum would have been jealous. With a polished stone façade and marble footings at its base, the stadium is a fitting tribute to man's imagination.

As we neared the gate I asked a stranger to snap our picture with the stadium towering in the background. I thought of the old movie line "If you build it they will come," uttered by Kevin Costner in "Field of Dreams". Did Mayors Rudy Giuliani and Michael Bloomberg use that line on owner George Steinbrenner to loosen up his purse strings? Or was it the tax-free New York City bonds they approved that clinched the deal? We'll never know, but I think Mayors Bloomberg and Giuliani sat in the first row behind the dugout on opening day. Coincidence?

We entered the stadium by the great hall, a huge atrium with banners of Yankee greats hanging in a row from the high ceiling. Gehrig, Mantle, DiMaggio, and Berra still looked strong beneath their pinstripes. The tune to Simon and Garfunkle's lyric "Where have you gone Joe DiMaggio?" played in my mind as I walked along, craning my neck. I pointed, gesturing to my son like the tourist I was. "There's Thurmon Munson, Don Mattingly, and Whitey Ford," I said. "I saw all these guys play."

Involuntarily I found myself lowering my voice. I glanced around and the throngs seemed to be unusually hushed—no swearing, no drunken swaggers. Is it the history of this place or the fact that the game has yet to begin, I wondered?

The game got off to a slow start. The Yanks managed only two hits through the first six innings against their old teammate, Carl Pavano, a frequently injured Yankee pitcher who got paid millions for sitting on the Yankee bench. I suspected he'd get shelled, but instead he turned into an ace, fanning aptly named Mark Swisher with the bases loaded. The Yankee rally fizzled with the Indians leading 3-1 in the seventh inning.

Don't feel sorry for me, for this day had a happy ending. Timely Yankee hitting returned. A pinch-hit home run by Jorge Posada put my boys ahead 4-3 and a bases-loaded double by unknown Yankee third baseman, Cody Ransom, put the game on ice. Final score 7-3 Yanks.

My son and I wandered around the stadium for a while, taking in the new sights. As we strolled past the players' entrance we saw broadcasters Mike Kay and John Sterling waiting for their cars. Jorge Posada drove by in a black Audi to the cheers of the children waiting for a glimpse of their hero. Alas, he failed to stop. I guess the idea of signing free autographs for kids is a thing of the past.

For those of you who plan to see a game this year, let me tell you of some improvements. There's plenty of kosher food, as long as you like Hebrew National hotdogs, and a Kosher Caterer pushcart was prominently displayed. The bathrooms are spotlessly clean (for now). Water fountains deliver frosty cold water and the water pressure is high enough so you don't have to kiss the fountain to get a drink. The infield grass is still an incredible shade of green, and the dirt just as dark as ever.

The Yankees still win a few and lose a few, but, happily on this day when I so wanted to reminisce about the good old days with my son, the Yankees won. As we began the long process of making our way back to Waterford, I thought not of the Yankee win, nor of their chances to go deep in the playoffs this year. I thought instead of the four hours spent sitting beside my twenty-seven-year-old son, and the pleasure of connecting over a shared passion. For, after all, whether I sit in the bleachers or behind home plate, whether the stadium is falling apart, or spanking new, isn't sharing the experience with my children what keeps me coming back?

THE ANNIVERSARY GIFT

With apologies to O'Henry

Part I

"You know, I love you more than ever," Sharon said.

"I do, too," Aaron said slowly, the tumblers of his mind clicking into place as he wiped the sleep from his eyes, searching desperately for that thread of memory that might explain his wife's affections.

Sharon's eyes flashed. She drew him close and kissed his lips. "I've got a surprise for you tonight." Then she bounced out of bed. "Sorry, I've got to run," she said on the way to the shower. "See you tonight at five."

Aaron fell back asleep. He woke to the sound of the alarm to find Sharon gone, off to her nursing shift at the hospital. He thought of her amorous kiss. *Couldn't we both call in sick, just once, mortgage or no mortgage?*

He stumbled to his computer and checked his emails. *"Congratulations!! You've won Radio WNYC's trivia contest: One ticket to tonight's World Series game sitting with Yankee legends.* Aaron nearly deleted the notice as SPAM. It was only after he called the station to check on the hoax, that the enormity of his good luck was confirmed.

He'd been glued to the TV every night for three weeks, watching the playoffs unfold. He knew Sharon watched to keep him company, but a real fan wouldn't go to bed in the fifth inning. Now that the Yankees were poised to clinch, a ticket was like baseball gold. *I'll be the envy of all my friends.* How many men could say they watched the Yankees beat the Phillies to win the World Series three rows from home plate? Sitting with the likes of guys like Whitey Ford, and Yogi Berra, no less.

It was only when he reached his office and glanced at his calendar that he saw the reminder he had written for the day, the previous year. "Tenth Wedding Anniversary. Get the matching heart earrings." Beads of sweat broke out on his forehead. *How can I tell her I'm going to the game? I don't even have money for a present... I am so dead.*

meanwhile...

Sharon entered the pediatrics wing like a diva greeting her public. She waved to doctors as she passed down the hall, the smile on her face a mirror of her growing anticipation. Oddly she thought of her mother.

"I warned you not to marry a sports fanatic. You deserve better," she had said on Sharon's wedding day. How I'd love to hear her apologize, she thought. But that would mean Sharon would have to call her mother—something she'd not done in a long while.

She pulled out her purse and rummaged for her wedding picture, running her finger over Aaron's image. *So, he's put on a few pounds, and maybe his hair is thinning just a bit.* Still, with her parents' miserable marriage, and most of her friends divorced, ten years together seemed like something worth celebrating.

"You must be crazy," her best friend said when Sharon told her of her plans. "That necklace is the only jewelry you ever wear."

"You don't know him like I do," Sharon said. Then she removed the gold chain with the little diamond heart from her neck and placed it in her pocket. Sure, times were tough. Pay cutbacks at the hospital coupled with their rising mortgage rate had produced plenty of stress. Keeping the house was their first priority. What difference did it make that they hadn't dined out in two years?

Later that morning on her break she walked across the street to Louies. "Money for your Gold," the neon sign flashed. She hesitated. Then she tried to imagine the look on his face as he saw her gift. *He'll die. He'll just die.* She went in.

"$1,000 for a pair of diamond earrings? You must be out of your mind," Aaron's best friend said when Aaron confessed his plan. "Most guys would sell their own mother for a chance to see the Yankees clinch. You're nuts."

All morning long Aaron could barely concentrate on his work, tortured by the decision he was contemplating. Then he thought of the way her lower lip would quiver when she saw his surprise.

"Sometimes you've got to make a sacrifice for someone you love," he told his friend with a shrug. "This is something I promised her a long time ago." Then he laughed—a hollow laugh, more like a disguised grimace. He'd lost his business, taken on three jobs, working sixty hours a week to pay their bills. He denied himself any extravagance, hoping to one day let Sharon cut back on her hours, maybe stay home and have a child.

During lunch he took the ticket from his wallet and ran a finger over the embossed gold lettering. Section 101, Row 3 Behind Home Plate. Only Rudolph Guliani might have a better seat. He thought of the night of his first wedding anniversary, the way Sharon gasped when he gave her the necklace. He took a deep breath and dialed the ticket broker.

"Yeah, I'm sellin'," Aaron said. "Best seat in the house."

After work Aaron trudged home. As he walked the two blocks from the subway, lost in thought, he imagined sitting at Yankee Stadium for the game that night with thousands cheering themselves hoarse. For a moment he wondered what type of fat cat would be sitting in his box seat. *I always dreamed I'd get to be at a World Series game.* He palmed the jewelry box in his pocket and a smile replaced his lost expression. He glanced at his watch and then quickened his pace, practically flying up the stairs of his third floor walk-up.

While he fumbled for his keys Sharon opened the door. "Happy Anniversary, darling," Sharon said, "I was worried. It's getting late."

"Yeah, well I had a little errand to run before coming home," he said. "Hey, how come you're not wearing your necklace?"

Her hand ran to the fake pearls at her throat. "Oh that… I just felt like wearing something different," she said, her eyes darting away.

Aaron shrugged. *Nine years wearing the same necklace, and tonight she decides to change?*

"I got you something. Hope you like it," she said and placed a pair of Amtrak train tickets to New York into his hand.

"How nice," he said, feigning excitement. The roar of the imaginary Yankee crowd faded in his ears. "We can use these some time to have dinner in the city… I got you something too. Close your eyes."

As she did, he removed the present from his pocket and popped open the box. "You can look now."

She opened her eyes and her mouth fell open. She put her hands to the side of her face. "Oh, Aaron. They're beautiful," she said as she held the earrings up to the window, the light flashing from the diamond stud ensconced within a tiny golden heart.

"But, Aaron, how can we afford these?" she said, beaming, already placing them through her earlobes.

"Nothing's too good for my girl," he said, placing his arms on her waist.

"And nothing's too good for you," she said.

"I love the train tickets," he said, forcing a smile.

"Glad you like them," she said, "Because if we hurry, we can still catch the 5:30 to New York."

He hesitated and the fine lines of his forehead deepened.

"Aw, gee honey, a trip for our anniversary would be nice," he said finally. "But, I'm beat, and you know there's a big game on tonight."

"Of course I know," she said. "But I won't let you watch it on TV."

"You won't?" he said, trying to conceal the panic in his voice.

"Of course not. What do you think the train tickets are for?" Then she handed him another envelope.

With his heart pounding Aaron took the envelope and ripped it open.

"A ticket to the Yankee game, tonight!!! What in the world!! Impossible! How did you do this?" he said, hyperventilating, a hysterical laugh building in his throat.

"Sorry it's only a bleacher seat," she said with a twinkle in her eye.

"But there's only one? How can I leave you alone on our anniversary?"

"You can't," she said. Then from behind her back she brought out another ticket and donned a Yankee cap. "I'll be sitting right beside you."

As Sharon went to get her coat her cell phone rang. When Aaron opened her purse to answer the call he found the pawn ticket. His face fell. But, as Sharon returned he slipped it into his pocket, resolving to make everything right by Chanukah.

"You're the greatest, baby," he whispered into her ear."

"So, are you," she said. Then they walked arm in arm into the cool autumn night.

Part II

The train ride to New York was a joyous affair. After all, it's not every day a man gets to fulfill a childhood fantasy like seeing a World Series game. The fact that the tickets were bleacher seats in the last row mattered little. Just the thought of being at the Stadium with the Yankees poised to clinch made the little hairs on the back of Aaron's neck stand on end.

Sharon linked her arm through his and nestled her head against his shoulder. "I still can't believe you got me diamond earrings for our anniversary," she murmured, her hand on the fake pearls around her neck.

He thought of the pawn ticket he had lifted from her purse. *I can't believe she hocked the matching necklace to buy me World Series tickets. She's the best...but how will I ever get the money to redeem it?*

Outside of the New Haven station the train slowed to a crawl. He glanced at his watch: 6:30- still time to get to the stadium in time to see the first pitch. Husband and wife talked of the future to pass the time. "Wouldn't you want to see a World Series with your son one day," she said. Aaron shrugged. After ten years without children he had all but given up. Besides, with the downsizing at work and the home mortgage under water, the thought of a child had been pushed from his mind. Still, when he glanced around the train and saw a man his own age laughing with a ten-year-old boy, wearing matching Derek Jeter uniforms, a pang ran through Aaron, but he said nothing. *Maybe one day.*

"Aren't I enough of a child for you?" he said, smiling, holding his World Series ticket beside his head, his eyes wide, with the unrestrained grin of a twelve-year-old.

"You are a child," she said. "Who needs another one?"

But when the young boy in the seat ahead hugged his father and kissed his cheek Sharon turned her face to the window.

The train lurched, and then slowed to a stop.

"Nothing to be worried about folks. Just a few minutes delay," the conductor said as he walked the length of the car. This is the Yankee Clipper due at the Stadium by game time or your money back."

Aaron looked out the window, and then glanced at his watch. Beads of sweat rose on his forehead. After twenty minutes his banter trailed off. The lights of the train dimmed, and then went out, leaving them in darkness. A collective groan peppered with expletives filled the train. "These tickets cost me a month's salary," Aaron heard someone say in a murderous tone. "I'm gonna sue Amtrak if I miss this game," he heard someone else say, anguish in his voice. The door at the end of the car slid open and the conductor, waving a flashlight down the aisle, held his hand up for quiet.

"Please stay calm," he said, in a wavering voice, with the demeanor Custer might have had before his last stand.

"Get this train moving, or else," a deep-throated voice retorted.

"Don't worry, honey, everything will work out," Sharon whispered in the dark, pressing Aaron's hand in hers. Aaron said nothing and bit his lip.

Minutes later the smell of smoke filled the train. A siren wailed in the distance, growing stronger in sync with Aaron's soaring blood pressure. *We'll never make it to the game.*

Then the doors opened and a high-pitched buzzer sounded.

"Everyone off the train," the conductor was saying. "This is not a drill." They walked the quarter mile to the New Haven station, too stunned to speak.

At the station a uniformed man spoke through a bullhorn. "Sorry folks, electrical fire. Another train is waiting to take you to the stadium."

The pounding in Aaron's head subsided.

"Looks like we'll make it after all," Sharon said as they stood in line to board. She squeezed his hand.

As they neared the train doors Aaron noticed the father and son in Jeter uniforms sitting on a bench. The man's face was creased with pain, while the boy sat with his hands covering his face, sobs wracking his thin body.

"What's wrong?" Aaron said.

The man shrugged. "I left my jacket in the train."

"So, buy a sweatshirt at the game. Hurry up or you'll miss the train. As it is we'll miss the first few innings."

The man took a deep breath. "You don't understand. My tickets are in the jacket. Now they won't let me go back."

"That's too bad," Aaron said to the little boy. "But there's always next year."

When the boy shook his head his little Yankee cap fell off, revealing what at first looked to Aaron like a very close crew cut.

"There may not be another…" the father said, his voice trailing off as his eyes glanced away. He stroked the boy's head, but the boy's trembling only increased with cries like a wounded bird emanating from his throat.

Sharon and Aaron exchanged glances. She drew close to her husband and put her lips to his ear.

"Chemo," she whispered with a nod towards the little boy's bald skull.

"All aboard!" the conductor shouted.

Aaron and his wife walked towards the train doors but then they paused. He glanced at Sharon and noted the strange look on her face. Together they looked back at the father and son sitting dejectedly on the bench.

"Are you thinking what I'm thinking?" Sharon said in a subdued voice.

Aaron could only nod, for the moisture seemed to have evaporated from his mouth. He approached the bench. Aaron thrust his hands into his pocket and handed an envelope to the surprised father.

"I can't accept this," the man said when he saw the two Yankee tickets.

"Yes, you can," Aaron said.

The man stood. He pumped Aaron's hand in thanks. Then taking out a checkbook he scribbled out a check. When Aaron refused the man folded it and stuffed it into Aaron's pocket.

"Last call," the conductor shouted.

"Take my card, please," the man said to Aaron. "I'm a headhunter. Call me if you ever want to change jobs. And may God bless you for your kindness."

The man scooped his smiling son into his arms and carried him onto the train.

"My God, this check is for twelve hundred dollars," Aaron said when the train pulled out.

"Enough to get a hotel room and watch the game?" Sharon asked.

Aaron nodded and put his arm around Sharon's waist.

That night fifty four thousand people celebrated at Yankee Stadium in frigid cold. Aaron and Sharon were not among them, for they were ensconced in a charming bed and breakfast in New Haven. They ate a scrumptious dinner in their suite—the only one with a forty-inch plasma TV. They drank a few beers and ate peanuts in bed, while they cheered for the Yankees until midnight.

"It was almost as good as being there," Sharon said when it was over.

"Better," Aaron said, lying just a little. Then he turned out the light and took his wife of ten years in his arms. "Happy Anniversary," he said.

Three days later Aaron redeemed Sharon's necklace, a gesture that led to another amorous adventure during the televised Yankee Victory Parade down Broadway.

On the first day of Chanukah Sharon came home from her physical exam with a surprise.

"I really am pregnant," she said to a disbelieving Aaron.

The science of pinpointing the date of conception is subject to great error. Still, Sharon and Aaron decided to name their child Derek for a boy, or Alexa for a girl. Sharon drew the line at Hideki.

Weekend Ski Trip; or How a Middle-aged Man Glimpses Mortality.

Want a great way to connect with your teenaged kids? Try skiing with them. It's a sure way of spending quality time in the great outdoors. You'll have the pleasure of their company. They'll open up…ok so don't expect miracles. At least you'll get to sit next to them on the lift for a while. And you'll know where they are. Those were my thoughts on a recent trip to Pico in Vermont.

"Come on Dad. The moguls aren't that bad," my eldest son says.

"Wait for me…" I say to his back as he careens toward a steep slope beneath the chairlift.

"Be careful," I caution my fourteen-year-old daughter. She follows me, her snowboard crisply grating as she navigates around fallen skiers.

I ski towards a trail sign that reads, "Upper Giant Killer," wince at the sight of the black diamond marking. What twisted sadist thinks up the names for these trails? I stop beside my son at what seems to be a precipice worthy of a crazed travel video about stunt skiing in the Rockies. My daughter stops beside me, spraying snow across the tips of my skis. Tall pines, laden with snow, line a ribbon-like trail that descends below.

I suck in a breath of subarctic air and cough. Moguls extend the length of the trail. Their soft curves look like a blanket that's been left in the dryer too long, resulting in a terminal case of static cling.

"You're kidding," I say to my eldest son, knowing full well that he can handle this terrain with ease.

"I can't take your sister down this," I say, imagining the call to my wife back in Waterford that I'd be making from the hospital.

"If she doesn't do moguls she'll never get better," he says. My daughter nods.

"I can do it. Don't worry," she says.

"You've done harder stuff," my son says to me, and smiles when he sees me hesitate. He takes off down the slope.

I think of my sore ribs. I've finally been able to lie on my left side without pain—a gift from the fall I took three months ago on another ill-fated ski adventure. How can I let my daughter do this? I look back up the slope, realize we'll have a tough climb if we want to take an easier trail.

"I'm old enough to make my own decisions," my daughter says, and edges toward the first mogul without looking back.

A man who looks sixty flies by me on a snowboard, carving beautiful turns. In seconds he is beyond the field of moguls and hurtling around a hairpin curve until he disappears behind a group of pines.

"Take it very slow," I say, reciting a silent prayer, glad my wife isn't here to see me capitulate. By now my daughter reaches the first mogul. For you non-skiers: moguls are rounded mounds formed by countless skiers as they turn at steep sections of the trail to avoid going out of control. As the season progresses the moguls become steeper and more treacherous, their raised centers often coated with ice.

Many skiers have seen their athletic careers end in the time it takes to yell, "Oh sh…" Orthopedic surgeons have enough to do without my family's business, I think, as I watch my daughter execute turn after turn, weaving between moguls like a boxer slips punches.

I take a deep breath, wonder if anyone will show up at my funeral, and turn my skis downhill.

"You must attack the hill," I say to myself in an Austrian accent, remembering a ski lesson from my youth, before the weight of responsibility and the fear of pain made me a coward.

I begin to hyperventilate. My skis seem to be turning themselves; some hidden autopilot has hijacked them.

"Ya, you must turn on top of the moguls," my phantom guide commands in Arnold Schwarzenegger's voice.

"I am doing it," a voice sings somewhere in my cerebral cortex, a voice that has lost its synaptic connection to memories of my most horrible disasters. Ahead, my daughter has made it past the moguls unscathed. Hallelujah! She is sitting on the side of the trail laughing with my son. I'm lucky they get along so well together, I think, as I slip backwards across the face of a steep mogul. I catch myself before falling, with the form of a novice bronco rider. I'm glad I can share this with my kids, I think, but by now my thighs feel like they're going to burst into flames.

"Great trail," my daughter says when I stop beside her.

"Nice job," my son adds.

"You guys are terrific," I say. "Would you go cross-country skiing with me this afternoon? (A gentler sport that I greatly prefer.)

My children look at each other and burst into laughter.

"Not a chance," they say... "You're such a girly man," Arnold Schwarzenegger whispers in my ear.

I downhill ski with the kids for the rest of the day, keeping up for the most part, avoiding disaster and trying to keep my kids from tempting fate. But I realize that something has changed. In a morning my daughter has gone from a tentative intermediate skier to someone who can do the black diamonds. Instead of waiting for her after steep slopes, she and my son now wait for me.

"Watch out, Dad. It's a little icy," she calls to me.

"Thanks," I say and follow her down the slope.

At a well-deserved lunch stop I look across the table at my son and my daughter. I picture a robin as it feeds its young, knowing full well that one day its little birds will fly away forever. I've only got another three years before my little girl goes off to college. So when she rises after a brief lunch to get her snowboard and says, "Ready to go, Dad?" I stand slowly on my sore fifty-year-old legs and say simply, "Ready if you are."

YANKEE FANTASY CAMP

I have always loved surprises, but most often I have been the one to bestow them on others. So when Barbara, my wife of twenty-six years, led me into a living room filled with smiling friends and family I was floored. My wife was beaming, always indescribably most beautiful when she's hiding something from me. "We've got a little surprise for you for your fiftieth birthday," she said with a mysterious grin worthy of Alfred Hitchcock on a rainy night.

I staggered back to a chair, still unsettled. I peered into smiling faces. I was stunned. Everyone was there, my four kids, my sister and parents, even my friends from the old neighborhood.

"But how?" was all I could muster, as Barbara unfurled a scroll and began to read an impish poem she'd concocted to mark the occasion. Everywhere faces contorted with mirth. I told myself they were laughing with me. I tried to catch the words, but I was still dazed—something about "Artie, the best part of you is that you're still a little boy, hope this gift brings you lots of joy."

Laughter erupted mixed with thunderous applause. My wife paused, nodded, and then turned to me with a small envelope in her hand. It was obvious I was the only one not in on the joke.

The opened envelope slipped from my hand. "Yankee Fantasy Camp!! Are you kidding?"

"Yep, you're going." My wife's serene smile told me this was no joke. I started to say something, but paused, suddenly aware that my response might color my marital relationship for the next decade. The pop of a camera flash blinded me. I imagined the sound that Roger Clemens' fastball makes when it slams into a catcher's mitt, just inches from my head. Those stories I told my wife about playing stickball in the old neighborhood, wanting to be a major leaguer till the age of twelve. *She must have taken it all seriously. They want me to play baseball for a week in Tampa with Yankee legends.*

"Honey, say something. Everyone chipped in for this. Don't you like it?"

I stuttered…what could I say? A long-winded speech seemed out of the question.

"I hope they don't hurt me," dribbled from my mouth. Again applause, slaps on the back. "Good old Artie. Always joking. You'll be great. Wish I could go too."

Before I knew it everyone descended on the hors d'oeuvres. I took my wife behind the wall and kissed her tenderly.

"Thanks for doing this."

"We all love you. You're going to have the time of your life."

"Yeah, it'll be great," I said, but suddenly I had this sinking feeling in the pit of my stomach. I pictured pitching to Mickey Mantle, may he rest in peace. A searing line drive hit me flush on the chin, shattering my teeth, further impairing my ability to speak.

"Oh, I can't wait," oozed from my lifeless body like blood from a fractured jaw.

"And I'm coming with you." My wife's smile extended from ear to ear, bathing her face in an angelic light.

I pictured her running from the stands, wailing over my crumpled body, while the grounds keeping crew sweeps around me doing the YMCA at appropriate intervals.

"That's the best thing about it. We'll go through this together," I said, making a mental note to check my health policy and get a lower deductible in the morning.

Why would a fifty-year-old man, who hopes to see fifty-one travel to Tampa to play baseball for a week with 72 like-minded Yankee fans? Is it that twelve Yankee stars of the past would be there to coach us? Is the thought of wearing a Yankee uniform for ten baseball games over a span of five days a powerful enough lure to bring businessmen, lawyers, and doctors out from behind their safe facades to discard three-piece suits and don the Yankee pinstripes?

As my wife and I rode the elevator down to the pool party arranged for the first night of Yankee Fantasy Camp in Tampa I almost didn't notice the diminutive man smiling to himself in the corner of the elevator—*ah another camper perhaps, although with the salt and pepper hair, paunch and rounded shoulders, he looked a little old to be involved in such foolishness.*

I thought of introducing myself, but how could I be sure—*maybe he's a businessman on a trip—seems to be a little out of shape to be playing ball.*

The elevator opened; we spilled out into the lobby. I stuck out my hand, "Hi I'm Artie Dean. Here for the Yankee Fantasy Camp?"

"As a matter of fact I am," he said with a broad smile that looked vaguely familiar.

"Where you from?"

"California," he said. His hand enveloped mine in a firm grip.

"Ever play in high school?" I asked.

"A bit," he said. "Don't get much chance anymore."

My gaze wandered toward the pool where middle-aged men were huddled in small groups. *Wonder if anyone famous is there?*

"Name's Al Downing," he said, then he turned and waved towards a man seated near the bar who looked like he must be Joe Pepitone's father.

My mouth fell open as I stared down at my palm.

"What's wrong," my wife said?"

"I just shook hands with Al Downing."

"Oh, is he someone?" she whispered.

"Ace of the Yankees pitching staff in 63. Used to throw 98 miles an hour."

"Can you still throw the ball that fast?" I asked him.

"Only if I'm in a car," the former Yankee great said. Then he excused himself and headed for his former teammates.

"Come on, I'll have them sign your balls." my wife said, cracking a smile.

I smirked and trudged after her, carrying my autograph notebook and the four balls I had brought from Connecticut.

"You think I should talk to them?"

"Of course, that's what they're here for."

Shyly I followed my wife. *These are Yankee legends...Downing, Pepitone, Blomberg...how can I talk to them?*

But I did, and they signed everything anyone pushed in front of them, and posed for pictures, and smiled and laughed and made sure that it was a week to remember forever.

On the first day I arrived at seven am at Legends Field, the Yankee spring training facility in Tampa, Florida, I was a rookie to end all rookies, a twelve-year-old boy trapped in a fifty year old's body.

I found my locker. *Is this for real? They want me to dress in Yankee pinstripes?* I nestled onto the bench. *Holy, cow, there's a Yankee uniform hanging in it.* I glanced around, trying to savor the experience, yet everyone else seemed to be dressed already. I donned the pants, belt, cleats and hat, nodded to my teammates, and tried to squelch the runaway gallop of my heart. My team, a cross-section of Yankee fanatics from around the country, included a former minor league pitcher, several high school standouts, and a former college catcher who had come with his thirty-two-year-old son.

A wave of nausea came over me; I tried to focus on my last game wearing a little league uniform, a one hit shutout I had pitched at the age of twelve. *Jeez these guys look good*, I mused as a man near me took a tin of chewing tobacco from his locker, then pounded his glove with an iron fist. My breath came in shallow gasps. *Wonder if I can still get my money back.*

"Come on, the game's going to start in twenty minutes," my nearest teammate said.

I can't believe this is really happening.

I walked on numb legs among my teammates through the tunnel, a broad passageway that led from the locker room to the field, the sounds of dozens of new cleats clacking spasmodically on concrete. Up ahead Oscar Gamble and Ron Blomberg strode side by side, their easy laughter echoing past me like a spring breeze waving the pennants at Yankee Stadium.

Ron glanced over his shoulder and called in his rambling southern drawl, "Come on you guys. This is your fantasy."

I fought the urge to hurl my breakfast. *I haven't played in nearly forty years. How the hell am I going to do this?* And then I saw the field, the grass a forest green that only Crayola could duplicate, a color so perfect that it may not exist anywhere else in reality.

"Better stretch," our coach, Marty Brown, said. I paused, letting my teammates pass me. I scanned the infield, an unblemished expanse of tan dirt.

"The Yankees play right here in spring training," I heard someone say. I caught a glimpse of my wife, video camera in hand, filming my every move. I waved hesitantly—let my hand fall limply to my side—my smile a wily cover to the terror eating at my heart.

The trainer started us off slowly with gentle stretches, then built to the big finish.

"All right, now touch the ground."

I tried, hamstrings as tight as the wire supports of the George Washington Bridge, wishing the grass would miraculously grow another foot. Grunts of defiance escaped all around me, although one particularly spry thirty two year old seemed capable of palming the ground. Laughter flickered across the trainer's face.

"Ok …make that touch your knees." (Each day as our aging spines became more rigid the goal was made more attainable…last day deteriorated to "touch your belt.")

"Where can you play?" our manager asked as we filed into the dugout. I pictured a soaring fly ball striking me on the side of the head.

"Infield, I guess, but I'd like to try to pitch," dribbled from my mouth." He smiled, looked me over, "We've got twelve men so you'll sit for now."

I nodded, watched my teammates take the field, my twisted insides relaxing just a tad.

I sat on the bench, marveling at the feel of my Yankee uniform, thankful that my new cleats didn't crush my toes.

The game finally began. I tried not to look at my wife who was standing behind the fence, camcorder in hand, waiting to capture any small triumph. As Hector Lopez liked to say, things started off slowly and then tapered off. Our opponents looked like Olympians, albeit with small paunches and a few double chins, but they could hit and our pitcher decided to nibble at the corners.

Two well-hit balls were snared and the runners thrown out. My teammates are great, I thought, settling against the wall, content to watch for the rest of the game. Unfortunately the umpire had a new set of glasses and Ron Shelton, our former minor league pitcher, now white-haired, but still trim and powerful, could not buy another strike.

"Three walks, sorry you got to take him out. That's the rule," the umpire said and our ace was done with two outs and the bases loaded.

Our manager walked to the mound, picked up the ball and stared into the dugout in my direction.

"Dean, you're in," he called.

I looked around me. No one else moved. I fought the urge to run back to the locker room and book the first flight back to Connecticut. The manager pointed at me and curled his finger. I stood slowly feeling like a deer caught in the headlights of his gaze. My legs advanced against my will and I wafted out to the mound like Casper the friendly ghost, without my spotless cleats touching the ground.

He handed me the ball. "Warm up."

I nodded, my insides set to explode, climbed up the mound and peered down towards the catcher. Wow, that's far, I thought as I heard my wife yelling in the stands.

"Oh my God, Artie's pitching. I can't believe it. He looks good in pinstripes."

I secretly prayed for the camera to run out of film. *Hope my wife doesn't show this to our children.*

But my first warm-up reached the plate, always a good sign, and the catcher yelled his approval, as did our entire infield.

"Come on, Dean, baby, you can do it. Just throw strikes."

After a dozen more tosses the umpire settled in, despite my desire to delay further. A huge man stood at the plate, pointing his bat in my direction. The moment was set. *Dean in relief, two outs, bases loaded, the twelve fans in the stands going crazy.* I looked around the field, as the runners took their leads. *I want to remember this moment forever, before I embarrass myself.*

I peered in at the catcher, ignoring the sensation that my heart was beating irregularly. The batter may have been a stockbroker or an accountant, but, to me, he looked like he ate guys like me for breakfast.

Just throw a strike, please, God, just one.

I took my best little league wind-up, my eyes on the mitt, arm whirling, weight coming forward, nimbly striding ahead without falling.

The ball zipped towards the plate, a fifty-mile per hour fastball, which seemed to sink from a lack of momentum.

"Strike one," bellowed the ump, as the ball plopped into the catcher's mitt.

The batter pounded the plate with his bat, infuriated that someone would dare to throw one right down the middle. My teammates yelled encouragement and a warm feeling spread into my chest. I am in the moment, a kid once more. Again the wind up, the pitch, but this time a mighty swing, the crack of the bat, a sizzling line drive to left, which mercifully hooked foul.

Thank God he didn't hit it at my head. Hallelujah. Two strikes…the batter takes his stance, crowds the plate, the angry scowl on his face tempered by a glimmer of doubt around his eyes. *Could it be that a lifetime of pitching to the kids in the back yard has prepared me for this moment?*

I look in for the sign, although I've only got one pitch. Everyone is screaming. *The windup, the pitch…Oh no! It's heading toward his head.* He dances away, but it's on the inside corner…called strike three; the batter drops his bat in disgust. Three outs.

I hear my wife scream "Oh my God."

Suddenly everyone is pounding my shoulders.

"Way to go, Dean."

I feel like I've won the World Series. In the dugout I find that I can't stop smiling, a fact which my teammates point out to me all week long. The manager sent me out for a second inning, and, then, even a third. To my amazement I stayed out there and despite some mighty hits no one scored against me. It's as if some all powerful little league angel has given me a drink from the fountain of youth.

The week flew by in a blur, two nine inning games a day for five days, capped by a game against the Yankee greats themselves in an old timers game. Even the Yankee hitters seemed to have difficulty hitting my pitches. I can only assume that they have never seen such anemic stuff and that the effort to conceal their laughter has taken its toll. The fact that they are all nearing sixty, have arthritic joints and a few artificial hips between them, also crossed my mind. But my wife said that I looked good in the Yankee uniform and that's good enough for me.

I garnered enough memories in a week to last two lifetimes, made friends with some wonderful people, my teammates, and somehow survived a pulled hamstring, a sore shoulder and a bruised hand. The Yankee greats proved to be modest, generous with their time and their praise, reminders of all that is good about the men who have worn the Yankee uniform and lived the life of professional athletes.

"I lived a fantasy for ten years as a professional baseball player," our coach Ron Blomberg said. "Now I want to see you live yours."

What a great attitude.

By now I have forgotten that my thigh muscles were so sore that I could not lift my legs to put on my pants. I'm left with the thought that I got to meet twelve former Yankee players who coached me and laughed with me, and made sure I had the time of my life. It turned out that my fantasy was not to be a Yankee legend, not to take a crack at the major leagues. As nice as it was to meet all the former players, they alone could not have filled a week with such excitement. The real fantasy was to be part of a team that needed me, to walk out onto a field of dreams, and, despite aging bones and graying hair, to be young once again.

Golf—The Game I Love to Hate

I often wonder what drives grown men and women to pursue the game of golf. If you are an enthusiast, please don't be offended. I mean no harm. Yours is a noble pastime, one I share, worthy of inclusion in any sportsman's repertoire. Not since the first caveman poked himself in the eye with a sharp stick has a better sport been invented. Having attempted to learn the game over the past fifteen years and having just walked off the course defeated, I feel the need to vent.

Why should the attempt to smash a ball into oblivion cause such frustration? Conversely, what's so difficult about gently tapping a stationary ball into a hole in the ground? After all, the little dimpled thing isn't moving. It's not like basketball where you're trying to heave a ball through a hoop while athletic men in pajamas attempt to swat your offering away. Imagine the rules of hockey applied to golf— angry men wearing pads and carrying sticks willing to punch out your lights if you dare approach the hole. Picture a game of baseball where success depends on your ability to strike a ball thrown at speeds approaching 100 miles an hour, knowing full well that if you strike that ball out of the park, you will have to run around the bases and get yourself all tired out. What's more, your worthy opponent on the pitcher's mound will likely aim a high hard one at your head the next time you take up your bat. Soccer fans know that even the most well intentioned offensive players are likely to get slide tackled, bumped and battered should they have the audacity to attempt to kick the ball into the goal.

Golf seems tame by comparison, and quite civilized. You can rent a little buggy to carry your clubs around the course while you look all over for the ball—very useful when you're navigating between the impenetrable jungle on the right and the deep dark forest on the left. Balls are readily available, sold in quantities of a dozen at a time—just in case you lose one on occasion…make that on many occasions. Golf courses often sell used balls that they fish from lakes. I recognize some of them and feel privileged to buy them back at a fraction of my original cost.

The equipment is fun to buy, available at pro shops and golf warehouses all over the country. You can buy clubs on the Internet, or sporting goods stores. You can even buy used clubs at a discount. I often wonder about those lonely clubs set up in the corner of the pro shop. Were they turned in because they didn't work? Are they faulty designs supplanted by newer technology? It's difficult to find a set of clubs that works right. From years of observing other players it seems very few people find adequate equipment. I know my clubs are lousy, with a mind of their own. Sometimes they work well. Other times I'm tempted to throw them in one of the many water hazards made from generations of golfers' tears.

Golfers like to play their game surrounded by nature's beauty. Golf can be very spiritual and nondiscriminatory. You'll often hear golfers invoke the deity whether they're playing on Saturday or Sunday. Golfers are pack animals and like to talk as they play. Walking 6 or 7 miles in groups of four and smashing holes in the grass with clubs of varying length often brings comments from those who pass by. I must be pretty good at cheering people up. Sometimes I hear other golfers laugh with delight after I hit my shot.

Golfers are socially and politically correct. Anyone can play—even if they have a handicap. I don't want you to think I don't have fun while I play golf. I do. I keep company with some wonderful people. We talk of life as we walk. We speak of our children and the challenges we face in our lives. Most days I'm disappointed in my score, as are my fellow golfers. I miss two-foot putts. Sand traps attract my ball and want to keep it forever. As soon as I think I'm playing well my game falls apart. When I started, I used to think that triumph meant losing less than a dozen balls. Now I crave improvement.

For, you see, the golfer who hits under a hundred wants to break ninety. The one who breaks ninety covets eighty, and the scratch golfer dreams of one day quitting his job and joining the pro tour. Perhaps it's striving to be the best we can be that sets us up for failure and ultimate frustration. Sometimes I swear that I'll never play again. Yet when the phone rings and my buddy says, "I've got a tee time," I always go along. Maybe it's because I don't want to disappoint my friends. Maybe I like to walk and it's going to be a nice day. But maybe, just maybe I think, I'll hit a great shot, or sink a long putt that'll make five hours of slow death worthwhile.

Sometimes Even When You Lose You Win

This July in New England seemed more like an extended trip to a rain forest than an endless summer searching for the perfect tan. As August ebbs, morning dew blankets the grass and the nip of September grasps the air. It is on mornings like these that my thoughts drift to the inevitable turn of the season, and the return of college students everywhere to their dormitories, leaving their parents to mourn their departure.

It is in this spirit that I offer you the fictional story of Harvey Neufield, a father very much like any other father who desperately wants to contribute to his son's future, while still unwilling to give up the past.

Harvey Neufield always prided himself on his athletic prowess. Certainly he was intelligent, you don't get to be the head of a prestigious law firm without top grades and a lot of hard work. But, at forty it was his physical activities that people marveled at; running mini marathons, biking with men twenty years his junior, winning tennis tournaments.

When his son, Aaron, showed an aptitude for tennis, Harvey felt certain the game would allow them to bond. By the age of nine Aaron began to accompany his father to the nearby park courts, where the elder Neufield would drill balls to his son's backhand, lob balls over his head, and feed the boy put away shots, hoping that one day the boy would love the game as he did. The boy thought his father was a modern day Achilles, invincible and invulnerable.

Over the years the two had their differences, as all fathers and sons do. But when there was something bothering Aaron, there was still their weekly tennis game. They would play and then talk, the boy often disclosing things about his life on the tennis court that he would never say in the living room.

"If I let you win, you'll hate me for it," Harvey would say with a wink to the twelve year old Aaron. They'd play each Monday night until darkness crept in, squeezing out an extra set when they could, the boy trying to somehow win his first match, the father relishing the company much more than his victories.

Time passed. The boy entered high school. He grew taller, put on lean muscle, and went out for the school tennis team. While he wasn't the best on the team he was always known for his hustle and his tenacity. The weekly game continued, often the mother driving out to the court to bring them back.

"You two are crazy to play in the rain," she would say as her favorite two men would pile into the back of the car. But as soon as she saw their smiles her criticism would wither.

As time went by the father-son relationship became strained. The boy became more guarded, as do so many teenagers. Anxieties about the world and his place in it were never far from his mind. Still, the weekly tennis game continued, but it was Harvey who now seemed more insistent that they not miss a week. The games became closer. Aaron developed a spin serve and a fierce net game. Still, as in previous years, it was always Harvey who was the victor. But instead of beating the boy 6-0, as he could have, he held back, letting balls go by him, keeping the match close. One night during their game Aaron thought he saw his father purposely hit the ball out on a crucial point.

"I don't need your charity," the boy said, with a seriousness that made Harvey wince. "If I catch you letting me win, I'll never play with you again."

Aaron entered his senior year. Their conversations took on a more serious tone. They talked (or should I say fought) over politics, discussed future college choices, and career possibilities. As in past years the boy remained reticent everywhere but the tennis court. The talk turned to SAT's and AP's, the alphabet soup that ambitious eighteen year olds live or die by. That October Aaron began to date a girl from the girl's tennis team. They became inseparable. When she applied to Stanford, Aaron put in an application as well. "That's one of the best schools in the country," Harvey told his son, with a sinking feeling, on the day Aaron was accepted. "But California is so far away…"

Aaron matriculated. Although Aaron promised to stay close the phone calls became shorter and the talk less and less consequential. When Harvey asked how things were, all Aaron ever said was, "Fine, just fine."

A year passed. When Aaron returned home in May, he received a hero's reception. "It's Monday night, got time for tennis?" Harvey said after dinner.

"Can I watch?" the mother said, although she had never asked before.

"Don't worry, I'll be fine," Aaron thought he heard his father whisper to his mother when he thought Aaron wasn't listening. He noticed the tufts of gray hair peppering his father's temples, something he'd never paid attention to before. When Harvey bent his knees to put on his sneakers, a loud pop punctuated his grunt. Aaron wondered why he never noticed the rounded slump of his father's shoulders and the way the pouches under his father's eyes had darkened.

Before playing the two men stood at the net. Instead of waiting for the game to end, Aaron's worries surfaced.

"I broke up with my girlfriend, I hate my courses and I'm thinking of dropping out."

Harvey nodded, the lines on his forehead deepening.

"We'll talk about that after the game," he said. "Everything will be all right."

The game began. Harvey seemed much more sluggish than Aaron remembered, always a step slower to the ball. His father's serve had lost its zip and after a few games it became clear that for every tactic Harvey tried, Aaron had an answer.

"6-0, that's set," Aaron shouted and pumped his fist, when the last point was over.

"That's the first time I've ever beaten you!" Aaron said as Harvey sank onto a nearby bench, his breath coming harder than the match should have required.

"Is something wrong?" the boy said, his voice breaking, as he wiped his forehead with a towel.

"You beat me fair and square," Harvey said. "I'm proud of you…but that's only the first set."

"I don't know Dad…maybe you better take a break."

"If you don't give me a chance to get even, I'll never play with you again," Harvey said, half in jest, but with a desperate sound in his voice.

The second set began. Even though Harvey seemed sluggish, Aaron started to make mistakes, hitting balls a foot or two long, and missing easy overheads at the net.

Harvey won the set 6-4 when Aaron double faulted in the crucial last game.

"No way, I would never throw a match," Aaron said when Harvey protested, but Aaron had to turn away to hide his smile.

"Let's talk about your college plans," Harvey said and put a hand around Aaron's shoulder.

As mother, father and son walked towards the car, Harvey had to stop to catch his breath. Aaron ran ahead to get the car.

"If you don't take that stress test this week, I'll kill you myself," the mother said, under her breath, an arm around Harvey's waist.

Aaron caught the gist of the conversation through the open car window, but made believe he was adjusting the radio. Harvey got into the back seat, closed his eyes, and immediately fell asleep— fortunate for Aaron, who couldn't control the flow of his tears or the way his hands trembled when he took the wheel.

A LITTLE LEAGUE FANTASY

A fantasy written with admiration for all the participants in Little League, Babe Ruth, American Legion and Girl's softball, players and parents both past and present. You know who you are.

Tommy Everyman sat on his hands in the dugout. He was glad he wasn't in the game. His team was down 1-0 going into the 7th inning. With his buzz cut and thick neck the opposing pitcher looked more like a marine sergeant than a twelve year old.

"Don't take it personally, son, but I've got to sit you for this one," the coach had said when they arrived at the field. After all, like Coach said, at nine he'd have plenty of years to play. So what if this was the State Championship game? So what if he was the only player on the bench and his parents had driven an hour and a half to get to the game? So what if the coach's son was pitching and his nephew was at shortstop?

"The important thing is winning the game for the team," Coach said.

Small, even for a nine year old, always polite and a little shy, Tommy wasn't the kind of kid to complain. But as he sat on the bench and his teammates took the field he felt as though his heart had sunk to the pit of his stomach. How many times had his mother driven him to practice? He glanced up into the stands and nodded to his father, once an all-star pitcher at Waterford High. How disappointed Dad looked whenever their eyes met. As Tommy watched the pitcher warm up, he felt his father's eyes boring into the back of his head.

Thoughts of his father saying, "You're not good enough to start," danced in his head. He stopped turning back and concentrated on the game.

The field was perfect. Big cities like Hartford had the bucks to keep the grass green. Instead of rock-strewn dirt, their infield smelled of fine Georgian clay, perfectly raked to a flawless surface, the foul lines as straight as laser beams from home to the outfield wall. Instead of bleachers they had seats!

The Hartford team looked like a squad of weightlifters. Tommy could swear he saw a five o'clock shadow on the first baseman's chin.

"Attaboy, no batter," Tommy yelled from the bench, his tiny voice drowned out by hundreds of Hartford loyalists in the seats.

The game progressed quickly. The opposing pitcher mowed down Tommy's teammates with fastballs on the corners. Yet the coach's son pitched the game of his life and despite some hot line drives and towering fly balls only one run came in.

When they reached the bottom of the seventh inning the score stood at one to nothing. As Tommy's team came to bat for their last licks, the coach put a hand on his shoulder. "If we get a man on I'll try to put you in as a pinch runner," Coach said. Tommy nodded and bit his lip, unsure if the gnawing feeling in his gut was fear or elation.

When the first batter struck out Tommy realized he would never get into the game. Yet Coach's son walked and the next batter beat out a dribbler to third. When the next pitch got by the catcher, runners advanced to second and third. An intentional walk was issued with hopes of setting up a double play. Coach's nephew, their best hitter, stepped into the batter's box with bases loaded and pointed his bat at the center field wall. But when he fouled the first pitch off his ankle he had to be helped off the field.

"You need a batter," the umpire bellowed.

When Coach pointed to the on deck batter the ump shook his head.

"If you got a sub you've got to use him."

Even from the bench Tommy could see his coach swallow hard. Then he turned towards the dugout, extended one finger and pointed at Tommy. Tommy shot off the bench and ran to home plate. "Just give me your best," Coach said. "And watch my signs. You're all we got." Then Tommy felt a pat on his backside and Coach trotted over to the foul side of third.

Tommy gazed at the pitcher who was sweating heavily.

"Let's get two," the catcher yelled. The outfielders crept in to the edge of the outfield grass to stop a ground ball from squirting through. Tommy glanced over at Coach who was rubbing the brim of his cap, the sign for bunt. Tommy squared up, but the pitch was low, as were the next two. He bunted the next pitch perfectly down the third base line, but it kicked foul at the last moment.

"Tough luck, runt," the first baseman said, as Tommy trotted back to home.

"Three and two," bellowed the Ump, and he settled down into a crouch. Tommy glanced over at Coach who wiped off the brim of his cap.

"Hit away?" Tommy muttered under his breath, his heart fluttering like a hummingbird's wings, his breath coming in shallow gasps. He pictured the face of his father and prayed for ball four, but somehow he knew that the next pitch would be a fastball right down the middle. "Oh, please, Lord, help me," he prayed. "I promise to be good to my sister."

The pitcher spat, and went into a full wind-up, his arm whirling forward and the ball flying towards Tommy in a moment that would live in his memory forever. It was the last thing he thought of when he died at eighty four.

For, in that split second that separates success and failure, winning and losing, joy and lament, our boy swung with all his might and met the ball squarely on the sweet spot of the bat. To the pitcher's horror, the ball sailed majestically over the head of the drawn in center-fielder, skipped off the grass, and rolled all the way to the fence. All three runs scored. Tommy stopped at third and his teammates mobbed him. As Coach carried him from the field on his shoulders Tommy caught a glimpse of his parents hugging each other. Coach set him down reluctantly, the joyous cries of his friends drowned out only by the thunderous beating of Tommy's heart.

THE JEW WHO WON A SUPER BOWL

I visited the University of Pennsylvania campus last weekend to spend time with my son and daughter. While there, I attended Shabbat services at the campus Hillel. I sat in the back with my son. Immediately, I noticed a large man nearby, dressed in a black coat belted at the waist. His salt and pepper beard flowed unconstrained down his chest, covering his starched white shirt and collar. His black hat obscured neatly cropped hair, the fringe more white than black.

A man dressed in Hassidic garb is not such a rarity at Penn Hillel, an organization that houses reform, conservative, and orthodox services in one building. Impressive cooperation, although each group has their own floor. At first glance he had an athletic build, a strong jaw, and the bearing of a man more youthful than his facial hair would suggest. He sat quietly, his head bowed towards his prayer book, absorbed in the service. Sitting amongst the other students he seemed somewhat out of place. I put his appearance out of my mind and tried to concentrate on the service. The reader began the blessing for the Torah service.

Then the Hassidic visitor stood. A Samson amongst mere men, this mountain of strength towered above all others. "I bet he plays center for the Mir Yeshiva," my son quipped. I nodded, estimating his height at 6' 7" with a build Wilt Chamberlain would have been proud of.

After the service we made Kiddush and then waited for lunch to be served at the Hillel dining room. My son disappeared with my daughter for a while and then returned to my table with a broad smile on his face.

"Hey, Dad, come with me. There's someone you have to meet."

I followed, intrigued by the whimsical twinkle in his eye. He led me towards a small circle of students with the tall Hassidic man at its center. Rabbi Levy, a young man who runs the Chabad house near campus, greeted me and held up a large ring encrusted in jewels.

"Ever see a Super Bowl ring?" he asked and placed a ring with the heft of a paperweight in my palm.

"Is this real?" I asked, wondering if the diminutive Hassidic rabbi might have powers I was not aware of.

"Of course it's real," he answered with a glance towards the tall Hassid holding court with the students. "This is Shlomo Veingrad. He won the Superbowl in 1992, with the Dallas Cowboys.

My eyes widened. An orthodox Jew in medicine, law, or accounting would raise few eyebrows, but professional football? I shook hands with the man and wondered how such a thing could be possible.

"Come to our minyan tonight," Rabbi Levy said. "Shlomo will talk about his experiences."

Who can pick up a good novel without reading the end? I had to know more, especially since my son is a Bal Teshuva and questions of faith always intrigue me. So, accompanied by my son, I attended the Chabad event and got to schmooze with Mr. Veingrad after davening the Maariv service by his side.

"Were you Hassidic when you played professional football?" I asked, trying to imagine him dressed in black coat, hat and long beard during a huddle.

He laughed. "No. Religion was not part of my life in those days. I became religious long after my playing days were over."

Turns out our unlikely champion played 7 years in the National Football League as an offensive lineman. He broke into the NFL in 1986, with the Green Bay Packers and was traded eventually to the Dallas Cowboys, where he played with running back legend Emmet Smith.

He won the Superbowl in 1992, and retired in '93. Shlomo, known as Alan Veingrad back in his playing days, tipped the scales at 285. He's a much more svelte 220 now at 46, and, although he seems quite gentle, I wouldn't want to cross him or break Shabbat in his presence.

He shared some stories about his playing days. He's been injured several times, had hip operations and ankle problems, all in the pursuit of his professional responsibilities. He told me how he met a Rabbi in Ft. Lauderdale who changed his life by bringing him to his home for Shabbat. He went back many times, began to study Torah, and eventually, with his wife, chose a Hassidic path for his family. But my favorite story was of his relationship with his father and their attempts to reconcile their religious differences. Alan's father, a conservative Jew, was always proud of his son's athletic endeavors, but balked at his religious transformation. Yet, with time, he became more accepting and began to attend services with his son. He took part in Shabbat at his son's home. Then one day, a few years before his passing, the elder Veingrad turned to his son, pointed to his kippah and said, "Alan, I was always proud of you when you played football, and especially when you won the Super Bowl. But I have to say I've never been more proud of you than I am today."

I left the Chabad house feeling quite moved. Not because Shlomo Veingrad was a Jewish football hero, and not because he became a very religious man from indifferent beginnings. Rather, I felt moved by his humanity, by his search for truth and a way of life that felt right. Most of all, I admired the way he changed his life without fear of criticism, and made sure to stay close to his family. Perhaps that's the best we can expect from our children even when they hear the beat of a different drummer.

CHAPTER 3

REFLECTIONS ON RAISING CHILDREN

Reflections on Raising Children

From time to time I have offered my invaluable advice to my children. Even when they were toddlers they accepted my gentle instructions with suspicion. Years ago I became used to their admonishments: "I'd rather do it myself, Daddy," when playing with Lego blocks. "No, meeee," shouted by an irate two year old with tomato sauce all over his face and spaghetti on his lap, as I tried to instruct him in the finer points of eating Italian cuisine with a fork.

In most cases I backed off. A parent quickly learns which battles can be won, and at what cost. In some cases my anxiety that they might be harmed by their decisions drove my intervention. Like the time I came home and found my oldest (he was six at the time) ensconced twenty feet up on a branch of a stately oak with a look of pure joy on his face. Other times my interference stemmed from an overprotective concern for family unity. "No, you cannot give your brother away to a different family!"

As my children grew up my advice was asked for much less frequently than it was offered. "Let me show you how to shoot a jump shot," was more typically met with polite silence, when it was complete admiration I was looking for.

"Make sure you study a practical subject— one where you can get a job," rarely provokes appreciation from college-aged children.

"You just want me to be like you," I heard chanted by my teenagers as a trump card during family discussions of their politics or life choices, as if this were a result to be abhorred. Anyone who has raised children can sympathize with the old joke: Insanity is hereditary. You get it from your children. Sometimes, after a heated discussion, I would think back to my own teenage years in the sixties. The country seemed to be on the verge of revolution at times. Protests and counter-protests about the Vietnam War, civil rights marches, and rebellion against the establishment seemed a weekly occurrence in New York City. The battle lines were drawn between generations. I remember confrontations with my father that ended in, "You'll do what I say because I'm your father." Times have changed. The thought of getting away with using that line on my children brings a smile to my lips.

Back then, I thought my parents, who had emigrated from Europe after the war, had no understanding of the important things in life. They worried about health. They worried about money. They worried about having a nice place to live. Above all they worried about raising moral children who could make a living and take care of themselves. At seventeen I worried about changing the world.

Remember the saying, "Never trust anyone over thirty?" Now that I am almost twice that age, I recognize that argument was short sighted.

My four children are pretty much on their own these days. Like many other parents who are empty nesters, my children are scattered around the country and the world. They come back during school breaks. We try to talk on the phone. My opportunities to give timely advice have diminished considerably. In one respect my children have followed in my own footsteps. They have learned to listen to their friends' and parents' advice and then make their own choices. Perhaps that's all I have a right to hope for.

I observed the third anniversary of my father's Yartzheit a few months ago. Sometimes I still feel like I owe him a call, as if I've been remiss in not updating him on how his grandchildren are doing. As much as I strained against the bit of conformity as a teenager, my worries in middle age seem to be much the same as those of my parents. I worry about how my children will carry on their Jewish heritage. I think about their chosen professions. I wonder who they will marry. I've stopped planning to change the world. That seems like much too big a burden to shoulder, better left to my children's generation. I've wound up with values much like my parents, despite so many years convinced I'd be different.

I wonder what my father would say if only he could read these words. Perhaps he'd offer some advice. Perhaps he'd nod and tell me I was doing the best I could, and that my children's lives were their own to live. Maybe he'd just laugh and put his hand on my shoulder and tell me he knew just how I felt.

A TREE GROWS IN WATERFORD

Nearly twenty years ago my nine-year-old son, Adam, came home from his fourth grade class at Solomon Schechter with an intriguing class project: Get an apple seed to germinate. Great idea, I thought at the time. Let the children see how hard it is to get things to grow. He wrapped a handful of seeds in damp cotton and kept them on the windowsill in direct sunlight. He checked them each day, watered and tended to them, much as we, his parents, fussed over his 9 year old needs. After a while the seeds opened, sending their fragile shoots out into the world. I still remember the wondrous look on his face as he pondered the miracle that we too often take for granted.

He transferred the germinating seeds into a paper cup filled with potting soil. He groomed and watered them each day, fretting that his pride and joy would receive all the sunlight and care it needed to turn into a fine healthy plant.

Adam's days were filled with a whirl of activities in those years: little league baseball, basketball. Like most parents, our days were spent shuttling our son from activity to activity. We sat on bleachers watching him play so often I could have sworn we developed permanent depressions where once only curves prevailed.

Within a few months the plant outgrew its small container and our son transferred it into a pot. It stayed in our kitchen for months, basking in the sun, gaining strength for the day when it might take its place outdoors.

During that spring our son seemed to be growing out of his clothes monthly. We replaced sneakers grown tight overnight. Jackets grew too small. Baby teeth fell out, replaced by their adult counterparts. I thought I glimpsed a hint of darker hair mixed with the peach fuzz above my son's lip.

Our son continued to water his growing apple sprig long after his school project ended. One sunny day in June the inevitable moment came. Adam went out into the back yard and planted the fruit of his labors in the soil. We worried about the hazards. What if the deer, so often seen in the area, found our son's six-inch apple tree no more than a passing treat? What if the man who mowed the lawn each week ignored the rocks placed around our tree and in an inattentive moment turned our treasure into a bit of mulch?

Adam continued to water his plant all that summer. It seemed to double in height overnight. We stopped worrying about the deer's appetite or an errant lawn mower.

Meanwhile, Adam grew like a weed. He played center on his middle school basketball team. We calculated that if he continued to grow at his current speed he would reach eight feet by college. His darkening peach fuzz turned into a mustache. He began to shave. Friends came and went. Our son was so busy we should have installed a revolving door in our house. In high school he took up track and soccer and tennis. His sneakers lasted for weeks instead of months. We sat on bigger bleachers, picking up splinters with other parents in similar circumstances. I had four children playing town sports, all on different teams. It seemed like the whirl of family life would never end. If I had five minutes to wolf down a sandwich before driving my kids to a game, I considered it a leisurely meal.

During Adam's high school years the tree managed without our influence. It grew with a mind of its own, branching, sending roots surging. Our son went off to college. We continued to watch out for his tree, but, with him gone it wasn't the same.

He returned once in a while. There were vacations, and long weekends. Quickly we realized we were more of a pit stop than a permanent home. One day we went to his graduation ceremony.

That summer the apple tree produced a single solitary apple, the size of an apricot. We treasured it and told all our friends the story of Adam's tree. Adam moved to Chicago for graduate school the summer that three apples appeared on his tree.

Seeing our son is so much harder these days. He's busy working towards his future. He wants to be a professor at a University one day.

Last year my wife and I joined the exclusive ranks of empty nesters. We've raised four children to adulthood. Every day when we look out our kitchen window we see that apple tree in our back yard. It's twelve feet high now, and if a lawn mower ran into it the mower blade would break. Yesterday my wife ran into the house. "You won't believe this!" she said breathlessly. "Come out back." I trudged out into the yard, my jaw dropping, my hands held to the side of my face.

She pointed to Adam's tree in full bloom for the first time ever with hundreds of apple blossoms opening in a canopy of red and white. I smiled at the thought of dozens of fine young apples growing in the back yard after all these years of waiting.

The tree makes me think of my four grown children, spread all over the country and the world, taking root in different soil. I wonder what they're doing, and of how fast time passes. I think of the joy of thirty years spent in Waterford raising a family, and I hope I'll get to see my children raise children of their own.

I can picture a scene, somewhere in the future, where my son returns home to show his own son the apple tree in my backyard laden with fruit. Perhaps his son will take a bite of an apple and wonder how such a wondrous thing could grow from a tiny seed. And I'll smile and watch the two of them, and wonder the same thing.

FATHER'S DAY STORY

When Frank Durango rose that morning the first hint of crimson haze was lighting the beaches that lined Pequot Avenue. He threw on white socks, sandy boat shoes, and a tattered sweatshirt that he claimed years earlier from his only son. *Should have thrown this out with the rest of his junk.* He fingered yet another hole in the armpit, and thought of throwing the sweatshirt away. He knew he never would.

He fixed coffee, drank it on the front porch as the paperboy biked up his driveway.

"Good Morning, Mr. Durango," the boy said.

"Oh, yeah, what's so good about it?" Durango barked with a dismissive wave of his hand.

The boy paused, then smiled the hopeful smile of the young still untouched by sorrow.

"Well, then, Happy Father's Day, anyway," the boy said. Then he turned his bike around and sped towards the next house.

For a moment an image of Frank Jr. flashed in his mind. *Wonder if he's still in California? Or if he's still alive after five years without word? Not that he'd ever call after what happened.*

Frank forced the thought from his mind, just as he did every morning. Then he grabbed the shaft of his metal detector and headed down to Ocean Beach. As the sun rose Frank worked the area nearest the boardwalk. A generation of New London schoolboys called Frank "crazy old metal head," behind his back. With the headset on, sweeping the sand for the occasional coin, Frank looked eccentric. He knew that. But crazy? Not yet.

He found solace in his task—something to fill the empty hours of each morning, after nightmares wrenched him from sleep. They always ended the same with his son calling for help in the dark. There wasn't much payback in the work, only the calm Frank got from repeating the same motion endlessly—his silent penance.

He found coins every day, chump change mostly, barely enough to buy his daily donut and coffee at the Dunkin Donuts on Ocean Avenue. Once he'd found a gold pen. Another time a high school ring, but mostly he found other people's discarded junk: rusted pen knives, buried beer cans, nameless keys to unknown locks.

Usually Frank let his mind go numb as he worked. Yet, on this Father's Day, as Frank reached the far end of the boardwalk, his mind flashed back to the night five years earlier.

He relived the sights and sounds of that night, the same as in his nightmares: the busted glass, the police sirens, his son's call to Frank, a frantic plea for help. *And what did I do? Let the kid rot in jail for the night. Thought he'd be scared straight. And he was. Only one problem: He never spoke to me again.*

As he neared the end of the boardwalk a shadowy figure climbed down from the lifeguard's chair. *Probably some drunken bum sleeping off an all night bender.* Frank continued scanning. He let his mind play out his favorite fantasy, imagined finding a 2 carat diamond, and using the proceeds to buy a ticket to California, where he'd track down Frank Jr., wherever he was, and bring him home. *He'll be 21 next month.*

As the shadowy figure advanced towards Frank, the metal detector went ballistic. Frank's heart quickened. He began to dig. The shadowy figure walked faster, fastening his hood tighter around his head to mask his face. Frank ignored the possible danger and dug, his pulse pounding. As the figure approached, Frank reached into the sand and pulled out a bracelet.

"Nice find," a voice called out.

Instinctively Frank clutched the bracelet behind his back, even though he knew at once it was worthless costume jewelry. He turned quickly, ready to swing the metal detector with deadly force if the stranger tried anything funny.
For some reason he paused, something about the way the man facing him cocked his head to the side.

"What do you want? I've got nothing," Frank yelled.

The young man drew back his hood and smiled, as Frank dropped to his knees in the sand. "Happy Father's Day, Pops." was all the young man said.

Ferries still ply the Thames River every day with eager passengers scanning the beaches. Bathers from all over Connecticut still flock to Ocean Beach on warm summer mornings to claim a choice spot on the sand. But they won't be seeing "crazy old metal head," any more. He's put away his metal detector for good. Most early mornings you can find him on his front porch, sipping coffee with his son, while the sun comes up on another day.

ASSIMILATION

Jewish newspapers and magazines frequently run stories about the decline of synagogue involvement. I read these with interest as I raised my four children— three boys and a girl. The articles are almost always written by Rabbis keen on keeping the Jewish people from disappearing through assimilation. Most recently the Pew report has put numbers to the issue through its thorough poll. Suffice it to say the Rabbis' warning is confirmed. Our children are turning away from religion in record numbers.

I view these reports with fatalistic acceptance. Having come of age in the sixties, I know it is hard to change the world. A nationwide trend away from religious observance is not so easily stemmed. Yet before we close the books on the issue I think we have reason to hope. The exodus may not be as complete or as permanent as some fear.

I am neither a Rabbi, nor an educator. My credentials as a social scientist are lacking. I grew up in an orthodox household, but chose to join a conservative congregation when I got married. Any standing I have as a commentator comes not from my scholarship, but instead from the fact that over my 60 years I have faced these issues myself, from both sides.

As a child of Austrian immigrants I wanted only to pursue the American dream, caring little for my parents' angst at my love for baseball and all things "goyish." They were disappointed at my disdain for Hebrew School and my indifference to synagogue attendance.

As a young man I struggled to find the right balance for my children. I recognized that I had already separated myself from my religious forebears. I reasoned that I wanted them to grow up as well rounded American children who happened to be Jewish. I sent them to the Solomon Schechter School in New London. They learned about our holidays. We built sukkahs on Sukkot and held Seders on Passover. Often, I recited Kiddush on Friday nights, and my wife made a nice Sabbath meal, even if we chose to go to the movies right afterwards. If the kids had a league basketball game we took them, Shabbat or no Shabbat. The children learned to read from the Torah and conduct services. They were bar/bat mitzvahed. As teenagers they all went to Camp Ramah every summer camp. We pushed them to take part in all things Jewish. We journeyed to Israel together.

By the time the kids went off to college, I reasoned I had done my best, and hopefully the kids would turn out to be just like me—mindful of my heritage— happy to follow along in the conservative tradition. I forgot to take into account one minor thing. My children all had minds of their own.

Two of my children became involved with the Maimonides program at their university. They began to study Judaism with renewed zeal. They observed kashrut both inside and outside their homes. They dressed modestly and began strict observance of Shabbat. One weekend my youngest son came home wearing a kippah and revealed that he had been teaching himself Aramaic so that he could study the Talmud in the language it was written. After graduation he enrolled in a Yeshiva in Israel to study Talmud, a path he followed for two years before coming back to the States. My daughter attended the same Maimonides program three years later and studied with the same charismatic Rabbi on her university campus. After a trip to Poland where she toured the concentration camps she, too, turned towards a strictly observant life.

I was mildly surprised, to say the least. Why would my children gravitate towards more strict observance when I had rebelled all those years ago? Wasn't there enough to satisfy them in our conservative synagogue? These questions kept me awake some nights, but above all my wife and I pledged to support our children regardless of their choices in life. We kashered our home so that the observant branch of our family would eat in our house. We began to pay attention to hekshers on the foods we bought. Whenever I visited my son over a weekend, my wife and I attended services at the shul of my son's choosing.

And what of my other two children? They took different paths. My eldest son joined a reform congregation. He married a wonderful young woman "who chose to be Jewish" by converting to Judaism. From what I hear, she is the driving force behind their involvement in the synagogue. They attend Friday nights, and, for the past several years, have organized the break-the-fast meal after Yom Kippur. I've been to their synagogue for a Kabbalat Shabbat on a Friday night, and it's a warm friendly place, filled with spirit.

My middle son and his wife hear the beat of a different drum. They prefer to be secular. They stay clear of organized religion on most occasions. At their wedding, although there were two Rabbis in attendance, they chose to have their parents conduct the wedding service. Still, they had a ketubah, a chuppah, and all the things required to make it a proper wedding in the eyes of Jewish law. Last Passover they held a Seder for 24 of their friends. In their personal lives they follow the precepts of Tikun Olam, helping others to live a better life. They choose to do it outside any religious institutions.

My point in giving you a glimpse of my family is to demonstrate the richness, and the diversity of their choices. None of them chose to live as their parents do when it comes to religion. They want to be different. I'm sure my four children have fascinating discussions on their ways of life and on how they view their upbringing. I'd love to be a fly on the wall and take in what they have to say.

My children have affected me in many ways. I had never attended services in a reform synagogue—now I have. I had never attended services in an orthodox Yeshiva, amongst men wearing black hats—now I have. As I've gotten older I seem to have gravitated back to our conservative synagogue—only with renewed commitment. I am more involved than ever.

I've come to realize that Judaism is not a static thing. It is there for us throughout our lives. When we are young and immortal we may not be as interested. When we have children, a sense of continuity of the generations comes knocking. And, as we approach our senior years, we may find additional comfort in our traditions and the belief in God.

I've become increasingly aware that there is a small but steady stream of Jewish men and women turning back to strict observance of Judaism—the so called B'al Teshuva movement. There is something inherently beautiful in our religion that will always attract and inspire people. As conservative Jews, we may not agree with their approach. We may not be observant in the same manner, and may not practice all the precepts. Still, I take comfort in knowing that Judaism holds such richness, such attraction, even if I do not follow every commandment.

I wish that, on some level, the different denominations of our faith could pool their resources—to help inspire future generations, for that is certainly the task at hand. Programs like Birthright, which sends young adults to Israel, seem to be on the right track. Educators need to reach our children in their later teenage years and young adulthood, when they no longer live under our roof and play by our rules.

We've been a people for more than 5000 years. During that time we've had our ups and downs—admittedly many downs. But for all we've been through, the Jewish people are still around when the mightiest empires have turned to dust. Let's hope that the challenges we face can be met with wisdom, compassion and commitment.

Leaving Home

Betsy threw her last few toiletries into her suitcase, ran a brush through the salt and pepper tussle on the top of her head, and stepped out into the damp cold that passes for a Connecticut November. The taxi pulled up the driveway. Betsy got in, not knowing when she might return. She'd decided long ago to be ready for this day. She'd packed a bag and kept it at the side of her bed. Never could pinpoint the day, but when it came she'd be ready.

Sam, her husband, worked at Electric Boat as an electrical engineer. He was working the night shift that month. It was a good steady job with lots of overtime when a new boat had to get done, but some days he felt like shucking the responsibility and taking off for the warmth of the Florida Coast. Three more years working 60 hour weeks and he'd be pretty to cash in on the pension. This new wrinkle had him worried. He'd argued, he'd pleaded, anything to keep Betsy from going.

"Betsy, you can't leave me alone like this," he said. "She's a hopeless case."

She'd blinked back tears, but when Betsy made a decision about something there was no possibility of changing her mind.

So, with battle lines drawn, and no possibility of compromise, Betsy gave the driver the fateful command that would send her so far from home.

"Providence airport," she said.

As the driver eased onto the highway and accelerated to cruising speed, Betsy lit a cigarette. She inhaled deeply, first one she'd had in the ten years since she'd quit. She thought of calling Sam, to give him one last chance, but what would be the point? When push came to shove she'd do what she had to do, no matter the consequences.

They arrived at the airport with her mind in a whirl.

"You need help with your bag, lady?" the cabbie barked as they pulled up to the terminal.

"Nope, take care of it myself," she said and took her bag from the trunk. *Just like I take care of everything.*

Six hours later Betsy's plane landed in Los Angeles. For a moment she imagined a crowd of well-wishers waiting for her at the gate, but no one was at the airport to meet her—*why would they be?*

She waited for her bag. She made her way to the taxi stand. As she waited for the next car to drive up she relived the fight she'd had with her daughter that night two years earlier.

"LA is no place for a girl like you. Stay with us. You and your boyfriend are always welcome."

"How many times do I have to tell you to stay out of my life?"

"But where will you live? How will you manage? You can't just waltz into town and land a job as an actress."

Her daughter's eyes flashed, her face sullen, the silence between them deafening.

"You need talent," Betsy had said, frantic to keep her daughter from making the biggest mistake of her life.

And that was the last conversation they'd had, until the call came.

"Where to Ma'am?" the driver asked.

"Burbank General Hospital," Betsy said. "As fast as you can. I've got to get there in time."

She sat back as the cab turned onto the expressway. She closed her eyes and tried to sleep, but an imagined vision of her daughter alone at the hospital rose in her mind. *Is she suffering? Lord knows there'd be pain, but will Frannie crack under the strain? At least if I'm there she won't be alone....and what if the worst happens?*

The cab slowed. Betsy barked through Plexiglass thick enough to stop a bullet, "Why are we stopping? I've got to get to the hospital!"

The cab driver checked the rear view mirror and rolled his eyes. In his thirty years driving the streets of LA he'd seen and heard everything. He got detached after a while. How else could he deal with the stress of people who think a cabbie can work miracles?

After a few minutes, the cab came to a full stop, salsa music playing from the radio, the cabbie drumming his fingers on the wheel.

Betsy looked at the license affixed to the divider between them.

"Please, Mr. Torres, can't you do something?"

Torres nodded. *What I wouldn't do for some medical marijuana.* Again he glanced at the lady in the rear view mirror. *Sure is pretty. But why do I have to fix everyone's emergency.* He scanned her features, the clear complexion and red and black business suit—hair in a bun, a Jewish star hanging from the delicate gold necklace around her neck. He noted the little pile of shredded Kleenex strips she'd been twisting in her lap. *Thank God I left Manhattan when I did. These eastern types'll kill ya.*

"Lady, relax, there's nothing we can do. This is California. You got to learn to relax or you'll drive yourself crazy. Nothing can be that important."

Betsy's lower lip quivered.

"But my daughter needs me," she said through clenched teeth. "Everyone deserves a second chance."

The cab driver shrugged.

"Do you have a family?" Betsy asked with hesitation.

"Had," Torres said. He thought of the years he'd spent in the marines. *Was I serving my country or getting away from all the fighting at home?* He thought of telling her how the post traumatic stress took its toll, but remained silent.

"Didn't work out," he said in a small voice after a long pause.

"Well mine didn't either and I need to make things right," Betsy said. "Can't you drive on the shoulder?"

Torres grimaced. "Whew, lady, ya want me to lose my license?"

Betsy's soft sobs wafted from the back seat. Torres scanned the expressway, the red brake lights stretching as far as he could see. After a few minutes he turned around.

"Lady, if I take the exit up ahead we'll be in East LA, could be better, could be much worse."

"Do it, anything. Just try to get me to Burbank Hospital in time."

Torres bit his lip. He recognized the look of a frightened animal in Betsy's eyes and something in his hardened heart softened.

"Alright, I'll try, but don't say I didn't warn you if it doesn't work."

Torres turned the cab onto the shoulder, sped the quarter mile past angry cars, their drivers flicking middle fingers as the cab flew by. He took the first exit off the expressway onto a street that looked more like a war zone than a suburb of the richest city in the country.

Torres' thoughts turned to the last time he saw his own daughter. *Let's see, ten years since the split. That would mean she'd be 18 by now. I missed her whole life.* The cab driver's vision became clouded. He blinked back tears. That's when he hit the first obstacle, a pothole the size of a cave. The cab shuddered, then swerved to the left while Betsy screamed, the cab upending garbage cans and sending trash flying.

"Hold on, lady," Torres yelled, his head bobbing like a prizefighter slipping jabs. The cab jumped the curb and hit a hydrant before it finally stopped.

Torres cursed the day he was born in Spanish—he always reverted to his native tongue when under stress. He shut off the engine and got out to check the damage.

Betsy sat in the back, but when she smelled smoke she jumped out in a hurry.

Torres grunted. "This'll cost me a month's pay," he mumbled when the front bumper came away in his hand.

Betsy's eyes grew wide, not with concern for the vehicle, but rather for the gang of six young men who were approaching the taxi from the other end of the street. "You have to help me reach my daughter," Betsy said to Torres, her voice trembling. "Please, she needs me."

"Let's move," Torres said, "Or we'll wind up in the hospital."

Betsy took off her heels and they began to jog down the street, slowly at first, but when the gang ran towards them, Betsy and Torres broke into a sprint, heading towards the gas station in the distance.

Suddenly three men carrying baseball bats stepped out of the darkness.

"What's your hurry, lady," someone was saying.

"Welcome to East LA," said another, and gripped her upper arm, his fingers digging into her flesh.

She glanced at Torres, her expression etched in fear and determination.

"My daughter, I have to reach my daughter," she said through clenched teeth.

Torres nodded and his eyes narrowed for, by then, the gang of six was close enough to see their faces. Torres broke and ran, eluding one man cleanly and stiff-arming another, running as fast as he could towards his taxi.

"Let him go," someone was saying. "We got enough to keep us busy."

Betsy stared helplessly, watching as her only hope disappeared into the taxi. *How will I reach Frannie?*

The taxi's lights flickered once, then twice, and finally came on fully, the roar of the engine no match for the pounding of Betsy's heart.

Then the taxi was doing a K turn and heading back towards the highway, the lights disappearing around a corner.

"Hey, you pretty fine for an older woman," someone was saying. Betsy closed her eyes, her mind consumed with thoughts of her daughter's face on the day she was born. She imagined one day they might be reunited, if not in this world, then in another. She wondered if she'd ever see her husband again. *Will he ever know what happened?*

The words of the Shema came to her mind and she silently recited the few words she remembered. *Please, Dear God, you can't let it end like this. Help me.*

Her hands balled into fists as she waited for the worst. She felt like she was going to pass out. A litany of her life's regrets passed through her mind in an instant.

Why did I let my daughter slip out of my life?

She opened her eyes to see a car creeping around the corner, its lights off. Then it crawled to a stop.

"Taxi man must be lost," someone was saying and the gang laughed. The laughter died when the car turned on its brights, roared into action, and then sped towards them with astonishing speed.

The gang members stood motionless, blinking uncomprehendingly at the approaching car as if it were an apparition. Within seconds the lights were upon them, the young men scattering.

Betsy fell to the ground. She waited for the impact. But, at the last moment, the car swerved and went by, wheels screeching. The car turned in a semicircle, exposing the missing fender of the yellow cab she'd thought she'd never see again. And there was a determined looking Torres at the wheel, his eyes ablaze.

"Hey, we gonna mess you up," Betsy heard one man say. "You shoulda run when you could."

Three young men ran at the car, smashing the windshield with their bats and reaching into the car to pull Torres out. Three more had chains wrapped around their fists.

But, then, the car door was opening. Torres rolled out and with a series of lightening quick moves upended two men and kicked the bats out of the hands of two others. Then he crouched behind the car, his arms steadied on the hood, a service revolver grasped in his hands.

"Let the lady go and I'll let you live," Torres was saying to the men facing him.

"You can't get all of us," one of them said.

"No, but I can get you," Torres said, and took dead aim. "Get in the cab, lady."

Betsy staggered to her feet, grimacing at the pain in her hip. She ignored the rip in her dress and the scraped knees and stumbled towards the cab. She got into the back seat. Torres opened the driver's door and slid behind the wheel, keeping his revolver trained on the gang members, who threw hate with their eyes. Torres slammed the door closed. He floored the accelerator. The car lurched, then sped away.

"You ok, lady?" Torres said when the gang was out of sight.

"My name's Betsy. Betsy Gould," she said. "Where'd you learn to fight like that, the Barrio?"

Torres took a deep breath, and let it out slowly. "Iraq, Desert Storm, and two tours in Afghanistan."

"Thank you. I'll never forget what you did for me."

"Next stop Burbank General Hospital," he said.

He maneuvered through deserted streets, navigating parallel to the highway until they were past the bottleneck. They got back on the highway and within minutes arrived at the hospital.

"Hey, lady, you're hurt," Torres said when he saw the way Betsy got out of the taxi. "I'll help you." And although she protested, he put an arm around her waist for support, and brought her into the lobby.

"Frannie Gould, please," she said to the elderly receptionist.

"She's in the maternity wing 4th floor. But you can't see her 'till she's delivered."

"I'm her mother," Betsy said with a tone that the receptionist didn't challenge.

Torres put Betsy in a wheelchair and maneuvered her down the hall.

When they got to the maternity floor, a security guard asked her to wait. "You can go now," she said to Torres. "You've been great,"

"I'm done for the night. I'll wait with you," he said.

Within minutes the double doors flew open and a nurse came out.

"She's asking for you," she said and ushered Betsy into the delivery room.

She held her daughter's hand and stroked the sweat-laden hair plastered on Frannie's forehead. They spoke not of Frannie's former boyfriend, nor of her stalled career. There would be plenty of time for that in the coming days and weeks while Betsy stayed on as the baby nurse and got reacquainted with her daughter. *Who knows, maybe Sam will have a change of heart and come west.*

Torres spent an hour in the waiting room. He replayed the events of the evening in his mind and wondered why he cared so much about this Jewish lady and her Frannie. Then his thoughts turned towards his own daughter. *How could I have let ten years go by without seeing her? What kind of man have I become?*

The nurse came out through the double doors and walked over to Torres.

"It's a boy," she said. And they want you to know they're naming him Tory Gould.

A smile came to Torres' lips. They ask if you'd leave your address so they can thank you and pay the fare.

"That won't be necessary. I've gotten my reward."

Then he rose and walked to the elevator. He got in his taxi and slowly drove away. When he reached the corner he stopped, opened the glove compartment and removed the plastic bag that contained the last of his dope. For a moment he thought of lighting up but then in an instant changed course. He threw the bag in the trashcan. He took out his credit card and approached what must have been one of the last pay phones left in Burbank.

"I'd like to place a long distance call to San Juan, Puerto Rico," he said when the operator answered.

To his amazement his daughter picked up the phone on the first ring. They talked haltingly at first; a spur of the moment decision can't erase ten years of neglect. But as the conversation continued and his daughter seemed more relaxed, Torres had the growing feeling that a second chance might be granted.

"No kidding, you got a partial scholarship to attend UCLA this coming year," he said after a long pause.

And, as Torres got back in his cab and eased out onto the highway, he thought that maybe, just maybe, there are some things that happen in life that just can't be explained.

A Bike Trip to Remember

Jason of Greek lore searched for the Golden Fleece. King Arthur had his Holy Grail. Odysseus labored to return home to his wife, Penelope, after the Peloponnesian War. So it was with mixed admiration and fear that I greeted my son, David's, decision to bike across the United States of America.

He mentioned it casually to my wife and me, as one might mention the decision to take a day trip to Ocean Beach.

"I'm planning a three month trip to cross the country by bike," he said, with a whimsical smile. My mind whirled, considering that my attempts to curtail my son's adventures have always met with failure, and he is almost thirty. I measured my response carefully. "But you're married," I said. "Does your wife know you're going?"

"Yes, and she's encouraging me." David said, with the look of a poker player holding four aces.

I paused. *A father's duty is to worry. Right? To consider the practical.* "What about your job?"

"No problem. I resigned, but they promised to hire me back in September. It's not so easy to find American computer engineers. That is unless the economy has a total meltdown while I'm gone."

An image of Ben Bernanke weeping at a Congressional hearing flashed before me.

"But, is it safe?" I muttered with the deflated feel of a newly punctured helium balloon. I pictured sixteen wheel trucks following my precious son down hairpin country roads.

"I'll be fine," he said with a patient air. He said nothing more, but his eyes darted away from my anxious gaze. I glanced at my wife, who seemed to be unusually calm, considering the gravity of the moment. "Why do you feel you have to go alone?" I asked, wondering what existential truth he might have learned that he might share with his parents. He shrugged. "I want to see the country. And I like to bike." I ran a hand through my hair, expecting clumps to come away in my fingers, searching for some bit of wisdom that might allay my fears. I found none.

"So you'll bike over the Rocky Mountains?" I said at last, with a tone of resignation.

"Yep, but first Ashford, North Carolina. Adam (my second son) is meeting me there. Then we'll bike a thousand miles together to Chicago. He'll go back to school, and I'll ride on alone."

"To California?" I said in a small voice, picturing a clan of hungry bears rambling after my sons on a deserted forest road.

"Eventually. First to Fargo, North Dakota, then Denver, over the Rockies, then Seattle, and eventually San Jose, where I'll dip a wheel in the Pacific Ocean after 6500 miles."

David smiled, the same smile I recognized from his childhood when he had fabricated an especially complex structure out of Lego blocks.

"Where will you sleep?"

"I've got a tent. There are campgrounds everywhere. Besides, in a pinch, I can always sleep in someone's front yard. People are friendly."

I felt thankful that Charles Manson is still behind bars.

I took a deep breath. "When are you going?" I said at last, calculating how many days I had to come up with more persuasive objections. "Not for another two weeks," he said.

I glanced at my wife, noting the way her pupils had dilated. "Be safe," I said for the lack of anything else.

I polled my friends, hoping for insights that might convince Dave to stay closer to home.

"When he looks back on this, it'll be the best thing he ever did," Harry Leiser, an avid cyclist said. Harry's been all over the world on his bike, places like New Zealand and California. Long distance cycling to Harry is like a walk to the grocery store for me.

"He'll be fine," Rabbi Carl Astor agreed, a man who can still keep pace with most bikers in the area. "Besides, he's young and strong," my sensible Rabbi said. "I think it's great."

Apparently so do David's coworkers at Mimio of Cambridge, Massachusetts. When he biked past his former place of employment thirty people came down to the street to give him a big send off. "Wish it were me," I can picture some of the men with children saying. "I wish it were you, too," I would have told them if I were there.

Dave left Boston, heading west, last Wednesday, the day tornadoes ripped through Springfield, Massachusets. A hailstorm greeted my son on his first day out and he had three flat tires, but fortunately no 200-mile per hour winds.

"A good omen," I emailed to David. "Won't get worse."

Now that he's off and biking, everyone in the family is excited, including me. He's set up a blog, linked with the GPS on his phone, that track his progress on a map. He's planning 75 miles a day as an average, with a few days off here and there to rest and see the sights.

I've been wondering what motivates so many people to undertake grueling challenges, when they could sit at home with a remote, watching Seinfeld reruns. Why do some people train for marathons, while, for others, a gentle hour-long walk suffices? Why bike 7000 miles when you could bike 7 miles a day for a thousand days? Why sleep in a tent in a forest by the side of a deserted road when the bed at home is so warm and cozy? I suppose such questions would be better asked of the men who climb Mount Everest, or Charles Lindberg, if he were still alive, or perhaps Lewis and Clark.

With his bike packed with some 40 pounds of gear, David seems ready for anything. He's got a small stove, a tent, a high tech sleeping bag, and solar batteries that keep his cell phone charged. The cell phone has a GPS function which gives him every map he could ever need, and it updates his position so that he knows where he is and where he's going at all times. (A metaphor for life, which his father can only admire.) He programmed his phone to update his position on the Internet, twice an hour, so we always know where he is. And he maintains a blog, and updates it with his impressions and occasional pictures, a sort of digital journal, which makes us feel that, in some small way, we are sharing the experience.

On his third day of biking, after sleeping in a state park, David passed through New Hartford, Connecticut. I left New London at 6:30 am by car and intersected David's path along Route 44 in the foothills of the Berkshires. I brought a bag filled with delicious muffins, a couple of vegetable omelets with hash brown potatoes, and a steaming mug of coffee. We sat by the side of the road munching on toast as cars whizzed by. He showed me his bike, and his solar battery pack. We talked about the next leg of his trip over the Newburg Bridge that leads into New York State over the Hudson River. I told him that his wife was a wonderful woman to support his decision. He looked energized, and happy, and strong. All too soon it was time for him to go. I waited while he packed up his gear. We embraced, and I kissed him on the cheek.

"Have a good journey," I whispered. *And stay safe.* He mounted his bike, headed out into traffic, and without looking back started up a steep rise.

I watched, as he grew smaller, a lump forming in my throat. My mind flashed back to an earlier time, when my son was a toddler. I used to put him in a seat mounted on the rear of my own bike and ride around the neighborhood. I had the illusion that I could keep my children safe and close to me forever. Those days have come and gone, as they must for all of us.

AN EPIC JOURNEY ENDS

Earlier this summer I reported on the start of my son, David's, bike trip across the country. Back in May, my wife and I exchanged clandestine glances as our eldest son detailed his plans. "I'm taking three months to cross the country by bike," David said with the calm of a man leaving to pick up a few groceries at the corner store. A father is supposed to impart wisdom, is he not? And keep his family safe. My mouth worked like a carp out of water, yet words would not come. A trio of objections was dismissed before I even got going. "My wife's encouraging me," "I think I can get my job back if I quit," and "Who knows when I'll get another chance. Besides people do this all the time."

An arduous journey into the unknown is not what a parent usually wishes for their children. Although Dave was soon to turn thirty years of age, he was still my son. A few of my friends, Carl Astor and Harry Leiser, men with long distance biking experience told me not to worry. "He'll be fine," they said as we ate breakfast one day before Dave left. Runaway tractor-trailer trucks rose in my imagination. I nodded, squirmed in my seat, and forced a smile.

Dave started out from Cambridge, Mass, on June 1st, packed down with 40 lbs. of gear on a touring bike he bought for the journey. On the second day he encountered violent thunderstorms that spawned hail. A tornado demolished part of Springfield, Mass, but left him unscathed. I drove out from New London to intersect his path and bring him a hot breakfast on his second day. We spent an hour together, in the Berkshire foothills, and ate omelets by the side of the road. He showed me his gear, and the solar charger for his cell phone. "Where will you sleep?" popped out of my mouth. "How will you eat?" questions hardwired by millennia of Dean ancestors, programmed to worry.

"In campgrounds, sometimes by the side of the road. We'll see," Dave said with a shrug.

"Make sure you drink plenty of water," I said, wishing I could squelch the Jewish mother that lurks beneath my skin. All too quickly it was time for Dave to go. He pushed out into traffic, rode up a hill, and without looking back was gone.

Through the miracle of modern technology my son kept in touch through the Internet. Most days he posted pictures and commentary on his blog. Friends and family kept tabs and posted comments in return that he could see. How times have changed. No more waiting in line at phone booths to place long distance collect calls to anxious parents.

Thanks to the GPS function on Dave's smart phone and some of his imaginative programming, I was able to pinpoint his location at any time of the day or night. In fact, using the computer's zoom function, I could see his virtual location on the road. By rotating the field of view I could see what lay behind or ahead. Alas, I could only see the road that had been recorded by satellite some time earlier, not Dave himself. Nor could I see what truly lay ahead. Perhaps that was for the best.

A direct route to California would be 3000 miles. Dave's course of exploration was far from direct. I suppose Lewis and Clark made some detours as well. He navigated through Connecticut and through parts of New York and Pennsylvania before turning south towards Ashville, North Carolina. The weather turned hotter. Dave met up with his brother, Adam, who flew in from Chicago. They were to bike along the Great Smoky Mountains together, then head northwest towards Chicago, where Adam would return to his life. After Kentucky, and Indiana, and Illinois, David would continue.

They camped in tents and biked through little southern towns. I followed their progress on the computer, and tried not to think of the final scene of "Easy Rider.'"Content to know that my sons were together, I slept easier. My wife plotted their trip on a giant map of the United States, connecting each day's destination with a red line that grew longer each night. Dave posted a picture of a bank thermometer that read 106. Adam kept up Dave's pace. I tried not to picture them racing down steep mountains, although I'm sure they had their little friendly competitions. They stayed in a few motels overnight. I checked the blog in my air-conditioned living room and hoped for a cold snap to sweep through the south. It didn't. Despite a heat wave, that would make any normal person long for winter, they persevered. After two weeks and 1200 miles they reached Chicago in blistering heat.

Dave lingered in Chicago for a few days, saw Lake Michigan, and then pushed west. He saw the gleaming arch in St. Louis. The roads through the plains of Kansas were flat, deserted and lined with corn. He made good time doing upwards of 100 miles a day on occasion. He grew a beard. He ate midwest beef and took in state fairs whenever he could, sometimes pitching his tent on the fairgrounds. Occasionally he stayed in inexpensive hotels, but mostly he was frugal.

He swam in community pools. People in the middle of the country were kind and eager to talk of his journey. They engaged him in conversation wherever he went. In Kansas, one man slipped him $20 and refused to take it back. "Just speak kindly of Yates Center," he said. Consider that pledge fulfilled. A man fixing a motorcycle on his driveway invited David to share a barbecue while Dave helped him work. People asked him to pitch his tent on their lawns. Others bought him a meal, just for encouragement. When stuck for a place to stay Dave would call the police and ask where in town he could camp out. People smiled. Dogs barked but never bit.

Dave reached Denver. He crossed the Rockies, the altitude as much a challenge as the hills. He crossed the Continental Divide 9 times, zig-zagging across Montana and Wyoming to see the sights. He saw Old Faithful in Yellowstone National Park and camped in the Grand Tetons. His pictures of snow capped mountains made my jaw drop. Then he aimed his bike towards Portland, Oregon, with plans to bike down the coast of California to San Francisco and then a finish at San Jose. Things were going well, yet fate has a way of intervening.

Somewhere on a rural road, 200 miles east of Portland, David was sideswiped by a gray minivan. Thrown to the ground, his helmet cracked, Dave managed to pop up in time to see the van driver slow down, then sped off. Dave could only lift a fist in protest. A passing motorist pulled over to help. An ambulance came, the paramedics prepared for the worst. Dave insisted on walking into the ambulance unassisted—a good sign, I suppose. X-rays of his hip and CAT scans of his inner organs were negative—no fractures. He was left with a wickedly sore hip and road rash across his back and left side.

"I wouldn't bike for two weeks," the ER doc said. "Keep those wounds clean."

Dave checked into a motel for two days. He licked his wounds, took painkillers and had his bike repaired. On the third day he started off again. He reached Portland a few days later, sore hip and all. He sent back a picture of his feet in the surf of Canon Beach on the Pacific Coast. Success!

"Come back home already my wife and I wanted to shout," but didn't. Dave biked down the coast, for two fabulous weeks. He saw the beauty of northern California and the Redwood Forests. In order to reach San Jose on time, he biked a hundred miles up arduous hills on his last day. He reached his sister-in-law's house, the termination of his journey, on September 2nd, his 4th wedding anniversary, a day before his 30th birthday. His wife Alicia and a group of friends were waiting with a makeshift finish line strung across the street.

I saw Dave for the first time in three months last week. His beard was gone, and although he looked a bit leaner, for the most part he was unchanged. My wife and I sat in rapt attention as David displayed his breathtaking photos, and reminisced about his trip.

I'm happy to say he's back in Cambridge with Alicia, his very understanding wife. He got rehired as a computer engineer at his previous position and, aside from a few scars, appears none the worse for wear. My wife and I sleep better, but when I look in the mirror I see bunches of gray hair that seemed to have sprouted overnight.

I'd like to write the end to this story, but I'm afraid I'd come off as a doddering overprotective parent. Instead I will paraphrase the last entry of Dave's blog, for after all this is his tale to tell…

I don't know how best to write any sort of epilogue or finale or summary of the trip. I never really got that "hooray, I've done it!" feeling, not even as I literally crossed the finish line. There was happiness and relief, but not a sense that I had accomplished a goal as of that moment.

And I guess that's what it comes down to. The stated goal was to "bike across the country", but it was the fun and adventure of the whole summer that I enjoyed, not simply the conclusion. There would have been something missing if I had fallen short of the ending, and was not able to claim that I had "biked across the country." The experience would have been far less had I put my head down and zoomed west as fast and direct as I could, as if the only important thing was to reach San Francisco.

That's why writing a conclusion only 6 days after finishing feels odd. If you've followed along, you have a pretty good sense of where I've been, what I've done, and how I've felt about things and people and places along the way. So, a literal summary of the trip isn't needed. What I've really done this summer is give myself an enormous trove of experiences that I can draw from for years to come, and it will be a while before I'll be able to look back and determine how "the trip" has affected me.

For my part, as Dave's father, I can only shake my head in wonder. I will try not to think of how I felt when I heard Dave was hit by a car. Instead I will celebrate his strength, his perseverance, and his achievement. May we each, in our own way, have a taste of that feeling some time in our lives, regardless of the size or nature of the challenge.

You can still see Dave's blog and the pictures of his trip at davebike.blogspot.com.

Snow White as Wool

The first snowflake fell with temerity, a single solitary fleck of frozen water, innocuous to the casual observer. Charlie Plotnik glanced at his watch. He wiped his forehead with his hand. *Still two hours to go.*

The flowers arrived; great bunches of white gardenias fastened with rose garlands. Three men who looked more like stevedores than florists carried a heavy structure to the front of the room. Charlie smiled as the men unpacked a crate and removed tree branches. He thought of the day he and his wife planted the foot high dogwood in the back yard to mark the birth of their son.

"We'll use the branches for his chuppah one day," his wife had said that beautiful summer day some twenty-five years earlier while Charlie tamped the mulch around the base of the tree. The boy grew like a weed (no pun intended). He seemed to grow out of his clothes overnight. In adolescence his sneakers wore out in a month, his pants seemed always a little too short. The little dogwood grew as well. Charlie watered it twice a day, pruned dead wood in the fall, and fertilized often. By his son's Bar Mitzvah, the tree was as tall as Charlie. By the time the boy announced his engagement, the tree was approaching the roof of the house.

Charlie glanced out of the window and noted the swirling wisps of snow.

"Where do you want the smorgasbord set up?" a man wearing a white chef's hat asked.

Charlie motioned to the corner of the room, where men were setting up long wooden tables. Charlie left to check on his wife in the dressing room reserved for family. The breath caught in his throat as he first caught a glimpse. He snuck up behind her as she stared into the wall mirror, frowning as she applied her lipstick. *She still looks like a bride.*

"Oh, Thank G-d you're here," she said.

He placed his hands on her shoulders, kneading the tension from her muscles. She reached back and put a hand to his face.

"Two more hours and our boy will have a wife," she said. He watched her lips in the mirror, the sweet smile belied by the slightest tremor of her lower lip.

"Everything will go fine," he said with calm assurance. He winked and took a deep breath, fighting to keep his rising anxiety from infecting his wife.

"Did the flowers arrive?"

"Check."

"Photographers?"

"Of course. Stop worrying. Everything's under control."

"But the snow? The forecast said we could get more than an inch."

Charlie took a deep breath. "They never get these things right," he said, despite the rising unease in his belly.

"Nothing will go wrong. We've got the best caterer in the state of New Jersey. The band could win American Idol, and the photographers won an award for best wedding video from Frumster.com. I told them all to be early. I won't let anything ruin this wedding."

"But what if it the storm doesn't stay offshore?"

He nodded, his broad smile vanishing, as he turned away.

"Stop worrying. Most of the guests live nearby, the caterer's already setting up the apple martinis and the bride and groom are posing for pictures. Most of the guests from out of town will sleep over if the snow gets too bad. I'll handle everything."

"Charlie Plotnik, that's why I married you," she said. She applied a dab of rouge to her cheeks.

"Just make sure you give the list of honors to the Rabbi before he starts the ceremony."

As he walked out the door he put a hand to his forehead. *The Rabbi? Wonder how the turnpike is?*

In the area set aside for the ceremony, a man was setting up chairs while he listened to a portable radio.

"Snow intensifying more than expected, remember to listen on the eights," Charlie heard as the weather forecaster finished his report and music resumed. *With all the Rabbis in New Jersey why did the kids have to insist on a man who lives in Philadelphia?* Outside, flakes swirled like a flurry of tiny yarmulkes pelting the picture windows. Charlie's cell phone rang with the first of many calls—people stuck in their houses—unable to make it to the wedding.

Meanwhile, a young man is pacing in the hallway. He thinks not of the snowstorm, which is now astounding the meteorologists with its massive drop in pressure. Nor is he thinking of the Rabbi, still navigating around cars spun out on the New Jersey Turnpike. He thinks only of the woman who will be his bride in another hour, and who, by mutual decision, he has not seen for the past week. For theirs is a traditional orthodox wedding with all that entails.

For Charlie time passes in a flurry of last minute activities. Then come the family photos. As Charlie and the family are smiling for the camera, the snow is piling up outside—3 inches, then 4—6 by the time the klezmer band begins to tune up. As the groom paces, Charlie watches the first guests arrive, their hats covered in snow, their coats tinged with celestial dandruff.

"It's the worst blizzard I've ever seen," one man says. "I could hardly see the road."

"Has anyone seen the Rabbi?" Charlie says to no one in particular.

The smorgasbord begins in earnest: great tureens of steaming pasta, succulent dumplings cooked to perfection, delicacies not seen in a generation. Charlie and his wife link arms and mingle, making small talk, too excited to eat. Charlie checks his watch every few minutes. *20 minutes to the ceremony and still no Rabbi. After all the planning what if he can't make it?*

Charlie goes to the window and stares out at what will soon become the biggest snow storm New Jersey has ever seen, The Great Blizzard of 2010 dumped 31 inches, made driving impossible, and forced a reluctant Governor to close the highways and declare a state of emergency.

But to those within the Plotnik wedding all that is irrelevant. The bride is beautiful, the groom tall and handsome. Charlie's heart is pounding as he sees a huge SUV with enormous snow tires pull up to the parking lot. A youthful man with a neatly trimmed beard, wearing a black hat, emerges and strides purposely to the door. Charlie is there to shake his hand.

"Rabbi, Thank G-d you made it," Charlie says, pumping the Rabbi's arm like an old fashioned water pump.

"Baruch Hashem. Nothing could stop me."

Within minutes the guests are invited to view the ceremony. The chuppah is perfect, lined with fragrant white flowers, interlaced with the branches of the groom's tree. The groom enters and walks towards the chuppah flanked by Charlie and his wife. Then come sisters and brothers, followed by grandparents. Finally the bride enters, her long white train trailing, escorted by her parents. By the time the ceremony concludes grown men and women are dabbing at their eyes.

"No one will ever forget this wedding," The Rabbi says in conclusion. "And G-d so loved this couple he sent snow white as wool to cover the earth in purity."

"A sage," Charlie's wife whispers to her husband.

"An optimist," Charlie mutters.

Later that evening as the wedding is winding down and people are thinking of how they will dig out their cars, Charlie pulls the Rabbi aside.

"I think this night shows that G-d has a sense of humor," Charlie says with a whimsical chuckle.

"Perhaps," the Rabbi says with a smile and puts a hand on Charlie's shoulder. "Or perhaps, Mr. Plotnik, there are things on this earth that are beyond our control. The sooner we recognize that the better."

Charlie nods and his smile fades.

"So let's drink a l'Chaim to the Bride and Groom," the Rabbi says. "They're married now."

Charlie's smile returns and he downs his drink in a gulp.

"Amen to that, Rabbi. And may they live to a ripe old age and have many children."

"Amen," the Rabbi replies. "And may they hold their weddings in July."

"The Times They Are A-Changin'"

"Did you know that I met your mother online?" I asked my son one day, a whimsical smile on my face.

He rolled his eyes, as teenagers are wont to do, once they reach the age when they realize their parents are electronically challenged. "Didn't you meet like in the sixties?"

"Seventies, early seventies," I corrected, shifting in my seat and running a hand through graying hair. (Each one well earned I might add.)

"Dad, the first personal computers weren't on the market till 1980," he said. "Internet didn't start till the 90's."

My mind went back to the Fortran Computer I once programmed back in high school—the large mainframe that took up the better part of a room and used punch cards. Rather than contradict my computer whiz and embarrass myself with the simplicity of those early machines I kept my protests to myself and continued my routine.

"No, really we met on line at the University of Pennsylvania."

Again his doubting eyes stared unblinking.

"It was the first day of class, and I was standing in line in the cafeteria. Your mother and a few of her girlfriends were in front of me. I said hello. The rest is history."

I stifled a smile, my corny sense of humor now fully exposed.

My son yawned. "On line. Very funny."

My face broke into a grin and I laughed. "She was really something in those days. Still is, you know. Why, I can tell you stories."

"Can I go now, Dad? I've got work to do."

"Aren't you on spring break?"

Ok, so I may have embellished this imagined exchange, but I'm sure if you've raised children and still remember when gas cost 32 cents a gallon, you get my drift. The rules of engagement have changed for our children in ways we could never have imagined when we baby boomers were coming of age. When I was in college in my twenties I knew I had to call my parents on Sundays and that was about the extent of our contact. Today, if you aren't tuned into Facebook, Tweeter, and Linkedin…well you're just not connected. Emails come and go, but an hour-long phone call, rarely. Our busy schedules put time at a premium. We eat fast food, jot off emails in seconds and cc all those who need to know. I don't mean to whine, but to mimic the Gen Xers, "It is what it is."

When we were kids, our parents could have probably regaled us with stories of how they first started using a telephone back in the day. Or the first time they saw a television, or the way our grandparents wrote love letters. Today's generation rarely uses the phone. They never write letters. Why else is our Post Office going broke?

Everyone in my family stays in touch by texting. Although I swore a few years ago I'd never get into that habit, I, too, now text. I have to. For, you see, my children rarely answer the phone when I call. (Can't be that they see that it's me calling. No, it's rather that they're really busy during the day…and night…and sometimes in the afternoon.) But they do answer a text—fast, easy, amazingly non-personal, with little catchphrases I've learned to understand…like lol for laugh out loud, when I've texted something incredibly witty. I like the lol response, no need to see someone rolling their eyes in person.

For a real treat try Skype. For the uninitiated, Skype is a program that turns your computer into a two way phone call with video. You can sit in your living room, see and speak with friends, relatives, bill collectors; you name it. The Jetsons would smile to see we're finally catching up.

I swore I'd never use Facebook—too impersonal, too modern. Yet, when I started getting requests to acknowledge friends, I relented. I've found people I lost touch with after 6th grade, keep in touch with Israeli relatives, and get a sense of what people want to post on their face book pages without writing anything on my own. I suppose I'm a Facebook voyeur.

Many people have met and married because of JDate, the online dating service for our tribe. Who would have thought such a thing possible back in the sixties?

I am part of a book club that has been meeting every month or so for the past dozen years. A few years ago the Kindle burst on the scene, a digital device that can store hundreds of books and display the prose on an electronic display much like a computer. I never thought it would catch on. I had always relished the feel of a book, the smell, the welcoming heft of its weight, each one a different size and color. How could an electronic device match all that? It couldn't of course, yet still, now at least half the members of my book club read on the Kindle instead of buying traditional books, myself included. I don't think the days of handsome bookshelves lining the walls are numbered, it's just that, for convenience, and travel, or entertaining oneself while on the treadmill, reading on an electronic tablet has its advantages.

So, dear readers, if you still use devices that connect with an RCA jack, realize that the technology is rapidly evolving. The days of the CD are numbered. Just as the vinyl record disappeared except from nostalgia shops, so will the CD vanish one day. Electronic devices and phones that store thousands of songs and videos have been on the market for some time and will likely become smaller and more powerful. Industry experts predict the personal computer will rapidly be replaced with the smart phone. Who can predict where technology will lead? Any device that makes it easier to stay in touch with my children, family and friends is welcome.

I am certainly no expert, merely a fellow traveler passing through time, amazed at the diversions along the way. To borrow from Bob Dylan, that ancient troubadour of my youth, "The times they are a-changin'."

FORGIVENESS

When the rain began, Ethan Pinchas hunched his shoulders and drew the filthy tarp that doubled as a blanket over his head. He desperately tried to hold on to sleep, the only respite he had from the nagging voices. He opened his eyes as the rain intensified, once again mystified by the turn of events that had wrenched him from the comfort of his suburban lifestyle. What had started as a passion for speculating on stocks, had turned into days of solitude spent foraging for food in Central Park.

The summer had been warm and dry, but there was an unmistakable chill in the air, and the water that dripped from the trees felt uncomfortably cool as it trickled through his hair.

Ethan rose. He rolled up the soaked tarp and placed it into his shopping cart, shoving aside his few remaining possessions. As he left the park an image of his father's scowl rose before him.

"You'll end up a bum just like your good for nothing friends," the apparition whispered.

This condemnation uttered so many years ago when Ethan was only twelve still seemed too harsh. *So what if I wanted to play basketball on Yom Kippur? I was a kid.* As he passed a store front along Fifth Avenue he caught a glimpse of his reflection, dressed in tattered clothes, his face smeared with grime, his hands magenta with the cold. His voices reiterated each one of his shortcomings: a failed marriage, abandoned children, an IRS suit that drained every last penny from his offshore account. *Happy now, Poppa?*

There's still a chance for you, a single voice maintained. Just go.

But look at me, I'm a train wreck. I can't.

You can. And you must.

Ethan slapped himself across the face, as if he could banish the voices forever.

"Don't tell me what to do," he growled through clenched teeth.

He noted the time on the bank building across the street: 6:20. Hurry, the voice said. Despite the battle raging within, his feet took him to the West Side, to the little shul tucked beside Riverside Drive. Husband and wives, their children in tow, were streaming up the street, hurrying to hear the first notes of the Kol Nidre prayer. They crossed the street to avoid Ethan, hushing their children when they pointed with laughter on their faces.

Normally Ethan would rather leap into the Grand Canyon than cross the threshold of a synagogue, yet, here he was, awaiting the moment of Yom Kippur.

Whether it was inspiration or the strange effect of going off his medications, Ethan hadn't a clue. He hid his cart behind some bushes.

"Hurry, we'll be late," a man shouted to his wife as the couple hurried by.

A voice in Ethan's head whispered. "It's never too late." *Maybe I'll get out of the rain for a moment.*

As Ethan approached the stairway to the shul, his knees buckled and he felt as if he might faint.

"Look at my clothes," he said to no one in particular, "I don't belong here." *Nonsense. Everyone belongs. Just go.*

He waited until the throng slowed to a trickle and then the streets were empty. He walked around to the back of the building where the muffled voice of the cantor, trilling like a bird, wafted from an open window. Calmness washed over Ethan, and he felt lucid for the first time in months. Alone and in shadows he felt secure. He mumbled what few Hebrew words he remembered, humming the tunes he had abandoned in his youth.

At the Al Chet prayer he closed his eyes and pounded his chest. *I have cheated. I have lied. I have taken drugs. I have stolen money. I have abandoned my wife and my children.* Can you forgive me? He waited for an answer but none came, only the chant of the Chazzan, with a tune no opera singer could match.

"Charity and good works can lessen the severity of the decree."

If only that were true, Ethan thought. He craned his neck to get a glimpse of the congregation through the window. He scanned the men and women dressed in their finest clothes, searching for the one man he wanted to surprise. The thought of entering the sanctuary filled him with dread. He remained on the outside looking in, his thoughts filled with remorse for all the mistakes he carried in his heart.

Ethan looked towards the faint sound of a scream in the distance. He stood and sniffed at the air, like a bird dog, turning his face towards Riverside Park. Normally he ran from trouble, but on this night his feet led him towards the sound. *Just go, his voice said.*

When he got to the park he hid behind a tree. He saw a group of five teenagers in hip-hop garb gathered around a twelve-year old boy wearing a blue suit. The teenagers played Frisbee with his yamulke. When the boy grabbed it they slapped him and shoved him back and forth like a rag doll. The young boy's eyes shone like a frightened deer before a pack of wolves. Ethan's first impulse was to run. He pictured being ensconced beneath his tarp on the park bench, *Safe, stay safe.* Then the words of the Chazzan melded with those of his own voice. "We ask for forgiveness."

Ethan felt his hands ball into fists." Stop that!!!" he screamed as he sprung from behind the tree.

The teenagers turned. They stared at him, and then began to laugh. But when Ethan reached down for a rock and threw it, their faces filled with anger.

"Hey, we gonna cut you up," the ringleader said and advanced towards Ethan, the bloodied twelve year old all but forgotten. The boy slipped away and ran for his life.

Ethan never was much of a fighter, and the months on a park bench had left him softer than ever. After the first few blows Ethan lost consciousness. Fortunately the young boy flagged down a passing police car as he ran. The officers arrived to find Ethan in a pool of blood. He awoke two days later in a private room at Bellevue Hospital.

The doctors in the psychiatric ward interpreted Ethan's intervention in the park as just another sign of his mental instability. They dressed him in clean whites and changed his sheets daily. He got 3 square meals a day and antipsychotic medications by injection. The voices stopped, leaving Ethan able to think without interruption for the first time in years.

A week later as the staff was arranging a transfer to a homeless shelter Ethan had a visitor. Ethan was drifting into sleep when the sound of familiar footsteps in the hall jerked him awake. When the sound of the footsteps stopped outside his room, Ethan held his breath. Then came a persistent knock. The man who entered Ethan's room looked much older than he remembered, stooped with age, his eyes pained with the troubles of life. At first Ethan could say nothing, but he sat on the edge of the bed, unable to meet the elder man's earnest gaze.

Past failures welled up in his mind, but words of apology seemed impossible.

"How did you find me?" Ethan said at last.

"I read the papers."

Ethan nodded. "I looked for you outside the synagogue."

The older man shook his head. "I know. That was the Rabbi's grandson that you saved."

The silence was deafening. Ethan held his breath. The elder man looked Ethan over, searching for the right words. Ethan stared at his feet.

Finally the elder man spoke. "It's time to come home, son."

CHAPTER 4

THE BIG PICTURE

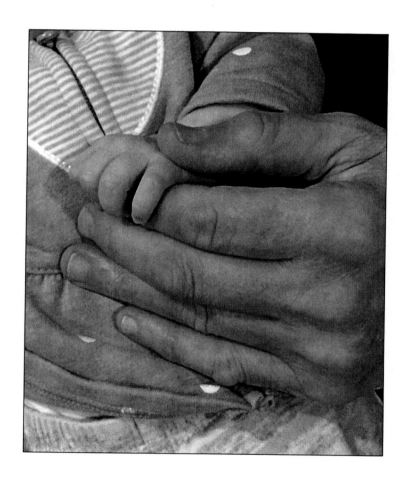

THE BIG PICTURE

Saul ate slowly over the kitchen table. He eyed the unopened letter from his daughter suspiciously while he chewed his lox and bagel breakfast.

"What's it been, two years?" He muttered. *Rachel only gets in touch when she needs money.* He wiped excess cream cheese from the corner of his mouth with the back of his hand. Then he glanced at the tiny manila envelope that contained the hotel reservation and airline tickets for San Francisco—his first real vacation in ten years, and a chance to see his beloved Giants in the playoffs. He knew he'd open the letter eventually, and discover her latest crisis, but, just for a few more minutes he chose to savor the fantasy of a vacation without having to worry about someone else.

He tried to read the morning paper, but his eyes kept drifting to her letter. He glanced at his watch. *Only a few more hours before I leave for the airport.* He ran his finger over the return address, his daughter's unmistakable chicken scratches revealing that she'd moved once again...to Nebraska of all places. *Wonder if she's still with that bum she calls a boyfriend.*

As he sipped his coffee, his eyes became unfocused, and his mind drifted to a happier time. His wife was still living, his daughter still the center of his universe, with her pigtails, her Barbie dolls and that adorable way she had of wrapping him around her little finger.

"Swing me, Papa," she shrieked, as he pushed her on the swing. "Higher! Higher!" she gasped on each return—her joy unrestrained by neither life's hard truths nor gravity.

If only life were that joyous all the time. He frowned when he thought of the nasty bump she sustained when she leapt from the swing, feeling the pain of her injury anew, his guilt over his failure as fresh as the day it happened. Like so many other disasters he had given advice, and been ignored. *She'll never learn.*

The phone rang. "So, Saul, you ready?" the voice boomed. "I can't believe we're really going."

Saul's hand slipped to his pocket, checking the wad of playoff tickets for the fifth time.

"Sure, sure, just packing a few things. Let me meet you at the airport, ok, Bernie?"

"What's wrong? You lost the tickets?"

"Of course not...its just that..."

"Look, Saul. This has been on our bucket list for a long time. Sometimes you gotta forget everything else and just do it. So what if your boss gives you a hard time for taking a week off."

"You're right. I will...its just that I got a letter from Rachel today."

A long silence followed. "She's doing it to you again, isn't she?" Bernie blurted at last.

Saul sighed. "I'm not even going to open her letter until I get back."

"Yeah, man, now you're talking. Why get upset? I can almost smell those stadium franks grilling."

Saul picked up Rachel's letter and placed it under the phone. Then he started gathering his things for the trip. He pictured his daughter the last time they met, with her biker boyfriend half covered by tattoos—quite a contrast from the nice Jewish boys he'd prefer. *Fat chance.*

His cell phone rang, announcing the cab outside.

He grabbed his suitcase, left his apartment, and double locked the door. Then, hesitating as the elevator arrived, he went back in the apartment, tucked Rachel's letter in his pant's pocket, and then rushed down the stairs to the waiting cab.

"Hey, mister, why so glum? You look like you lost your best friend," the cabbie said, while Saul settled in the back seat.

"JFK," Saul muttered, his thoughts in the past.

He replayed his last encounter with Rachel and her biker—them both drunk and in jail, Saul left to bail them out, as if it was his duty to clean up her mistakes, with no questions asked.

Who in their right mind goes skinny dipping in the Hudson River across from a police station?

Saul stared out the window, a hand to the side of his face. As they turned off the highway towards the airport he took a deep breath. Then he slipped a hand into his pocket and drew out Rachel's letter.

❖   ❖   ❖   ❖   ❖

Inside the terminal Bernie was pacing in front of the baggage counter.

"Come on Saul, they'll be boarding in a few moments. Good thing you're here. The flight is overbooked." Saul's eyes swept the floor and he bit his lip.

Bernie frowned when he saw the unopened letter in Saul's hand. "You're pale."

Saul nodded. They walked to the waiting area and Saul slumped into a chair, while Bernie sat in the adjoining chair.

"So, open it already," Bernie muttered, holding his hands to the sky as if beseeching the Almighty for intervention.

Saul ripped open the letter and withdrew its contents: a small index sized picture and a handwritten note. It's time we were a family again, the note read. Saul's eyes were moist as he fumbled for the photo. It slipped onto the floor and came to rest on Bernie's shoe.

Bernie picked it up, but Saul snatched the picture away like a man being denied his last meal.

"She's in trouble again, and there's a child."

"We better board," Bernie said, as the loudspeaker announced their flight.

Saul stared at his longtime friend. For a moment he pictured sitting in seats behind home plate at a Giant's World Series. He could almost smell the salt air at Fisherman's Wharf, and taste the franks at the ballpark—Hebrew National of course. But when Bernie nudged him towards the line of people waiting to board, Saul resisted. Then he thrust his hand in his pocket and pulled out the playoff tickets. "You go, and sell my tickets at the park. You can send me the money."

"Saul, you're crazy! A chance to see the Giants in the World Series comes once in a lifetime. You can visit after the World Series."

"I know. You'll have to tell me all about it," Saul shouted as he began to run towards the ticket counter, hoping to exchange his boarding pass for the next flight to Omaha.

"Some things in life are even more important than baseball," he muttered, glancing over his shoulder as Bernie disappeared past the loading gate.

When the airline steward announced that a ticket was available three standby passengers rushed forward to make a claim. And the triple air miles Saul received for turning in his seat to a grateful airline more than paid for a first class round-trip ticket to Omaha.

Saul sat waiting for his new flight to board with many more questions than answers. What type of maelstrom was he heading for? Would his daughter ever really change? He read the note again and again and stared at the photo. *She needs me.*

But it wasn't until he was halfway across the country that a broad grin lit his face. *I've got a grandson.*

Part 2

As his plane sped towards Omaha, Saul's mind went over the details of the previous 24 hours. Conflicting thoughts wrestled within. Giving up on seeing the Giants' playoff games at Candlestick Park had been easy—so what if he'd waited 25 years to have the time, the cash, and the opportunity. Letting Bernie down at the last minute had been harder—a good friend, even with all his mischegas. Would Bernie ever forgive him for abandoning their plans at the last minute?

Saul opened Rachel's letter once more, and fondled the small photo of his new grandson. It's time we were a family again. Is it possible these were Rachel's words, the same wild girl who'd given him sleepless nights since she turned twelve and boys began to turn their heads as she passed? Saul blocked out any negative thoughts, at least for the moment, and reveled in the image that he would soon be holding his grandson. *He looks a bit like me around the eyes. Imagine, a full head of hair and he's only a month old.* Saul put Rachel's letter in his carryon bag, but placed the photo in the shirt pocket over his heart. *If only my wife had lived to see this day.*

Once on the ground, Saul marched towards the baggage claim, slowing his pace as he thought of the impending reunion. After their last encounter Saul had thought he'd never hear from Rachel. And he had sworn to himself never to trust her again. Now, just three years later, here he was again, like a marionette on a string, dancing to a tune of Rachel's composition. He tried not to think of the hole in his retirement fund. *This time it'll be different.* And just as that old familiar sinking feeling wrenched his gut, he heard her call his name, and the years of resentment receded. "Papa, we're over here."

Earlier that week:

"He's our only chance to put this thing right," Paul was saying to a distracted Rachel. She sealed the photo in the envelope and scrawled the address. The thought that he might refuse never entered her mind. He was her father, despite the acrimony. When all seemed hopeless there was always someone to turn to, someone with arms spread wide and an open pocketbook, even if the bailout came with a sermon. Yet this time it was different. She'd gone to the well so many times without thinking. What if one day the well ran dry? She glanced once again at her sleeping son and placed the stamp in the corner of her letter. "Everything will be all right," she said. "He'll come," but she averted her eyes when a thin smile came to Paul's lips.

❖   ❖   ❖   ❖   ❖

At the sound of Rachel's voice, Saul's heart quickened. He tried to call out, but could only manage a whisper. "Rachel, my, my," he marveled. "And what have we here?" He stretched out his hands and Rachel put the baby into the crook of his arm. "Say hello to Zaidi," Rachel said. Saul blinked several times, his vision clouded, his eyes brimming. "He looks like you," she said.

She kissed her father quickly on the side of the face and put her hand on his shoulder.

"Paul's waiting outside in the car. We've got a lot to talk about."

Saul swallowed, but said nothing. *What kind of a Jewish name is Paul?* He thought of asking if there'd been a bris, but decided to keep that question for another day. He put a finger in his grandson's hand, and the baby's fingers closed, with surprising pressure.

"Does he have a name?"

"We call him Jo Jo, but his real name is Joseph."

Saul smiled a weak smile. *Joseph*—Saul's father's name—a name he thought he'd never hear again. "I like that."

The pressure on his finger increased and little Jo Jo's legs began to kick, the hint of a smile rising on the infant's face.

"He knows me already," Saul said, a broad grin creasing his features.

"Either that, or he's got gas," Rachel said, and took the child from the new Zaidi's arms.

Saul chuckled at the gentle burp that escaped Jo Jo's lips.

"Adorable," Saul whispered with the enthusiasm a new grandfather exhibits when observing the miracle of bodily functions.

"I am so happy you sent me that letter."

For a moment Rachel's face went blank, but aware of Saul's grin, she returned a polite smile.

"We better go outside. Paul hates to wait."

Saul kept his impression of Paul to himself: a serious man of few words, but definite opinions.

Their conversation was to the point; "How long was he staying, how was the weather back east, did he have a retirement adviser handling his finances?"

What kind of career is a venture capitalist?

When Saul began to gush about his grandson, Paul said nothing, glancing briefly at Rachel who stared down into the folded hands on her lap.

"He's all right," Paul said at last, and then fell silent, his hands tightening on the steering wheel as they merged onto the highway that would bring him to their home.

They drove up a circular drive to a redwood paneled home reminiscent of a Frank Lloyd Wright masterpiece.

"Why, this is sensational," Saul said.

"You have to keep up appearances, you know," Rachel said, but she fell silent after Paul clicked his tongue.

"I'm going out for a nightcap," Paul said as soon as they were inside. "Don't wait up."

Once ensconced on the couch Saul noticed a purplish, green bruise on the inside of Rachel's arm.

The conversation was cautious at first, like a couple of old sparring partners holding their punches.

"No, he's never hit me," if that's what you're thinking, Rachel said, when she caught her father staring at her bruise.

"That never entered my mind…it's just that the mark looks like the fingers of a hand."

Rachel's tears fell unrestrained. Saul reached out and held her while she blurted out her troubles. "He's a good man…just down on his luck at the moment."

"We've all been hurt by the recession," Saul said. "But money isn't everything. With two good hands and a will to make a living, he'll get by."

"We're dead broke, Papa. This house is a rental and we're being evicted next week."

Saul blinked rapidly. "I see," he said cautiously…*and this is where I'm supposed to step in like a white knight to save the day…for the umpteenth time.*

"I could lend you a bit each month to help with the rent, if that's what you're thinking—say four or five hundred?"

Rachel bit her lip, averted her gaze, and stared at the baby sleeping in his basinet.

"Paul's got a business opportunity in South America—in the mountains of Columbia to be exact—a coffee plantation."

"I see," Saul mumbled, the illusion of his newly reunited family evaporating all at once.

"Paul says Bogata's no place to bring a baby."

"Well, don't you have a say in all this? Talk to your husband. You could all come and live with me back east."

"Paul and I aren't married," Rachel said in a small voice. Then she paused, the prolonged silence painfully awkward. "He wants me to put Jo Jo up for adoption, but I won't. He says I could ask you to take the baby for just a few months, of course. I'll come back for him as soon as the business takes off."

Saul felt as if he was on a rollercoaster on the precipice of the highest rise, about to plunge into the abyss. He felt short of breath, his mouth turned to sandpaper, struggling to respond to the enormity of his daughter's request.

"I don't know what to say. I'm nearly sixty years old. A baby?"

"Paul says we need $250,000 to do it right. It'd be a loan not a gift. I'm begging you, Papa. My life is on the line."

Mine too.

Part 3

That night conflicting thoughts pounded at Saul's mind. He tried to sleep but the thought of Rachel's momentous request made his stomach churn. On the one hand, the baby was his flesh and blood, not a ping pong ball to be shuttled back and forth. *How can I commit to taking care of an infant at my age? What if Rachel followed Paul to Columbia and never returned?*

He tried to remember the last time he'd changed a diaper, the last time he'd prepared a bottle. Then there was the bucket list—all the places he wanted to see, things he wanted to try before age and disability came to call. What of the skydiving lessons—the trip around the country to see one baseball game in every park? He had saved all his life, denied himself an extravagant life style, thinking that one day he'd be able to retire and live life more fully. The image of a gray haired senior citizen schlepping a baby to a Yankee baseball game seemed comical to say the least. What of the fantasies of meeting a younger woman—maybe getting married again…how could he possibly balance a new relationship with the demands of raising a child? And what woman in her right mind would want to get involved with an AARP card carrying widower with a newborn in his house?

On the other hand, 60's not really that old. Men older than that had fathered children of their own, had become president, had started great corporations. Didn't Abraham, the patriarch, father a child with a woman of 90? Perhaps he was making too much of Rachel's request—a simple babysitting arrangement that would end when Rachel and Paul made their fortune and returned triumphantly to New York. But what if that's not what happened, and Rachel's track record of disappointments were a lifelong pattern not soon to be remade.

I'll have to say no. What am I, some sort of fire brigade to be called in only when the house is burning down? On the other hand I could give Jo Jo a good start in life, arrange a bris, see to it the child knows he's Jewish.

Early the next morning Rachel knocked timidly on the door of the extra bedroom where Saul had spent the night.

"Are you up, Papa?"

He opened his eyes, aware at once of the aroma of brewing coffee, and the sizzle of salami and eggs frying on the stove—his favorite indulgence—the dish Rachel used to prepare for him when, as a teenager, she knew she had gone too far.

He threw on a pair of slacks, passed a hand through thinning hair, and plodded to the kitchen. He ate ravenously, while Rachel sat silently at the table, her head propped on her hands, staring at Saul intently. As he finished a second helping and sipped his coffee Rachel cleared her throat. "Well, Papa, have you made a decision?"

"I've been giving it a lot of thought," he began. "It's a difficult request, and I've decided to…"

"Yes, Papa, so you'll do it?"

"Well, I was thinking…"

Saul's pronouncement was interrupted by the wail of a hungry infant. Rachel ran to her bedroom and within a few moments returned with Saul's grandson and a bottle of formula.

"Here, Papa, why don't you feed him?"

Saul cradled the infant in his arms, and placed the nipple of the bottle to the child's lips. He latched on immediately, the cries subsiding with a heavy sigh, as if a two month old's morning hunger was the most important issue of the day. Saul gazed at the suckling infant and felt a tingle in the area of his heart.

At that moment heavy footsteps pounded on the stairs to the apartment. Then the door flew open. Paul thundered in, his clothes disheveled, obviously intoxicated.

"Rachel, get me my morning coffee," he ordered, avoiding Saul's hardened gaze.

Part 4

Rachel went to prepare the coffee, her face drawn. Saul continued to feed his grandson, Jo Jo, keeping his eyes on the infant's suckling lips, yet painfully aware that Paul was staring at him,

When Rachel returned with his coffee Paul cleared his throat. "You're good with the child," Paul said with sudden charm, the kind some people can turn on and off like a lamp on a cold winter night.

"It's been a long time."

"Nonsense, I can see you're a natural. Jo Jo should have a chance to know his grandpa. Hate to put the child with foster parents while we're in Columbia."

Saul glanced immediately at Rachel, who bit her lip and avoided her father's gaze.

They sat in silence until the baby finished his bottle and then Saul handed Jo Jo back to Rachel.

"I hope you've decided to help Rachel with our little proposition," Paul began.

Saul squirmed. *$250,000 for a plantation in Columbia—nothing little about that.*

When Saul failed to answer Paul smiled with all the charm of a used car salesman.

"Look, I understand. This is all coming so quickly. You have every right to be cautious. But I've come up with a solution that protects your interests while furthering our own."

Saul's eyes widened. "I thought you needed my retirement savings."

Paul hesitated. "Technically, yes, but what if the deed to the coffee plantation in Bogata is in your name?"

"My name?"

"That's right, it's a win-win. The property will remain in your name, until which time we pay back the full 250 K. That place is worth all of a million. If we don't make good, you keep the plantation."

Saul glanced over at Rachel, who shrugged, her expression blank. Again Paul turned on a smile so big that every tooth was exposed.

Saul shifted in his seat. He looked again at Rachel, and at little Jo Jo now asleep in her arms.

"All right, I'll do it," he blurted. Paul's face lit up. He put a hand on Saul's shoulder. "You won't regret this."

Saul managed a weak smile as Paul stared into his eyes.

"And you'll take Jo Jo?" Paul said in a manner that was more a statement than a question, his breath laced with gin. "At least until we get on our feet."

"Is this what you want?" Saul said to Rachel. She took a deep breath, and turned to look at Paul. When she turned back towards her father her eyes were moist, but she nodded her head yes.

Saul glanced once again at the sleeping child. *I'll call him Joseph like my father.* "Yes, of course I'll take him. He's my own flesh and blood."

❖   ❖   ❖   ❖   ❖

The next few days were a blur of activity. Paul handled all the paperwork.

"Why cut the lawyers into the deal?" he said when Saul asked how the money would be repaid. "Everything is in your name because you're putting up the money. There are big profits in coffee these days. You've got nothing to worry about."

One night Saul dreamed of a smiling "Alexa Hente," the advertising gimmick of all those coffee commercials of the sixties—only in the dream when he smiled he looked a lot like Paul.

"You have nothing to worry about," the smiling coffee grower with the best beans said. He handed a canvas sack of beans to Saul as proof. But when Saul opened the sack, instead of savory beans, he found only a swaddled Jo Jo with a dirty diaper. Saul awoke in a cold sweat, but resolved to keep his fantasies to himself.

Rachel spent their last week together instructing Saul in the care of a baby— how he likes his bath—how warm to make his bottle—all the minutia that makes for good parenting.

Saul hired Mrs. Cohen, a woman in his building who had raised seven children, to help with Jo Jo when he came back to New York.

Plane tickets were bought, plans were made, few of which involved Saul. It was soon clear that Rachel and Paul were focusing on their future in Columbia now that little Jo Jo was out of the picture.

Things went well back in New York. Mrs. Cohen, a handsome widow a little younger than Saul, took charge. Saul arranged for a bris, and began to call little Jo

Jo, "Joseph," who didn't seem to mind. Saul's friend Bernie came for meals often, and kept Saul company most days while he took care of the child.

After a month small packages began to arrive at the apartment sent from Rachel. At first they were rolls of fives with a few tens mixed in. Later the packages were thick pads of twenty dollar bills with a few fifties. After six months there were weekly rolls of hundreds with descriptions of their new life in Columbia.

"Everything is going great," Rachel wrote. "Hold onto the cash for us. All the coffee buyers down here pay in cash."

Little Joseph rolled over and began to crawl. By the end of a year Saul's loan was almost repaid as Joseph began to take his first steps. Then the money and the letters stopped. Saul tried to call Rachel's cell, but only got a recording. He left a message and waited for a reply.

Early one morning, about a week later, there was a sharp knock on Saul's door. Startled, little Joseph erupted in terror. Saul picked up the child and went to the door.

"Mr. Saul Kaplinsky?" A man in a uniform said, ignoring the child in Saul's arms.

"Yes, that's me," Saul said, unsettled by the man's aggressive tone.

"I'm here to search your apartment."

"There must be some mistake, I've done nothing wrong," Saul said. He was about to slam the door in the man's face when he noticed the letters DEA stenciled across the man's jacket.

A matronly woman stepped out of the shadows and walked towards the door.

"Sergeant Murphy is here to take the child. I'm afraid I've got a warrant for your arrest."

Part 5

The words fell like hammers on Saul's disbelieving ears, but it was not until the police officer had removed little Jo Jo from Saul's arms, that he began to glimpse the import of what was happening.

"You have the right to remain silent," the arresting officer said, while he led Saul towards a police van parked outside the apartment. "If you cannot afford a lawyer one will be appointed for you."

The sound of Jo Jo's screams made Saul's pulse pound.

"What! No! You can't. This must be a mistake! You can't take my grandson! Rachel!!!! No!!!"

Three policemen with hands on their firearms surrounded Saul. The back of the van opened revealing a man with a shotgun held across his chest.

"Get in the van," he said, in a voice that did not leave room for further argument.

"This can't be happening," Saul muttered.

"It can and it is," the officer with the shotgun said, with indifference.

"We've been tracking your drug money for almost a year."

"Is that what this is all about? You're making a big mistake. Since when is investing in a coffee plantation illegal?"

The officer's deadpan expression gave way to a sneer.

"Coffee plantation money, now that's one I haven't heard before. Make sure you tell that one to the judge. He can use a laugh."

❖   ❖   ❖   ❖   ❖

Saul's nightmare intensified over the next few hours. He spent the night at Rikers Island in a cell with a cross section of New York's most hardened criminals. Rapists, burglars, and pimps eyed him with disdain.

"What kind of scum sells drugs to little kids?" a man apprehended while strangling his own mother whispered under his breath. Then he drew a finger across his throat with a nod towards Saul. "You're mine, baby."

Saul glanced away. He imagined himself carved like a Thanksgiving turkey by this grinning psychopath. *"What'll become of Joseph?"*

The arresting police officer appeared at the cell door, prompting the mother strangler to retreat into the shadows. "You get one call," the officer said to Saul as he led him into an alcove down the hall. Saul reached for the telephone on a rusted metal desk. He dialed Rachel's number. *Please answer....please.*

Somewhere in Columbia Rachel's cell phone was ringing. The DEA surveillance team centered in Bogata intercepted the call, and recorded Saul's pleading voice.

"Rachel, if you can hear me, you've got to help straighten this mess out.... Wherever you are, you've got to come back. They've taken Jo Jo."

But there was no answer. Rachel and Paul had long since fled. Saul left a message, unsure whether it would ever be heard. He shuffled back to his holding cell consumed with the worry that he would never again hold his grandson on his lap.

When Bernie heard of Saul's predicament he went straight to Buddy Schwartz, a childhood friend to them both, and arguably the best criminal attorney in all of New York City. "He's being framed by his own daughter," Bernie said, while Buddy put a hand to his forehead.

Buddy came to Rikers Island the following morning. As Buddy read off a list of the charges Saul's jaw went slack.

"Racketeering, money laundering, tax evasion, for starters..."

"They told me I'd be investing in a coffee plantation," Saul said, his eyes unfocused.

Buddy paused and stared at Saul over the rims of his bifocals. Then he scratched his head. "Who do you think you are? Alexa Hente?"

"Rachel would never intentionally hurt me."

"That may be, but your name is on the deed to the biggest opium farm in all of Columbia."

Saul's eyes bulged. "They paid back all of my $250,000."

"Drug money. Bet they made ten times that amount for themselves."

An image of a cell door clanging shut rose before Saul. *"Why should Joseph suffer for my stupidity?"*

Saul spent a half hour detailing everything that had happened since Rachel introduced him to Paul.

Buddy drummed his fingers on the desk. "The Feds need someone to pin this on….if only you could lead them to those responsible. You'd walk."

Turn in my daughter and future son-in-law? "Even if I knew where they were, I could never."

Buddy shrugged. "I'll see what I can do. The kid will be raised in a foster home. You're looking at a minimum sentence of fifteen years if we get a plea bargain."

Saul felt as if he were going to pass out. *In fifteen years Joseph will be sixteen. He'll grow up not knowing who I am. How could Rachel abandon us?*

❖   ❖   ❖   ❖   ❖

Previously, in a corner of a tiny mud hut hidden in the mountains outside of Bogata, Paul and Rachel were arguing when Saul's solitary phone call came in from the prison.

"They've taken Jo Jo," Saul was saying.

"Don't touch the phone," Paul said, "if you know what's good for you."

Rachel put a hand to her right cheekbone, still swollen from their last disagreement. She tried to calculate the odds of running out the door and escaping once and for all, but did not move a muscle, the words of condemnation stuck in her throat. Sure, she'd let her father down, time after time, but she always figured she'd make it up to him one day. Now, with everything gone wrong, on the run with a man she feared, the chance of a happy ending seemed infinitesimal at best.

"Saul takes the rap. We slip out of the country and start fresh somewhere else. What could be sweeter than that?"

Rachel's eyes brimmed with tears. "We'll never see Jo Jo."

Paul ignored her plaintive sobs. If he'd learned one thing about women, it's that they expect a strong hand…anything else and they'll walk all over you.

Rachel spent the night tossing and turning in her straw cot—quite a difference from the satin sheets and antique Louis the 14th furniture they'd left behind back at the plantation. Still, when the Feds come a knockin', ya better get rockin'—at least that's what Paul always said. She watched him now on the other lone cot, noting the bulge of a pistol strapped across his chest—a habit he'd gotten into once they went on the run.

She waited for the rhythmic snoring that always signaled his deepest sleep. Then she rose from her cot and slipped down the hall. She thought of cracking his skull with the frying pan in the kitchen—too risky—and besides there might be a better way to get even. She tiptoed to the door, then retreated to Paul's nightstand, grabbing a small black item with silent desperation. Paul stirred for a moment and she froze. But then, as he settled back and turned towards the wall, Rachel continued to the door. She glanced in every direction for the best way to run. Finally, she went out into the cool night leaving with nothing but the clothes on her back, a renewed sense of purpose, and Paul's cell phone in her pocket.

Part 6

Rachel stared into the jungle with trepidation. She'd followed Paul to Columbia without question, after all, he was her son's father, and who knows, perhaps he would come through with a marriage proposal eventually. When he lost his temper from time to time, Rachael tried to pretend she was invisible, that the slaps were not really aimed at her, only at Paul's frustration for not being able to provide a better life for his family. She put up with his wild schemes, yet when they left the coffee plantation, Rachel could no longer rationalize that the cash deals Paul made each day were victimless crimes.

Rachel always suspected Paul's get rich schemes were perched on the border between deception and dishonesty. But when the money kept rolling in, albeit in tens and twenties, it was easier to turn a blind eye than confront him with her suspicions.

She stepped out into the night without much of a plan, other than the burning desire to flee. Nestled in a mountaintop refuge, there was no one within miles. A pack of wild dogs howled in the distance. She looked down a road lit only with the glimmer of moonlight, and strode with purpose towards the town some 5 miles away in the next valley. She knew there were drug gangs living in the mountains who would slash her throat in an instant if they thought she might give evidence to the authorities. On the other hand, if the police found her first a hail of bullets might end her strange odyssey.

An image of little Jo Jo's face rose before her. She imagined the aroma of Desitin and baby powder, and the way her baby always smiled after his bath. *How could I have left Jo Jo to follow a man?* In that instant of revelation tears flooded her eyes. She had made so many bad choices in her life that she half expected things would go wrong. As she descended she pictured her father's disappointed face when he agreed to take care of Jo Jo. *How could I have left him for his first year of life?* She bit her lip. *I'm hopeless.*

When she had traveled a mile, the glare of headlights somewhere down the road sent Rachel scampering into the brush.

Maybe I could slip back to the hideout and pretend I never left. She put a hand to her pocket and felt for Paul's cell phone. A pickup truck passed, with armed men in the back, heading towards the cabin. She felt it difficult to breath, as her mind whirled, unsure of her next move. *I should warn Paul.* The thought of never seeing her son again overcame all other fears. When the truck was well past she stepped into the road, looked towards the cabin, and then down towards the lights of the town. Then shots erupted, and in a moment of clarity, she glimpsed her chance to make things right. She turned her back on the cabin and began to run down the road.

Meanwhile, Saul, increasingly frantic, still locked in jail, with the evidence mounting, put a hand to his forehead, as his attorney droned on. *I'll never see Joseph again.*

"Still no word," the attorney was saying. "I'm afraid you're the only patsy the DA has. If they can't find Rachel or Paul…you've got to give them something, anything that might lead to your daughter's arrest."

Saul's eyes widened. After two weeks in prison his hope that his incarceration was all a colossal mistake had given way to a growing fear that he would likely spend the rest of his life in prison. Still, he'd refused to talk about his daughter, afraid to give the police information that might put her life in jeopardy. The attorney wagged a crooked finger.

"Give me something, even her cell number might help get you a lighter sentence." Saul shook his head. "She won't let me down…not this time."

The attorney nodded. He'd defended well-intentioned men like Saul all of his professional life. He knew better than to contradict a father's hopes for his daughter, no matter how misguided they might be.

"Besides, they'd never keep their cell phones. They're not stupid."

The attorney shrugged. "There's another matter we've got to discuss. They've placed your grandson with a nice couple in Park Slope, Pete and Candy McCarthy. They hope to adopt."

The Anglo-Saxon names made Saul wince. The image of his grandson as a five-year-old opening presents under a Christmas tree made his breathing quicken.

"I've got to be around to raise my Joseph," Saul muttered.

❖   ❖   ❖   ❖   ❖

The sound of the pickup truck barreling down the road sent Rachel diving into the brush. Thorns tore her flesh. Palm fronds scraped her face, as the pop pop pop of automatic gunfire sounded. Bullets ripped the asphalt where she had been standing seconds earlier. She found herself on all fours, holding her breath, her face in mud, as the echoes of gunfire rippled through the valley. Then there was silence. She lifted her head and turned towards the road. A lone voice screamed in Spanish—a voice Rachel recognized as Paul's—the words a slew of curses she knew could only be meant for her.

Within seconds shots sprayed through the palms above her head, the firing indiscriminate, the flash of gunfire sparking in the night. The curses stopped after a loud grunt, then a moan like the sound of air being let out of a balloon. She put a trembling hand over her mouth to keep from screaming.

Then suddenly men were running from the bush on all sides of the road, their weapons drawn.

"Stop! DEA!", she heard one man yell just before a blast sent him hurtling backwards.

Rachel lay prone on her belly, and buried her face in crossed arms, while gunfire raged all around her.

Part 7

Rachel's mind focused on an image of her infant son, *Will I ever see him again?* As she faced a violent end to her all too brief existence, a litany of her failures rose in her mind. She had never been a religious person, had scoffed at her father's attempts to interest her in Judaism. Her idea of being Jewish was identifying with Woody Allen movies. When she was thirteen and her father insisted she attend Yom Kippur services, she had smiled her devilish grin and replied, "If God wants me to pray on Yom Kippur, why doesn't he ask me himself?"

The fighting intensified, with Rachel the prize. A grenade exploded across the road. A volley of automatic weapon fire shredded the tree limbs above her head. The smell of cordite and gunpowder filled her nostrils and brought tears to her eyes. *How could I ever think I could get away from Paul?* Then Paul's cell phone began to vibrate in her pocket. She fumbled to turn it off, terrified that if it rang she'd be targeted. For a few moments there was silence. She thought of throwing the phone deep into the forest, but she hesitated, afraid that the information it held might be her only salvation. *I've got to make this right.* Then the sound of a helicopter reverberated above, making her chest vibrate while the trees danced. She lifted her head and peered into the night, the helicopter's search light illuminating scattered bodies. She caught a glimpse of Paul lying on his side in a gully by the road, his hands clutching his gut, his head flailing from side to side.

"She's over here," she heard someone yell. She lowered her head, and began to mumble a prayer—the only one she remembered from the Rabbi's failed attempts to get her through her Bat Mitzvah.

"Shema Yisrael Adonaj Eloheinu, Adonai Echad...."

❖   ❖   ❖   ❖   ❖

Back at the prison Saul's meetings with his lawyer had become increasingly more contentious.

"I will not sacrifice my daughter, and that's final," Saul was saying.

This time the lawyer just shrugged. "Your name is on the deed to land producing opium. The DA's got enough evidence to send you away for the rest of your life. Your daughter got you into this; don't expect me to get you out."

Saul shook his head.

"At least give the Feds her cell phone number or her location. Otherwise, Saul, without proving that your daughter set you up, you need a miracle."

Saul put a hand through hair that seemed thinner than ever. He nodded solemnly, and swallowed.

"I can't...don't you understand? I just can't."

As the lawyer scribbled some notes Saul's mind drifted to a happier time when Rachel was twelve and his wife was still alive. On Sundays he and Rachel would set out from home early in the morning on their bikes, intent on biking to the bagel shop a few miles away. New York City drivers being deserving of their reputation, Saul would always have Rachel bike on the inside, closest to the curb, while he maneuvered on the outside closest to traffic.

"I want you in the sheltered zone," he would always say when Rachel protested, eager to be free of parental rules. It became their joke...the sheltered zone...a fantasy of Saul's...as if any father could keep their child completely out of harm's way. As the years went by and Rachel's penchant for the unconventional emerged, Saul longed for those simpler times when a bike trip through city streets was all he had to deal with.

"She's got to stay out of jail," Saul muttered.

The lawyer's eyes burrowed into Saul's.

"And she will. The DA's after the big time operators, not some love-crossed pawn caught in the wrong place at the wrong time." For a time the lawyer fell silent while Saul's mind whirled.

"Do it for little Joseph. You want him to grow up in a foster home? Don't you want him to know his mother and his grandfather?"

Saul pictured little Joseph being baptized by his new foster parents. He hesitated, but as the lawyer was about to leave, Saul scribbled a number. "All right I'll cooperate. This is Paul's cell phone number. Rachel's phone went dead last month."

The lawyer strode from the room and within minutes came back with an official of the DEA carrying papers. "Don't you want to read them before you sign?" the official said.

"As long as Rachel's got a chance," Saul said.

"You realize what this means for you?" the lawyer said. Saul swallowed hard and nodded.

❖   ❖   ❖   ❖   ❖

Rachel lay on her belly, mouthing a prayer. Suddenly the shooting ceased. She peeked through half lidded eyes to see a set of mud-caked boots before her face. *The drug lords will kill me for sure...after torture, or worse.* She waited, while the sound of men running towards her position sounded from all sides. Then she heard the sounds of rifles being drawn. When she looked up she saw gun barrels pointed at her head and men in camouflage jackets lit by the glare of a helicopter searchlight.

She shut her eyes and waited for the bullet that would end her life. There was silence, then the cackle of a hand held radio. "Copy that," she heard a man say. "Stand down."

Then she felt someone shackling her hands behind her back.

"You have the right to remain silent. Anything you say can and will be used against you."

Rachel moaned. The handcuffs cut her wrists, and the humiliation of being taken into custody was more than most young women could bear without breaking down. But Rachel's mind was not focused on incarceration. *Maybe I'll see Jo Jo again.* And my father—*I've got to make this right.* As they loaded her into a waiting jeep an image of Paul writhing in a gulley rose before her. She felt neither pity nor remorse, only the hope that she'd never face him again.

Part 8

Hoisted into the helicopter by a steel cable and then crammed into a corner, Rachel sat dazed. The DEA men surrounding her stared with suspicious eyes, their weapons on their laps, fingers on triggers. The ping of a stray bullet ricocheting off the armor plating of the helicopter's underbelly set her teeth on edge. She glanced out the window and saw ragged men illuminated only by the helicopter's searchlight, running towards the chopper. A man in camouflage fatigues was setting up a mortar on a tripod.

"Go, go, go!" the commander in charge barked and the helicopter began to rise, the men below craning their necks to follow its flight while the trees whipped.

"Kill that damned light," the commander ordered, and the scene on the ground went black.

Within seconds a flash of light on the ground sent a mortar round streaking upwards. The missile barely missed the chopper, but took the top off a nearby tree. A whooshing sound shook the chopper and then the sound of small branches scraped against the outer metal skin. The chopper seemed to shudder, wobbling for a moment, like a wounded animal, before leveling off.

"Head for base," the commander ordered, his voice cracking, as automatic weapon fire sounded below. His walkie-talkie squawked.

"Copy that," the commander replied. Then the chopper turned 180 degrees and began to accelerate, heading towards a cluster of twinkling lights in the distance.

Rachel closed her eyes and tried to picture her son's face. Her teeth chattered. Tears rolled down her cheeks, and then, in a fashion she couldn't remember at any time in her life, her chest began to heave while silent sobs wracked her body.

An hour later Saul's lawyer entered Saul's holding room with a broad smile across his lips.

"They got her, and she's unharmed," he was saying. "She'll be back in the States by tomorrow. She knows nothing about the deal. She'll get off with probation."

Saul's eyes went wide. A vision of his little family, rose in his mind—little Joseph swinging between him and Rachel as they walked along the boardwalk at Coney Island. *If only that could happen.* He'd written her off to insulate himself from disappointment for so many years. In light of his decision to plead guilty to get a lesser sentence for Rachel, the loss of his retirement money seemed the least of his worries.

Meanwhile, Rachel's interrogation went forward as planned: processing in Bogotá, extradition to the U.S., all under the watchful eyes of the DEA and Colombian authorities. It was only back in the States that the real questioning began.

"I really don't know," she found herself saying again and again. "Paul never filled me in on details."

"You didn't know that your husband ran the biggest opium plantation in Colombia?"

"He said we grew coffee."

"Then why run from the DEA?"

"Paul said they were IRS agents looking for back taxes."

"If the DEA didn't find you first you'd be dead in a ditch. Ever hear of the Medellin Drug Cartel? They don't like to leave loose ends."

Rachel shrugged, and glanced at the handcuffs on her wrist. "I'm not sure this is much better. How did you find me anyway?"

"The phone."

Rachel replayed the events of her capture—*the phone began ringing just before the DEA closed in....*

"Your father's tip let us locate the phone. It's called triangulation."

"Its called betrayal." Rachel shuddered. *How could my father turn me in?*

The two interrogators exchanged a glance. The one in charge nodded.

He held up Paul's phone. "Your father made a plea deal, and the contacts on this phone are part of that deal. We need to know what you know about everyone your husband did business with."

Rachel said nothing.

"The drug lords were out to kill you. The phone number that your father gave us saved your life."

The color drained from Rachel's face. "If you call thirty years in prison a life."

Again the interrogators glanced at one another. "You'll have to talk to your father."

Rachel's eyes narrowed. She pictured her father sitting at home in his apartment while she broke rocks on a chain gang. She drummed her fingers on the desk and stared at her jailers without blinking. *I hope I never see that dirty rotten bastard again.*

❖   ❖   ❖   ❖   ❖

Saul had another meeting with his lawyer.

"They'll let you see her alone as soon as she's back in the States," the lawyer said. "Two days, maybe three."

Saul nodded, the grin on his face lighting features that had become increasing haggard. An image of walking arm in arm with his daughter while pushing little Joseph in a stroller popped into his mind. He laughed softly. This was the first bit of good news in his nightmare.

Perhaps that's why the rancor of their reunion was so hard to take.

Rachel stormed into Saul's holding cell like a crazed animal. Not since she'd thrown a temper tantrum at eleven had Saul ever seen such fury. He put up a hand as if to fend off the sting of her accusations, but it only seemed to make her more angry.

"I did it for you," he was saying. Her spittle sprayed his face as she unleashed a string of diatribes normally reserved for the bleachers at a Yankee/ Red Sox game.

"You gave me up, so you could get off—probably want to keep me from Jo Jo— get me locked up for the rest of my life. What did I ever do to you?"

Saul stared wide-eyed. *You lied, took my pension, landed me in jail.* He struggled to remain calm. It had always worked when Rachel was a child. She'd blow up like a summer squall, vent her anger, and then crawl up to her room for a nap. But now, Rachel was no longer a child, and an ember of anger fanned into flames in Saul's mind. He struggled to keep from shouting, for that had never worked before.

"You don't understand," he mumbled.

Rachel leaned close to Saul's ear. "Traitor... Judas."

Something deep within was working itself loose. He began to shake; his hands trembled. *For this I agreed to go to jail for fifteen years?* When he tried to reply he could only stutter.

Rachel's contorted face was before him, taunting, accusing, her eyes full of hate. "I wish you were dead," Rachel hissed.

That was when Saul lost all control. His right palm swept out as if to slap Rachel squarely in the jaw. For that instant he wanted to hurt her like she had hurt him so many times—snap her back to reality. Whether a father's physical retribution would have an effect on a girl like Rachel will never be known, for the blow fell well short.

Rachel laughed, but then, when she saw the look on her father's face, she fell silent.

A squeezing pain gripped his chest, as if an elephant were suddenly standing on his ribs. He no longer felt his legs, and his breaths came in short gasps.

"Papa, you're turning blue," Rachel was saying, her furious expression replaced by one of shock.

Then the room was spinning. He fell like a sack of potatoes, landing with a sickly thud on the concrete floor.

For a few seconds all was silent, but for Rachel's shriek. She retreated to a corner of the cell, her hand over her mouth. She felt the old familiar guilt she had fought as a child. Her first impulse was to run to her father's side, to nestle his head in her hands. Instead she stood mute. Then the door clanked open and the lawyer and two guards ran into the room. One guard placed handcuffs back on Rachel's wrists, while the other hovered over Saul.

"Do something," Rachel wailed.

"What have you done?" the lawyer was saying.

"He's not breathing," he shouted. Then he reached over and thumped Saul's chest with a clenched fist.

"Still nothing," he said after checking for a pulse in Saul's neck. Then, with Rachel watching in stunned silence, the two guards began CPR on Saul's limp body.

Part 9

As they carried Saul out on a stretcher, Rachel remained in the corner of the cell. She stared unblinking, her hands shackled behind her back. With the anger that had fueled her outburst spent, she stood eerily detached, as if she were viewing a movie, not her father's struggle for life.

It had always been this way with her father—the shouting, the all-encompassing fury, the compulsive need to squelch his disapproval imagined or otherwise. When he got talking about religion, whew boy, that's when she really blew her top—like the time Saul insisted on Jo Jo's bris, or Saul's pressure that she attend Shabbat services with the family, back when her Mom was alive and there was a reason to try and be civil.

"Borderline personality disorder, with manic-depressive tendencies," the shrink at college had called her outbursts. "You need help dealing with conflict." Whether it was her lack of health insurance, or the way she threw her cup of coffee in her therapist's lap, it really didn't matter. They cancelled her appointments.

She tried to suppress the violent images that plagued her from time to time. "I can work out my own problems," she was fond of saying whenever her actions brought catastrophe. Rachel always chose to escape rather than confront her demons. She was beautiful and men overlooked her quirkiness, judging her more for her looks than the idiosyncrasies of her mind.

Too often she hopped from one man to another whenever her anxiety got too intense. She chose to hide her pain, rather than admit her shortcomings. Some men understood and so she stayed for a while. Others, like Paul, used the back of their hand instead of trying to understand her anguish. She chalked her failures up to bad luck in the past, calling on her father only when things looked hopeless.

As the cell door swung closed her mind reeled. An image of Jo-Jo's face rose before her, and the ashen pallor of her father's face as the guards carried him away. *I'd rather die than spend my life in jail, alone, without someone who cares about me.*

❖　❖　❖　❖　❖

The medical officer on call bolted upright when the call came in. As an overworked third year psychiatry resident doing a rotation in the New York City prisons, Dr. Jacob Katz was used to challenges. Still, nothing could have prepared him for the challenge he was about to face.

"Prisoner 5520 found unresponsive," the guard was saying as they brought Saul's stretcher into the makeshift infirmary.

"Put him down here," Jacob Katz said, discarding a book on mood disorders, indicating a stainless steel bed on wheels that doubled as transportation to the morgue when things didn't go so well. Jacob grimaced when the guards dumped Saul's body onto the gurney.

"Poor guy," Jacob muttered. If only you'd gotten here while the chief resident in cardiology was still on duty, maybe you'd have a chance, Jacob Katz was thinking, as he noted the lack of a pulse in Saul's neck.

Katz normally dealt with feelings of isolation and anger in his patients, not a complete cessation of vital signs. Still, this was a teaching rotation, and with NYC budget cuts, attending physicians were few and far between.

"I'm afraid I'm all you've got," Katz said, when the guards gave him a quizzical look.

"Should we transport him to the morgue?" the guard asked with a shrug, "or call for ambulance transportation to Bellevue?"

Katz took a deep breath. *What would be the point of a twenty-minute ride to an emergency room when there are no vital signs?*

"Damn budget cuts," Katz muttered.

"I guess it's the morgue, then" the guard said, beginning to wheel Saul away.

"No wait," Katz said. "Let me try something first." *After all this is supposed to be a teaching rotation.*

Katz sprang to the medical supply cabinet and rummaged around in the top draw. Finally he found what he was looking for—an oversized hypodermic syringe loaded with adrenaline that looked like it was meant for a horse. The guards took a step back as Katz approached Saul's body. With the decisiveness that would, one day, propel Katz to the head of his profession, he ripped open Saul's shirt and unsheathed the needle. Then, after feeling for the breastbone with his opposite hand Katz plunged the hypodermic fully in to the hilt, and deposited its contents directly into Saul's heart muscle.

"Well, it was worth a try," the guard said when Saul remained motionless.

"Here goes nothing," Katz said, and brought his fist crashing down on Saul's chest. Startled, the guards staggered backwards. "What the…"

Katz stared expectantly. Then he bent down to check for breath sounds.

"Still nothing. Might as well get going." He covered Saul's body with a sheet.

The guards were wheeling the bed away when Katz heard the cough.

"Out of my way," Katz said and ran to the side of Saul's gurney. He stripped away the sheet to find Saul's eyes wide open—staring, inquisitive eyes, filled with pain.

Katz stared in wonder. "You have no idea how lucky you are."

Saul stared at the ceiling, blinking back tears. *Rachel. Oh my sweet little Rachel. I did it for you, only for you.* Then an image of his daughter's fury rose in his mind, and he began to weep.

❖   ❖   ❖   ❖   ❖

While Saul struggled for life Rachel seethed. Images of her violent capture by the DEA and their fight against the drug lords rose in her mind—the gunfire, the mortars, a glimpse of Paul writhing in pain, his hands over the gunshot in his belly. A trained professional might have diagnosed post-traumatic stress reaction had he been there to see Rachel rocking in the corner of her cell. Certainly the guard knew something was wrong, when he looked into her eyes and saw nothing but a vacant stare.

Despite Rachel's detachment, images were flashing fast and furious in her mind. The shock of her father's collapse was like having a scab ripped off her emotional wounds. *It's all my fault.* The accumulated traumas of her life overwhelmed her defenses. Hurts, real and imagined, her father's disapproving scowl, the slap of Paul's open palm across the side of her face, all rose to the surface.

Mixed with the recollection of explosions and gunfire came snippets of psychic horror, perhaps more horrible. She imagined that Paul might still be alive, hungry for revenge and coming to the prison to kill her. *What if he's got s knife?*

Rachel's breath came in shallow gasps. Her heart raced, her physiologic systems reacting to the turmoil in her mind. Behind her unresponsive eyes she relived the maniacal accusations from Paul's obsessive rants, the crash of a fist on her face, the taste of blood in her mouth.

Someone was shaking her now, shouting very close to her face, yet her mind chose to draw away. She heard Jo Jo's first cry, mixed with her own sobbing, reliving the birthing pains so intense she wanted to die. A single voice fought through the images, and the voice was her father's. *What kind of a person leaves her baby?* Through the fog of her delirium she heard the cell door swing open and then clang shut.

Yes, better to die now, her body seemed to be saying, her pulse over 200, her blood pressure skyrocketing as she lay on the floor of the holding cell. And despite her youth she truly might have died, had not Chief Resident Jacob Katz intervened.

"Stand back," he was saying, and the guard jumped away. He took her blood pressure, then measured her pulse, trying to stay calm despite his own agitation. "She's having a panic attack," he said to the guard. He'd seen it all before, just never this severe. For a moment he allowed himself a look at her face—she was beautiful, despite the red flush and the spittle on her lips, her raven hair plastered by sweat to her forehead. Then the convulsions began, her head rolling from side to side while her arms and legs shook.

"Lady, don't die," the guard was shouting. She seemed to focus on Jacob for an instant, struggling to say something.

Jo Jo, I want Jo Jo.

Then the syringe was in Katz's hand. He rolled Rachel on her side, while the guard gripped her arm.

"Haldol IM," Katz said, as if that information would matter to the guard or his patient. "Stay with me," he shouted.

Rachel felt the jab in her shoulder, felt the sting of the fluid forced into her body. She writhed on the floor, her anger rising to full force, held down by two powerful men.

"What right do you have?" she said through clenched teeth. "Get your damn paws offffffffffff," she yelled. "Who the hell are you?"

"You're going to be all right, I'm a doctor," Katz was saying, his eyes riveted to the fullness of her lips. "Try to relax. You need time to heal," he said in a voice full of compassion.

She fought to respond. *Is my father dead? Who will take care of my son?*

But before she could speak the lid was descending on the steaming cauldron of her thoughts. Her eyes closed and her arms went limp at her side.

Part 10 - Conclusion

Rachel slept for 12 hours. When she awoke, her body ached as if she'd run a marathon. A man who looked vaguely familiar entered the room and took her pulse.

"You had a close call," Dr. Katz said. "You need rest." When he saw the panicked look in her eyes he put a hand on her shoulder.

Suddenly she thought of her father. She saw the pain in his eyes, sensed his fear, as he collapsed to the floor, his hand on his chest.

"Did I kill my father?" she asked Katz in a small voice.

"Dead? God forbid!" Katz explained the details of his treatment, the adrenaline to the heart, the thump on the chest, the last ditch effort that worked despite the odds.

"Your father had an arrhythmia, an irregularity in the rhythm of the heart. Happens sometimes with great emotional upset. He's going to be fine."

The thought of facing her father sent a shiver down her back.

"When's the trial?"

"That's not my call," Katz said, and his eyes darted away from her gaze.

Meanwhile, in another part of the hospital, Saul was in recovery after doctors implanted a pacemaker in his chest.

"Where's Rachel?" was the first thing he said after the nurse took out his breathing tube.

An armed guard advanced to the bedside. "The DA wants a meeting with you and your daughter. You'll see her then."

Saul grimaced. The thought of sitting opposite Rachel made his pulse quicken. *She must think I sold her out.*

Two days later…

The District Attorney sat on one side of a mahogany desk, Saul and Rachel on the other. The DA had the look and demeanor you'd expect in a 50's crime show on TV-crewcut, hard chiseled features, neatly pressed slacks and jacket. He opened a drawer and placed a cell phone in a worn leather case on the desk.

The little hairs on the back of Rachel's neck stood on end. Her hands balled into fists. *That's Paul's phone.*

"We need your help to find and prosecute Paul and his drug ring," the DA said.

Saul's eyes brimmed with tears but he said nothing, his eyes on his hands shackled in his lap.

Rachel's lip quivered. An image of Paul writhing in the road, holding his belly, flashed in her mind.

"Paul's alive...and free...but how?"

"The drug cartels are pretty good at treating gunshots in Bogata. He got away in the confusion when we picked you up."

Rachel glanced at Saul. She pictured Paul in a drunken rage the last time he slapped her around. *What's worse, prison or the possibility of facing Paul again?* She turned back to the DA, her heart pounding. "Why should I help you? So you can keep me locked up for the rest of my life?"

"Who said anything about life in prison?"

"But my father…the deal. I go to prison and he goes free. Do you think I'm stupid?"

The DA's all business manner softened. He took a deep breath and shook his head. He spoke slowly, as one would to a child.

"Don't you realize your father agreed to a sentence of 15 years to keep you from going to prison? He said his grandson needed a mother, and a chance at a normal life."

Rachel's eyes flew wide. *I thought he made a deal so he would go free.* She stared at her father who was sniffling now. She thought of little Jo Jo, pictured an imaginary scene with her father, walking along the boardwalk at Coney Island with the child between them. *That'll never happen if Dad goes to jail. I've been such an idiot.*

"Let me explain your options," the DA said.

Saul's mind drifted as the DA prattled on about probation, and community service and things that the lawyers would fight over later. *Was I such an awful father to want my daughter to live a respectable life, to raise her son as a Jew? Is this how it ends, with me in prison and Rachel free to gallivant around the country again? I only wanted her to have a decent life.* He turned to stare at his daughter.

Rachel returned a half smile and a nod, as if reading Saul's thoughts. Then she put a hand on his shoulder.

"I have one scenario where you both can stay out of jail," the DA was saying.

"Tell us everything you know about Paul and anyone he ever associated with. Identify the contacts on his phone. Then testify against them, and make sure we put them all away for a very long time. I'll see that you both get immunity."

"We won't go to jail?" Rachel said.

"I said you'd both go free. And you'll have joint custody of the child."
Rachel was smiling now. *Jo Jo. I'll get to raise Jo Jo.* But then, amidst this new hope, Rachel pictured Paul in a rage. She'd seen enough movies to know that the bad guys too often murder the stool pigeon.

"It's a chance to save your father," the DA said. "Of course there's always some risk."

"I can't tell you what to do," Saul said to Rachel, but the tears in his eyes told a different story.

Rachel pictured a car exploding as she turned the ignition. She wondered if she could live in the same house as her father, and raise little Jo Jo together...at least for a while.

"After the trial, we'll put you in a witness protection program. It's a chance to start over."

Rachel hesitated, for she sensed this was the biggest decision of her life, and for once there wasn't a man to tell her what to do. She took a deep breath, and pondered the choices. Perhaps this new clarity was the result of her new anti-anxiety medication. Or perhaps it was her determination to take responsibility for her life. Either way, for the first time in a long while, Rachel no longer felt fearful when she thought of her future.

❖   ❖   ❖   ❖   ❖

Rachel held up better than the DA ever expected, despite the murderous looks from Paul during the trial. Paul was convicted on all counts and sent away for three consecutive twenty-year terms. Rachel resolved never to date a loser again...she had Jo Jo to think about.

When the trials were over, the DA offered Saul and Rachel the possibility of two locations for the witness protection program. The first was in Lancaster, Pennsylvania, living with an Amish community—quite a few Federal protection witnesses were there, building barns and living the Mennonite lifestyle.

The second opportunity was a chance to live in Borough Park, Brooklyn, not too far from where Saul grew up.

"Living within an orthodox Jewish community might be interesting," the DA said, when Rachel balked at the first choice. "You'd live in a duplex apartment with the cousins of a man I think you've already met...Dr. Jacob Katz, one of the psychiatric residents in the New York prison system. Of course you'd have to send your son to one of their schools. A yeshiva I think they call it. Believe me a drug dealer would never think to come looking for you in Borough Park."

For a while Rachel said nothing. Her mind grappled with the two possibilities.

"I can't imagine living in Pennsylvania, on a farm," she said.

Saul was determined to let Rachel make this decision for the both of them which ever she chose, as long he got the chance to be with little Joseph.

Saul fought to suppress a smile as the DA went over the details—kosher food, modest dress, and all the rules that made Borough Park a closed community.

Finally, the DA folded his hands on his desk. "It's the last place a drug dealer would ever look. You and your child would be completely safe, but I want you to know that you'd have to fit in. They take Judaism very seriously."

Rachel threw her hands in the air. "Ok, I'll live with the Jews in Borough Park. They can't be **that** strict."

❖ ❖ ❖ ❖ ❖

It took a few days to process the paperwork and put things in order. Rachel, always used to a change in venue, adopted her new persona with unusual enthusiasm. She scoured the Borough Park shops for calf length dresses, bought a wig to cover her hair, and threw her designer jeans in the trash. She checked Dr. Jacob Katz's Facebook page, and realized he was single. She began to think of this new wrinkle in her life as a great adventure.

True to his nature, Saul was more cautious. Despite his desire to maintain Jewish traditions he'd never considered a life of strict observance. Even as the DA escorted them to their new apartment, Saul pondered a future, living with Rachel, in a new community without his old friends. *What have I gotten myself into?*

At the apartment, a cramped 2nd floor walkup, Saul sat in a chair absorbed in thought, half listening to the DA's instructions. "Blend in with your neighbors, attend Sabbath services. Don't do anything that might set you apart," the DA was saying.

Rachel looked radiant, a flush on her cheeks, her eyes sparkling at the thought of a new life, despite all the rules.

Saul took a deep breath. He'd lived alone for so long, that now, when faced with the reality of a crowded household, a sheen of perspiration rose on his forehead. Someone knocked at the door. Saul walked to the door and opened it wide. Then his hand went to cover his mouth.

"Hello, Mr. Rappinsky, I'm from Social Services," a woman said as she placed a one-year-old into Saul's open arms.

Saul opened his mouth to call Rachel, but the words caught in his throat. He held the boy up to the ceiling and then brought him close to his face, reveling in the chance to hold his grandson after all these months. "I love you, Joseph."

At first the child's face fell, as if he might cry, having grown unaccustomed to Saul's voice. But then, as the stubble on Saul's chin tickled the child's neck, little Joseph burst into laughter. Rachel and the DA came in from the other room.

The child put a hand on Saul's chin and pulled at his wispy excuse for a beard.

"Poppa," the child said, and giggling, placed his other hand on Saul's nose. Rachel embraced her son. "Jo Jo, it's Mommy." The newly reconstituted family stood together laughing. Rachel turned to Saul with tears in her eyes. "You never gave up on me after all I've done. Can you forgive me?"

Saul nodded and kissed her on the cheek. "That's what fathers are for."

The DA bade farewell and, with the woman from Social Services, headed for the door. "We'll be in touch," he said.

Saul smiled, and, after handing the child to Rachel, walked with the DA down the stairs and onto the sidewalk. "Thank you for all you've done," Saul said, as he walked the DA to his car. When they passed a group of young men wearing black velvet kippahs Saul whispered under his breath, "It's just that when I asked for a Jewish community, I was thinking of Scarsdale or Boca Raton."

The DA shrugged. "You never know about these things. Sometimes in life you get more than you bargained for, sometimes less. Take care of your daughter and your grandson. They need you."

Saul smiled. "I'll take that under advisement, District Attorney Morgenthau."

"Be well, and mazel tov," the DA said. Then he winked. "And remember, if there's anything you need, I live right up the block."

The End....at least for now.

Requiem for a Heavyweight

I checked the scale that fateful morning, the day after Passover as I always did. My eyes nearly bulged from my sockets. *This is impossible. How can a person gain a pound a day?* Memories of this Passover's delicacies leapt to my mind: the matzah slathered in butter, sprinkled with salt, macaroons of multiple description, almond, chocolate, chocolate chip. And what of the matzah brei breakfasts? (Matzah soaked in eggs, fried golden brown on the griddle.) I suppose I could have lived without the generous helping of maple syrup (kosher for Pesach of course). While a nice touch, the extra sprinkling of sugar on top might be considered excessive. And who can resist chocolate covered matzah—a breakfast staple that would have been relished by our ancestors as a well-deserved manna of distinction. As for the metal tin of Barton's caramel covered almonds, no need to dredge up the particulars of how they disappeared in my festival of indulgence.

I leaned to the left and shifted my weight to my heels, a sure fire maneuver that usually reduced the scale's readout by a few pounds. Hedge as I might, there was no assuaging my guilt. I had gained 8 pounds over Passover.

"So how'd you do?" my wife inquired from the bedroom, her lilting voice casual and non-accusatory.

"Water weight, I must be retaining fluid," I muttered,

"Doesn't matter, you're so active. You'll take it off in no time."

I threw on my trousers, fumbling as I tried to force the button through its mated hole.

What the...! I nearly accused my wife of shrinking the pants in the wash, but kept my tongue. I glanced into the mirror. Despite the additional stretch of the forgiving elastic hidden in the waistband there was no camouflaging the distortion of my newly developed silhouette.

As I drove off to work, images of past diets rolled in my head: Atkins, shmatkins, my forebears might have said. "A man of your age needs a little meat on your bones. Otherwise you'll get sick." My mind wandered to the all-vegetable diet that had once erased thirty pounds from my frame in three months. I resolved to make a nice root stew for dinner, but the concept faded almost as quickly as it had appeared. Weight Watchers, Thins In, Slim Fast, where are you when I really need you?

At work I checked my email. "Lose ten pounds a month without dieting and without exercising," the come-on proclaimed. *Click here for this incredible offer of all natural ingredients, guaranteed to let you shed those unwanted pounds, and give you back the body you always wanted.* My hand hovered over the delete key, but then, in a moment of weakness tinged with desperation, I opened the too good to be true offer.

What I read astonished me. "You may be harboring a hidden gene that makes it impossible to lose weight," the pitch began. "Through no fault of your own this gene abnormality has imprisoned you in a seesaw of gain and loss. Get off the rollercoaster of fad diets with the new gene therapy solution at Dr. Quakenbush's Weight Loss Clinic."

The ad gave an address and phone number which I will refrain from publishing to prevent a stampede to Dr. Quackenbush's place of business.

After work that evening I beat a path to Dr. Quackenbush's office, as if my feet had a mind of their own. I parked down the street, unwilling to take the chance that someone I knew might recognize my car. I strolled along cautiously, glancing into shop windows. I found Quackenbush's office and entered.

A woman well into her eighties greeted me. "Are you here for the weight loss or the age reversal therapy?" she croaked. I put a hand over my newly formed paunch, as if comforting an old friend. "The weight loss," I muttered. "Didn't know they could slow down aging."

"Dr. Quackenbush can do almost anything with gene therapy," my octogenarian receptionist intoned. "He's wonderful," she said with a knowing grin.

"Yes, ahem," I coughed. "I'm sure he is. I'd like to make an appointment."

"Of course you do." she said. She checked her computer screen, and clicked a few keys. "This is your lucky day. I think the doctor can see you now."

I nodded hesitantly, and then filled out a few forms, agreeing to hold Quackenbush harmless should my results not be typically wonderful.

Once inside a young nurse took my vital signs, had me pee in a cup, and took a clipping of my hair. Then she prepared to take a vial of my blood.

"For the gene sequencing exam," she said, when I gave her a quizzical look. Fifteen minutes later a man in a wrinkled white doctor's coat entered the room. He gazed at me without blinking, and then, after a brief explanation, began to measure the girth of my neck and my waistline.

"Yes just as I suspected—the weight gain gene. I'm afraid you have it."

"I do? Well, how do I get rid of it?" I blurted. "Your ad says weight loss without exercise or diet."

Dr. Q's concerned manner brightened. "We'll come to that in our next session," he said. "First I have to run a few tests. Can I take a swipe of your credit card?"

I nodded my head and forked it over. In return he gave me an appointment for the following week and handed me some reading material.

I couldn't wait for my next visit. During the week I gained another two pounds. *Hey, why skimp on my portions when I was going to be reborn through gene therapy?*

At my next visit Dr. Q began his explanation at once.

"Did you know, our Paleolithic ancestors stored fat, so that, when deprived of food, they could slow their metabolism to a nearly imperceptible crawl? That's why we gain weight when we overeat. It's hard-wired into our DNA." I nodded, hanging on his every word.

"My gene modulation will change all that," he continued.

"So when do I start?" I said with a jerk of my head. He eyed me suspiciously, as if deciding on whether I was gene therapy worthy. At last he nodded. "I'll need another swipe of your credit card."

I forked it over. "I thought I paid last week," I said with a shrug.

He smiled as he took the card. "That was for tests. This is for the gene therapy itself. I tailor treatment individually for each of my patients."

He handed me a DVD. "Study this presentation and return next week. You'll get everything you have coming to you at that visit. You'll eat to your heart's content and never gain weight, effortlessly and without exercise."

I went home immediately, DVD in hand. I cancelled my gym membership and ate a pint of Ben and Jerry's Dark Chocolate with Pralines Ice Cream to celebrate the rebirth of the new me.

By my next visit I had gained another 3 pounds and was getting increasingly anxious to start my treatment.

Dr. Quackenbush ushered me into one of the treatment rooms where a device that looked like an open coffin awaited.

"Is that what I think it is?" I asked.

"Yep, the TD2000, newest innovation in gene therapy."

I swallowed hard. "Yes, of course, but it looks like a...tanning bed."

Quackenbush laughed. "Yes, I suppose to the uninitiated. That's like saying a rocket ship looks like a Model T Ford. The TD2000 has been modified to use ultraviolet radiation to alter your genetic makeup. "Wear these goggles and get in."

I did as I was told, and when the twenty-minute timer sounded I went home. My skin was tingling and I felt a little nauseous. I ate a bagel with cream cheese to settle my queasy stomach. By the following week's appointment I had gained another two pounds and raccoon-like white circles had formed around my eyes.

"You know, my skin's been a little tender and red," I said.

"Good, that's how you know the treatment is working," Dr. Quackenbush said. He handed me the goggles, helped me get into the TD2000, and left the room.

The following week I fought an intense craving for Jarlsberg Cheese on English muffins. To my dismay, my weight ballooned another 2 pounds, and I noticed a definite darkening of my skin.

I resolved to share my disappointment with my doctor and called my credit card company to see if I could rescind the previous charges for Quackenbush's treatment.

When I arrived back at the clinic for my confrontation the door was padlocked and the office dark. When I called the office a recording said the office was closed until further notice. All the police would tell me was that Quackenbush had been closed down for impersonating a physician.

I'm starting back at the gym this week. I might try spinning. I'm reserving my elliptical trainer for sure, and I'm considering weight loss alternatives of my own, like having my jaws wired shut. As for Quackenbush's treatments I never did get a refund. He skipped town ahead of the Feds. I was reminded that nothing worth doing is easy and that if something sounds too good to be true it probably is. A bit of wisdom is all I got from my well-intentioned gene re-sequencing…that and a moderately good tan.

A Farewell to Rabbi Astor

I came to this community in 1981, nearly 32 years ago, with my wife and 6 month old son in tow.

"There's a new Rabbi coming," I heard from my father-in law. "And I think he plays tennis. Why don't you call him?"

A tennis playing Rabbi, now how could that be? The only Rabbis I had ever seen in my youth were white-haired, bearded men approaching their sunset years. The Rabbi who ran my Hebrew school when I was a child was a strict disciplinarian, who several times game me the back of his hand. Still, I was new in town, anxious to make friends, and if this new Rabbi Astor had a decent game, I would try not to hold his rabbinical training against him.

So, after a few phone calls back and forth we met. And we played—right here on the Mitchell courts in New London. And, truth be told, I was crushed, the weakness of my tennis game exposed, my wimpy backhand destroyed. After the game we talked. I found out more about the Rabbi—his time in Wayne, New Jersey—his education at Penn and the Jewish Theological seminary. He had a wife and three young children. His newborn son, Donny, was only a few weeks older than my son, David.

Our lives intersected in many ways beyond the love of sports. Often, young men relate through activities. They talk while doing something manly, as if the act of conversation were not enough. Somehow, through our many days of tennis, stickball, basketball, and golf, I'd like to think that we forged a friendship. He guided me through so many of the momentous moments of my life. When my sons were born, Rabbi Carl Astor was there, with his considerable skill to perform their bris.

Our friendship grew through the sports we so loved, but at every step of my religious life Rabbi Astor and Sharon were there. When my daughter was named, of course it was Rabbi Astor who performed the ceremony. He taught at the Schechter school, which my four children attended. He prepared them for their Bat and Bar Mitzvahs, helped assure that they would grow into adulthood knowing only the gentle guidance of a kind spiritual leader. He performed the wedding for my eldest son, David, and watched my second son Adam walk down the aisle last May. It's hard to believe that 32 years have passed, but the last days of Rabbi Astor's tenure are upon us.

Some people approach retirement with trepidation, some with relief. I believe Rabbi Astor should be proud of the years he gave to our community. Last week, as

I sat in the sanctuary during the tribute for his retirement, I was amazed to see how much our Rabbi has impacted his colleagues. Ministers, Priests and other Rabbis were in attendance. It was a most unusual Shabbat service, but, then again, it's not every day that a congregation says goodbye to a leader of such long standing. Two choirs from nearby churches sang hymns during the service, Rabbi Rosenberg of Temple Emanu El spoke in tribute. A Priest spoke of the pleasure of having Rabbi Astor as a friend and colleague all these years. Reverend Benjamin Watts of the Baptist Church gave a warm hearted farewell, recounting all the years that Rabbi Astor had been involved in Martin Luther King Day commemorations and the impact he had on the black community. Reverend Watts likened Rabbi Astor to Rabbi Abraham Theodor Heshel, a champion of social justice who marched with and supported Martin Luther King in his fight for civil rights. I don't know if Rabbi Astor was blushing, but I felt proud to know that my friend and spiritual leader was so well thought of outside of the Beth El Community.

Imam Mangi, the former head of the Muslim Center got up to speak. He acknowledged that over the years he and Rabbi Astor had some difficult discussions. I can only imagine, since Rabbi Astor is a tremendously strong supporter of Israel, and Mangi may have had other thoughts. But in the end he was proud to count our Rabbi as his friend. "He made me a better Muslim," Mangi said in conclusion. I glanced at my wife, but said nothing, feeling a sense of pride to see my Rabbi praised so sincerely.

After the service I looked around the sanctuary, by now packed with almost 400 well-wishers. Present were Beth El members I normally see only on Yom Kippur, representatives of the hospital where our Rabbi serves on the ethics committee, and a plethora of former congregants who made long trips to return for the weekend's festivities.

The tribute made me feel good about Beth El and my fellow Jews, knowing that Rabbi Astor had, in his quiet measured way, represented the Jewish Community so well. For 32 years he's been our spokesman, an example of tolerance and good citizenship to the community at large. He's been our steward through all of our life cycle events, in sickness and in health. For some he lent an ear when no one else would listen. For some he gave a word of consolation when their grief was so overwhelming that no consolation seemed possible. He taught us about Judaism, either by sermon or by example. I can still picture him rollerblading his way back home from services on Shabbat, in the freezing cold, or the pouring rain, all to avoid driving on the Sabbath.

In all the years I've known Rabbi Astor, he never once chastised me over religion, never once asked me to come to services more often or to be more observant. Being around our Rabbi and his wife, Sharon, I picked up a thing or two about being committed to family. I learned about helping those who needed help, about visiting the sick. I learned about bringing God into your life and about living your life with humility.

I know that in a more jovial moment the Rabbi might say "Artie, with your athletic skills you have every right to be humble." And I might laugh and insult his backhand, or tell him he's lost his golf swing, just when he needs it for retirement. Men are not so good at giving compliments even when those compliments are well deserved. So, when I reflect on Rabbi Astor's effect on my life I will always think of him kindly. I will wish him well, and hope that he never strays far from his home here in New London. In closing I will tell him something he may be surprised to hear since so much of our relationship revolves around competitive sports. I will simply paraphrase the words of one of the speakers at Rabbi Astor's retirement tribute. He made me want to be a better Jew. And in the final analysis isn't that something a Rabbi can be proud of?

WHAT'S HAPPENED TO OUR HEROES?

Let's face it. Our nation loves heroes. We love to create them and we love to tear them down. Whether in politics or sports, we idolize those who we really don't know. We elevate them to heights of fame. We plaster their names on election posters.

As a boy I used to collect baseball cards, hoping to find that magical Mickey Mantle or Roger Maris card buried beneath a stale stick of gum. I thought John F. Kennedy was the answer to all our nation's hopes and aspirations. As far as I was concerned, at age 10, he could do no wrong.

Yet, time and time again, our heroes turn out to have feet of clay. Stories of Mantle's indiscretions are legendary. His difficulty with alcohol may have been exceeded only by his affairs with women. Rumors persist that President Kennedy had his mistresses secretly brought into the White House, Marilyn Monroe among them. To tell you the truth, I would rather turn a blind eye to the scandals. I prefer to remember the arc of the ball after Mantle crushed another home run. I choose to remember how Kennedy made us feel, full of hope, intoxicated by the certainty that the future would be better than the past.

Today's rich and famous toil under the additional burden of 24/7 news organizations that crave dirt. When scandal strikes why is it so difficult to look away? The German term Schaudenfroide springs to mind—the pleasure one has at seeing the misfortune of others. If we weren't watching why would news shows devote hours to discussions of Tiger Wood's infidelities? Why was Bill Clinton's legacy besmirched by impeachment? Why did John Edwards become the laughing stock of American politics? Why did we roll our eyes when Governor Mark Sanford disappeared for a tryst to Argentina when he claimed to be hiking the Appalachian Trail?

When then Governor of New York, Elliot Spitzer, famous for stamping out corruption, showed up on the list of a call girl's clients why were we so fascinated? Why does disgraced Governor Blagojevich, who tried to sell Obama's vacated senate seat, still make headlines?

We remember Pete Rose for his gambling problems, not his prowess on the field. When someone mentions Barry Bonds do we think of his home run records or picture him injecting steroids?

Tiger Woods, at his recent press conference, apologized for his indiscretions and stated, "I thought the rules didn't apply to me." I find his words to be most revealing. Could this be the moral failing that links all our fallen role models together?

Most ordinary people try to make their mortgage payments on time. They pay their taxes. They trudge off to work. They try to raise honest, hard-working children, and hope for a better world. They take solace in their spouses and their families. They usually shun the limelight. They worry about their children, not their public persona. They may not be better people than the fallen-from-grace rich and famous, but at least they don't have to answer for their failings to the entire world.

Human nature demands that we follow leaders. Fortune awaits those who can sink a buzzer beating three point shot in the NBA finals, or catch a Hail Mary pass in the end zone. We pay for tours of the homes of Hollywood stars, and elect political leaders whose words inspire. When they are exposed as cheats and liars we feel betrayed, but can't stop watching.

Maybe we should be more selective in our adoration. Let's honor the teacher who helps their students achieve. Let's honor parents who sacrifice for their children. Let's put academic excellence on the same pedestal as sports figures, and pay homage to those who take care of us when we are sick. And, let's realize that fame and fortune isn't the only way to measure success.

YOU CAN'T GO HOME AGAIN.

Washington Heights, in the fifties and sixties, was the quintessential melting pot of New York City. Its mix of nationalities seemed all inclusive: Italians, Irish, African Americans, Puerto Ricans, and Jews all rubbing shoulders in a square mile plot of concrete, filled with school yards and basketball courts. While the migration to the suburbs decimated the area in the early seventies, generations of Jewish children trace their heritage to those sometimes-mean streets. Such luminaries as Henry Kissinger, Dr. Ruth, and even our own Jerry Fischer, once called the "Heights" home.

Reunions are a tricky thing. Memory can play havoc with reality, leaving the experience wanting. So it is with a sense of appreciation and remembrance that I offer up this simple story, for I too claim a Washington Heights pedigree.- Artie

The sense of smell is one of our most underappreciated senses. Often a smell triggers a vivid memory, conjuring up thoughts and feelings long buried beneath our protective armor. So it was, on that June day, when I drove Mr. Rubin home from dinner a day before our sixth grade reunion. I know it's unusual for ten-year-olds to get together forty years later, but we were a most unusual group of individuals. I took a few turns off of the West Side Highway and entered a darkened street. I felt my heart quicken.

A group of young men in baggy pants and oversized shirts stood drinking beer and laughing in a small group, blocking the entrance to his building. Up the block a torrent of water gushed into the street from an open hydrant.

"Let me walk you up," I say.

"No that's all right," he says. I know those kids. They won't give me any trouble."

I nod, but I park and escort him toward the front door anyway. At 82 he's lost a step or two and the imposing frame I remember in grade school is now bent and frail.

The brass numbers on the front of the building are tarnished so badly that I can't read them. I glance at the street sign, "Audabon Avenue." I feel a strange sense of foreboding, my stomach lurching as if I'd been dropped down an elevator shaft at the Empire State Building.

"You don't have to do this," says Mr. Rubin, but by now I'm along for the ride for my own reasons. The elevator door opens. We step in. The stale smell of urine confirms what I have suspected from the moment that we turned onto this street.

"Is this one-forty five?" I ask.

161

He nods. "Right, one forty five Audabon,"

I slump against the elevator wall. As we pass each floor on the way to the sixth a rhythmic chime hammers at my memory. Everything seems as in a dream: the agonizing crawl of the elevator, the muted flash of yellow light as we pass each floor, the claustrophobic iron box that passes for an elevator, but, above all, the pungent smell of urine.

"What's wrong? You're so pale," Mr. Rubin says, as we reach the sixth floor, and the door opens.

"Nothing," I say, but my breath comes quickly, in shallow gasps. The single bare bulb in the hallway is swaying and the tiled floor is rocking as we walk down a narrow corridor. Mr Rubin puts a hand on my arm.

"Are you all right?" He says.

"I don't know," I say in a whisper and stagger against the wall. My hands and feet are tingling. I can feel a cold clammy hand at my throat and there's an elephant crushing my chest. "Hard to breath."

"Let's get you inside," Rubin says in a voice that echoes from a distance.

I hear voices shouting in the hall. I try to stay on my feet, but my legs have turned to Jello. Then there is only darkness and silence.

A roaring in my ears startles me and then a pulsating squeal. Abruptly, the sound ceases only to be replaced by a rumble that intensifies. I recognize the sounds of a subway on the elevated tracks outside the apartment. Why does it make the monitor clipped to my chest beep faster?

"Oh, good, you're up," a uniformed man says as he bends over me.

Mr Rubin hovers nearby. There's a blood pressure cuff on my arm and I am laying on a couch in his living room.

"Am I having a heart attack?" I ask.

The uniform chuckles, and then shakes his head.

"You fainted. See it all the time. You'll be good as new in a few hours. Good thing I'm not a rookie or you'd wind up in intensive care for the night."

I struggle to sit up, feel whoosie and slump onto my back again.

"Whoa, fella, better stay down for a while. Keep your feet up," the officer says, propping a pillow under my ankles. He places something beneath my nose. The pungent fumes make me cough. I take a deep breath, and tears fill my eyes.

"Usually see this with a bad emotional upset. Did something shock you?"

I stare at Rubin. He shrugs.

Nausea overcomes me. I turn my head to the side and deposit the evening's meal on the spotless Persian rug beside the couch. The uniform jumps away, chuckling. "Don't worry…. I'm used to that too."

"I grew up in this building," I say. "Haven't been back in forty years."

The uniform shrugs. "Sometimes those are the worst shocks. Maybe you'll feel better in the morning."

I spent the night at Rubin's apartment in a spare bedroom down the hall. I slept poorly, haunted by dreams, strange specters dancing like a pinwheel around my head. I wake in a cold sweat to a horrible scream, an intense flash of light bursting before me, sure that a nuclear blast has detonated beyond the window. As my mind clears I sense no searing heat, no collapse of the building around me, just an eerie calm. The rumble ceases, the sun streaming into my eyes through cracked Venetian blinds at the window. I rise and close the blinds, noting the graffiti covered steel subway car still paused at the platform far below. Then I stumble back to bed, ignoring the growing roar of the train as it leaves the station.

As a young boy, in the early sixties, I had woken often to the grinding squeal of steel wheels on rails, the orange orb of the morning sun peeking between concrete buildings and searing my ten year old flesh to a crisp. Or, so I imagined in the seconds between sleep and consciousness, sure that those civil defense drills we had at school were no laughing matter. Years later pundits would mock the seriousness of our middle aged teachers who took those disaster drills in deadly earnest.

"So, remember boys and girls, when that air raid siren sounds, make sure you crouch as I've shown you, put your hands behind your head, roll into a ball, placing your head firmly between your legs, and then remember, as you hear the sound of the blast, to kiss your little tush goodbye."

Nan Zucker would sit at her desk, defiant to Mr. Rubin's pleas.

"This is stupid. I'm not doing it," she'd say.

I'd glance at her from my crouched position. Foolish little girl, I'd think. She won't be ready when the big blast comes. And who in those years dared to ignore a teacher's commands? Yet she never got into trouble for her prepubescent defiance. In fact, after the first confrontations, Rubin often let her go to the bathroom unescorted before the drill, a twinkle in his eye, happy to avoid a meaningless showdown. I often thought she was his favorite.

My desire to please often got me into trouble, rather than appease the powers that ruled my world. Maybe that's why my life's been so confusing. *When you follow the rules shouldn't you sometimes win the game?*

Mr. Rubin brought me tea with two sugar cookies. I sat on the couch and sipped the tea, but passed on the cookies. They reminded me of the offerings at a shiva call, the somber visit one makes to the family when a close relative dies.

Rubin's face looked pinched. His eyes narrowed as he watched me from a chair across the room.

"Is there someone I can call?" he said with concern.

"No, no, I'm fine now. Really," I said, but the rhythmic pounding of a migraine rose behind my eyes with a beat Mick Jagger would have envied.

I washed in the bathroom, thanked Rubin, and then went downstairs. The bright sunlight of mid-morning made me squint and the pounding in my head was unrelenting. Every car on the street looked like a reject from a body shop, yet they all had that urban security blanket "The Club" fastened across their steering wheel. I looked up the street anxiously for my old Saab. By some miracle it was still parked in front of the apartment building where I had left it. I suppose even crooks have higher standards.

I slid into the driver's seat and then fumbled in the glove compartment for the Imitrex self-injection syringe, the little godsend that would soon make my throbbing head bearable. I glanced around the street aware that, in this neighborhood, a cop would more likely arrest me for shooting up than believe that the little needle in my arm was a migraine cure.

After a few minutes the pounding headache subsided. I called my wife and tried to explain why she couldn't reach me at the hotel last night.

"No really, Brit, I must have fainted. You can call the EMT's if you don't believe me. I told you. I didn't go anywhere else. I spent the night on Mr. Rubin's couch. Why do you think I'm hiding something from you?"

She didn't answer.

"Brit?"

I heard a click, then silence. *What good are cell phones if they don't work when you need them most.*

I fumbled in the glove compartment. Hidden behind the owner's manual I found my nightguard, the king's ransom priced piece of plastic my dentist fitted to cut down on my grinding. Seems I'm wearing all the enamel off of my teeth.

"Any alternative?" I had asked my dentist.

"There's always psychotherapy," he answered in his nasal voice, a thin-lipped smile peaking from the corners of his mouth. "Might cut down on your headaches."

I opted for the nightguard—seemed less expensive than a shrink. Lot of good it did me half forgotten in the glove compartment. At least I hadn't lost it, like I seem to do with most important things in my life.

Since it was Saturday I decided to stay in the city until the reunion on Sunday instead of driving to New London and back. There'd be the usual scene at home— probably take a week for the ice to thaw. Besides, didn't the EMT tell me to take it easy for a while? Maybe I'll take a look around the old neighborhood while I have the chance, I thought.

I called home again. I felt strangely relieved that the answering machine was on, but I could almost feel Brit's anger, and imagined her sitting cross-legged at the kitchen table, biting her lip when she heard my voice on the speakerphone.

"Hi, honey. Pick up if you're there…I'm gonna catch up with a few people in the old neighborhood. Be back Sunday night. I'll come in quietly if I'm late…Brit are you there?"

I would have left a detailed itinerary, but the machine must have run out of tape. "Love you, too," I said to a dial tone. I hung up the phone, and began to make a mental list of the places I wanted to visit during my little two-day adventure. This is going to be great, I thought, but a rising sense of disquiet brought a sense of breathlessness that I could not explain.

Part 2

I couldn't stop thinking about what happened to me the previous night. I'd never fainted before. Everything had gone fine at dinner, a modest affair at Ben's Deli on Thirty-Fourth Street, just across from Madison Square Garden. I spent a few hours talking with people I hardly recognized, using the usual lies about how great I was doing. "I want to hear all about you," was my best line—one that never failed to win friends and influence people. At least it got the spotlight off me for the moment. And people do love to talk about themselves. I'm relieved not to dwell on my disappointments, afraid that if I started talking I might not stop.

The food was great. Can't get that stuff in Connecticut. I decided to forgo the Atkins diet and stock up on pastrami on rye. No, I didn't ask for lean. And then the matzoh ball soup. Enough salt to rival the Dead Sea. Forget the blood pressure. Is there a carb rebound effect that would explain my fainting, I wondered? No, I was fine at the restaurant. Even took home half a pastrami sandwich. Then I drove Mr. Rubin, my fifth grade teacher, home to save him from taking the subway… was fine in the car…started to feel jumpy when I pulled up to the old apartment building. I didn't know Mr. Rubin had moved into my old building thirty years ago…didn't recognize where I was until it was too late…and then the urine smell. Why had that triggered everything?

The next day I decide to walk to my old elementary school, P.S. 152, a mile up Broadway from the George Washington Bridge. I head toward Nagle Avenue, past the bodegas and the pawnshops, the bail bondsmen and the massage parlors. Gray exhaust spews from a bus at the corner, filling my lungs with enough toxic fumes to bring the EPA out in force.

Throngs of people hurry along the streets, each scurrying somewhere. I stare into their blank expressions hoping to see a familiar face, but they look straight ahead, their lives insulated from their neighbors in crowded anonymity.

New London, Connecticut, lays only 100 miles east along the Long Island Sound, but it could be a thousand, or on another planet for that matter. Not that I don't like where I live. Who would get bored of all that open land, the forest, the fresh air? And two miles from my home the sea beckons. How many early mornings have I walked along the Ocean Beach boardwalk, thinking of nothing but the peace and the calm, the seagulls my only companion. *I wouldn't trade that for the world. Even so, why do I feel so alive after one day back on the streets?*

Old memories, long buried, rise like specters, yet, mixed with the apprehension of a walk down Broadway is the adrenaline rush of new possibilities.

After forty years you make certain attachments. You reach a comfort zone. People know me in New London. I've got friends, acquaintances…my wife. There's an old cliché about an old horse that can guide the milk wagon home even when the driver has fallen asleep. At twenty I left the city filled with the seductive promise of endless possibilities. Now I'm that old horse, unable to alter my course, even though the path is unbarred.

At the intersection of Nagle and Broadway stands the fortress wall of Fort Tryon Park overlooking the Hudson River. Once the young nation's stronghold against the British, the fort straddles a granite ridge, the highest point in Manhattan. I glance up the hill. A flag still snaps briskly atop the flagpole where my father and I fed pigeons near the canons of the revolution when I was five. It must be ten years since I've spoken to him. I picture him as a young man, his big hand enveloping mine as we strolled through the park. I had to reach up to hold on, but his warmth flowed around me like a protective blanket. If he ever caught a glimpse of the terrors that surrounded us he might not have chosen a destination so lightly. *Funny, but I didn't even think of telling him I'd be in the city...what would be the point? But I don't want to think about that now.*

I cross Broadway headed for the park as if caught in a trance. A car horn blares. A taxi swerves to avoid a young woman with a stroller, then speeds to get past me before the light turns from yellow to red. I freeze. I shake my head, snapped out of my middle-aged musings by a near death experience.

"Hey," I yell, but the taxi driver guns the motor, leaving me only with the smell of burned rubber and the memory of his middle finger extended to me in a New York salute. *Ah, City life. How could I have left this all behind?*

I enter the park, walk down paths worn thin by generations of immigrant families who came to Washington Heights to escape their own brand of misery. On wooden benches sit old men, an occasional mother with a baby carriage, and a lone vagrant stretched across a bench asleep. Pigeons coo and peck at scraps of bread thrown by children. One boy stamps his foot, and then runs at a flock of birds, scattering them with omnipotent delight. *Could these humiliated pigeons be direct descendants of those I fed as a boy? Why don't they fly to some friendlier shore?*

I walk on until I reach a secluded area. I sit on a bench, lost in thought. I can't stop thinking about my father. As a boy of seven I would wait in our tiny New York apartment for him to return from work. Every night around six, I'd hear the clang of the elevator door, then the sound of his footsteps growing louder in the hall. His key would wiggle in the lock. I'd yell to my mother, "Daddy's home." Then the door would fly open and he'd be standing there, a newspaper folded under his arm, his face drawn from the hour-long subway ride from the Garment District on 34th street. In the early sixties there were no air-conditioned subways. The cliché 'packed in like sardines' was probably coined for the city's transit system. (On a summer's day make that steamed sardines.) His face would light up when he saw me. Then he'd drop his paper, crouch, and spread his arms.

"Daddeeeee," I'd scream as I took a running leap, sure, beyond all doubt, that he'd catch me. He'd shake with laughter, struggling to stand with my arms clasped around his neck.

My mother would scowl. "Be careful, you'll hurt your father."

But he'd lift me like a wave lifts a twig. Then he'd swing me around and deposit me where he'd snatched me on the worn living room tiles.

"Acchh, Dad's got a bad back," my mother insisted.

"It's all right," he'd say. "I'm fine." But, often he'd stagger to the turquoise chair in the living room and collapse in mock exhaustion, the plastic slipcover squeaking from his two-hundred-and-twenty-pound frame.

"One day you'll hurt yourself," she continued. "The boy's too heavy."

He'd laugh. "Don't be silly. That machine gun I carried in the war—now that was heavy. This little bit of gefilte fish is as light as a feather." Then he'd tickle me under the armpits till I'd scream.

On Friday he'd be home early, especially in the winter when the sun set around five and the Sabbath started early. Even his Syrian bosses at the showroom respected his early departures.

"What'd you get me?" I'd squeal, beginning our weekly ritual, more sacred to me than the Kiddush we would say later that night.

His smile would vanish. "Get you something?" he whispered, looking far into the distance as if there was something important he'd forgotten like the secret hiding place of some fabulous diamond. "Oh, I didn't have time," he'd mumble, but I'd see that his hands were clasped behind his back.

"No, Daddy you did, you did." And I'd run to him trying to get my hands behind him, but he'd hold me off with one arm, his strong hand covering my chest.

"Really Daddy, What did you get me?" I'd shriek.

"What did I get you? With people starving in China? I got you nothing, nothing, you hear me? Nothing!" By now he couldn't contain his laughter and it would pour out of him in great gulps. He'd let me push him onto the couch. He'd raise his eyebrows, the whites of his eyes popping from their sockets in a mock imitation of a mad Hitler.

"Ya, nothing, I got you nothing, nothinnnnnng, drawing the last syllable out like Sargeant Shultz in Hogan's Heroes, my favorite TV show in those days.

I'd jump onto the couch, try to run my hands around his belly, to reach what he was hiding behind his back, but he'd lean away from me. Then he'd explode, his words torn apart by laughter.

My mother would stand at the dining room table, watching this weekly spectacle unfold, an apron around her waist. She'd fold her arms across her chest, a whimsical smile on her face, the smell of roasted chicken wafting enticingly from the kitchen.

"Narrashkite," she'd mutter, the Yiddish word for silliness. Then she'd shake her head and go back to the kitchen to check on the dinner.

"It's done," she'd say, closing the oven door. "Come to the table. It'll get cold."

My father would nod as he might have once done to his commanding officer in the British army. "Ya, a minute."

Then his hands would emerge from behind his back, but he'd palm whatever the secret delight was between his fingers. Immediately I'd attack, prying his fingers apart, unable to contain myself.

"Nothinnnnng. You hear me? Nothinnnng." He'd erupt again in laughter.

"Enough already. You'll disturb the neighbors."

"All right, But it feels good to laugh."

Finally his hands would open.

"A soldier? You got me a soldier?" I'd say, my hands clutching the perfectly painted tin soldier above my head. "Oh Daddy, thank you, thank you, thank you!" Then I'd throw my arms around his belly, never able to clasp my hands fully behind his back.

He'd stop laughing and stroke the top of my head. For that moment all was right in my world.

"Alright, make Kiddush," my mother would say with the hint of a smile on her lips. Then she'd place a Manishewitz wine bottle and three Kiddush cups on the table.

"Ya, ya, what's the hurry," he'd say, still running his hand over my hair. But under her watchful gaze he'd soon extricate himself from my embrace.

❖   ❖   ❖   ❖   ❖

A dog's bark snaps me from my memories.

Someone begins to scream—a muted wail so desperate that Alfred Hitchcock might have orchestrated the scene. I scan the path from which I entered the park. People are strolling along the path, but no one seems concerned.

"Ayeee," again a scream, but this time louder. The hairs on the back of my head bristle against my collar. My eyes focus on a secluded thicket of trees about a hundred feet away. From behind a tree a little arm protrudes, then a little hand clutching an ice cream cone, chocolate ice cream running onto the fingers. A figure steps out from behind the tree. It's a little kid. Can't be more than four or five. His lips tremble. He holds a shaking hand out as if to ward away a demon. Then I see the dog, a pitbull as big as the kid. The dog paces silently, its teeth bared, its stubby tail erect, never taking its eyes from the child.

"For God's sake, where are the parents?" I groan, frantically searching for someone to take responsibility. If only I could find a cop, I think, but I seem to be the only witness to this impending catastrophe.

I picture the saddened look on Brit's face when she sees me in intensive care. Then I stoop to pick up a rock.

"Shhh, don't be scared, it's all right," I say as I approach the boy. His mouth drops open, his eyes wide with terror. My heart pounds to a staccato beat that rivals a psychotic drum solo.

"Come to me," I say, but the boy stands frozen, shaken only by his building sobs. The dog snarls. Then it makes a mock charge, stopping two feet before the child. I can see the dog's huge teeth and pink tongue. Again the child shrieks, and drops his cone.

Why isn't anyone coming?

"Help!" I yell, sure that my intervention will bring the death of us both. *Why am I doing this?* I consider backing off, reporting the incident at the nearest police station, but something about the look on the child's face spurs me on as if I have no choice.

I never take my eyes off the dog, now so close I can see the saliva drooling from its mouth.

"Easy now, easy, don't do something stupid," I say gently, as much to the whimpering child and the dog as to myself.

The dog whirls towards me, its teeth flashing. I'm about to throw the rock, when I remember the pastrami and rye in my pocket. I drop the rock, thrust my hand into my pocket, and pull out the half sandwich that I brought home the other night.

"Here boy," I coo, letting the wax paper waft away in the breeze.

The dog's mouth snaps shut, the frenzy instantly gone from its eyes, replaced by a look of questioning wonder.

"Fetch," I yell, then toss the sandwich away, the seeded rye slices separating and sailing like Frisbees, the greasy meat falling into a clump of leaves in the untamed woods beyond.

The dog scampers after the pastrami, mercifully forgetting about me. I rush to the child, who is hyperventilating. I swoop him into my arms. He doesn't struggle, and I run with this sobbing child away from the woods to the bench where I was a moment ago so peacefully ensconced.

"Hold it right there," I hear from behind me, as I'm about to deposit the kid on the bench.

"Put the kid down!" commands a uniformed officer, as I turn around to face one of New York's finest.

I smile. "Thank God you're here," I say, and place the child gently on the bench. I turn back to the officer, ready for his words of thanks, but instead of congratulating me he crouches, draws his handgun, and points it at my chest.

"You sick mother," he says, with disgust, and then spits at my feet.

"I heard someone yell for help."

"That was me," I say. "I saved him from a pitbull." I gaze into the woods after my pastrami, but all is quiet—no sign of the dog.

"Officer, I saved this kid, ask him." I say, but the cop looks at me like I'm a convicted murderer.

"You'll have plenty of time to explain, you pervert," he says. "Now hands up. I'll read you your rights."

I raise my hands slowly, and glance at the child on the bench, who is curled into a fetal position, sucking his thumb, the broad forehead and wide eyes of a Down's child now so obvious on his face.

Part 3

The cops at the 32nd precinct give you only one call. I thought of calling Brit, but it's a three-hour ride from New London. Besides, I knew she'd probably keep her answering machine off all weekend, a most effective way to express her anger at my leaving for the reunion. In this case her passive-aggressive play might be more detrimental than our usual psychodrama. And, considering the growing chill between us, how could I explain that I'd been charged with child molestation, kidnapping, and reckless endangerment in a ten-minute phone call?

I glanced at my watch—five o'clock. I thought of calling Mr. Rubin. He'd been so helpful the night before. How could I expect my fifth grade teacher, a man of 82, who I'd last seen forty years earlier, to come bail me out at the police station?

There was only one person I could call, although it was the hardest call I'd ever made. I dialed the number from memory.

"Ya, hello. Who is it?" came the response. In the background I heard the theme of Beethoven's Ninth—Ode to Joy, always his favorite piece.

"Vate a second," he murmured. The music faded to a whisper.

Beads of sweat formed on my upper lip. I struggled to speak. "It's Sam," I said in a hoarse voice.

Silence greeted me. "Who is this really?" he repeated after a long pause, his voice cracking. "Don't tease an old man."

"No, Dad, I wouldn't. It's your son, Samuel."

I hadn't talked to my father in over ten years. After our last fight I resolved to wait until he called me before I'd speak to him again. Every year I thought of calling him on his birthday—I never could bring myself to dial his number.

"Vat's wrong, Shmulie?" he said without a hello.

I hesitated, thought of hanging up. *He still insists on calling me Shmulie.* "How are you?"

"Nu, How should I be? At seventy five I'm just happy to be on this side of the ground."

"How's Mom?"

"Fine, fine, we're both fine."

"That's good…" My saliva turned to dust, my tongue a size too small for my mouth.

"So you wanted to apologize before we're both dead?"

I said nothing. At forty five I felt ten again.

"Brit all right?"

"She's fine…it's just that…"

"You're in trouble?"

"I'm in jail at the 32nd precinct, Dad."

Silence. Each second seemed an eternity. "I'll be there in a half hour," was all he said.

Bail was set at $250,000, probably as much as my father had saved in a lifetime of pinching pennies. He posted the bond without so much as a word. This is a big mistake, I thought. For some reason everything he did, every little movement annoyed me, as if he'd arranged my humiliation and my worthlessness had finally been proved beyond a doubt.

I got into his car, the same '85 Oldsmobile he'd bought fifteen years earlier. It still looked new. I glanced at the dashboard. The odometer was just shy of forty thousand.

"Car still looks good," I said.

"I take care of my things." He stared straight ahead as he drove, the muscles of his jaw bulging, his fingers white as they clenched the steering wheel.

We drove in silence until we reached his apartment building, the rent controlled twenty-story building we'd moved to when I was six, a step up from the squalor of 145 Audabon Avenue. He pulled to the curb. Then he turned to me, ran his hand over his eyes as if to wipe away a bad dream.

"So, tell me. Vat happened."

"It's all a big mistake." I explained with the uneasy realization that my story sounded preposterous. Yet, he listened without interrupting, something he'd rarely done when I was a teenager living at home.

"You need a good lawyer," he said. "You should call your brother."

I felt that old familiar pang under my ribcage. I shook my head.

"The police will clear it up in a few days."

"Ya, but the child can't talk, so how will they clear it up?"

"You think I'm guilty! Don't you?"

"Doesn't matter what I think. It matters only what a jury thinks."

His face was a mask, but as he spoke his eyes glistened.

"People will vouch for me. Twenty years teaching high school has to mean something."

"School, schmool. That means nothing. When Hitler rounded us up, character witnesses didn't help much."

I bit my lip. Still the same old mindset, I thought. *Sixty years after the holocaust and he still thinks everyone is out to get him.*

"This isn't Germany, and the police **want** to straighten this out."

"Is that what you think?" he said, a single tear escaping his lower lid and cascading down his wrinkled cheek.

"I didn't do anything to deserve this," I said, my voice rising more in the form of a question than a declaration.

"If you say so. But what'll you do when the school board gets wind of the investigation?"

I got out of the car and slammed the door.

"Come up, your mother wants to see you," he said.

"You think I did something wrong with that kid?" I said, almost yelling, my hands folded across my chest. I noticed an old lady cross the street to avoid us.

My father got out of the driver's side door slowly. The tears were gone, his face hardened to match my own.

"No you didn't do anything wrong. Not today…but when a man turns his back on his faith and his family, God remembers."

Part 4

My father's words suck the air from my chest like an uppercut to the solar plexus.

I don't know about God, but I certainly remember when the rift with my father began all those years ago....

I sit at my desk in Hebrew School, watching the second hand sweep slowly across the face of my new Timex, the one I got for my tenth birthday a week earlier (the watch that takes a licking and keeps on ticking.) Our teacher, Mr. Goldfarb, is droning on about some fine point regarding the Sabbath. I glance through the lone window obscured by the collective grime of generations of unwilling students. The window is opened six inches as a treat on this first day of spring to let in some "fresh air."

As the stale odor of decaying books and vacant minds rushes out a sprinkling of teenage laughter seeps in. Some Irish kids are playing stickball on Bogardus Street. *If only I could get out of this place.*

Mr. Goldfarb's voice fades, replaced by the imagined voice of Mel Allen, the legendary Yankee sportscaster doing play by play at the Stadium. I slip my treasured Mickey Mantle card from my pocket and place it on the prayer book before me.

"Yes, ladies and gentlemen, you heard right," Allen says. "It's the bottom of the ninth, bases loaded, and two men out. Yankees trail the Red Sox 5 to 2."

The fans are going crazy as yours truly, Big Shmulie, leaves the dugout to pinch-hit for Mantle.

My hands clench an imaginary bat. The smell of newly mown grass and pine tar is strong as I wait for the pitch. I set my feet. The ball looks as big as a basketball coming in. I can see the slow rotation of a curveball, but it's aimed at my head. I fight the urge to bail out and wait for the break. Then, as it drops over the plate, I swing with all my might, my hips and shoulders working together with the power of a well-oiled pile driver. The crack of the bat sends electricity through the crowd.

"That ball is well hit," Allen screams. "Ted Willliams goes back to the wall." I hold my breath. "Williams looks up. That ball is going… going… gone, a home run!

I break into my homerun trot. The fans explode with delirious cheers. I laugh with delight as Mantle himself hugs me when I cross the plate with the winning run.

"Just what is so funny, young man?" booms Mr. Goldfarb.

The cheers disappear, replaced by stifled snickers from my classmates. I look up from my desk to see Mr. Goldfarb standing above me, one hand on his hip, his index finger wagging in front of my nose.

"Wipe that smile off your face!"

I try, but a drop of his spittle hits me in the face and I burst into laughter. "All right. That's it. You're out."

Goldfarb, a bony man with fingers of steel, grabs me behind the neck and levitates me from my chair.

"What's this?" he says and lifts my precious Mickey Mantle card off of my prayer book. He flexes it between his fingers. I pray he doesn't rip it, making it worthless, but I say nothing.

"I'm sorry," is all I can manage. I reach for my card, the pride of my collection, but he snatches it away. "You'll get this back at the end of the year," he says.

Yeah, and pigs are kosher.

Goldfarb drags me to the front of the class by my neck, kicks open the door, and shoves me into the hall.

"You stay there until I come for you," he says to the laughter of my classmates. Then he slams the door in my face. Goldfarb loves to play this little game. He never hits you. That would be too easy. Instead he leaves you in the hall for the Rabbi. If Goldfarb lets you back into the class before the Rabbi catches you, you live another day.

My heart shrivels in my chest. I hide between the narrow strip of wall between the closed classroom door and the Rabbi's office. If Rabbi Weiss finds out I've been kicked out again it's the end of me for sure. I stand silently, glued to the wall, a lump in my throat. I hold my breath and listen to the gentle murmur from behind his closed door. *He must be on the phone.*

"Yes, two dozen luluvs is good. Fresh ones, you hear? And I'll pay ten dollars each and not a penny more. And I expect your usual donation to the Rabbi's fund." He hangs up the phone and starts to hum Hava Nagila.

I rub my cheek. I can almost feel the sting of the back of Weiss' hand. A smack won't be half as bad as the pain of seeing my father's disappointed face.

From within the Rabbi's office I hear the squeak of a swivel chair, then heavy steps towards the door. *How can I be a major league hitter with my arms twisted out of their sockets?*

The door opens. I close my eyes and imagine Nan Zucker crying at my funeral. The phone rings again. I open one eye and see the tips of Weiss' perfectly polished black loafers.

"Interruptions. Always interruptions," he murmurs. The shoes pivot and disappear back into his office.

"I thought I told you never to call me here," he whispers. Then a pause and the door closes again.

For God's sake get it over with! String me up by my thumbs, flay me alive, pluck out my eyeballs. Don't make me wait out here on the edge of the crater of hell. Will I be buried with my Mickey Mantle card? And who'll inherit my comic books? I try using telepathy to summon my 137 pound savior, but the door to the classroom remains closed, as invulnerable as Superman's Fortress of Solitude.

Please, Mighty Goldfarb come for me now. I swear by all that's holy to never laugh in your class again.

I sneak down the hall to the boy's bathroom and hide, my mind seething with escape plans. Ten minutes later I hear a door slam and heavy steps advance towards my temporary enclave. The whistled refrains of Hava Nagila grow louder. I scamper into a bathroom stall, shut the door, and hold my breath. The polished black loafers appear in the stall beside me. The Hava Nagila stops, replaced by the sounds of a man content on his throne. I step onto the toilet and crouch, my torn Converse sneakers hugging each side of the rim in a frenzied fight for survival. I wonder if it's a sin to pray in the bathroom. I'm turning blue, but I can't take a breath. I think of JFK's funeral, think of my Mother crying—anything to keep from laughing.

The sound of natural gas escapes from the stall beside mine. I clasp my nose and mouth to stop my howls but tears fill my eyes and my insides are about to explode. All is quiet for a minute. I remove my hands from my mouth. I take a tiny breath. I've got myself under control. I think I'll survive.

Then "Oy...Vey is Meer..."

Suddenly it's as if Mt. Vesuvius has erupted. My chest heaves. Both hands over my mouth cannot stem the tide. Laughter escapes me like water breaks through a dam that's been breached. I'm shaking so hard that my feet slip from their perch. My right foot lands in the toilet bowl. I freeze. The toilet bowl next door flushes. I wait to see Weiss's head appear over the side of the stall, but I see nothing. The Hava Nagila resumes, then sounds of receding footsteps... the close of a door.

Could it be the Rabbi's half deaf? Perhaps God does intervene in daily life.

I sneak back to the classroom thinking that by now Goldfarb will let me back in. Rabbi Weiss's door is closed, but as I take my position between the Rabbi's office and the classroom, the Rabbi's door opens a crack and a deep voice says,

"Can I see you for a moment, Shmulie, if it's not too much trouble?" I enter the Rabbi's office with my eyes on the floor. Weiss lets me wait while he finishes reading a page from a Talmudic text open on his desk.

He's short and squat, powerfully built for a Rabbi. His head seems to blend with his chest as if God forgot to give him a neck. "So, my boy, kicked out again?" He strokes his beard and shakes his head.

I take a deep breath. *Maybe he's in a good mood today.* "Yes, Rabbi."

His smile broadens, revealing worn yellowed teeth like the jaws of an aging shark.

"What'd you do this time?"

I edge imperceptible towards the door. *If I run would he catch me?* As if he can read minds, he stands, walks past me, and shuts the door.

"I laughed, Sir."

"You laughed? I see." Again he strokes his beard and nods, contemplating my fate as if Solomon the Wise never had such a difficult decision.

"Shmulie, Shmulie, Shmulie. What will I do with you?"

"I shrug." *Let me live another day... I hope.*

His face is so close I can smell his cigar breath. The muscles of his huge jaw bulge as if he's working up to a snack.

I back towards the closed door.

"Don't be frightened," he says, advancing towards me, his smile gone. He places a meaty paw against my cheek. "I know you won't give Goldfarb any more trouble."

"No, Sir," I say and nod.

"Shmulie was my father's name," Weiss says with a grin. He drops his hand from my cheek. *He's letting me go!* I start towards the door, but a flesh colored blur crashes into the side of my face. I try to stand but my legs collapse.

"I think we understand each other now," he says. Then he sits and begins reading his text, ignoring me sprawled on the floor.

I feel the taste of blood in my mouth. I struggle to stand, fighting back the tears that are blurring my vision.

"I'm glad we had this little chat," Rabbi Weiss says, his smile gone.
I nod, edge out the door. My watch face is broken. I run the three blocks to my apartment building, tears streaming down my face, spitting blood, and swearing to never again set foot in a house of worship.

❖   ❖   ❖   ❖   ❖

"Why are you crying?" My father asks the moment he gets home from work.
"I got hit."

He sits next to me on the couch. "Who did this?" he asks, his lips drawn, his eyes full of concern.

"Rabbi Weiss," I say quietly, avoiding my father's gaze.

My father's eyes bulge as if he's been choked. He swallows hard. "The Rabbi did this?" he mutters. I nod, content that now at last justice will be done. I imagine Weiss in solitary confinement.

"And what did **you** do?" my father asks, a frown creasing his forehead.

"I didn't do anything."

"You did nothing and he hit you?"

I nod.

My father glances at my mother who stands by his side, her face pale as New York snow before the soot turns it gray.

"The Rabbi's a learned man," my father says. He wouldn't hit you without a reason." My mother puts a hand to the side of her face.

I shrug, still believing my parents will have the Rabbi arrested.

"I laughed."

"You laughed at a Rabbi? Unthinkable!"

My mother bites her lip, but says nothing.

I stare into my father's face. *How could he side with Weiss?*

"I'm never going back!" I say, tears filling my eyes, my swollen lip throbbing. "I hate that place."

"You'll go back tomorrow and apologize to Rabbi Weiss," he says, his face turned to stone.

I can't speak; I'm trapped in a nightmare.

"You have no respect. When I was a boy no one ever insulted the Rabbi. My father would have beaten me with his belt. Why can't you be more like your brother? He never gets into such trouble."

Even now, when I need my family's help more than ever, those memories linger. And that wasn't the last run in with Goldfarb either, nor the last time I disappointed my father, not by a long shot.

"So, it's settled," my father says, as soon as we're in his apartment.

"You'll go see your brother tomorrow. Josh is still the best trial attorney in Manhattan, whether you like it or not." I fight the urge to roll my eyes.

"From where I stand you need all the help you can get."

Part 5

After a sleepless night I head down towards Josh's office, replaying my father's words again and again: *"Why couldn't you be more like your brother. He's still the best attorney in New York, whether you like it or not."*

The faded card my father gave me read 107 Fifth Avenue, one of the ritziest addresses in Midtown Manhattan. The case against me seems ridiculous, yet without a good lawyer, I know I'm in big trouble.

"I'm here to see Josh Rappinsky," I say to the security guard at the front desk as I hand him my brother's card.

He turns it over, a puzzled look on his face.

"I'm afraid Mr. Rappinsky hasn't worked here in 2 years."

I track my brother down to a run down office building in the lower east side. I hadn't seen him in almost twenty years, not since I married Brit, and the interminable rift with my family began. His clothes are immaculate as ever, his hair a little thinner than I remembered, but my eyes are drawn to the tremor in his hand as he reaches out to shake mine. The years have not been kind to Josh: a broken marriage, disowned by his kids, ethics violations with the New York Bar.

His manner remains reserved as always, the curl of his upper lip a match to his condescending manner. To my relief he dispenses with the small talk and gets right down to work.

"Your problem must be pretty bad to look me up," he says.

I lay out my troubles in a strained voice, my hands darting like sparrows. I detail my fainting spell at the smell of urine in my old building the previous day, continuing right up to my debacle in Fort Tryon Park. He stares at me without blinking.

"The cop caught you with your arms around a Down's kid in the park?"

"I told you, a pitbull was stalking him, about to rip him to shreds. I distracted the dog by throwing him my pastrami sandwich, and carried the kid to safety. For my efforts I should get a medal. Instead the DA called me a child molester."

"Alleged child molester, there's a difference. And despite the absurdity of the whole thing, you've got to mount a defense."

"So, you'll help me?" I say, holding his gaze. I don't have much money, and Brit's not talking to me."

"We'll see, he says. "You get what you pay for. I haven't tried a case in five years."

"But Dad said you're still the best attorney in New York."

He chuckles and rubs the back of his neck. "In his mind I can't do anything wrong."

I take a deep breath. *And he thinks I can't do anything right.*

Two days later I meet with Josh again. He looks as if he's come back from a funeral. "What's wrong?" I ask.

"What's wrong? **What's wrong?** He repeats, his voice rising. "You didn't tell me the kid was the nephew of Rabbi Weiss."

"I didn't know," I said, my eyes wide. "Does that matter?"

"Everything matters when there are no witnesses, and the kid can't talk. Character can make or break this case and Weiss is testifying against you."

I never thought I'd hear that name again, let alone face him in court as my accuser. My long list of run-ins with the man rises before me. I sink into a chair.

❖　❖　❖　❖　❖

A week later, I sit in the front row of the courtroom with Josh beside me. The room is packed. My father sits in the back row, his face a hardened mask. I catch the gaze of Rabbi Weiss, but his eyes dart away. He is older, and his hair now snow white. But the disdain in his eyes makes the small hairs on the back of my neck stand on end.

The DA lays out his case, efficiently reiterating the facts. The arresting officer parrots the DA. "I caught the defendant kidnapping a child," he says. The grand jury sits stone-faced.

"Circumstantial," Josh mutters. I picture a door slamming closed in my darkened cell. Josh had refused to let me take the stand in my own defense. *And they never looked for the dog.*

"The state calls Rabbi Weiss."

Weiss dredges up a series of my childhood indiscretions.

"In all my years as an educator this boy was the worst child that ever went through Inwood Talmud Torah Hebrew School."

He hashes up episodes any normal person would have long forgotten. He makes my youthful rebellions sound like diabolical indiscretions of a depraved maniac.

"Shmulie Rappinsky did not deserve to have a Bar Mitzvah. He routinely broke the Shabbat. He ate non-kosher food in front of the synagogue. He couldn't even recite the morning prayers. He had no respect for authority."

That was thirty years ago.

Josh rises slowly when the DA sits. Weiss eyes him suspiciously and shifts in his seat.

"So Rabbi Weiss, we all can sympathize with the difficulty of teaching young children, and I sense your frustration. But that was long ago and Samuel Rappinsky, although not observant, has led an exemplary life. He's married and holds a teaching position in the New London School system."

At least for now.

"A man who turns his back on his family and his people is still a bum."

I roll my eyes, and again glance at my father in the back row. I imagine him running forward and lifting Rabbi Weiss out of his seat by the lapels of his Armani suit.

"Mr Rappinsky tells me you beat him in Hebrew School."

Rabbi Weiss feignes indignation. "Never."

"He says you regularly bullied and slapped the students."

Weiss strokes his chin. "Children need a firm hand. They need discipline. I was trying to prepare the next generation to carry on our traditions. But I never, ever raised a hand to any child."

I glance at my father who covers his eyes with his hand.

"Even so Rabbi, in America one is presumed innocent until proven guilty. And your testimony, damaging as it is, does not prove guilt. Why are you so bent on destroying my client?"

Weiss stands in the witness box, his jaw muscles bulging, his mouth contorted in a smirk.

He looks around the room. Then he points an accusatory finger in my direction.

"I'm sure of his guilt because my nephew told me what happened."

Josh takes a step backwards as if he'd been slapped. "I'm told the boy is mute," he says.

Weiss' lips form a tight-lipped smile, not unlike the sardonic snarl I remembered when he'd haul me out of class all those years ago.

"He makes himself understood with gestures. I understand him completely. He told me Shmulie Rappinsky accosted him in the park. Rappinsky deserves to be put away for good."

Pandemonium erupts in the courtroom. The judge pounds his gavel. I feel as if I'm suffocating.

The hint of a smile plays at the corners of Josh's mouth.

"So, Rabbi Weiss, you'd have us believe that on the strength of your word as a man of the clergy that Shmulie Rappinsky is guilty?"

"I'd stake my reputation on it."

A roaring headache pounds in my temples. *That's what I get for using my own brother. I'll be seventy before I get out.*

But instead of looking defeated my brother bounces and whirls as if he has no doubt of my innocence. I was waiting for some brilliant bit of oration, something to make the grand jury doubt a man whose list of academic pursuits and rabbinical scholarship put him on the short list as the next chancellor of Yeshiva University.

"The defense rests," is all Josh says. "But we reserve the right to continue tomorrow, and we have some additional witnesses to disclose to the court."

Outside my father is waiting, his old Chevy idling at the curb, his eyes full of pain.

"I didn't do it," I say.

My father's eyes narrow. "Please, don't say another word. Just get in the car."

Part 6—Conclusion

My father and I ride home in silence. That night I barely sleep. The next day the grand jury would determine whether or not to try me as a child molester. *How under God's heaven have my youthful transgressions come to this?* Finally, near dawn, I drift into a nightmare-ridden sleep.

I stand alone in an empty courtroom. A voice from the heavens intones, "The Supreme court in now in session."

My accuser, Rabbi Weiss, in his best Yom Kipper kittle, wags a finger in my face.

"Shmulie Rappinsky, you were the most pathetic excuse for a Hebrew School Student I have ever seen."

I try to protest but my words dry up in my throat. Weiss' spittle hits me square in the face.

"We have prepared a 5 count indictment:"

"1) You willfully disregarded the laws of the Sabbath by playing Little League instead of attending Junior Congregation." *I couldn't help it.*

"2) You preferred stickball to the study of Chumash." *I couldn't help it.*

"3) You laughed at your teachers." *I couldn't help it*

"4) You disobeyed your father so many times he gave up on you." *I shouldn't have.*

At this point a divine voice intervenes, which sounds amazingly like my father's, **"You married outside your religion."**

I rise to protest, but find I have lost my voice. I stumble backwards as if I've been hit with a sledgehammer, beads of sweat covering my forehead. *Ten years together, and she doesn't even return my phone calls.*

"There's still time."

My mind reels. *What can it all mean?*

"There's still time!"

I sit bolt upright in bed, my eyes wide, unsure for the moment where I am. My father stands motionless at the foot of my bed.

"Shmulie, you'll be late for the trial. There's still time."

I wipe the sleep from my eyes. "My name is Sam," Dad.

The second day of the grand jury trial convened. When the prosecution called Rabbi Weiss again he nearly vaulted to the stand.

I stare at the age spots on the back of his hand. The memory of his forced smile rises before me.

The fact that I was on trial for child molestation while this monster was testifying against me made me want to retch. *I wonder if he knows how many of his students have lost their faith. With all the kind, supportive Rabbis I know in New London, how is it possible that a man like Weiss flourishes? How many young Jews has he turned against religion in the name of his discipline?*

Meanwhile my father sits in silence in the back row, his eyes bloodshot, his face worried.

Josh sits quietly at my side. Is his enigmatic smile the practiced facade of a brilliant lawyer, playing his hand perfectly, or rather the phony veneer of an incompetent, washed-up hack? The next few hours will tell. And where are the witnesses for my defense? Why had Josh refused to discuss his plans? My brother's jest, "You get what you pay for," only heightened my angst. And his refusal to put me on the stand in my own defense irked me to no end. What did he mean when he said, "Sam, you were always your worst enemy."

Weiss continues his diatribe against me, as if my indiscretions as a Hebrew school student had been uniquely responsible for the assimilation of the American Jewish community. And his accusations, that I kidnapped and molested his mute handicapped nephew, seem more and more like the ranting of a desperate man.

Finally Josh rises.

"So, Rabbi, you'd have us believe that on your interpretation of your nephew's gestures we should convict Samuel Rappinsky and send him to prison."

I glance towards my father who sits stone faced, listening to the Rabbi's venom.

"A rotten apple spoils the whole bunch," Weiss says, smirking, his gaze blazing on my forehead.

"I see," Josh mumbles, his smile gone. "Unfortunately for your brand of justice, who is rotten is yet to be determined. Rabbi Weiss, we want the truth, only the truth."

Had I been such a disappointment? I knew marrying Brit would strain our family bonds, but ten years without a phone call from my father seems excessive. Brit hadn't returned any of my phone calls. Does she even know I've been arrested?

"You can't handle the truth!" Weiss yells as he pounds his hand with his fist. "Assimilation is finishing the job that Hitler started. Before long there won't be a Jewish people."

The courtroom is stiflingly warm with grime caked windows last opened during the forties. As Weiss continues he rolls up the sleeves of his dress shirt.

As I stare at Rabbi Weiss I notice the faded number tattooed on his forearm. The skin is scarred and hairless, as if a failed attempt at cosmetic surgery could not erase the sign of this man's torment. *Is that really what this is all about?* I place a hand to my forehead and sink deeper into my chair. To my recollection I had never seen the number on Weiss arm. *Had he always worn long sleeves when he ran the Hebrew School?* A door opens at the rear of the courtroom. I turn to find the source of the commotion. Three men file in quietly. They look in my direction. One man dressed in Buddhist robes waves. Something about them tweaks my memory, as if I'd known them many years earlier, yet I can't place their faces. Rabbi Weiss stops in mid-sentence and follows the men with his eyes, his mouth agape.

"Who are they?" I whisper to Josh.

Josh covers his mouth. He leans towards me. "Don't tell me you don't recognize your Hebrew School classmates."

Again the door opens and a slender silver-haired woman enters. Her face is hardened as if to ward off great pain.

"And that's the former Mrs. Weiss," Josh continues. Rumor has it she divorced the old goat ten years ago claiming physical abuse. His kids won't even speak to him."

Rabbi Weiss' face has gone pale. His words trail off in a whisper.

"The defense may cross examine," the judge intones.

Josh rises and saunters towards Rabbi Weiss' subdued figure.

"What would you say if I told you we have witnesses who will testify that you brutalized the children at the Hebrew School you administered between 1960 and 1967?"

Weiss says nothing.

"And what would you say if we were prepared to have your former wife testify to your violent temper."

Again, Weiss says nothing. He stares towards the silver-haired woman as if she were an apparition.

The door at the rear opens and Mr. Rubin, my fifth grade teacher slips in. "We will present a former public school teacher who will testify that Mr. Sam Rappinsky was one of the best English students he ever had, and that the students from your Hebrew School were some of the brightest children he ever taught at P.S 152.

Before Weiss can answer Josh motions towards a guard at the back of the courtroom. He opens the door and a young boy with the look of a Down's child enters flanked by a man and a woman who, by the way they lovingly hold the boys hands, must be the boy's parents. The boy lets go of their hands, runs to my side and lays his head on my shoulder. Suddenly the room sounds more like opening day at Yankee Stadium than a courtroom.

The judge pounds his gavel. "Silence! Order! Or I'll clear the courtroom."

"And finally, Rabbi Weiss," Josh continues when the furor dies down.

"What would you say if I told you that your nephew is here with the help of his parents to refute your testimony."

Weiss looks as if he's been shot. He motions to his attorney. Weiss whispers in the man's ear, as his attorney nods, a solemn look on his face.

"Your honor, Rabbi Weiss wishes to withdraw his accusations," the attorney says.

"In that case I have no other recourse, but to acquit. Case dismissed. Mr. Rappinsky you have thirty days to file a motion against Rabbi Weiss for perjury.

Well-wishers surround me as if I'd won the Nobel Prize. I glance around to see Mr. Rubin talking to my father. My father's face is slack. Rubin talks while gesticulating in my direction. Josh walks over and whispers something in my father's ear. They fight through the crowd and exit the back door.

Outside Rubin, Josh, the three Hebrew School buddies, and my father are standing together. I fight my way through the crowd. Finally I stand before them. My father looks as if he is really seeing me for the first time.

"I'm sorry," he says. "I've misjudged you."

"I'm sorry too," I say. We embrace.

A taxi pulls up to the curb. A beautiful woman pays the fare and gets out. It's Brit. I can see she's been crying.

"Am I too late?" she says.

"No, my darling, it's never too late. I'd like you to meet my father."

With hope in my heart I turn towards my father. He hesitates for a moment, while I hold my breath. Then he opens his arms and gives her an awkward hug.

"We have a lot of catching up to do," he says.

"There's nothing I'd like more," Brit says.

Later, at a quiet moment at my father's house, my father sits down beside me.

"So, Josh tells me you could prosecute Rabbi Weiss for perjury. Would you really do such a thing?"

I laugh, and shake my head. "Not really."

"Because you don't want to go through the ordeal?"

"No, quite the contrary. I'd love to turn the tables. It's just that most of what happened back then was kid stuff, and actually Rabbi Weiss described it pretty accurately. There comes a time when you've got to let go of old hurts. And I never knew he was a survivor of Aushwitz. He never talked about it in front of his students."

My father nods. "Sam, there's one more thing I want to ask you in private before you head back to Connecticut." He glances at Brit.

"Anything you can say to me, you can say to Brit." She puts a hand on my shoulder.

He shrugs. "Well, all right then. Do you think Brit would ever...you know, would she ever…"

"Would she ever what?" I say.

"Would she ever…you know… convert to Judaism while I'm still alive."

I blink rapidly, my pulse racing. *Just like my father to get right to the point.*

I cough, trying to respond, but I stammer horribly.

Brit puts a finger to my lips. She smiles. "I might consider it."

"After all this time? Why didn't you say so?" I sputter.

"Samuel Rappinsky, you never really asked me. And especially now that there's someone else in the picture, who knows?" She smiles again, one of those enigmatic smiles that made me fall in love with her in the first place.

"What do you mean? There's someone else," I say, bristling.

"Sammy, I'm two months pregnant," she says. I've had my head in a bucket for the past four days. Why do you think I put the answering machine on? I came to New York as soon as I got your messages. I'm so sorry you had to go through this all yourself."

My jaw gapes open. My eyes are moist. I feel as if my head is going to explode, but there's a sense of immense pleasure growing in my chest. I glance over at my father, who is grinning from ear to ear.

"So I'll have a grandchild," he mumbles. "If it's a boy he'll have a bris."

Brit laughs. "We'll see, Mr. Rappinsky. Some things are God's to decide."

"Please, Brit, call me Dad."

CHAPTER 5

HOLIDAY BLUES

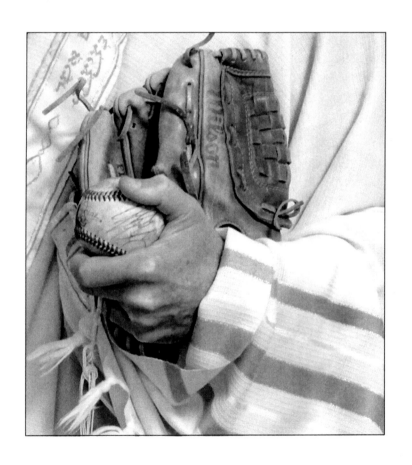

A PASSOVER STORY

The day before Pesach was a busy one in the Katzburg household. Josh and Michelle were thrilled to host although the work would be endless. Like so many modern day families the Katzburgs had become used to their scattered family. Jacob lived in Chicago, Rebecca in London, and their youngest, Isaac, lived in L.A. He attended the San Jose School for Comparative Religion when he wasn't backpacking the Himalayas or hitchhiking through Europe. Yet, on this particular Pesach, they were all going to be together.

As the day wore on the preparations intensified. Josh set the table and Michelle began to bring out the delicacies of a bygone era: stuffed derma, pickled herring, gefilte fish made from scratch, and the always popular brisket a la Michelle, made with raisons and cinnamon. Of course, this year she had added a series of tofu based concoctions in honor of her returning children, vegans one and all.

The phone rang a few minutes past noon. Josh swallowed hard as soon as he heard the raspy voice he knew all too well. "It's Dad. He's coming tonight. Something about giving me a gift."

Michelle nodded, but Josh noted the way her lower lip trembled when she forced a smile. As the patriarch of the family, Abe Katzburg could always be relied upon to share his opinions at any family gathering. With his heavy Austrian accent, his often-repeated stories of the holocaust, and the faded number on his forearm, he stood in strict contrast to his more liberal grandchildren.

"I hope he doesn't get into it with Isaac over his Palestinian girlfriend," Michelle said to Josh as she mixed the marror.

He smiled and came up behind her, placing an arm around her waist.

"I'll talk to Dad. But, you know, when a man gets to be 90, there's no telling what he might say or do."

She nodded and took a deep breath, letting it out slowly. "I don't want him upsetting the kids. They are who they are. Why try to change them with stories of the past?"

Josh kissed the back of her neck. She wriggled away, her hands smeared with chopped apple and nuts.

"The kids will be here any minute. Go chop the bitter herbs instead," she said, laughing, as she motioned him towards the cutting board.

As Josh chopped he pictured the previous year's Seder with its verbal fireworks, and a gnawing anxiety chewed at his insides. *Please, Dear God, get me through this evening.*

As Isaac walked up the driveway of his parents' home, dueling emotions rose in his mind. It had been a year since they'd last seen each other. They used Skype once a month, and as long as they didn't talk about his choice in women they had peace—a cold peace, but a peace nevertheless. Isaac raised his hand to ring the bell of his childhood home. His throat felt parched, and a sinking sensation gripped his insides as he heard his father's familiar footsteps approaching on the other side of the door. He thought of his family gathered around the Seder table, gorging on food, celebrating their ancient rites, while draught stricken refugees in Africa were starving. *Dear God, if you exist, get me through this evening.*

Abe Katzburg got out of the taxi with effort. At 90 my children should come to me, he mused. Still, as hard as it was to make the trip from Miami, at his stage of life there was no telling how many Passovers he'd have to set things right.

"Why the sad face, mister?" the taxi driver said in a Russian accent. Abe's eyes glimmered. He took a cloth handkerchief from his pocket and blew a note that rivaled a shofar blast.

"You wouldn't understand," Abe said, picturing his doctor's face when he delivered the latest bit of bad news.

"It's not easy to admit you've been a liar all your life."

The taxi driver carried Abe's bag and set it beside the front door while Abe shuffled forward.

"Just be ready to come back in an hour if I call you."

Abe knocked on the door with a fist covered with age spots, and waited for the door to open. *Dear God, please get me through this Passover.*

Isaac and his grandfather, Abe, spent most of the afternoon debating the changes in the Arab World.

"Why do you always interpret world events by their impact on Israel," Isaac said in exasperation. He waited for Abe's response, his anger rising until, glancing over, he realized that the gentle murmur was his grandfather's slumber.

By eight Josh called his family to the table. "Let's start the Seder," he said. As was their custom the Katzburg family took turns reading from the Haggadah.

"We were slaves in Egypt and God took us out with a mighty hand."

"And Pharoh assigned heavy labors," Rebecca read.

"We should each feel as if we were redeemed from Egypt," Abe continued. "I know what it's like to be a slave."

He noticed the scoffing expression on Isaac's face as he passed the Haggadah, but Abe said nothing. Soon it was time for the four questions.

"You're still the baby," Rebecca said to Isaac.

Instead of reading, Isaac put his hands up to get everyone's attention. "I don't see the relevance of reliving an ancient story when there's no evidence it ever happened."

Abe put a hand to his chest as if he'd been stabbed. He glanced at his son, Josh, and for a moment held his gaze, until Josh flushed and looked away. Abe held his anger in check and pointed to the Haggadah. "Just the same, make an old man happy. Do the four questions for us, won't you?" he said in a tone that was hard to refuse.

Isaac took a deep breath and rolled his eyes as if dealing with a child.

"How can we celebrate our freedom when the Palestinians have no hope in Gaza?" Isaac said, his eyes flashing.

"Is that what they teach you in that fancy university?" Abe said under his breath.

"Please don't make a scene," Josh said, his lips pursed, staring first at Isaac, and then at Abe.

"I'll do the Questions," Rebecca said.

When she continued with the story of the wicked son, Abe tried not to think of his grandson. Later as they ate the meal Abe felt a gnawing pain down his left arm.

"Dad you look a little pale," Josh said.

"It's just my arthritis acting up," Abe said, rubbing his elbow. "I'm fine." But, when he thought no one was looking, he popped a tiny pill beneath his tongue.

The Seder continued. Isaac made sure to drink four full cups of wine, and his earlier defiance seemed to fade.

Abe sat beside Isaac. "So tell me about graduate school," he said. Isaac spoke at great length.

"How will you make a living teaching Comparative Religion?" Abe said, ignoring Isaac's murderous stare. "I never had a chance to study. Hitler took that from me. Just like he took my first wife and my daughter."

Abe's eyes became unfocused. He continued to pour out his memories. Josh's eyes fluttered and then narrowed. Within a minute his head slumped forward and he fell into a deep sleep. Whether it was the wine or the fact that Josh had heard Abe's stories one time too many, who can say? One by one the grandchildren made excuses to leave the Seder table. Rebecca had a headache. Jacob had jet lag and went to bed early. Michelle went into the kitchen to start on the dishes.

By the time they were ready for Elijah's cup only Isaac and Abe remained. Isaac went down the hall and opened the front door. When he returned Abe cleared his throat.

"Hitler never took my first wife and he never took my daughter," Abe croaked, in a feeble voice.

Isaac's eyes flew wide, for his grandfather's lost family had long been a taboo subject.

"Grandpa, what are you saying? Of course you lost your family."

Abe put a hand to his forehead. "No, that's just what I told you and your father. My first wife left me in '48 and moved to Jerusalem with our daughter."

Isaac's mouth sagged open. He sat silently for a long while.

"Why tell us now, Grandpa?"

"My first wife died last month, without ever talking to me again."

"I'm sorry," Isaac mumbled.

"So am I, but I came from Miami to tell you face to face while I still have the chance. I've lived a lie."

Isaac waited, while Abe struggled to get out the words.

"...I got a letter from my daughter. We've been in touch. She wants to reunite with my side of the family. Isaac, you have an aunt who wants to meet you."

Isaac's mind reeled.

Abe took a small sheath of faded pictures from his breast pocket. "Since you're the traveler. I want you to bring these pictures of me with my daughter as a baby to Israel. Let her know she really had a father."

Isaac stared at his grandfather, and blinked back tears. Not for the wonder of gaining an aunt or her four grown children who would be a joy to Isaac for the rest of his life. The tears were instead for his tortured grandfather, who, true to his reputation, had turned yet another Pesach on its ear.

THE SEDER MUST GO ON

"The Seder starts on time, no matter what," Grandpa Rosensweig said. "That's the way it's always been, and that's the way it's got to be now. If our people let hardships stop them in the desert where would we be?"

Then Charley heard a click. "Must be trouble with the satellite," he said to his wife, Amy, who was staring at him from the other room with that "Can't we stay home just this once," look on her face.

The winter had been one of the worst on record: snow piled five feet high, subzero temps, winds buffeting those brave enough or foolish enough to venture outside.

"Who ever heard of holding a Seder in a snowstorm?" She said, "and in April no less."

Charlie shook his head slowly. "I know, I know, but it's just that he's..."

"Rich," Amy said without a smile.

"I was going to say old. He means no harm, and he's the only Rosensweig left from the family that survived the war."

Amy tapped her foot slowly; she'd heard the shpiel before, how grandpa walked twelve miles in a snowstorm to escape the Nazi's and then crossed the Alps into Switzerland on foot. He told that story every Passover and, no doubt, they'd be hearing it again...that is if they made the 60 mile drive in a blizzard.

"Besides, David's applying to grad school next year, wouldn't it be nice if Grandpa helped with the tuition?"

Amy bit her lip. She thought of all the times Grandpa Rosensweig threatened cutting off her husband's inheritance if he so much as disagreed with the overbearing patriarch.

"Why does he insist on reading the entire Seder himself in Hebrew? Why stay up 'till one in the morning, and then drive through the night just to please him?"

"Look, David's taking the train from Philly direct to Penn station and then the LIRR right out to Grandpa's. How would it look if he goes and we don't show up?"

"What if no one else shows up?" Amy said. "You'll risk the LIE in a blizzard for nothing."

"You know the rest of the family will be there, they all live out on the Island."

And so it was that Charlie and Amy headed out for the Seder in a freak snowstorm.

"God help us," Charlie muttered under his breath, as soon as they got out of the garage.

189

The trip that normally took an hour took three. The roads were awful. They careened out of control three times, dug themselves out of a snow bank once, and arrived at Grandpa Rosensweig's only fifteen minutes late. Charlie's hands were half frozen, his face beet red.

"Well, it's about time," Grandpa Rosensweig said, pointing to his watch. "Everyone else is here, except your son, David."

❖ ❖ ❖ ❖ ❖

When David got off the train the wind was howling. Ice pellets peppered his face. He wanted to run to the taxi stand to make sure he got one, but he stopped to help an elderly lady, who was struggling with her suitcase. As he reached the taxi stand he saw the last one drive away.

David stood under the overhang of the station, buffeted by the storm, waiting for another taxi to arrive. He tapped his foot and checked his watch, mulling over his conversation with his father the previous night. "Don't embarrass me in front of Grandpa, and for heaven's sake be on time."

The memory of the previous year's Seder rose in his mind. He pictured the way his grandfather's jugulars stood out on his face when the topic of his studying Creative Writing was raised. Then came the argument that erupted over Israel and the West Bank...*what a disaster. Perhaps I should stay away from politics this year.*

David checked his cell phone...*I'm late already.*

His thoughts ran to his recent discussion with his college advisor.

"Be true to yourself," the man had said, as if that would wipe away David's angst over choosing a career.

"Just remember, life is not a dress rehearsal."

As David shivered he pictured himself in a big downtown law firm, corner office, secretaries and junior partners hanging on his every word. Was that his father and grandfather's dream, or his? A sinking feeling came over him and for a moment he felt as if he were free falling in the runaway elevator of his life. He stamped his feet. He blew into his hands—still no taxi.

Then a car horn blared. The window of a black Cadillac with fins opened. "Hey, young man, where are you going?" said the old lady whose bags he had carried. David gave the address. "Get in," said the woman. It's not far from my home."

❖ ❖ ❖ ❖ ❖

The old lady pulled the ancient Cadillac to the corner and David got in.

"This is awfully nice of you," he said, brushing the snow from his coat.

"I don't want to miss my family's Seder."

"It's nothing. Vere I come from ve help von another," she said with a sad smile, in an accent that spoke of another world.

"Are you a student?"

He nodded. "I want to be a writer."

"Very ambitious. My first love vas a writer," she said. "But he never finished anything. Became a businessman. Pity really."

David studied her face as they talked. Despite the lines and the features that gravity was reclaiming, he could tell that she was once quite beautiful.

"My family wants me to study law or medicine."

"Also nice. But the world has a lot of lawyers and doctors already. Great writers…not so much," she said with a laugh that revealed a gap toothed smile with a single gold cap on a lower front tooth.

"If you are meant to write, you should write," she said. "Don't let anyone deter you. It's your life."

The snow fell in great swirling sheets, and the Cadillac slowed to a crawl, the visibility all but zero.

"Wish Grandpa Rosensweig felt the same," he said.

"He once did," she muttered in a voice too low for David to make out.

They continued to talk and by the time the car approached Grandpa Rosensweig's, David felt a bond forming with this elderly lady that would be hard to explain to his buddies back at the dorm.

"Why don't you join us at the Seder," he said, although from her accent he couldn't be sure if she was Jewish. "Mrs….?"

"My friends call me Elsa," she said, and extended a tiny gloved hand.

"Perhaps I'll stop in later. You never know. But you'd better go in. You can't keep the Seder waiting."

Once inside the family descended on David like the cloud of locusts they would soon be discussing. Elsa's Cadillac disappeared in a swirl of snow.

"Thank God you made it? What happened? Are you all right? This blizzard will last two days."

David recounted his strange odyssey.

"A black Cadillac?" Grandpa Rosensweig said with a far-away look.

The Seder began. As the wind howled outside, the Rosensweig menagerie recounted the story of the Exodus. Grandpa Rosensweig recited in Hebrew, but he hurried along with an air of distraction.

David feigned interest, but his thoughts were on his muddled future.

During the meal Grandpa began his interrogation. "So what law school is our college boy applying to?" he asked.

David glanced at his father, who shook his head ever so slightly and put an index finger to his lips.

"I'm not sure what I'm doing yet," David said in a whisper.

"There's no time to waste," Grandpa Rosensweig said. I've decided to fund your education, as long as you finish law school."

"Wonderful," said David's father.

"Fantastic," said David's mother.

David mumbled thanks, but averted his eyes from Grandpa Rosensweig's intense gaze.

"You know, I never had all the advantages you have…never got to do all the things I wanted. Had to earn a living. No one ever gave me anything. Did I ever tell you how I escaped the Nazis through the Alps?"

Before waiting for an answer Grandpa launched into his story. The family sat in silence, and listened, as they did every year, as if hearing of Grandpa's escape for the first time.

The afikoman was found, the final blessings recited, when David stood.

"I can't live a lie. I'm not going to Law School," he said in a loud voice, staring directly at Grandpa Rosensweig, who knocked over Elijah's Cup, spilling wine onto the white tablecloth.

"I want to be a writer."

Silence descended over the table. "A writer doesn't make much money," Grandpa said, his eyes flashing. "You'll starve…unless you're a great writer."

"I hope to be. I'm accepted at the UCLA program for Creative Writing."

Grandpa Rosensweig studied the determination etched in David's face. Then he looked around the table, for all eyes were watching.

"I once wanted to write," he muttered. Then he fell silent, as if mulling over his own choices in life.

Later that night David opened the family photo album that Grandpa kept in the living room. He became aware of Grandpa Rosensweig watching from the opposite corner of the room.

"Maybe you'll write my life story," Grandpa Rosensweig said. "I still want to give you that tuition money."

Grandfather and grandson sat together and poured over the photo album, Grandpa Rosensweig recalling countless relatives who perished in the War. David's attention was drawn to a faded picture of his Grandfather as a young man, with his arm around the waist of a beautiful girl, her gap toothed smile and the single gold crown on her lower front tooth impossible to ignore.

"I will write your story, Grandpa, whether you give me money or not, under one condition."

"And what might that be?" Grandpa Rosensweig said.

David tapped the picture. "I choose the subject and you tell me the truth."

For a moment David thought Grandpa Rosensweig might keel over on the spot, and renounce his promise, for his face turned purple and the neck vessels stood out from under his starched collar. But then he smiled, and calm seemed to settle on his face. "Why not?" he said at last, and put a wrinkled hand on David's shoulder. "It's never too late."

Grandpa Rosensweig sank into a chair. David closed the photo album and sat facing his grandfather.

"Tell me about the girl in that picture."

The elder Rosensweig fidgeted in his chair, his eyes darting to the photo album, while he put a trembling hand to his lips.

"I never saw that photo before...not sure how it got in the album. That was so long ago…ancient history. What difference could it make?"

David's eyes narrowed. He had heard the stories about the family's origins in Poland when he was a kid from his father—the deportations, forced marches, concentration camps—Grandpa Rosensweig's escape through the Alps. David had heard of the world left behind, the great grandparents slaughtered, the cousins never heard from again, the seething anti-Semitism that would have wiped the Rosensweig lineage off the face of the planet. But never, in all the years of family gatherings, had anyone ever mentioned the girl with the gap-toothed smile.

"Did I ever tell you how I met your grandmother while I was working at the Concord? 1947, it was, or maybe '48. I was a bus boy, she was a guest…spilled a plate of borscht on her white dress, don't think she ever fully forgave me 'till the day she died. Now there was a woman who could hold a grudge!"

"Yes, Grandpa, you told me," David interrupted, for once Grandpa got up a head of steam on a story, there was as much chance of altering the conversation as stemming the flow of the Mississippi.

"But now tell me about Elsa."

Grandpa drew in a deep breath and then coughed, a great hacking expulsion, as if he might expel a distasteful memory while clearing his airway. He drew out a handkerchief and wiped his mouth.

"How could you know her name? I've never spoken of her to anyone."

"She gave me a lift to the Seder."

Grandpa's mouth fell open and his upper denture nearly fell from his mouth.

"You are mistaken," he mumbled. "Can't be." Then he turned away from his grandson, his face pale, his hand trembling.

"She definitely knew you. Said you could have been a writer if you stuck to it."

"Feh, don't kid a kidder," Grandpa said, settling into the chair, his head leaning back. Whether it was his advanced age, the late hour, or the Seder's four cups of wine, Grandpa's eyelids drooped and he began to snore. David rose, placed a cushion beneath the old man's head and slipped out of the room. As soon as David left the room, Grandpa's eyes fluttered open, and a smile came to his lips, for the vision of young Elsa had never left his thoughts.

❖   ❖   ❖   ❖   ❖

It was long ago, the winter of 1938, to be exact, when that picture was taken of an 18 year old Aaron Rosensweig and his 2nd cousin Elsa, posing by the banks of the Danube. Grandpa Rosensweig looked down at the age spots on his hands, and the pleated reptilian skin that had lost all remnants of elasticity along his arms. He shook his head, took a deep breath, and wondered why the decay of his 90-year-old body had not muted the pain Elsa's memory still held. Although he had bottled his passions for so many years he allowed himself once again the bitter-sweet torture of remembrance….

Her parents were against it from the start. That was indisputable. They'd grown up in the same town, in the same extended menagerie of siblings and cousins and friends. In the spring of '38, they became inseparable.

"The boy's a good for nothing," Elsa's father said, the day Aaron asked for her hand. "He'll never amount to anything, never give you the finer things in life."

"But he makes me laugh, Poppa," Elsa said. "And I love him. Besides, he's a wonderful writer. He's working on a novel."

"You're not....you know…"

Elsa's eyes flashed. "No! I'm not!" But although she did not yet need larger sized dresses her clothes already felt tight across her waist.

"No matter. I forbid it!"

Aaron was despondent. Disregarding your family in matters of the heart was not easily forgiven. And so, while the Nazis were planning to annex his country, Aaron came to Elsa with a plan.

"We'll go to America," he said. "I have a friend who can get us forged papers. He'll get us a train ticket to Salzburg and then on to Brussels. From there to England and then we'll take a freighter to New York." Elsa smiled, and put her arms around his neck.

"I would follow you anywhere," she said and kissed him passionately. She was about to tell him of her condition, but then thought better of it. *I'll tell him when we're out of the country.*

A week later plans were in place.

"Meet me at the train station at 7 am and don't be late," he said.

The next morning Elsa had to wait until her parents left for work. She wrote them a note and slipped out of the house, with nothing but the clothes on her back.   Meanwhile Aaron paced back and forth on the train platform.

"Ach, 6:55. Where is she?" he muttered.

        The train pulled into the station. *Still no Elsa.*

His heart was pounding when the conductor cried, "All aboard!"

The seconds seemed hours as the station clock ticked towards 7:00. Aaron showed his papers and got aboard, his eyes still glued to the far end of the station. *Could it be she changed her mind? If I get off I'll miss my chance.*

Then, suddenly, Elsa appeared. The train began to move. Elsa ran towards the train, but the stationmaster stopped her and asked for her papers. By the time the matter was settled the train was picking up speed, with no chance for Elsa to board.

As Aaron went by he tossed Elsa's ticket out the window, and shouted, "Take the next train. I'll wait."

Whether Elsa heard he couldn't be sure.

He reached Salzburg, and spent the next 24 hours roaming around the town, for there was only one train to Salzburg each day. Finally he slept on a park bench. The next day he went to the station to wait for Elsa. His heart ached, for the thought of losing Elsa was like losing his own life.

What he couldn't have known was that although Elsa got the ticket, her father found her note about leaving the country when he came home unexpectedly at lunchtime. The family was mobilized. Her father found Elsa at the station, brought her back to the house, and locked her in her room for the next week. He ripped up the ticket to Salzburg and threw it in her face.

Aaron waited for two weeks, hoping against hope that Elsa would somehow make it to Salzburg. Finally, he lost hope. When he heard that a group of young mountaineers were taking refugees to safety across the Alps to Switzerland he scraped together every last cent that he had and joined the next group.

Through incredible hardship he made it across the Alps and eventually on to America, although his thoughts were always with Elsa. He tried to find out what happened to her, but by then the iron boot of the Nazis lay firmly across the throat of Europe. He abandoned his dreams of being a writer and never finished his novel, for Elsa had been his muse. He turned his mind towards making a fabulous living in business, wishing, perhaps subconsciously, that despite losing Elsa, he would still prove Elsa's father wrong. He never got over his hatred of cold weather and developed an obsession for being on time.

❖   ❖   ❖   ❖   ❖

A gentle hand was shaking Grandpa Rosensweig.

"Grandpa, wake up," David said. "It's midnight, time to go to bed."

"Elsa was the love of my life," Aaron Rosensweig said, feeling more energized than he had in years. "She believed in me. Wanted me to write. I want you to know all about her."

Grandfather and grandson talked half the night. "You know, it's been seventy two years to the day since she missed that train. Sometimes I still see her in my dreams."

"But Grandpa, I'm telling you, she gave me a lift to the Seder."

Grandpa Rosensweig put a hand to David's cheek. "My sweet boy. I believe you, but it couldn't be her."

"And why not?" David said.

The old man smiled sadly. Elsa died in the camps. I went back to our town after the war. Nothing was left of our houses.

"That doesn't prove anything."

The next day Grandpa Rosensweig took a long nap in the afternoon, gathering strength for the second Seder. When he didn't come down on time—most unusual, the family was worried. They found Grandpa in a fetal position, his eyes glazed. He never spoke again and when he passed away six months later David found that a trust had been established for his education many years earlier with no restrictions on his choice of career.

David dedicated his free time to researching his family tree, and eventually went back to the town where his grandfather was born. He studied what documents he could find and, to his amazement, did in fact, find that Elsa had been killed during the war. What astounded him most of all, however, was information from newly released Nazi records that showed that Elsa had born a child. And that child's name was Aaron.

The news set the Rosensweig family on fire. They hired an investigator. Little Aaron had survived the war. He was almost 70, living in Canada, a father of four, a grandfather of twelve, totally unaware of the nature of his family origins. When David and his father travelled to Ottawa to rekindle family ties, they were met with open arms at the airport by a group of twenty.

As for David, he became a novelist and a Professor of English at a prestigious

University. He published, and critiqued, and flourished. He never did find Elsa again, although for years he looked throughout his grandfather's neighborhood, showing her picture as a young woman to anyone who would listen. No one had ever heard of her.

But, in winter, when snow blankets New England, David likes to take long walks, and, with a glimmer of hope, looks for an old lady driving a black Cadillac.

The End

A Yom Kippur Tale

Part I

The phone rang. Richard hesitated, then reluctantly answered, knowing full well that anyone worth talking to would have sent a text.

The monologue began.

He slumped in his chair, immediately recognizing the sputtering voice on the other side of the line. He swallowed slowly, and stole a furtive glance at Monica, his on again off again girlfriend, sitting cross-legged on his bed.

"Yes, Mom, of course I'm going to services at Hillel this Yom Kippur," he said finally. "I would never forget."

Then came the usual barrage of probing questions that he had learned to handle with one word answers.

"So when are you going to tell Uncle Mortie you'll go out with his friend's daughter? She's right there at your college. You can't leave a nice girl like that hanging."

He pictured the last time he had seen the young woman in question, a shy girl with dark brooding eyes and a mouth full of braces.

"What part of no don't you understand?" he wanted to say, but remained silent.

"Well, anyway, you'll see her when you come home for Thanksgiving."

It was only after he ended the call that he checked the calendar on his smart phone. "I've got tickets for the Coldplay concert tomorrow night with Monica at the arena," he muttered under his breath. *I'll have to miss the concert to go to services.*

"Is something wrong?" Monica said.

A pounding headache rose in his temples. He thought of explaining 5000 years of tradition and the complex relationship he had with his parents.

"You wouldn't understand," he said at last.

"That's ok," she said. "I gotta get to class anyway." She gathered her books, and flounced out of the room, planting a peck on his cheek as she passed.

"See you at the concert tomorrow night," she said. "I've been looking forward to this all semester."

Richard nodded, avoiding her gaze. "Yup, me too," he said quietly.

"Then maybe I'll have you over to my dorm afterwards, for a midnight supper," she said.

"Uh, huh," he said, his voice cracking. "That'd be great." After she left, Richard sat on his bed wondering whether he could find a local synagogue that had afternoon Kol Nidre services. He pictured the look of disappointment on Monica's face if he dared back out of their date and a cold sweat formed on his forehead. *There has to be a way.*

Later that morning, Richard sat in the back of his math class while his calculus professor droned on about integrals.

"So the key is to define your values," the professor said. "And don't forget our next class is cancelled for observance of Yom Kippur, the Jewish holiday, so the quiz is postponed as well."

One of his non-Jewish classmates glanced at Richard and flashed a thumbs up, as if Richard's religious convictions were instrumental in the professor's decision.

"Way to go, Dick," the boy said, while Richard winced.

On his way to the cafeteria Richard's mind whirled. As a child he had strained against his parent's strict religious observance. Yet he had never, ever, entertained the possibility of missing Kol Nidre services—just as he would never think of ordering a ham and cheese sandwich with a glass of milk. It just wasn't done in his mostly Jewish suburban town. But now, away at school, with all the freedom a university education provided, the choices were not as clear.

The burly man behind the cafeteria grill turned to him as Richard neared.

"We got a special on turkey BLT."

Richard stared at the steaming grill, the rows of bacon sizzling like sirens to shipwrecked sailors.

"I'll pass today," Richard said, aware of a vague nausea.

Back at the dorm the talk was all about the upcoming concert.

"It'll be awesome," said the girl in the room next door. "Last year they played till midnight."

When Richard returned to his dorm, his roommate, Ruben, was stuffing clothes into a backpack.

"What's up?" Richard said.

"Going home for Yom Kippur. Mom would kill me if I didn't."

"You're such a wuss," Richard said, laughing.

"You're staying and going to Hillel, aren't you?" Ruben said.

"Yeah, sure," Richard said, averting his eyes.

"Well, L'Shana Tova then," Ruben said, completely serious, and stuck out his hand. Have an easy fast."

Richard shook the offered hand, smiled weakly and then patted Ruben on the back.

"If you talk to God in shul put in a good word for me, will you?"

Ruben nodded. "I'll see what I can do, but you're a difficult case."

Part II

When his roommate, Ruben, left, Richard tried to smile, yet the rising tension in his face produced no more than a sneer. He sat at his desk, turning the tickets over in his hand. He imagined sitting at the Coldplay concert with Monica that night. "We'll have a midnight supper," she had said when she left. He could only imagine what delights might follow. A cold sweat rose on his forehead. *Kol Nidre starts in three hours. ...Mom'll never know.*

He tossed the tickets onto his desk and lay down on the bed. He began to read his calculus text, for although the exam was cancelled because of the Jewish holiday, he'd have to take the exam the following day. His eyelids began to droop as he read the algebra that so often put him to sleep. *First define your values.* He struggled and the numbers began to swim on the page. The book fell to the floor and Richard began to dream.

His mother was dressed in black, a soiled handkerchief held to her mouth, while his father paced the floor wearing a torn coat, as one who mourns the dead. Hung prominently on the wall above a wooden casket was a large painting of Richard at his Bar Mitzvah, on the table a newspaper with the headline "Fire at Coldplay Concert."

The door opened and a gray haired, bearded man with a face like a hawk ,entered. *Rabbi Finkelstien?*

"This boy was possibly the worst student I've had the misfortune to teach in the Hebrew School. Eats bacon, skips Kol Nidre services, goes out with all manner of women. You go into hock to send him to the finest university, and this is how he repays you. It's a shonda."

His mother began to wail. "Yes, a shonda!" she shrieked.

His father nodded, a scowl on his face. "I'll bet he didn't even fast."

The ringing cellphone woke Richard with a start.

"Hey, its Monica. Pick me up at the dorm, ok?"

He pictured Monica in the skimpy top she liked to wear on their dates. He dismissed his dream as a weakness, another example of how his parent's antiquated principles had left him a bundle of contradictions. He threw on his best pair of baggy ripped jeans, ignoring the rising tension that plagued his every decision.

As he walked across the quad in the shade of the setting sun he passed students in sports coats hurrying towards services. They glanced at him as they passed, and, although they said nothing, he chose to take a detour towards Monica's dorm to avoid the Hillel building.

Monica looked positively hot. She squeezed his arm and kissed his cheek, brushing her fingernails briefly against his chest. He forced a smile.

"Guess what I prepared for our midnight supper?" Monica said.

Richard shrugged.

"Lobster salad," she said with a triumphant jiggle of the best endowment in the university.

Richard took a deep breath and let it out slowly. If he were back at home this would be the time he and his parents and his family would be eating a big dinner before they went off to synagogue for Kol Nidre. There'd be all his favorites: roasted chicken, veal cutlets with mushroom and peppers, and his grandmother's exceptional flanken. He'd eat till near bursting to lessen the difficulty of fasting for Yom Kippur.

A high-pitched laugh escaped his lips as the memory of his dream flashed across his mind. "Midnight supper, lobster salad… how nice."

"What's wrong? You don't sound excited."

"Of course I'm excited…it's just that…"

"Just what?" she said, raising her eyebrows, the hint of her disappointment like a knife in his ribs.

"It's just this darn headache," he whimpered, placing the tips of his fingers on the sides of his temples.

"Aw, poor baby. Let Momma fix," she said in a throaty voice. She motioned to the lone chair in the room, and stood behind him while he sat. Then with strong hands she kneaded his neck. Then she ran her hands down his arms, nestling against his grateful shoulders.

"That is so much better," he purred, thoughts of chicken and flanken and the images of his grieving parents banished from his mind, at least for the moment.

She paused, and, after disappearing into the kitchenette, returned with a small bowl filled to the brim with what Richard assumed was lobster salad.

"Eat for Momma," she said, feeding him like a child and giggling, finishing off the appetizer with a brief kiss on the mouth.

"We better get going," she said after a while. "Can't be late for Coldplay."

Richard nodded and got up reluctantly, surprised by how good the lobster salad tasted. He wondered whether the Yom Kippur fast had already started, but refused to look at his watch.

"Yeah, sure, let's go," he said. As they walked through the Common he steered away from the Hillel building, taking a less traveled route to the Arena. They took their seats quickly, for the show was about to start. The lights dimmed. Multi colored strobe lights flashed across the domed ceiling. The sweet smell of forbidden substances wafted across the arena.

When an acquaintance on his right offered Richard a funny looking cigarette he took a drag, coughing and hacking at the harsh burn in his throat. A woman with tattooed arms, sitting in the row ahead, passed a bottle in a brown paper bag to Monica. She drank steadily, smacked her lips and passed the spiked wine to Richard. He drank, although the time for Kiddush at his parent's home had long since passed. The crowd began to stomp and hoot, begging for Coldplay to start.

Finally, when it seemed that the arena might erupt in a riot, one mighty bass chord rang out, followed by a long pause. Then to the screams of the crowd, a riff of such intensity erupted, that might wake Beethoven from his grave.

A swirl of fog enveloped the stage, the smell of smoke strong in Richard's nostrils, while sparks shot along the floor. The audience loved it, but Richard's pulse quickened. *Is this part of the act?*

As the band pounded out its rhythms Richard's head began to spin. He wasn't really sure whether it was the wine, the lobster salad, the smell of smoke, or thoughts of his dream that brought on his nausea. Even in the dim light Monica could sense that something was wrong when Richard doubled over, his hands over his mouth.

"I'm sick," he muttered when Monica put a hand on his shoulder.

After a few seconds of rubbing his back Monica's hand fell away and she leaned back in her seat.

"This is my favorite song," she said, her head bobbing in time to the beat. "Get into it."

The color drained from Richard's face. The room began to spin. He rose and mumbled, "I'll be back."

Monica nodded. "Do you want me to go with you?" When he shook his head no, she turned back to the stage, her face etched in ecstasy.

He jostled along the row of bouncing teens and ran to the bathroom, shutting himself in a stall. The smell of smoke was still strong when he emptied the contents of his stomach.

After missing most of the concert, he returned to the aisle where Monica stood clapping her hands and swaying.

"I've gotta go," he yelled above the music. "You can stay if you want."

Monica's rapture fell away. "No, I'll go if you want."

They left together, but the evening was ruined. Little was said on the way back to campus. He thought of recounting his dream, but Monica appeared distant.

"I'll call you," he said.

"Whatever," Monica said. Then she turned away.

Instead of a midnight supper, Richard returned alone to his dorm. He awoke on Yom Kippur morning still vaguely nauseous, and resolved not to eat for the rest of the day. He spent the afternoon shivering in bed. When he awoke in a cold sweat near evening he decided to wander down to Hillel. He arrived in time for the final Neilah service, and sat in the back. When someone put a prayer book in his hands, he opened it to the correct page and followed along. After an hour his nausea subsided.

The final shofar blast sounded. At the break-the-fast buffet he ate ravenously.

A pretty girl with dark eyes jostled against him as they both reached for the tuna salad.

"You're Richard, aren't you?" she said when he stooped to pick up her plate. Then she smiled. "I'm Rebecca."

A glimpse of this girl as a high school co-ed with braces flashed in his mind. A broad smile broke out on Richard's face. *This couldn't be the girl Uncle Morty was always talking about, could it?*

"Oh, there you are," a tall boy with terminal acne said as he maneuvered his way back to the girl's side, who still had her gaze trained on Richard.

The newly formed trio sat together in a corner, and Richard found that, try as he might, he couldn't stop staring into Rebecca's eyes.

"Why don't you meet me at the Simchat Torah party next week?" Rebecca asked both boys when they parted. "We can use some help setting up."

Conclusion

A week later Richard rose early. He leafed through his calculus textbook. As he read the symbols that used to make his eyelids droop, the equations began to make sense. He worked the problems at the end of the chapter and cross-referenced the answers.

"Not bad," he muttered. "There might be hope for me yet." At five thirty he dressed in the only dress shirt he owned and headed down to Hillel. He nodded to the students who were walking en masse towards the party.

"Chag Sameach," Ruben said, slapping him on the back, as he snuck up behind Richard.

"And to you, too, you dork," Richard said. Then his cell phone rang. It was Monica.

"Gotta take this," Richard said, "You go on ahead. I'll catch up."

"Ok, guess I can move some tables with Rebecca and Yonnie."

"I need you," Monica said in a raspy voice.

Richard hesitated. This was what he had dreamed of all semester.

"Right now," Monica said. "My roommate went home for the weekend."

Richard glanced at his watch. "I don't know. I gotta help a friend."

"So what am I, lobster salad?" she said, laughing. "Get your butt over here!"

Richard took a step towards Monica's dorm and then paused.

He glanced towards Hillel. An image of Rebecca setting up folding chairs with Yonnie, the tall pimple faced youth, rose before him. Although he tried to ignore the feeling, a growing resentment made him grind his teeth. Richard imagined himself sitting together at services with Rebecca and eating tuna fish sandwiches. She was the kind of girl you brought home to your parents. *Maybe we'd hold hands by the end of the semester.* Still, what would be the point if she was with another guy? He thought of calling Rebecca to make excuses, but realized she wouldn't have a phone on Simchat Torah…yomtov and all that. He entertained the thought of setting up tables with Rebecca and then heading over to Monica's. He glanced at his watch and thought of Monica's plea. *"I need you…"* How can I give up a sure thing? There'll always be another Jewish holiday.

He half walked, half ran to Monica's dorm, Rebecca and the Simchat Torah party all but forgotten. When he checked in at the desk a burly security guard asked for his ID. He ran a hand to his pocket with a sinking feeling in his gut. "Left it back at my room. But hey, you know me. Someone's waiting."

"You can call them to come down."

"Cell phone's back at my room."

"Well now, that certainly is a problem."

He tried to walk through the security gate, but the guard blocked his way and put a hand on his tazer gun.

"No ID, no entry."

"But I'm a student. You've checked me in ten times before. I'd have to go back across campus to get my ID. Please, this is important."

The guard smiled a gap toothed grin, a gold tooth gleaming. He gripped Richard's shoulder with the hands of a linebacker, and turned him around. "And I'm supposed to care? No exceptions!" he said.

Richard rolled his eyes. Now that he had made a choice the idea of missing out on Monica's offer turned his cheeks crimson.

"Fine," he said. Then he ran all the way back to his dorm. As he passed Hillel he heard singing. He stopped long enough to see a group of dancers run out into the street, clapping their hands in celebration. Then came his roommate, Ruben, holding a scroll while Rebecca and Yonnie linked arms and danced a wild hora as if they were possessed. Richard took a deep breath and picked up his pace. *Just as well.*

When he arrived at his room he retrieved his wallet and ID and grabbed his cell phone. The 5 new calls from his mother made the breath catch in his throat. *That's a new record.* He sat on his bed, prepared for all the recriminations that would surely follow. His mother had this thing about talking before every Jewish holiday that made him feel like a perennial five year old. *Why ruin my night with guilt?* He slipped the phone into his pocket without opening the voicemails. *I'll smooth it over later.*

On the way to Monica's dorm he paused again at Hillel. Dancers held hands in a circle, their heads thrown back in laughter, while Rebecca, Yonnie and Ruben whirled counterclockwise in the center. *Fine, they deserve one another.*

Finally, Richard arrived back at Monica's dorm. With the ID burning a hole in his pocket he waited behind 5 other students, the guard's motions deliberate and measured. Richard tapped his foot and bit his lip, glancing at his watch until finally he got through.

"It's my job," the guard said, when Richard flashed his ID and passed through the gate with a scowl on his face.

"No problem," Richard said.

"Hope she's worth it," the guard said when he thought Richard was out of earshot.

"I do too," Richard mumbled, as he repeatedly pressed the elevator button, determined not to glance back at the guard.

Alone in the elevator Richard smoothed his rumpled shirt and sniffed at the armpits, painfully aware that the run had left him gamier than a pickup basketball game at the gym.

As he approached Monica's door sounds of laughter wafted down the hall. He knocked. The laughter ceased. He hesitated, then knocked again. Footsteps sounded, punctuated by the sound of a bed frame scraping along a wooden floor. The door flew open. Monica stood before him, her hair disheveled, a half filled glass of rum in her hand.

"Thought you weren't coming," she said, her words slurred, a look of surprise on her face.

"It took longer than I thought, my ID…the guard…it's a long story."

"Yeah, well, whatever. Bruno didn't have any of those problems."

Richard looked beyond Monica to the figure reclining on the bed in the corner of the room. Immediately he recognized the brute who'd put his arm around Monica when they met on the Common.

Richard's forced smile disappeared. "I'll go."

Monica grabbed his arm. "Don't be silly. I told you I need you," she said with a seductive smile. "This is a job for two men."

Richard's heart pounded as she led him into the room. He had heard rumors about things like this, but now that it was upon him his instincts said run. *This is too crazy.*

"I thought I told you I was moving off campus."

Richard's eyes flew wide. He shook his head like a man in a trance. He stared at the packed boxes piled about the room.

"And besides, Bruno can't move all this furniture by himself."

Richard spent the next two hours struggling with furniture and boxes that would exhaust a professional mover. Monica was in the shower when the job was finally done.

Bruno pounded Richard's back and pumped his hand.

"Hey, thanks, man. You're not really that bad of a guy."

Then he led him to the door.

Monica shouted, "Call me," from the confines of the bathroom, and before Richard could respond Bruno closed the door in his face.

Richard sulked back across the Common, with nothing but a backache as a souvenir. He decided not to walk past Hillel. He plopped onto his bed and put a hand over his eyes. He pictured Rebecca and the young men at the party. *How could I have been such an idiot?*

He dozed for a while when the cell phone rang. Without thinking he answered.

"Yeah, of course I was going to call you back…no I didn't know you were trying to reach me."

There was a long pause on the other side of the line.

"Rebecca's mother's been trying to reach Rebecca since yesterday, but her phone must be off for the Jewish holiday. Uncle Morty thought you might be able to find her. She hangs out at Hillel a lot."

"I know."

"What do you mean, you know?"

"I met her last week at Hillel."

His mother's silence spoke volumes, for he'd refused to take her number from Uncle Morty often enough that he'd stopped offering.

"Richard, I'm afraid Rebecca's father had a serious heart attack. They want Rebecca at the hospital right away. Do you think you can find her?"

He hesitated. The thought of seeking out Rebecca after the way he had stood her up brought a tightness to his throat. Still, although he'd tried hard to take a walk on the wild side, inwardly he felt relieved to be free of Monica.

"Of course I'll tell her. Leave it to me."

Richard found Rebecca alone in the lounge of Hillel, folding chairs and cleaning tables after the big Simchat Torah party. She glanced up as he approached, biting her lip and then turning away. Richard said nothing, but he took the sponge from her hand and began to clean the table. They worked together for a few minutes, and the frown lines around her eyes disappeared.

He sat her down on a lounge chair and sat by her side. Then he told her, as gently as he could. He handed her his cell phone, and her eyes filled with tears.

She called home. Then she laid her head on his shoulder and cried.

"I've got a car. I'll drive you home," Richard said when her sobs ceased.

Rebecca nodded. She went to get a few things at her dorm. Richard finished cleaning up. Then he went to get his car.

Rebecca said little during the first two hours of the drive, and Richard thought it best to keep his questions to himself. They arrived at the hospital at two in the morning.

Rebecca grabbed her bag and got out of the car.

"Thanks," she said, distractedly, and walked towards the main entrance.

Richard was about to drive away when she returned to the driver's side. She bent over towards him and kissed him softly on the cheek.

"I'll never forget what you did for me tonight," she said. Then she walked towards the entrance and was gone.

Richard drove to his home, only a few miles away. He had a late night snack sitting and talking to his parents like when he was back in high school. In the morning his mother made him a mushroom and onion omelet with Swiss cheese— just the way he liked it. Then she kissed him on both cheeks and they embraced.

Back at school Richard knuckled down with his studies, especially calculus. When the next quiz was returned, Richard received an "A" and a comment from the professor scrawled across the front page: "Good work. I see you've learned a lot."

Rebecca returned to school a week later, her father on the road to recovery. When she bumped into Richard on the common, they sat on a bench and talked for an hour.

"I'd like to see you again," Richard said when Rebecca rose to go to class.

"That would be great," she said with a warm smile.

"I suppose you'd like to meet at Hillel," he said.

She hesitated, her smile diminished. "Maybe…but if you really want to go out I love Ethiopian food and there's this great jazz-fusion band I've been dying to see at the arena."

Richard laughed. "If you insist, Rebecca."

"My friends call me Becca."

"Becca it is," he said, grinning from ear to ear.

As Becca walked away, he followed her with his eyes, intoxicated by the sense of well-being that emanates from those who anticipate endless possibilities. And, once and for all, he made a mental note to apologize to his Uncle Morty.

'Twas the Night Before Passover

With a nod to Charles Dickens.

Joshua Stiglitz sat alone in Grand Central Station and fumed. A powerful Nor'easter had cancelled the evening's trains, leaving Joshua stranded. He was not a man who tolerated failures, be they personal, mechanical, or those explained by fickle whims of nature.

As a partner at a large investment firm in Manhattan Joshua oversaw 200 employees. He demanded perfection from himself and those around him—no matter what the cost. From the top of his perfectly coiffed hair to the tip of his Prada shoes, he was a man who craved success, unable to forgive anyone who put family concerns before the good of the company. That morning he let the ax fall on twelve brokers. "Prune the deadwood or lose the tree," he was fond of saying, when anyone questioned his financial decisions. To celebrate the cuts in payroll he had planned a quiet evening alone at home, reading the Wall Street Journal, and sipping a bottle of champagne that he saved for such occasions. Despite his triumph he felt uneasy all day, as if he was overlooking something, a financial report or a deadline, something that might invite havoc if ignored.

He ran from the station towards the taxi stand as the wind howled. The soaking rain drenched him in seconds, sending a chill up his spine, which only served to intensify his anger. A glance at the line of stranded travelers at the taxi stand confirmed his worse fears. "This is a disaster," he muttered. *No trains, no buses, and not a cab to be seen.* As he walked to the end of the line he clenched his teeth and a pounding headache rose in his temples. Just then an ancient black Mercedes drove up to the curb—a gypsy cab with the words "In God We Trust, All Others Pay Cash," painted across its doors. As the line of travelers turned with hopeful eyes the tinted window rolled down a few inches. A beckoning hand pointed an accusing finger at Joshua.

"Hey, mister," the taxi driver hissed with a Yiddish inflection. "Need a ride?"

Before the others in line could protest Joshua climbed over a low metal barricade and jumped into the back seat of the cab. A man the size of an NFL lineman turned from the front seat. He wore black pants and a starched white shirt, with a grey beard and earlocks flowing down the sides of his face. A black velvet yalmulke sat on his head.

"Vere to?" he said.

Joshua gave his address.

"Fancy shmancy, Scarsdale, no?" the driver said, picking a remnant of his chopped liver sandwich from between his teeth. "But aren't you going to your brother's in Brooklyn for the Seder? It's been five years."

Joshua's eyeballs nearly bulged out of their sockets. Seder? Brother? *So that's why I felt uneasy all day.* The image of the unopened invitation that he tossed in the trash flashed in his mind.

"You should at least have read what he had to say...Joshua," the driver said over his shoulder as he stopped at a light.

"Do I know you?" Joshua said, although a man as powerful as the driver would be hard to forget. He glanced at the name on the photo I.D. displayed next to the meter. *Mordechai Cohen, Member of the Guardian Angels, Brooklyn Chapter, since 1974.*

The driver glanced at Joshua in the rear view mirror. "It's never too late to get your life in order."

Joshua's hand trembled as he reached for the door handle, struggling to escape. "What business is it of yours, and how do you know my name?"

"Ven a man forgets his family and his people it is my business."

Meanwhile, in a tenement apartment in Borough Park, Shmulie Stiglitz donned his white kittle and straightened the collar of his white shirt. He scanned the contents of the silver Seder plate, the one his great grandfather brought from Poland for his first Seder in a strange new world. "Hardboiled egg, check, parsley, check, charoset and lamb shankbone, double check." All was in order for the Passover Seder, even if Shmulie spent the last of his unemployment check. Pity there wasn't enough to buy meat. He took a deep breath and put a hand over his eyes. *May God see it in his wisdom to cure little Avraham and may this be the month I get another job. Amen.*

He straightened the twelve chairs around the table: one for each of his eight children, one for his wife Rifka, another left empty for Elijah the Prophet, and of course the last for his brother. He positioned the oxygen tank for the six-year-old, Avraham. *Elijah is more likely to show tonight than Joshua.*

As Joshua struggled to open the taxi door the handle came off in his hand. The driver chuckled softly and nodded, as if he'd seen this all so many times before. The stoplight changed. The black Mercedes accelerated, dodging cars like a test run at the Indianapolis 500. The blur of skyscrapers gave way to dingy apartment buildings. The car stopped. The driver got out, opened the back door, and pulled his cringing passenger from the back seat. Joshua shrieked. "Where are you taking me?"

Passover past

The driver grinned. "Don't you recognize your old neighborhood?" Then he pointed towards the sun, hanging low on the horizon. "Still two hours to the Seder, but first let's see a bit of Passover Past." He folded his hands over his chest and stroked his beard. The street disappeared and Joshua found himself in a crowded apartment, the one he endured as a child. The room was filled to bursting with his relatives, the familiar aromas of matzah ball soup, brisket, and roast chicken wafting from a kitchen complete with his mother's hummed rendition of "Sunrise Sunset."

Joshua put a hand over his face as if to blot out the memories—the nosy cousins, the obnoxious aunts smothering him with kisses he never returned. He remembered the night he forgot the words to the four questions and ran crying from the apartment, ashamed at his failure and the muffled laughter, unwilling to accept his parents' words of consolation. *I'll never fail again. Who needs family anyway?*

Before he could run from the room a hand like a vice grasped him by the neck and lifted him like a roasted duck hung in the window of a Chinese restaurant. "We're not done," the driver said in a voice like thunder. Then he stroked his beard. Instantly the scene changed to a group of teenagers sitting at a wooden table, singing Chad Gadya off key. A seventeen year old Joshua sat stone-faced, sweating profusely as he turned to Sharon, the love of his life (or so he thought).

"Will you go to the Junior Prom with me?" he stammered, his heart pounding.

The silence was endless, broken finally by the girl's flippant reply, and the sound of her laughter. "I'd rather drink poison."

Passover Present

Then, again, he felt the iron hand on his neck and the sensation that he might pass out. The scene changed, and then the driver murmured, "Witness Passover Present." The vision of Shmulie Stiglitz's crowded apartment in Brooklyn came into focus. Eight scrawny children with sallow eyes sat around a table laden only with boxes of matzah and a single jar of gefilte fish. The father removed a cloth from a plate of hard-boiled eggs, and lovingly passed one to each child. "Sorry there's not more," he said to his wife, avoiding her gaze, "but the butcher put a hold on our credit."

"Eat, Tatelah," Shmulie said to little Avraham, the diminutive son who sat by his side with an oxygen line beneath his nose. Shmulie scooped up a morsel of gefilte fish and held it enticingly before his son's pursed lips.

"Ach, the boy hasn't eaten a decent meal in months," Shmulie said. He glanced at his wife's blood shot eyes.

"May Hashem help us," she murmured.

"If only we had the money to take Avraham to that specialist," Shmulie said under his breath. Then he turned back towards his son and stroked the boy's cheek, managing a weak smile, while fighting back tears.

Unseen, Joshua's eyes flew wide. He placed a hand to his forehead. "I never knew things were so bad...why didn't he come to me?"

The driver nodded. "Oh, but he did. You've chosen to forget."

Joshua swallowed hard. The image of his last confrontation with Shmulie rose before him. He ran a hand across his mouth as if to wipe away the bitterness of their argument.

"You were best friends as children," the driver said with unexpected tenderness.

Echoes of Joshua's admonition to his brother five years earlier reverberated in his mind. *Get a job, and stop asking for handouts. If you had any sense you wouldn't have had so many children!*

"I had no idea…" Joshua muttered as he turned towards the driver.

"He doesn't want your pity," the driver said. "Now come. We're running out of time. There's still Passover Future to see."

Before Joshua could protest an iron grip grasped his neck. He closed his eyes. The feeling that he might faint returned as an icy wind chilled his bones. When he opened his eyes he was back in his apartment. He poured himself a glass of scotch and sank into a leather chair. The images of the day played continually on his mind, but as he continued to sip his drink his capacity for denial returned. *Could it all be a nightmare?*

Passover Future

The scotch sent a warm glow through his chest. He closed his eyes and his head fell to the side. For a long while there was only blackness. Then a frigid wind passed through the room, jolting Joshua awake. Instead of his comfortable living room he stood on the outskirts of a desolate cemetery. Nearby, his brother stood, shaking with emotion, the words of the Kaddish rolling from his lips. "Yiskadal, Veyiskadash…"

The driver appeared at Joshua's side from out of nowhere.

"Who died?" Joshua asked, searching the driver's hardened features for a clue.

"I'm sure you know, don't you?"

Joshua raised his open hand as if to ward off a demon, for it's not every day a man attends his own funeral.

"But where are all the mourners? And there's no Rabbi."

The driver smiled. "A man who gives nothing in life is quickly forgotten."

"This can't be right. Where are the two hundred people who worked for me? You've got to help me!"

The driver smiled once again and pointed to his watch.

"If you hurry you can still make the Seder."

"All right. I'll go." He tensed for the iron grip, but none came. "Aren't you taking me?"

The driver laughed. "This is where we part ways, my friend."

He pointed towards the corner.

Joshua frowned. "The subway? You want me to ride the subway to Brooklyn?"

But there was no answer—only the sound of the gravediggers hard at work and the rustle of fallen leaves in the whipping wind. The rain turned into sleet.

On his way to the subway Joshua ducked into a kosher butcher shop, just as it was closing. An hour later he arrived at his brother's apartment. Joshua's teeth were chattering, but a new fire burned within his chest. Despite the weight of the five roast chickens that he carried in his arms Joshua had the lively step of a much younger man. He knocked once and then burst through the door.

"Shmulie, thank God you're still here. Am I in time?" he stammered.

Shmulie's jaw sagged open and Rivka nearly fell from her chair, but they ushered Joshua in as if he were expected. After the dinner little Avraham hid the Affikomen. Instead of the quarter he normally got from his father the little boy received a $25,000 check from his newfound uncle.

"I know you're my brother, but I can't accept charity," Shmulie said shaking his head and glancing at Rivka.

"Who said anything about charity? As my new financial consultant you'll be working long hours. Consider this a Passover bonus."

He glanced at Avraham. "We provide full health benefits and there's an educational benefit—college tuition for all your children. Don't make me beg you!"

For a moment there was silence. Then pandemonium erupted around the table, drowning out Shmulie's feeble protest, little Avraham's laughter, and Rivka's gentle weeping. In fact, throughout the Jewish neighborhoods of Brooklyn, the streets were silent and nearly deserted, but for the roar of a Mercedes engine and the self-congratulatory chuckle of Brooklyn's Guardian Angel on his way to find a new fare.

A YOM KIPPUR STORY

This Yom Kippur Benny was hoping for something more. Some shred of inspiration that might explain the awful year that was just now concluding. As the service continued he leaned forward with his elbows on his knees and covered his eyes with his hands. His thoughts ran towards the events of that year, the mere thought of which made the little hairs on the back of his neck stand on end. He squeezed his eyes tight, as if to obliterate the tears that now welled up behind his eyelids. That was when his beloved wife of twenty years gave him a love tap.

"You're embarrassing me," she said, the jolt of her elbow in his side rivaled only by her sharp tongue. He looked down the row at his three teenage children, each of them stifling their laughter. Clearly, their father's discomfort was the highlight of their morning. He mumbled an apology to the old woman who was staring at him from the next row. He stared at the Torah Scrolls on the bima, his face turning a shade of magenta. His attendance at synagogue three times a year was to set an example for his children. The thought of praying to God never entered his mind.

The service continued at a snail's pace. He thought of bolting. Perhaps a walk in the woods, or a run on the beach might calm the tightness that now rose within his chest. The Rabbi strode to the bima. "Today is the day God judges us," the Rabbi began. All thoughts of a timely escape vanished. How could Benny walk out on the Rabbi? What kind of message would that send to his children? Even worse, what would his clients think of him, sitting in clusters throughout the congregation?

So he settled back in his seat, the plush cushioned upholstery comforting him far better than the hard wooden benches of the synagogue he attended in his youth. While the Rabbi talked of redemption Benny replayed the logic of his decision. *Too much work. Things would never be the same.* He glanced down the row at his wife, her lips pursed, a hardened look about her eyes that seemed to have become permanent since their big blow up. *Why won't she understand?*

"Spirituality is in the person, not the service," the Rabbi was saying. "If you want to be a better person look inside your own heart." Benny glanced at his eldest son. *Wonder what he'd do if it was me.* The boy turned towards his father. "Hey, Pops, when can I go?" the boy said, with a bored beyond belief expression only a high school student can master. Benny's thoughts drifted back to the events of that year. He replayed the rift that had torn his family apart. He had talked his dilemma over with all of his friends—to the man he had their full support. Still, while his decision made perfect sense why did he find it so difficult to look into his wife's eyes? *If only things could be as they were.*

"And, so, my friends," the Rabbi said, as he concluded. "For true forgiveness you must make amends to those you have wronged."

Benny put a hand to his throat as if he were suffocating. "Air, I need air," he mumbled as he staggered from the sanctuary. He tumbled into the cool September afternoon, and took a walk along the beach. He passed his favorite house overlooking the water, a little bungalow with a view of the Sound and a for sale sign on the lawn. So many times he and his wife had strolled past that house and dreamed of watching the sunrise from the front porch. He shook his head and chuckled. The recession had certainly knocked that dream off its foundation.

We'll be lucky enough to keep our own house.

Lost in thought, he pondered the future, college tuition, job uncertain, and now this? He looked out over Long Island Sound at a tiny sailboat barely making headway against a choppy sea. "That's like my life," he muttered. Somehow his feet brought him back to the Synagogue.

"All those who want to pray before the ark, may come up to the bima," the Rabbi was saying.

Instead of taking his seat Benny headed for the front.

As he stood before the ark, he stared at the Torah Scroll. Aside from his own Bar Mitzvah, he'd never been as close to its worn parchment. Certainly, filled with 500 souls the synagogue was warmer than usual, but that wouldn't explain the beads of sweat on his forehead. He put a hand over his eyes and uttered the Shema. When he returned to his seat his wife gave him a sour smile.

"The kids want to go home," she said.

He nodded. "I think I want to say some prayers."

"Suit yourself," she said, with a look of surprise. "But it's almost one."

"I'm staying," he said. "I've got a lot to think about. Come back for Neilah."

She nodded, and put a hand on his shoulder, the first physical contact offered in months.

"Are you all right?" she whispered. Her face seemed to soften. She looked into his eyes, and for once he held her gaze.

"I'll be fine," he said. "See you later?"

She nodded, and then he was alone. As worshippers fled the synagogue, Benny remained. He followed every prayer. When the Rabbi announced a break for the afternoon Benny stayed in his seat. He thought of his children. He pictured the day of his wedding, right there on that very bima.

Later that evening his wife returned for the closing Neilah prayers without the kids. He smiled to see her in a simple dress, her hair pinned back, without makeup, looking more beautiful than when she dressed to the nines. She sat by his side. She closed her eyes while she recited the prayers—something he hadn't seen her do in years. While he pounded his heart for the Al Chet prayer, she did the same, watching him from the corner of her eye.

As the service ended the Rabbi raised a ram's horn that seemed longer than he was tall. A hush fell over the synagogue. The single blast blew loud and long, hovering over the congregation in its last waning moment, the Rabbi's face purple with effort.

"May this year be better than the last," Benny said with a weak smile, turning towards his wife. She said nothing, but when Benny got on line for the break-the-fast buffet, his wife took his arm.

That night Benny slept through the night for the first time in months. He rose before sunrise. He made some phone-calls, and when his wife came down he had breakfast waiting.

"Take a drive with me this morning," he said, "and don't ask questions."

They drove south on 95 towards New York City. She was convinced Benny had some hair-brain scheme to surprise her, as if taking her to a Yankee playoff game at the new Stadium might mend their broken fences. Maybe she gave him too little credit—perhaps a dinner and a Broadway show—a nice try, but hardly a fitting restitution. It was only when he took the Fairfield exit that her breathing quickened. She sat bolt upright in her seat and stared at the side of his face. He put a finger to his lips and the hint of a smile played at the corners of his mouth. They took the winding roads she had come to know all too well that year. *A Sunday morning visit instead of golf?* She thought. *Now there's a first.*

They parked in front of the long brick building marked Administration.

"You go on ahead," he said, I've got some things to attend to."

She smiled, trying to hide her puzzlement. She walked down the hall, glancing back at him as he approached the nurses' station.

A half hour later he joined his wife.

"Well, well, look what the cat dragged in. How are you Lenny?" his father-in-law said. Benny managed a weak smile. "I'm Benny, Dad."

"Lenny, Benny, whatever," the old man said, wiping the scrambled eggs from his upper lip.

"Why are you bothering me on a Monday?" the old man said. "Shouldn't you be at work, supporting my grandchildren?"

Benny set down the suitcase the nurses had packed. Then he glanced at his wife, and took a deep breath. "Dad, you're coming home with us," he said. "I'll get your walker."

The ride north on 95 was unusually quiet. His father-in-law sat in the back, except for an occasional chuckle at completely random moments. Benny drove as usual. Instead of trying to nap as she often did, his wife sat snuggled by his side, her head resting comfortably on his shoulder.

Benny thought of practical things. The extra help they would need—no more weekend getaways, all the changes they would have to make. As he drove along the Merritt Parkway, he mentioned none of these, but for some reason he kept thinking of the faded Torah he had prayed before on Yom Kippur.

When they got home Benny's wife brought her father inside, while Benny went to the trunk to get the old man's suitcase. Before he reached the house the door swung open. His wife approached with tears in her eyes. She put her hands on each side of his face.

"Thank you, Benny," she whispered with a smile that lit her face.

"You're the best." Then she kissed him on the lips.

"But your father," he stammered when she moved away.

"Don't worry, he'd better get used to it," she said.

For the first time in months he put his arms around her neck and drew her close. When she didn't resist he kissed her mouth for a long time. In that moment Benny was oblivious to his new responsibilities, oblivious to the way his life would be changing in the coming days. And, as usual, Benny was oblivious to his children, who were fist bumping each other behind the foyer windows, as their parents held hands and walked back towards the house.

CELEBRATING CHANUKAH

Rufus stared at the stack of used tires, each no larger than the sandy haired boy he used to protect. He sniffed at the stale breeze laced with bus exhaust and the pine scent of the Christmas tree beside the stack of used tires. He surveyed the bleak urban landscape of his South Bronx street corner and wondered. *Is this all there is?* He wagged his tail at the burly man shuttling back and forth between the tires and the street, but, as always, there was no response, just a dissatisfied growl far more fearsome than his own. From time to time the man would select a tire, wrap it in plastic and then bring it to the sidewalk where smiling men would hand over handfuls of green paper. Rufus knew it was his job to guard the tire shop at night. This he did in exchange for the man's stale leftovers—when there were some and when roving dogs didn't steal his portion.

Each night Rufus slept in a little wooden shed chained to a stake. Through rain or snow, his sole purpose was to bark if men were stealing the tires when the burly man went away in his pickup truck. Sometimes, especially on cold rainy nights, Rufus wondered if he had always been chained in the tire shop. He had no memory of any other existence. Somehow, however, Rufus knew deep in his animal soul that he belonged somewhere else.

One morning a man wearing a yarmulke stopped for a tire. His car radio was playing the Dreidel song... "dreidel, dreidel, dreidel, I made it out of clay..." Rufus sat up and wagged his tail. When the man came close and reached out, Rufus nestled against the man's hand and inhaled deeply, the scent of fried latkes filling Rufus with longing.

The smell seemed to jar something in Rufus's memory, an image perhaps, or a memory, although who can say what went on in Rufus' collection of instincts and learned responses. A picture appeared in Rufus' mind of mornings with little Doug, the scent of frying onions and potatoes filling a warm kitchen. He sat on his haunches and closed his eyes, his stub of a tail tapping the ground with thoughts of a warm fire and little Doug's hands buried in the fur behind his ears.

"Don't ever leave me, Rufus," the boy would say and snuggle his nose next to his. Then Rufus would sneeze and the man and woman who took care of the little boy would laugh and laugh. In the story that played in the space between Rufus' ears everyone was smiling. One day there was a big fuss in the house. People came to the house in droves. Doug hand fed Rufus little scraps of fried potatoes. "Look, Rufus likes latkes," the father said.

"We can't have Rufus in the house for the Chanukah party," the mother said.

Next thing Rufus knew he was out in the back yard, with a plate of the warm potato things on a dish. That was the last thing he could remember. When he woke he was chained to the stake in the tire store.

As the days went by and the weather turned colder Rufus dreamed of his old life. Images of running after a tennis ball in a lush meadow filled his head. Sometimes he pictured sleeping besides a roaring fireplace in the den with the little boy's head resting on his belly. In his dreams there was always plenty of food—delicious scraps of meat, pieces of cheddar cheese, and bits of real beef plopped in his bowl or fed to him with a warm hand.

One morning the burly man slapped Rufus in the head while Rufus slept. "Wake up, ya lousy mutt. It's Christmas."

Suddenly, the memory of Rufus' life came flowing back. His family was having a Chanukah party. He was in the back yard eating delicious latkes. That's when another dog appeared and snatched a latke. When Rufus jumped over the fence to follow, the burly man hit him with a baseball bat and threw him in the back of his truck. Then he drove away.

Rufus hung his head low and pawed at his chain. His memory of a better life seemed so long ago. He became consumed with one thought. *Where is my little boy and will I ever see him again?*

For two weeks after Rufus disappeared, Doug's parents tried everything to get him back. They posted rewards throughout Westchester with pictures of Rufus. They visited animal shelters. They went door to door and asked everyone in a radius of two miles whether they had seen their precious dog. Their efforts were to no avail. Rufus was gone without a trace.

"Rufus must have run away," the father said after a month. "We'll get you another dog."

"I don't want another dog, I want Rufus," little Doug wailed. He lost interest in his toys. He refused to go to preschool. He woke with night terrors.

"The child is depressed," the family doctor said after a few months. He needs medication. They tried medication. They tried therapy. Nothing helped.

It had been a full year since Rufus disappeared and Chanukah was again approaching.

"Let's play dreidel," the father said.

"Help me make latkes for the Chanukah party, Doug," said the mother as she stood over a bowl of grated potatoes.

Doug shook his head. He moped around the house, his thoughts consumed with memories of his beloved Rufus. *Will I ever get to hug my dog again?*

Conclusion

Each day Rufus remembered more of his previous life, dreaming each night of his glory days with his little boy. A passerby might laugh if he saw how Rufus' tail would thump, as he slept. Most nights he dreamt of the little boy's head on his belly, imagining the smell of frying latkes in the kitchen. Each day Rufus awoke hungry, faced by the same awful truth. *I'm chained to a stake in a tire store.*

Rufus ate scraps, when his new master remembered to leave food. Occasionally he barked at a stranger or another dog, but, other than these few interludes, his days were tedious. The man cared only for tires and Rufus was meant to guard them at night. That was the only reason the man kept him alive. A metaphysical analysis might reveal that Rufus' life was meaningless, but dogs rarely examine the existential questions of the universe, preferring instead to concentrate on the things that they can control, like their next meal. That, perhaps, is where Rufus' luck changed.

One day the man who always fed Rufus put a big sign up. "Closed for Christmas," Rufus heard the man mutter after he took a swig from a bottle wrapped in a brown paper bag. As always the man padlocked the gate and turned off the lights. He staggered as if he might topple over. Instead of leaving Rufus a few scraps for dinner, on this night he went right to his truck.

"The man must have a treat in his truck," Rufus thought. To his great disappointment the truck roared to life and the man drove away, while Rufus' stomach growled.

That night a group of men cut the lock and snuck into the tire store. Rufus barked for all he was worth, for, although he was consumed by hunger his instincts were still intact. As the men walked towards Rufus he smelled a strong odor of meat.

"Shut that dog up," someone was saying, while men started carrying snow tires away. Another man approached Rufus and dangled a slice of salami just out of his reach. Rufus's eyeballs nearly popped out of their sockets, for aside from latkes, salami had always been his favorite food when he lived with the little boy. He wondered if perhaps the men had come to feed him, and he ceased his barking. But instead of dropping the salami, the man hurled it into the street. Then another man cut Rufus' chain with bolt cutters. "Go get it, boy," he heard someone say. He ran into the street. He gobbled up the salami, his stub of a tail wagging, the tires all but forgotten. When he circled back to the tire store the men were gone and there were a lot fewer tires stacked up around the yard.

Rufus stood beside his broken chain and put his paws over his head. He pictured his master and a gnawing feeling rose in his belly, this time born not of hunger, but of fear, for he knew instinctively what failure felt like. His ears drooped. His tail fell between his legs. Then it began to snow. Sometime near dawn Rufus fell asleep. As before he dreamed of his little boy, pictured running after a ball in a lush green meadow. Around noon he woke to the sound of Christmas carols sung by teenage girls. When the girls moved on so did Rufus, for the bonds of poorly fed guard dogs are tenuous at best.

As Rufus sauntered through the unlocked gate, the distant scent of frying onions and potatoes reached his nose. He sniffed at the air as might his wild ancestors of passed millennia and pictured his little boy. His internal GPS strained with every passing moment until finally, his resolve intact, he set his sights north towards Westchester and ran steadily in search of a better life.

Meanwhile, in the Morgenstern household the mother and father had little time to concentrate on little Doug, who seemed to be mopping around worse than ever.

"Help me decorate the living room, Doug," the father said. "Our Chanukah party starts tomorrow at noon."

"I can't play with you now," the mother said, "but you can help me fry latkes. We need about three hundred."

Reluctantly, Doug stomped into the kitchen, for all he could think of was Rufus.

Rufus ran through the streets of the Bronx, awash in snow, trailing his broken chain. When he reached the Hudson River he crossed onto the Parkway and ran along the shoulder. Every few miles he would pause and sniff at the air, the familiar scent growing stronger by the minute. He reached Scarsdale. He pawed at the ground, for the smell of latkes was strong in that town, but somehow Rufus knew to move on. As the hours slipped by, he ran slower and slower, the broken chain like an anchor in the newly fallen snow. He ran through the day. He ran through the night until finally he reached New Rochelle around noon the next day. He sniffed at the air, his canine senses guiding his every move. His paws were numb, his belly empty, and a fever raged through his body. All he could picture was the little boy's head nestled on his as they sat before a roaring fire. *And there had to be latkes.*

The guests were streaming into the Rubinstien household, for this was the last day of Chanukah, and, as always, the Rubinstiens always threw the best Chanukah parties. It seemed like the entire community was invited. Grandparents, cousins, and neighbors choked every nook and cranny of the house. The older children played dreidel; the menorah burned brightly. The parents drank Vodka gimlets and smiled, talking of politics and money, but nothing remotely interesting to the little boy, Doug, who moped around wishing they would all leave so he could be alone.

"The latkes are served," the mother announced with much fanfare and everyone made a beeline to the kitchen, for Mrs. Rubinstien's latkes were famous in the community.

"Why can't every day be Chanukah," a little girl said, her lips smeared with sour cream, her mouth alive with the unforgettable taste of onions and potatoes fried in oil.

"Buy yourself something nice," one of the grandparents said and slipped a twenty-dollar bill into Doug's hand. The little boy looked at the bill and nodded, suffering through the mandatory kisses, unable to think of anything he really wanted for Chanukah besides Rufus.

As the day wore on the candles burned low. The latkes were eaten and the dreidels put away. Finally the guests left.

"I'm hungry," the little boy said.

"Didn't you eat any latkes?" the mother said. The boy shrugged.

"Well, then help me make one more batch," the mother said. So they went into the kitchen and fried up the last of the latke batter.

It was at just about this time that Rufus stopped a quarter mile from Doug's street. He had long since stopped running and could barely walk, shivering with the cold. He sat beside a hydrant and closed his eyes, for the scent of frying latkes had gone cold. I'll never find my little boy. He fell into a sleep of exhaustion. He dreamt of the tire store, he dreamt of his little boy, and finally he dreamt of that last Chanukah party and the plateful of latkes. When he regained consciousness he thought he might still be dreaming, for the scent of frying latkes was strong once again. Rufus rose with renewed vigor. He shook off the snow; he licked at his front paws till there was feeling once again. And then, as quickly as he could, he scampered the rest of the way to his little boy's house, following the scent of onions and potatoes as only Mrs. Rubinstien could prepare them.

Finally Rufus was before the house. He barked, a tiny bark, for the journey had left Rufus a shadow of his former self. He pawed at the door.

There was a commotion inside the house while Rufus barked with all the strength that remained despite his exhaustion. His little stub of a tail thumped for all it was worth. Then the door was opening, the mother and father gasping while the little boy nudged past his parents.

"Can this really be possible?" the father was saying.

"I can't believe it," said the mother.

Rufus passed out.

When Rufus awoke he was nestled in the boys arms before a roaring fire. He licked the boy's hand. He nuzzled the boys face. The room was warm as was the space in the boy's chest that had, for the past year, grown cold.

"I love you Rufus," said the boy.

If Rufus had the gift of speech he would have indeed said the same. Instead he thumped his little tail on the hardwood floor. He thought fleetingly of a life filled with play and love and imagined the boy's hands buried in his fur. But there'd be time for all that later. A plate of Mrs. Rubinstien's latkes was before him, and Rufus hadn't eaten in days. He swallowed the latkes whole and then sat on his haunches...the boy would have to wait. And while the family laughed and little Doug hugged his mother, Rufus did what any red-blooded dog would do on the last day of Chanukah; he wagged his tail and waited for another plate of latkes.

A SEDER STORY

When Charlie Roman left the New London train station the sun was just dipping below the horizon. *Still time to make David's Seder.* Disquieted by leaving the City when there was so much paperwork to be done Charlie prided himself on always being in control. As an emergency room physician at a midtown hospital Charlie relished out-thinking and out-working the competition. That's why at the tender age of 35 Charlie had been appointed head of the ER when most of his medical school buddies were still trying to start a practice.

Of course, there was a price to be paid for Charlie's meteoric rise. His 100 hour work weeks left little time for socializing. So, while his contemporaries married, Charlie concentrated on his career. While his old roommates were learning to change diapers, Charlie was learning to negotiate Medicare contracts. While his former friends were watching their kids at Little League, Charlie was planning the next hospital merger.

"There'll be plenty of time for that kind of thing when I'm head of the hospital," he told his aging parents in Boca Raton on his last biannual visit.

The fact that Charlie accepted an invitation for a Passover Seder from his college buddy, David, and his wife, was a departure from his secular life. Charlie had not attended a Seder since he left home for college. His only memories of Passover was his undying resentment at being forced to recite the four questions.

Perhaps he agreed to attend a Seder to please his oldest friend. Perhaps it was a chance to leave the frenzy of his Upper East Side neighborhood, if only for a few days, and see New London again. Certainly it wasn't the Aish.com web site that proclaimed, "Celebrate the Miracle of Passover," for Charlie Roman was not a believer.

Despite his protests to the contrary, Charlie only accepted after he heard that David's sister, Rose, would attend as well. They had met only briefly at a wedding a few years earlier at Beth El Synagogue. Charlie brushed away David's hint at a romance as easily as one would brush away a wisp of hair from one's forehead. But truth be told, as Passover approached, Charlie began to daydream about meeting the dark-haired Rose.

The cab ride took Charlie down Pequot Avenue, along the water where ferries crisscrossed the sound, and the mournful moans of the Ledge Light foghorn sounded like some celestial shofar announcing young Charlie's arrival. He craned his neck as they passed the Lawrence Memorial Hospital. *How quaint.*

When Charlie knocked on the door the Seder was just beginning. After the introductions and a few awkward hugs Charlie took his place in the empty chair beside Rose. David's young son sang the four questions while Charlie stole glances at Rose's hands.

"Great Miracles happened there," David read from the Haggadah.

"And God took us out with a strong hand," said Rose.

Charlie ate karpas when prompted, maror when reminded, all the while daydreaming of his big hospital meeting on Monday. He drank his cups of wine when Rose insisted, and read from the Haggadah when Rose turned towards him expectantly. But despite his outward engagement, Charlie Roman's mind was far away. *I can't believe they're going to do the whole Seder! This could go on all night!*

As the evening continued Charlie and Rose had a chance to talk. Rose told Charlie about her plans to spend a year studying in Jerusalem and eventually teach Judaic studies.

"I want to make a difference in the world," she said, "and Judaism is a big part of my life."

Charlie nodded politely, glanced at his watch frequently, all the while thinking of the reports he'd have to read to make up for taking a few days off. When Charlie described the innovative changes he'd made to the hospital's insurance claim processing Rose stifled a yawn.

While David's son went to hide the afikomen, David began a discussion.

"How do you feel about miracles, Charlie?" David said.

"I'm afraid the Mets don't have a chance, this year, if that's what you mean," Charlie said, trying to diffuse his metaphysical angst.

"That's not much of an answer," Rose said.

"You don't think any of that stuff ever really happened, do you?" Charlie said, pointing to his Haggadah, and chuckling.

"The only miracles here on earth are the ones made by man. I'm afraid I don't believe in God."

David glanced away. Rose put a hand up to cover her eyes, but crimson rose on her cheeks. The guests at the table fell silent.

Eventually the Seder continued. Although Charlie thought of leaving, he stayed, the four cups of wine having made him quite drowsy. He avoided any further talk of the Almighty. As the guests expounded on the Haggadah text, Charlie's eyelids began to droop. *What am I doing here?* When the Seder continued after the meal Charlie excused himself, found a comfortable seat in the living room, and fell into a deep sleep.

It was sometime around midnight, as the guests were walking to the door, when Rose scooped up some charoset with a scrap of the afikomen and swallowed it whole. Seconds later she put a hand to her throat, a coarse raspy sound coming from her chest. She pointed to her mouth, a froth of saliva on her lips. Then she collapsed.

"She's choking," David yelled as he ran back to the table. He checked her mouth. Her tongue seemed enormous.

"Call 911," he yelled.

The guests ran around like chickens without heads, clucking wildly.

"Rose, dearest Rose, God help us!" David yelled, as he shook her limp body.

The tumult around the Seder table aroused Dr. Charlie Roman from his Manishewitz induced coma.

"Stand back!" he commanded.

The crowd of guests huddled around Rose's prostrate figure parted to let Charlie pass. "Get me a flashlight. And make it quick!" he shouted as soon as he saw her swollen lips and the bluish hue of her skin.

"She's having an allergic reaction."

Then he swept her mouth with a forefinger. Finding nothing, he pinched off her nose, put his lips over her mouth, and attempted to give her CPR.

"She needs an airway," he said to no one in particular.

Ignoring the guest's cries he took a pen from his pocket. He unscrewed the top and discarded the ink cartridge. Then, stabilizing Rose's Adam's apple between two fingers he plunged the tip of his dismantled pen deftly into her neck. Blood spurted. The guests screamed. David's wife fainted. But as soon as the pen's hollow tube pierced Rose's throat the air streamed back into her struggling lungs. Within a half minute her eyelids fluttered, and then opened.

Charlie put a finger to his lips and smiled.

"You can't talk, Rose, but you'll be fine. You need to go to the hospital."

Rose nodded, never taking her eyes from Charlie's. Just then the paramedics entered. They placed Rose on a stretcher while Charlie stroked her hand. He rode to the Lawrence and Memorial hospital in the back of the ambulance and directed her care until she was stabilized and eventually discharged in the morning.

David was eternally grateful, as was Rose when she heard all the details of her resurrection. In a story with a fairy tale ending one might expect Rose and Charlie to fall madly in love, but in truth their world views were far too different to portend happiness.

Rose never forgot the wild Passover Seder at her brother's home. She bore a slight scar on her neck to remind her of Charlie's quick thinking. She had herself tested for food allergies and, when she married and had Passover Seders of her own in Brooklyn, she substituted pecans for the walnuts in her charoset. Each day she thanked God for sending her an emergency room physician in her time of greatest need. She was known by all for her kindness and her joy for life. Each year she invited strangers without a place for a Seder to her home. Although she always included an invitation to Dr. Charlie Roman, he never showed up at her door.

As for Charlie, he, too, remembered his time in New London. When the wire services picked up the story of his "New London miracle," he became a national sensation. He remained single for most of his life and he never became the head of the hospital as he imagined. He chose instead to shed administrative duties for patient care in the new emergency clinic that would one day bear his name. When his parents passed away in Florida, he decided to change his name back to Romansky. After many years, Rose introduced him to her doctor, a middle-aged female internist who shared his workaholic mentality. They married and his new wife gave birth at the age of 46, to a beautiful baby girl. While he never became "a believer," he and his wife decided to hold Seders on Passover so their daughter might know something of her Jewish heritage. Each year Charlie would lead and his daughter would read the four questions. When they reached the part about miracles in the Hagaddah Charlie would pause, and although he still had his doubts, he would tell the story of Rose and his last Seder in New London.

A CHANUKAH STORY

"Yes, Mom, of course I didn't forget Dad's Yartzheit," he said, drawing a sharp breath, hoping she didn't hear the hesitation in his voice. "Yes, yes, I know. Maariv services tonight, Shachrit tomorrow morning. Of course I'm going to services. He sank back into his chair and listened for the next five minutes, a typical conversation between mother and son.

"Uh huh, of course I'm listening," he said after a while. "Why don't you see the doctor again if your cold's so bad?"

Shirley Morgenstern continued, laying out the full litany of her physical complaints, the dark green sputum, the ache in her hip, the way the neighbor ignores her in the elevator. He listened like any good son would, entering a response only when the pause on her end required a retort. His mother had moved to Florida two years ago, a year after his father passed, leaving him up north, still tethered by the phone if not by the umbilical cord.

Finally, the list of her disappointments turned to her son.

"So, Benny, when are you going to meet a nice Jewish girl and settle down?" she said. "Get out of that crummy town while you can. Move here to Delray to be near me. Get married, give me grandchildren. A nuclear physicist can work anywhere. Show some initiative."

He closed his eyes, and raised a hand to his forehead, the throb of his headache gnawing into his skull.

"Thirty-four years old and unmarried, what are you waiting for? If your father were still alive he'd straighten you out. Who knows what kind of women you run around with? And don't forget to get tested."

"Yes, Mom," he said, holding the phone further from his ear. "I will."

"I can still tell Rabbi Finkelstein that you'd like to meet his daughter."

He stifled a laugh as his mother recited the list of Lila Finkelstein's virtues. "She's not for me. I gotta go Mom," he said at last, although he suspected she continued talking long after he hung up.

Mentally exhausted, he massaged his temples. He thought of his father, gone for three years, a quiet, hard-working man of few words. The memory of a long-ago fishing trip with his father flashed across his mind. He was eighteen and preparing to leave for college. They sat on the bank of their favorite fishing spot at Horseshoe Lake. His dad wasn't the type to give advice unless asked, but on this particular day he offered.

"When you meet the right girl, you'll know," his father said, with the hint of a smile creasing his lips. "Until then, don't run around with trash at that fancy college of yours."

Truth be told, Benjamin hadn't exactly been chaste at the University, nor in the years since. And his choice of partners did not always please his mother. He dated girls with names like Jones and Hanrahan, when his mother preferred names like Cohen and Schwartz. Benjamin's kind smile and puppy dog eyes attracted women who heard their biologic clock ticking. "Face it, chick magnets like you should never settle down," his coworker at the lab liked to say, whenever Benjamin took up with a new girl. But, what felt like conquest when he was in college, had turned stale and tired. He began to envy his married friends, lingered to play with their children whenever he was invited to dinner.

So, it was with a heavy heart that he made his way to the synagogue that night for his yearly Yarhtzeit visit for his father. He parked his car and sat in the parking lot. Normally the crowd that straggled in was decidedly mature. Yet on this night, young couples with children were strolling hand in hand to the synagogue steps. Laughter and giggles burst forth from impish faces etched in wide-eyed excitement. Benjamin stared at these unlikely minyan goers, the parents much his own age. *Sixty people can't all be here for the evening minyan.* He thought of bolting, heading home without saying Kaddish, but the guilt of having to lie to his mother gave him pause.

As he entered the synagogue he noted a brightly colored sign. "Chanukah Party Tonight." He took a deep breath. *This'll take all night.* He almost turned back to the parking lot, but the rich aroma of fried onions and potatoes hung over the lobby, making his stomach growl. An image of his mother and father making latkes together when he was a kid rose in his mind.

Rabbi Finkelstein nodded to him as they passed.

"So good to see you," the Rabbi said with unusual enthusiasm. "You too," Benjamin muttered with downcast eyes.

The Rabbi smiled. "Can you help us in the kitchen? We've got more mouths to feed than I planned for."

Benjamin shrugged. "I just came to say Kaddish for my father," he said, his eyes darting from the Rabbi's gaze.

"Of course, of course, minyan after the Chanukah Party. Now, go, please, help us make latkes."

Benjamin trudged to the kitchen. He surveyed a scene of quiet determination, as two elderly men made latkes at a snail's pace. A single tray of perfectly browned latkes was all they had produced in an hour and a half.

"I'm here to help with the latkes," a young woman said as she entered the kitchen behind Benjamin.

Ben turned to face the newest forced laborer, but the words stuck in his throat. Her almond shaped green eyes flashed as she smiled. "I'm not usually into organized religion," she said, but there are fifty hungry people out there." Ben's pulse hammered in his ears. Almost against his will, he glanced at the fingers of her left hand, noting the absence of a ring. He smiled awkwardly, his eyes riveted on her full lips as she spoke. With a toss of her mane of dark hair she walked towards the stove, taking up residence beside the two elderly men. Benjamin followed her to the pile of onions and potatoes waiting to be grated.

"I like a man who knows his way around the kitchen," she said.

Any thoughts of an early exit were forgotten as Benjamin began to grate onions into a large bowl. He grated potatoes until he felt he was losing all feeling in his fingers. Although the onions brought tears to his eyes he stayed at his post, chopping and dicing, smashing eggs and mixing with astonishing vigor. His newfound latke partner fried rows of latkes on the griddle, stacking them on waiting trays. Periodically the Rabbi would appear, carrying away the fruits of their labors to the hungry minions waiting in the social hall.

"More, we need more," he would say again and again, smiling at his two latke specialists.

As they worked they talked. The time sped by, and, by the time four hundred and thirty latkes were finished, Benjamin knew everything about the completion of his cooking partner's doctoral thesis at UCLA.

"So, you'll be staying back east?" Benjamin asked, his voice cracking.

"Well, that depends on a lot of things," she said, her eyes darting from his gaze.

His hand jolted suddenly and his knuckles scraped along the grater. "For God's sake," he shouted as drops of blood stained the latke batter.

"Here let me have a look at that," she said, and drew him towards the light. "Just a scrape," she said after washing and blotting his injured hand under the kitchen faucet. His heart began to pound at her touch, so that when the Rabbi appeared and said, "time for minyan, you've done enough," he hardly heard.

"You'd better go," she said. He nodded and with a towel clutched against his raw knuckles he went to find the minyan. When he saw her sit down in the back near the end of the service he smiled. He tried to stop glancing at her, and tried to focus on the memory of his father, as he waited for the Kaddish to start. As he always did during the Kaddish, he pictured the fishing trip with his dad when he was eighteen, one of the happier moments of their relationship.

When the service was finished he walked into the hallway. His fellow latke maker was waiting.

"I can't remember the last time I made latkes," she said. "Maybe my parents' insistence on all things Jewish turned me off...but I enjoyed meeting you."

"Me too," he said, hesitating. She smiled and turned to walk away.

"Want to get a cup of coffee?" he blurted.

"I'd love to."

As they walked down the stairs together they carried with them the aroma of onions and burnt oil. Chance meetings being what they are, who can say whether the seed of their encounter would one day bear fruit. But, as Benjamin walked to his car, the memory of his father's advice surfaced in his mind. *When you meet the right girl, you'll know.*

Meanwhile, back in the synagogue, the maintenance crew was cleaning the kitchen. Exhausted children where being gathered up by their parents, content with the best Chanukah dinner the synagogue had ever hosted. As was his custom Rabbi Finkelstein was the last to leave. He took one last look around the hallway, and ducked into his office to make the long distance phone call he never thought he'd make.

"Hello, Mrs. Morgenstern, Rabbi Finkelstein here. You were right about the whole thing. It worked like a charm."

He listened for a while as the excited matron of Delray giggled and cackled into the phone.

"Right now, they're on their way to have coffee," the Rabbi said.

"I always liked your Lila," she said.

"And I always liked your Ben."

"Happy Chanukah, Rabbi."

"And a Happy Chanukah to you, Mrs. Morgenstern."

GLOSSARY

Affikomen: —literally the middle piece of three special matzahs used during the Passover Seder. Often children hide this during the evening and receive treats or cash in return because the Seder cannot be completed without it.

Al Chet: —prayer asking for forgiveness from God (atonement) traditionally chanted on Yom Kippur.

Aleinu: —short Jewish prayer that marks the end of a prayer service.

Assimilation: —the process whereby a person or groups culture comes to resemble those of another group. Especially significant in America where immigrant societies become "Americanized."

Bar Mitzvah: —a ritual of passage for Jewish boys when they turn 13 years old and become counted as an adult in the eyes of the Jewish community, Usually marked by a religious service and a big party. Girls can have a service called a Bat Mitvah

Bima: —an elevated platform holding a reading table usually in the front of a synagogue, used to rest the Torah or the Book of the Prophets (Haftorah) during prayer services.

Borachu: —prayer of praise in Jewish worship.

Bubby: —affectionate name for a grandmother.

Chag Sameach: —Jewish greeting, literally "Happy Holiday."

Chanukah: —an 8 day Jewish holiday commemorating the rebellion and eventual victory over repressive Greek rule.

Charoset: —delicious ritual food used during the Passover Seder, traditionally made with apples, cinnamon, chopped walnuts, and sweet wine

Chazzan: —Person who chants or sings Jewish prayers in front of the congregation.

Cholent: —traditional Jewish stew usually of beans, meat, spices, and potatoes, often served during the Sabbath. Cooked on a slow flame or crock pot set out the day before so as not to begin cooking on the Sabbath itself.

Chummash: —yiddish, a printed form of the Torah scroll used in prayer service

Chuppah: —Hebrew, a canopy under which a Jewish couple stand during their wedding ceremony.

Daven: —Yiddish term, to pray.

Final mem: —the thirteenth letter of the Hebrew alphabet, final mem is a form of the letter mem used at the end of a word.

Flanken: —Yiddish, traditional Jewish dish of meat taken from the short ribs of beef, usually boiled or stewed and often served with horseradish. It is a treat for special occasions.

Gabbi: —Hebrew, a person who assists in the running of a synagogue prayer service, especially when reading the Torah.

Goyish: —somewhat disrespectful adjective referring to non-Jews or any practice considered typical of non-Jewish (gentile) people.

Haftorah: —Hebrew, Weekly selection from the Book of Prophets read after the Torah Scroll on the Sabbath.

Hassid: —Hebrew, a member of a religious sect founded in Poland in the 18th century characterized by its emphasis on mysticism, prayer, ritual strictness, religious zeal, and joy.

Hekshers: —markings on food packages that denote kosher food acceptable by the religious authorities.

Hora: —Hebrew, joyous circle dance often performed at Jewish weddings, Bat and Bar Mitzvahs.

Kaddish: —A hymn of praises to God performed in Jewish worship. The mourner's Kaddish is a special form said by the bereaved each day for a year after losing a loved one. Can also be said on the yearly anniversary of death.

Kashrut: —Hebrew, the dietary laws for Jews, those laws determining whether food is kosher.

Ketubah: —Hebrew, the formal marriage contract in a Jewish wedding ceremony, often a document displayed in a Jewish home.

Kiddush: —a blessing said on wine usually before a meal on the Sabbath or a Jewish holiday.

Kippah: —Hebrew, head covering worn by Jewish men; yarmulke.

Kittel: —a white robe used by orthodox Jewish men as a ceremonial garment, worn by a bridegroom at his wedding ceremony, his burial, and on High Holidays

Klezmer: —traditional Jewish folk music of Eastern Europe, played by small bands at weddings and Bar Mitzvahs.

Kosher: —prepared according to the Jewish dietary laws.

Koshered: —to make kosher, when referring to meat, prepared according to the Jewish dietary laws.

Kugel: —traditional baked casserole most commonly made from egg noodles or potatoes, sweet and savory, often served on the Sabbath.

L'Shana Tova: —Hebrew, Common greeting on Rosh Hashanah (the Jewish New Year) meaning, "Have a good year."

Lamb shank bone: —usually roasted and placed on the Seder plate at Passover. Symbolic of the special sacrifice prepared as a meal the night before the ancient Hebrews left Egypt in the Exodus.

Maror: —bitter herbs or horseradish eaten by Jews at the Passover Seder to symbolize the bitterness of slavery at the hands of the Egyptians.

Matzah: —Unleavened bread (flat, unrisen) used by Jews during Passover instead of bread. It symbolizes the unleavened bread the Jews ate when they left

Egypt in a hurry.

Mazel tov: —"Good Luck"

Mazel: —Hebrew/Yiddish, literally, "luck."

Minyan: —For orthodox Jews a group of 10 adult men necessary for prayer services, often involving the reading of the Torah—for Conservative and Reform Jew—ten adults be they men or women.

Mishegas:—Yiddish for craziness.

Motzi: —A blessing said before eating bread.

Neilah: —The closing prayer service on Yom Kippur, the holiest day of the Jewish Year.

Oy a Bruch: —a Yiddish expression expressing disgust, misery, or disaster, often used when a person is at their wit's end.

Pareve: —A food prepared without meat or milk according to Jewish dietary laws and therefore able to be eaten with either one.

Parsha: —any of the sections of the Torah read in the synagogue during religious services.

Passover: —8 day Jewish holiday commemorating the Exodus from Egypt in biblical times. After 400 years of slavery the Jews became a free people under the leadership of Moses.

Rebbitzen: —Yiddish, the wife of a Rabbi.

Rosh Chodesh: —Hebrew, the first day of every month marked by the birth of a new moon, considered a minor Jewish holiday.

Rosh Hashanah: —Jewish New Year celebration lasting 2 days, a very serious time when Jews are mindful of the upcoming Holiday of Yom Kippur only 8 days later.

Sanctuary: —a sacred place usually within a synagogue where people worship.

Schlepping: —Yiddish slang, to haul or carry something heavy or awkward.

Seder: —The traditional family dinner on the first two days of the Passover holiday, commemorating the Jewish Exodus from Egypt.

Shabbat: —the Sabbath, a day of rest for traditional Jews when they attend synagogue prayer services and read from the Torah Scroll.

Shagitz: —A non-Jewish male, somewhat disrespectful term.

Shema: —one of the oldest Hebrew prayers repeated at every worship service, affirming faith in one God. It is perhaps the most universally known Hebrew prayer.

Shin: —the twenty first letter of the Hebrew alphabet.

Shonda: —Yiddish, Shame, or shameful, often expressed as, "It's a Shonda."

Shpiel: —a lengthy extravagant speech or argument intended to persuade people, often by a salesman.

Shul: —Yiddish for synagogue.

Siddur: —a Jewish prayer book.

Simchat Torah: —Hebrew, Jewish holiday commemorating the completion of a full year of reading the Torah Scroll, and the start of a new cycle of weekly readings.

Sondek: —literally the one who holds the baby during the bris (circumcision) celebration performed on the eighth day after a baby boy's birth. It's a big honor to be asked.

Suf: —the last letter of the Hebrew alphabet.

Sukkah: —a temporary hut or booth constructed for the weeklong celebration of the Jewish holiday Sukkot. Often decorated, symbolizes the time God sustained the Jewish People in the wilderness after the Exodus from Egypt.

Talmud Chacham: —Hebrew, Jewish scholar of the Talmud, books interpreting the Torah and the law handed down orally in biblical times.

Tikkun Olam: —Hebrew, literally, "repairing the world." Suggests humanity's shared responsibility to heal, repair, and transform the world.

Torah: —The Law of God as revealed to Moses and recorded in the first five books of Moses (the Jewish Bible), in the synagogue the Torah scroll is read on the Sabbath and other holidays.

Yad: —a thin pointing device, often silver, used to point to the words written in the Torah scroll as the reader recites.

Yahrzeit: —yearly anniversary of a loved one's death when Jews come to the synagogue to say the Kaddish prayer. One also lights a memorial candle at home

Yiddishkeit: —Yiddish word meaning Jewish tradition, culture, character or heritage.

Yom Kippur: —The day of Atonement. The Holiest day of the year when Jews envision being judged by God for their deeds.

Yom Tov: —Hebrew, literally, "Good Day," but in normal usage denoting a Jewish Holiday.

Yud: —the tenth letter of the Hebrew alphabet.

Zie Gezunt: —Yiddish phrase for "Be well."

ABOUT THE AUTHOR

ARTHUR DEAN

Arthur (Artie) Dean was born in the Washington Heights neighborhood of New York City. After finishing a BA at New York University in 1974 he attended the University of Pennsylvania for his dental degree, where he met his wife Barbara. After a residency at Albert Einstein Medical Center in Philadelphia he trained at Boston University until 1981 to become a Periodontist, a specialist in dental implants and gum diseases. He has been practicing in Groton, Connecticut since 1981.

While his scientific training may not be relevant to his writing career, certainly raising his four children was. In fact his storytelling truly began while putting the kids to bed. In the Dean household bedtimes were an elaborate affair. Artie told "chose your own adventure," stories each night and the children would choose the outcome. As his four children entered adolescence their desire for bedtime stories understandably waned. But their father's imagination did not. He began to write stories and essays for both the *Waterford Times* newspaper and the *Jewish Leader* of Eastern Connecticut.

His column "My Two Cents," has appeared biweekly in the *Jewish Leader* for the past ten years. This collection includes a variety of stories from the "My Two Cents" column and sports related essays originally printed in the *Waterford Times*. Three of the stories: "My Father's Shoes," "The Kiddush Cup," and "A Family Found," were published in the *Masorti/Conservative Judaism magazine*, an international publication distributed to members of the Conservative Movement throughout the United States and Canada.

Artie lives with his wife, Barbara, in Waterford, Connecticut. He continues to write, and Barbara edits all his work. Currently he is working on a novel. He plans to publish another collection of short stories next year.

CPSIA information can be obtained at www.ICGtesting.com
Printed in the USA
BVOW04s1949040116

431670BV00004B/62/P

9 781935 656401